PRAISE FOR *Best European Fiction*

"Best European Fiction 2010 . . . *offers an appealingly diverse look at the Continent's fiction scene.*" **THE NEW YORK TIMES**

"*The work is vibrant, varied, sometimes downright odd. As [Zadie] Smith says [in her preface]: 'I was educated in a largely Anglo-American library, and it is sometimes dull to stare at the same four walls all day.' Here's the antidote.*" **FINANCIAL TIMES**

"*With the new anthology* Best European Fiction . . . *our literary world just got wider.*" **TIME MAGAZINE**

"*The collection's diverse range of styles includes more experimental works than a typical American anthology might . . . [Mr. Hemon's] only criteria were to include the best works from as many countries as possible.*" **WALL STREET JOURNAL**

"*This is a precious opportunity to understand more deeply the obsessions, hopes and fears of each nation's literary psyche—a sort of international show-and-tell of the soul.*" **THE GUARDIAN**

"*Dalkey has published an anthology of short fiction by European writers, and the result,* Best European Fiction 2010, *is one of the most remarkable collections I've read—vital, fascinating, and even more comprehensive than I would have thought possible.*" **BOOKSLUT**

"*Here's hoping to many more years of impossibly ambitious* Best European Fiction *anthologies.*" **POPMATTERS**

"Readers for whom the expression 'foreign literature' means the work of Canada's Alice Munro stand to have their eyes opened wide and their reading exposure exploded as they encounter works from places such as Croatia, Bulgaria, and Macedonia (and, yes, from more familiar terrain, such as Spain, the UK, and Russia)." **BOOKLIST** STARRED REVIEW

"[W]e can be thankful to have so many talented new voices to discover."
  LIBRARY JOURNAL

"If Dalkey can keep it up, this could easily become the most important annual literary anthology in America." **NEWCITY**

"[W]hat the reader takes from them are not only the usual pleasures of fiction—the twists and turns of plot, chance to inhabit other lives, other ways of being—but new ways of thinking about how to tell a story."
  CHRISTOPHER MERRILL, PRI'S "THE WORLD" HOLIDAY PICK

"The book tilts toward unconventional storytelling techniques. And while we've heard complaints about this before—why only translate the most difficult work coming out of Europe?—it makes sense here. The book isn't testing the boundaries, it's opening them up." **TIME OUT CHICAGO**

"Editor Aleksandar Hemon declares in his preface that at the heart of this compilation is the 'nonnegotiable need for communication with the world, wherever it may be,' and asserts that ongoing translation is crucial to this process. The English-language reading world, 'wherever it may be,' is grateful." **THE BELIEVER**

"Translations account for less than five percent of the literature published in the United States. This is the first anthology of its kind, and after reading it you may be so furious that such quality work has been kept from you that you'll repeat that stat to anyone who'll listen." **PASTE**

"Does European literature exist? Of course it does, and this collection of forty-one stories proves it." **THE INDEPENDENT**

BEST EUROPEAN FICTION 2012

EDITED AND
WITH AN
INTRODUCTION
BY
ALEKSANDAR
HEMON

PREFACE BY NICOLE KRAUSS

BEST EUROPEAN FICTION 2012

DALKEY ARCHIVE PRESS

CHAMPAIGN · DUBLIN · LONDON

ISBN 978-1-56478-680-7
ISSN 2152-6672

www.dalkeyarchive.com

Funded in part by the Arts Council (Ireland) and
the Illinois Arts Council, a state agency

Please see Acknowledgments on page 455 for additional
information on the support received for this volume

Printed on permanent/durable acid-free paper
and bound in the United States of America

Contents

evil

Preface

Around the time these stories were being gathered from Europe, Keith Richards published his autobiography, *Life*, in which he tells the story of growing up on the Dartford Marshes in England among smallpox hospitals, leper colonies, and insane asylums. One day, another kid emerged out of the precipitous atmosphere, skinny with big lips, carrying under his arm some rare and coveted records by Chuck Berry and Muddy Waters that otherwise Richards had no way of hearing; the rest is history. In other words, the Rolling Stones were born out of scarcity and longing, which may finally be what makes them old-fashioned. Scarcity built Greenwich Village—and forged friendships, bands, art movements, and communities of culture as far back as culture goes—but now the flocked-to village is Facebook and the condition is overabundance, and befriending has devolved into a means of staking out one's coordinates in infinity. Anyone can listen to, look at, or access almost anything at any time now, and a search is something finished a fraction of a second after it began.

But literature refuses the instantaneous on every level, and so while the proportions have changed radically in other mediums, in literature they've remained relatively unchanged: we still can't read anything we want unless it happens to have been written in a language we're proficient in, or a heroic and self-sacrificing effort has been made by a (usually) nonprofit publishing house and a (always) nonprofit translator. One might say that growing up in America right now with an appetite for contemporary Polish, Chinese, or Portuguese literature isn't so unlike growing up as a blues fan on the Dartford Marshes in the 1950s: only 0.7% of the books published annually in the States are translations of literary fiction and poetry, and you'll never hear about most of them unless you're lucky enough to cross paths with a skinny kid with big lips clutching a well-thumbed copy of *The Literary Conference* by César Aira, *Life on Sandpaper* by Yoram Kaniuk, or *Animalinside* by László Krasznahorkai, to mention just a few published concurrently with *Life*.

As someone who is indebted to translation for the majority of her transformative reading experiences, for me an anthology like this is a godsend. Things would have turned out differently for me if the writings of Bruno Schulz, Zbigniew Herbert, Yehuda Amichai, Joseph Brodsky, Franz Kafka, Jorge Luis Borges, Georges Perec, Italo Calvino, Danilo Kiš, Thomas Bernhard, Bohumil Hrabal, Edmond Jabès, and David Grossman, to name just a few, had not come down to me at an impressionable age, first through the almost impossibly narrow chute provided for literary translations into English, and then via a series of lucky accidents. These writers demanded of me many things. But collectively, they offered a view onto a homeland I might have had a chance of belonging to, something that neither my experience growing up in America, nor any similar group of American writers, had ever given me. I am not exaggerating the case, or maybe I am exaggerating only a very little, to say that had it not been for my encounter with them I might now be a shoe salesperson in the Americana shopping center on Long Island, near where I had the small misfortune to grow up; at best, I might have become a lawyer.

Not an insignificant number of those writers arrived to me thanks to Penguin's "Writers from the Other Europe" series edited by Philip Roth between 1974 and 1989, which introduced America—and me—to some of the greatest twentieth-century writers we'd never heard of. At that time it was the Iron Curtain that stood between us and the literature of Central and Eastern Europe; now it's free-market capitalism and the tyranny of the best seller: if nothing else, the irony is impeccable. And yet while those of us who live by books have become gluttons for bad news, everything is not doom and gloom.

More than thirty years after Roth imported Milan Kundera, Primo Levi, and Bruno Schulz in his suitcase, the brilliant American writer who has taken it upon himself to smuggle us a new crop of writers from Europe hails not from Newark but Sarajevo: history and chance blew Aleksandar Hemon to America and muscled him into English, which was nothing short of a windfall for us. In fact, anyone who follows contemporary American literature—i.e. much of the world— will have noticed that a growing portion of the most talented young American writers now making their mark on our national literature weren't born in this country or into this language; like Hemon, many of them only arrived here as adults or near adults. The American stories and novels they write are as much about China, Russia, or Nigeria as they are about here, or they are about Peru, India, and Serbia refracted through the prism of here, or about here reflected through the mirror of there. What seems clear is that these writers' flexible sense of identity doesn't hang on any one hook. The intertwining of nations and cultures, in the best of their work, encourages surprising reinventions of the form. If we didn't know better—if translation statistics weren't what they are, and we hadn't recently witnessed just how enormous a store some still set in the ambition for a Great American Novel that captures the essence of our *national experience* at the very moment it is being lived—we might even have been fooled into thinking that, two centuries after Goethe imagined it, the era of *Weltliteratur* had arrived on these shores at last.

But we are not talking about novels here; we're not even talking about America. It is our luck to be talking about short stories—a form whose physical diminutiveness has saved it from the expectation of carrying nations on its back, leaving it free to do as it pleases—and about Europe, the ideal of which Milan Kundera once boiled down to "maximum diversity in minimum space." If this anthology were looking for a subtitle, it couldn't do better than that. Here you will find stories told from the perspective of a horse in the Second World War ("I, Loshad'," by Jiří Kratochvil), a dog in the afterlife ("This Strange Lucidity," by Agustín Fernández Paz), or, in one of my favorites, a group of children in an orphanage left to fend for themselves when their director is forced to leave indefinitely ("The Children," by Noëlle Revaz). There are rambunctiously imaginative stories about girls laying giant eggs, but there are also chillingly realistic stories about rape, murder, pedophilia, war tourism, a man who survives a bus bomb, a mother who drowns her child, and one woman's lonely and graphic battle against death on the floor of her kitchen.

The singular power of literature lies not in its capacity for accurate representation of mass commonalities, but its ability to illuminate the individual life in a way that expands our understanding of some previously unseen or unarticulated aspect of existence. Kundera, still pondering the diversity of Europe, even went so far as to argue that geographic distance is preferable when it comes to judging literature, as it obscures the smaller, local context and allows the reader to view the work in the large context of world literature, which he saw as the only true way to perceive its aesthetic value, its potentially radical newness. If so, then we, the American readers, might just be the ideal readers for these European stories. But let's not get ahead of ourselves. At the very least, for those looking for an escape from the Dartford Marshes, here's our chance.

NICOLE KRAUSS

Introduction

As I write this intro in the summer of 2011, much of the world economy is in the middle of a nosedive, on the heels of crises precipitated by unfettered greed and stupidity; unemployment is on the constant rise; the euro is on the verge of collapse; the Syrian government is massacring its citizens, while the civil war in Libya continues unchecked; on the streets of Israel hundreds of thousands of protesters are expressing their righteous anger; Great Britain is on fire, riots having spread from London to other cities—and the list of troubles does not even begin to end there, nor is there any reason to believe that the fall would be calmer than the summer. A reasonable person might hence justifiably ask: why bother with reading contemporary European fiction? Indeed, why bother with literature at all?

Well, the short answer is: what else can we do? Literature opens our eyes to the horrors and the beauties of the relentless flow of calamities we call the world. Permit me to submit as evidence Danila Davydov's (Russia) story "The Telescope," in which a man survives what seems to be a terrorist attack and crawls out of the wreckage blind, only to end up opening up the entire universe to someone else. After I read "The Telescope," I thought: "Tweet this, motherfuckers!" for Davydov's masterpiece is ample evidence that there are vast spaces of human experience that could be covered and comprehended only by means of literature. If you need further proof of the essential value of intelligent fiction, take Bjarte Breiteig's (Norway) "Down There They Don't Mourn," which addresses the malady of the heart that is not unrelated to the recent terrorist massacre in his homeland. Or take Michael Stauffer's (Switzerland) "The Woman with the Stocks," whose opening sentence brings into vision the human order that modern capitalism has all but torn apart: "The woman with the stocks had a mother." And if you have started to think that love is something that can be done only on the Internet, read Maja Hrgović's (Croatia) "Zlatka." These are, of course, just some of the offerings from this year's *Best European Fiction*, which has yielded, I'm happy to say, a rich literary harvest, even if the richness made for a tormentful selection process.

The writers in *BEF 2012* convinced me—yet again—that literature is the best way to stay truly engaged with the immensity of human experience. This year, we decided to forgo the abstract alphabetical ordering and organize the anthology around the things that matter. Hence the selections are grouped thematically, whereby the themes are recognizable as fundamental aspects of existence: love, desire, family, thought, art, home, work, evil, etc. Literature is an inherently democratic (if utopian) project, capable not only of dealing with the onrushing train of history but with the ever-demanding questions of sheer being alive as well. The intention of the thematic organization was thus not to reduce the pieces to one general issue—for great writing is irreducible—but rather to engage them with one another, to put them in the situation of dialogue and to show what we have always known: the infinite variation of human experience, which can never be spent or diminished to a tweet, is the true and only domain of literature. What you can find in this book is not only great, relevant fiction, but also—and perhaps most importantly—a sense of kinship in the belief that human lives, thoughts, and feelings always matter.

So, if what is happening in the world baffles you or scares you, you need to read some books. *Best European Fiction 2012* would be an excellent place to start.

ALEKSANDAR HEMON

BEST EUROPEAN FICTION 2012

love

PATRICIA DE MARTELAERE

My Hand Is Exhausted

There are faces she never forgets. There are different kinds of reasons why she never forgets a face, although there's probably no single reason really, such as why she likes blue or chocolate or Bach, but then, on the other hand, that just seems completely necessary. The faces that Esther never forgets have nothing to do with the people who sport these faces. They're sitting immobile in front of her, the people, in the wicker armchair roughly five meters away from her, under Gao Qipei's tiger, back inclined toward the window, so that they appear like stencils cut out of the daylight. They are stiff and unnatural. Their legs crossed, hands convulsed on the armrests, lips pressed tightly together, they fix on some arbitrary point on the wall, the doorknob or the coat hook, for example, and try in the meantime to maintain an interesting look in their eyes. It never works. After half an hour, they get cramps in their legs, their hands tingle, and the corners of their lips begin to tremble. Their eyes become misty and stupid, as if hypnotized, helpless lambs. From time to time one of them complains the next day that he dreamed the whole night about the doorknob. That's how it goes; everything lingers, without it having the least bit of meaning, the brain works that way.

Esther also sits and looks. She is waiting for the moment that the face comes loose, like the postage stamp from a letter soaking in water. It always comes loose, one faster than the other. These are the faces she collects, the others don't concern her. It's about the moment a face becomes a mask, harder and more inflexible than itself, more real than itself. Or the moment a look merges into a landscape, deep, wide, but impersonal. She used to collect real landscapes. As a child, she had about ten of them, for nighttime in bed. She closed her eyes, framed the blackness, and copied the lines she had stolen while on holiday from real landscapes with a fluorescent finger. The most beautiful was that of the dunes, with fresh ridges blown by the wind in the sand, in the hollow a clump of beach grass, and in the bottom left-hand corner the rusty knots and spikes of barbed wire. The most difficult was the Swiss alpine landscape, not only because of the capricious shapes of the mountain peaks, the twenty-five tops of dark green spruces against the empty, elevated air, and the speckled bodies of nine cows on the mountain meadow, dotted here and there, but mainly because of the cable cars. The difficult thing about the cable cars was that she had been in one and the landscape had moved. What she remembered seemed like photos of a city at night, with ribbons of light through the streets, where departed cars raced through one another.

Esther only drew the outside. A landscape doesn't have an inside. You can plow through it, you can explore its most forsaken corners, you can get lost in it or live in it. But it's never the inside. A landscape begins with dissent and stretches from there on out. It ends when it seems to agree.

They become talkative, one and all. It comes from being silent for a long time, the hoarse throat, the drafty stillness in the head. But it also comes from being afraid, afraid of the portrait. They do want to be as they appear. Sometimes they hardly dare look, but they look all the same, all of them. And they are all disappointed, no matter what, whatever it is, however they are. Shouldn't that chin be a little sharper? they ask in despair. Isn't that nose much too long? But they can't draw; they're powerless in front of their very own face. They can comb their hair, or squeeze a pimple on their nose, or frown or straighten the shoulders. But on paper, they're useless. That's why they try it with words, at afternoon tea or during a quick break.

Esther is washing her hands at the small white basin behind the painter's easel.

She asks if it's the first time they've posed for a portrait.

It's always the first time.

She tells them they have an interesting face.

Come on, they say, hopeful and delighted, it's boring, everyday, nothing special.

Honestly, says Esther. It's got something, it's got character.

And then, of course, they tell her their entire life story, from childhood to unhappy marriage, from bed to bed, desire to disappointment, and all in the hope that it might change something, that Esther might make an adjustment here or there, that she might make the chin sharper, the nose shorter. They hope she will paint the portrait of someone as he is when he is loved, that she will draw everything that isn't there, and that it will be there all the same.

Esther lets them talk and listens. She listens, very carefully, but actually she's not listening. Listening is a form of looking. Watching how a face changes when the lips form words: I've always been lonely, or I never found what I was looking for. The face becomes serious and melancholic, as if it immediately believes what the lips are saying, just like that, and yet something isn't right, something's not completely sincere.

Esther despises them, one and all. Especially the self-motivated crowd, the ones that come of their own accord to have her draw or paint them, and are even willing to pay for it themselves. But also the ones that have been sent by family members or friends, for an anniversary or a birthday, she despises them too. She even despises the ones she asks herself. The writers and actors who come and pose at her request, complaining all the while that they don't have the time or that they think it's ridiculous but they come all the same. She despises them because they come all the same. The only ones she doesn't despise are the ones who don't come, because they don't come. The ones who come are mostly men. The only men in Esther's life, but they are many. And they stay, just as long as she wants. Once in a while there's a man who keeps coming back after his portrait's done. Then she pushes him with profound contempt into the chair underneath Gao Qipei's tiger and starts drawing his portrait anew. Sometimes there's a man whose lips reveal, over coffee or during a break: I thought about you. Then she looks carefully at the changing face, the traces of desire, the sign of faith, the onset of emotions. But she does not change a single line.

Gao Qipei was a Chinese painter who painted with his hands. Every painter paints with their hands, unless they have no hands, then they try with the feet or the mouth. But Gao Qipei painted by hand alone, without a brush. Chinese painters are so sick and tired of the brush because they have to write with it all day long so that there's no longer any difference between writing and painting. That's why Gao Qipei started painting by hand alone. It is an unusual tiger, impressive and endearing. A tiger from the rear, a little sheepish, with the chubby backside of a bear, but still with great dignity. As a child, Esther kept trying to turn the painting around, to see the tiger's head from the other side. That's what her mother says; every time she visits Esther's atelier and sees the tiger hanging there. In that way it's almost become the truth, impossible to distinguish from a memory. But Esther doesn't believe it's true. As a child she would have been much too scared to see the tiger's head, even if she did believe it was on the reverse side of the painting. She does remember the television screen, which isn't a television screen in this memory but rather a hutch with two white rabbits, and Esther as a child slipping carrots into the back of the set for the animals.

Esther sees them coming through the windows of her atelier. She likes to see them coming, especially the first time, when they're still new. The unfamiliar people on the other side of the street, looking for the house number, and then crossing over, nervous and excited. Frequently they comb their hair just before ringing the bell, which is of course ridiculous, as if they expect it to be reproduced lock for lock. Esther doesn't hurry to open the door for them. Sometimes she lets them ring twice, especially if it's a man she might just find a little attractive. Then she would have preferred not to open the door at all.

He finds the neighborhood particularly pretty. The house is stately and impressive, the weather chilly for the time of the year. She ascends the steep, spiral staircase in front of him, two stories up.

It's the custom, he says, for men to go first on stairs.

I know, says Esther, while she holds her skirts together at the knees. In elevators too, apparently.

That's a throwback to the days when elevators were not completely reliable. If the cage was open and you stepped in, there was always a chance you might crash to the ground, and then it was better if a man crashed to the ground, a lesser loss.

Everyone finds the atelier spacious and sunny and the view magnificent. None of them wants something to drink; they've just had breakfast, perhaps later. They stand there, boorish, in the middle of the attic, with their jacket and overcoat still on and their hands in their pockets. Esther lets them stand there. She messes about behind the painter's easel, rips a sheet of paper from the roll, and attaches it to the plank.

Where should I sit? they ask. What should I take off?

If she were now to say: stay where you are, they would do it, for hours and hours on end. And if she were to say: everything, they would do it, like the hired models at the art school, but then with an unutterable shame, and shame makes them unusable. It is impossible to draw a naked man if he's ashamed. Shame occasions shame. Love, on the other hand, does not occasion love. It's the eyes in particular that make it difficult. If they had no eyes it would probably be simple. They would have to be blind, one and all.

It's better without the glasses, says Esther.

Then I can't see a thing, he says.

But he obediently removes his glasses and places them on the wicker table next to the armchair.

You'll forget them, says Esther.

He winks and slips his glasses into his breast pocket.

Without the glasses he appears vaguer, half rubbed-out, a little blurred. He looks like a man waking up in a bed. Although Esther has never seen a man wake up in a bed; first there would have had to be a man who fell asleep in the bed. But a man asleep in a bed isn't much different from a man asleep on a train, and that much Esther has witnessed, and also how they wake up. The question remains, how do you know which man it is?

Godfried H., he says.

He pretends to be a stranger, as if there were no possibility she might know who he is, no possibility she might recognize him from photos and interviews.

But how do you know which one it is? Is it the man with the lopsided head against the grimy brown curtain, with his hands folded over his belt, the gleaming yellow wedding ring, his blue checked shirt open at the neck, with gray chest hair? Is it the man with beard and balding head, sitting rigidly with eyes closed, bolt upright, as if meditating, vigilant, as if furtively peeking between his eyelashes, but with his mouth open slightly, as though perhaps asleep? Is it the man called Peter? With crew-cut dark hair, pale complexion, and dark eyes, restless hands with broad hairy wrists? Is it the prince, the beggar, the knight, the dragon? You're only sure if they appear to know the magic word, and they all seem to know it. They are all the one, but she alone is not, not in this fairy tale.

You have a very interesting face.

I know. Comes in very handy.

It has character, something special.

My face, sure, pretty much.

Esther washes her hands again. She detests even the slightest traces of paint or charcoal on her hands. She washes them thirty times a day, sometimes halfway through a mouth or a nose. She would have preferred to be able to draw or paint under a running tap, then everything would wash off immediately, if that were possible. Or to paint with a sort of remote control, or with the eyes only, without hands. It's actually a miracle she ever started to paint in the first place.

She's at the kitchen table, hates making a mess. Pots of paint arrayed before her, immaculate, never used: yellow, green, blue, and red. And next to every pot of paint a jar of water, a paintbrush, and a rag. Every paintbrush neatly rinsed and dried after every session. And after every rinsing, to the sink for fresh water. How is it ever going to be possible to learn to mix colors, to allow impurities?

He's sitting reasonably still. Sometimes they find it difficult, sitting still. They keep crossing their legs, scratching, folding their hands open and closed. Peter at the cello, hands on the strings, the only way to keep him immobile. This one's doing it unassisted. He's almost too still. There is nothing about him that moves. He hasn't blinked once in half an hour. A fly crawls over his hand and there is no reaction to show that a fly is crawling over his hand. He begins to look like the motionless watchman at the wax museum, the one you want to shake to see if he's real.

He is a writer. Painting doesn't interest him. He doesn't even look at his own portrait. It's your portrait, he says, of me.

He once had the idea to make written portraits of people, for a fee and all that. He saw himself doing it, sitting on a street corner somewhere or on the Place du Tertre in Paris, between the painters and the sketchers, to have passersby pose for him on a stool for ten minutes while he portrayed their face in words. Like the description of a fugitive on the news: oval face, short chestnut hair, green eyes, bushy eyebrows, plump lips, a birthmark on the left cheek. Or, alternatively, the psychological approach: troubled look, melancholic eyes, serene forehead, sensual lips, willful chin. Or more romantic: a look of intense but unfulfilled desire, soft fleshy lips like a pouting child, but callous ridges along the cheeks, suggesting pent-up frustration, stubborn, dogged. Comparison with animals also works well: head like a mole, haddock eyes, rabbits' teeth. Esther has never painted animals. In addition to tigers, Gao Qipei also painted spiders, dragonflies, and shrimp. They all look human.

She's busy with an ear. It's a small ear, close to the skull, so that the dark—but here and there graying—hairs around the temples gently fall across it. The ear itself looks soft and downy, a few longer hairs growing in the middle, the earlobe partly attached. Under the ear, stubble from shaving, the short, broad neck, the dark blue silk shirt with the top button open.

Is it a listening ear? He doesn't like music, he says. He doesn't care what CD she puts on; he won't hear it. He says: music is like wallpaper in a room, it's background, you don't look at it. Nobody ever asks: do you like wallpaper?

He stares at the doorknob without batting an eye and doesn't budge an inch. But if he doesn't listen, then what does he do? If he doesn't listen, doesn't see much without glasses, and doesn't move, what does he do? Think? Feel?

He stares motionless at the doorknob. Will he dream about the doorknob? Esther knows all about it, how staring evolves into imagining. But it remains strange and inexplicable that the eyes look and the hands draw what the eyes see. It's like typing a page in typing class with the keyboard covered, without knowing what you're actually doing or whether it's right or not.

Now she has his ear. She looks at his ear on the white grainy sheet of rice paper. It's clearly his ear. It's an ear you could cut off, out of desperation or in surgery.

And why does she like blue? Blue is the color of Yves Klein's flower, a blue sponge on a lanky stem, cheap, noxious blue ink, screaming and helpless. She is standing in the middle of the spiral in the Guggenheim, and the Guggenheim also looks like an ear, a giant ear pressed against the heart of Manhattan, listening for a pending disaster. It's this color blue.

The oleander, he says, about the budding red oleander in the window alcove. It sounds as if he is announcing the title of a poem he's about to recite.

The oleander is one of the most poisonous plants in existence. The flower itself isn't poisonous but the leaf is. One single arrow-shaped blade is enough to send any adult to the grave, irretrievably. And yet, the sun soaked *avenidas* of the Italian Riviera, teeming with sauntering suicides, are lush with blossoming white, pink, and red oleander trees. And the resounding corridors of schools full of vigorous school children are adorned with unsuspecting oleanders in white plastic flowerpots, moved outside to the playground at the beginning of spring, the moment when suicides are, statistically speaking, at their peak. But nobody knows this. The oleander leaf is incredibly tough and hard. It would be easier to cut your wrists with one, so to speak, than to eat one.

Sometimes she clamps her jaw shut so hard that her teeth hurt. Then she has to force them apart and she thinks: it's from keeping silent for so long. At lunch, if she's alone, she performs a whole battery of relaxation exercises to combat hoarseness, although there's nothing wrong with being hoarse if you rarely speak anyway. Chewing with broad, round movements, as blatantly as possible, with the mouth wide open, first to the left, while the lower jaw makes a grinding circular downward curve, then the same to the right, like a cow chewing its cud. Yawning is also good for the vocal chords, a sort of inner ventilation. For the neck muscles, which suffer terribly from the long periods of sitting still behind the painter's easel, it helps to rest the head on one side, against the shoulder, turning to the rear, then in a slow curve to the other shoulder, and finally letting it fall forward before starting again in the opposite direction. It strikes her every time she does this just how heavy a head is to carry. For the wrists: bend the hand forward and then backward like a robotic child waving good-bye.

Peter the Deleter, she called him—because his mind always deleted whatever wasn't actually present. He forgot everything, immediately. One day he arrived at the conservatory without his cello. Lost somewhere along the way, he said with a broad grin. They tramped all the way back to his room, five of them, but the cello wasn't there. Then he remembered the sandwich he'd bought at the bakery on the corner. There they were, cello and sandwich.

I have a fantastic memory, said Peter. Because, he said, and I quote a well-known philosopher, memory is the capacity to forget.

With this same memory he forgot names, dates, and promises. He forgot where he had parked the car, forcing them to search half the city in the middle of the night. He sat waiting two hours early in the wrong restaurant for the wrong girl.

Forgetting, he said, was a precondition for happiness.

He forgot his wallet one day, left it on a bench in the park and never found it again. But even that was quickly forgotten, so! Esther, he said. You'd be better off forgetting me.

As a consequence, zealous and obedient, she started right away, at night in bed, her quilt high over her ears, her knees pulled up and her ice-cold feet rolled in her long nightgown, to delete Peter. It didn't differ much from desiring Peter, it was just that Peter could no longer be part of it. Deleting Peter was nothing more than an exercise in concentration, a technique like yoga or Zen, a question of rhythmic breathing and muscle relaxation. Alas, deleting Peter turned out to be more exhausting in the end than desiring him once had.

After a while, forgetting becomes a matter of course, like old age. Esther sees a woman in the mirror, forty-five, a matter of course. There's no technique necessary. But it is an exterior woman, with an adulthood that continues to be strange and unrecognizable inside.

Some painters maintain that the lines on their own faces are also carved on their own hands, so that whoever begins to draw a face blind automatically draws a self-portrait, much to his or her surprise. The question is, how can the hand know from inside how the face should look from the outside? It's already strange enough that a head should appear to know so many things, especially the things that come from the body, like someone dreaming about a lump in her belly, who feels no pain and knows nothing about any lump but afterward turns out to actually have a lump in her belly.

The woman she sees is unquestionably an ugly woman, and that's a shame. It's a woman with short, wiry curls of an indeterminate color between drab brown and dark gray. She has a long, pointed nose and dark deep-set eyes with high eyebrows. Her lips are thin and a little too tightly pressed together over teeth that are too big, the cheeks pale and gaunt, the neck long and thin. But she paints herself as a woman who sees herself, and thus with that look in her eye, a look from elsewhere. For that reason alone she paints herself other than she is, because she becomes other when she looks at herself and paints herself. Something disappears.

One of the men she's drawing writes letters in which he says how beautiful he finds her. When he comes, they never say a word about the letters. The first time Esther wrote him back. She wrote: I'm sorry, some things are simply not possible, that's how life is. But when he comes, it's as if he never wrote those letters and certainly not her who wrote that reply. She draws him in three-quarter profile, with his eyes facing the door. He is a handsome man in every respect, raven-haired and dark-eyed, but when she draws him, he's not a man anymore. There is no difference between a man and a plaster statue, a bowl of fruit or a sansevieria. It's always the same pencil she holds in her hand, and what she feels is never more than the smooth surface of the paper.

She reads his letters quickly, hurriedly, standing by the mailbox; she doesn't even take the time to go inside. She reads them and re-reads them, over and over, searching for what they contain; she can't get enough of what they contain. She reads that she's beautiful, that he is waiting for her, and that he cannot sleep. She hopes he will always write to her. But when he comes, he's not the same and all she can do is draw him.

She can only draw Peter too. Draw and delete.

And Peter in love. Jumpy, difficult to draw, as if his contours wouldn't stay still.

Esther, he said, in that tone. I've met someone.

Who is she? she asked. Do I know her?

Yes, he said. Her name begins with E.

And in that short second, the possibility that it would be like the movies, the veiled declaration of love, initially misunderstood, the doubt, the certainty that it had to be someone else, the impossibility of so much happiness.

She knew precisely who it really was.

I hope we can stay friends, he said.

Yes, of course, said Esther, sheepishly.

Friendship's more important, no matter what, Peter would later say.

Yes, of course, said Esther, self-assured.

Peter's sorrow was magnificent to draw. It gave him dark rings around his eyes that already looked like charcoal, and an ashen hue that was the same as that of the paper. To cap it all he had never sat so still, his restless hands motionless on his lap, heavy, as if it were impossible to lift them. Real robot hands, the kind you find in the sketchbooks for beginners, where they explain how to draw hands, beginning with a broad cube as a palm, to which you attach each finger in the form of three articulated cubes, the phalanges. The sadness penetrated into every fingertip, yet still it wasn't such a terribly awful sadness, because Peter forgot quickly and Elisabeth was easy to forget, and he still had his friends, and his cello, which he left behind from time to time.

I don't understand it, he said. She said she loved me.

Love passes, said Esther, intending, she presumed, to comfort him.

And she thought: I must remember that, love passes; it might indeed comfort someone, especially if one is the one who loves, which also passes.

But real love? Might as well say: life passes. But real life? Yes, real life also passes. And there is no other life than the life that passes. And it's not even a question of: the longer it lasts the more real it is. Children who die a crib death have really lived, if for an instant; length of time is absolutely not the test.

And then his shoulders shuddered all at once. With men that's a sign that they're crying. A crying man is impossible to draw; it's even worse than a naked man.

Esther stood up and went to wash the charcoal from her hands. She hoped that it would be over by then. With men it's over quickly, it's a moment of weakness.

But not with him, not then. When she turned he was sitting there sobbing like a child. She went toward him and rested her cold, still damp hands on his neck. He threw his arms around her as if it was love, and it was indeed love, just not love for her.

Later he said: I'm sorry.

You can stay the night if you want, she said.

You're sweet, he said, but better not.

At the door he kissed her again, something he had to do, then.

This shouldn't have happened, he added, while he kissed her.

No, said Esther. Not like this.

Not like anything, he said with his mouth on her neck.

No, said Esther. Of course not.

It happens every day, every second, more often than people die or are born: people are rejected. If it's not clear what rejection is, it depends on what one wanted. Varanasi or Lourdes. People go to Lourdes from far and wide, the sick, crippled, the incurably handicapped, looking for a miracle, a cure, a new life. People go to Varanasi from every corner of the world, lepers, the lame, the incurably sick, looking for a redeeming death, liberation into the great nothingness, and they lie down in rows on the banks of the Ganges and feel rejected by eternity because it won't let them in. What is rejection, anyway?

The sketched body of a man at the door, that's what he was. As long as he was sketched standing there, it was impossible to say whether he was coming or going. He came in. After standing at the door for a long time and hesitating, he finally came in. It was a man who had returned, you could see it immediately. Rather, it was the portrait of a man who stayed.

No man had ever remained so still for her as this one, now, in the wicker armchair, under Gao Qipeï's tiger. He's not stiff or tense, he's completely relaxed, motionless as if asleep with his eyes open. He appears to be absent in his body. When the telephone rings he's undisturbed and doesn't even take the opportunity to scratch himself or adjust his position.

It starts to rain, heavy, black droplets on the zinc roof of the atelier, and he doesn't seem to notice. She would like to take a look inside his ear to see if anything's vibrating there. And if his heart is beating, if he's breathing all right. Conversations while listening to the rain, that's like the title of a book written about Gao Qipei by a contemporary. Somewhere inside it says: "I heard that when he painted tigers he pressed his elbow in the ink in order to portray their crouched position prior to pouncing on their prey."

She doesn't know him. She hasn't read a single one of his books. She knew his name, of course, and his face from photos. And now she knows his ear, his neck, his nose, his chin. And words come from his mouth that probably existed first as thoughts in his head, and she knows them now too. But she doesn't know him. He's somewhere inside, if he's there at all. She has the impression no one is there, as if she is sketching a sketch.

Actually she already met him, very briefly, he probably won't remember. That evening in the theater, each with a friend who knew the other, leaving them suddenly next to one another on the way out. It was after that particularly terrible play with a young actor playing Nero, and she asked him if he found it terrible too.

He said it was all right.

You're not serious, she said.

He smiled.

I only half listen, he said, maybe that's why.

Are you joining us for a drink? he asked.

No, she said.

No is actually the most beautiful word. Esther repeats it as often as possible, out loud, in the dark, as lovers do with I love you. *Je t'aime.* *Ich liebe dich. Te quiero.* No, *non, nein, njet.* And then there's that song, *Je suis une poupée-hee-hee, qui dit non non non non non non.*

He has blue eyes, surprisingly blue for someone with dark hair. He says he was blond when he was a child. Next time he comes he brings a photo as proof, twelve years old, short pants, a sweet boyish smile, and, indeed, blond hair, although it's not so clear in black and white. He didn't wear glasses in those days.

His eyes seem different without glasses, deeper, bluer, hazier, as if he had just been swimming underwater or peeling an onion. But his eyes are impenetrable, they only reflect. You can see in them what they themselves see and nothing more. And what they see is the doorknob. Still, he's not really staring, he's only looking, with a strange, penetrating, questioning gaze, at the doorknob.

Blue is the deepest color. It is the color of the sea and the night as dawn approaches. It is a color that appears like velvet, like violets, and like desire. That song, *Bleu, bleu, l'amour est bleu.*

Not always, he says when she asks if he always wears silk shirts.

He always wears the same shirt because he thinks it's easier for her to draw.

It makes no difference, she says. Shirts are all the same.

People too, he says. Why bother painting them then?

It's not about people, Esther says, it's about drawing as such.

Actually, it makes absolutely no difference to her whatsoever, what she draws. It just gets a little monotonous if she draws the same thing all the time and it doesn't help her technique. What's nice about drawing different people is that you also get paid more than once. And that they all think their face is extremely exceptional, that it must almost be a privilege to be allowed to draw it.

People are vain, says Esther.

Especially writers, he says.

But your face, says Esther, there's something about it, something very special.

Come on, he says, irritated, I'm actually very shallow.

His cheeks are soft, a little pliable, with deep furrows running from the nose to the corners of his mouth. The nose is neutral, neither big nor small, neither a hawk nor a button, an ordinary nose, short and blunt. He wears a moustache and a beard, but cut very short, so that it looks more like a well-tended way of not shaving for a couple of days; not the rough stubble of the more nonchalant types. On his upper lip and chin the hair is dark, but on the lower jaw and the cheeks it's grayer and even completely white here and there. He has four children, two boys and two girls; they came evenly, in turns: boy, girl, boy, girl. He and his wife had intended to stop at two, but then a third came along and his wife thought four would be better.

Anna likes everything to be even, he says.

A strange notion, says Esther.

She also sees a lot of strange people, Anna, he says.

And a writer, says Esther, lives for his work, of course.

So you'd think, he says.

For writing, says Esther, women, and drink.

Women don't interest me, he says.

Then there's only drink, Esther concludes.

Moderately, he laughs. Everything in moderation.

Do you think it exists? asked Peter.

They were in a rowing boat in the middle of a lake, scorching sun and the incredible blue of a cloudless sky with a ripple-free reflection. It was summer, the summer of Elisabeth, when Peter suddenly appeared unable to forget and kept returning again and again to the same thing. He sat at the back of the boat with his knees hoisted up and his big hands with their broad wrists on the paddles. Set off against the blue, he looked like a prisoner condemned to forced labor. You could easily have imagined a ball and chain around his ankles, preventing him from running away, or here on the lake from jumping into the water and swimming to the bank. Although he could easily have let it drag him to the bottom, help him end his life, if he had wanted. Peter the galley slave, with his pale complexion and his crew-cut, flattop hair. Esther dangled her hand over the railing in the water and watched the ripples undulate, the irregularities vanish from the surface. Water is the most difficult thing to draw; it's like light turned hard, almost a mirror.

No, she said.

TRANSLATED FROM DUTCH BY BRIAN DOYLE

MAJA HRGOVIĆ

Zlatka

My head was hanging over the hair-washing basin like a drooping pistil. With her soft, sensually slow circular movements Zlatka made her way through the wet mass of my mane all the way to the roots. Pleasure spread down my neck in the form of goose bumps; I closed my eyes. Naturally, the tips of her fingers were seductively certain of their work.

Later, she sat me in front of a large mirror. In it I caught sight of well-thought-through scissor snips munching at the cracked tips of my hair, and two crinkles incised into the corners of Zlatka's mouth as she said, "I'll get that mane of yours in order."

■ ■ ■

I lived near the train station in a neighborhood built many decades ago for the families of railroad workers and machinists. Like tombstones over grave mounds, hardened chimneys rose from parallel rows of elongated one-story buildings. Decaying, hideous buildings made of concrete, separated by narrow tracks of municipal ground and an occasional wild chestnut, shivering before the sudden passage of express trains from Budapest and Venice.

My apartment blended in perfectly with the picturesque sorrow of the neighborhood; it grew out of it like a twig from a gnarled, old mulberry tree. I had two rooms at my disposal, but one smelled of damp and worms so badly that I gave up on it. I slept, read, and ate in the other, larger room, in which I was—perhaps because of a red futon, the only new piece of furniture in the apartment—less often overcome by the feeling that someone had recently died there. The wardrobe looked like a vertically placed coffin into which some-one very clever had installed shelves. A large square window opened upon yet another horrible one-story building and just barely let in enough light to give me a sense of what I was missing.

The cold crept in through the worm-eaten window frame, and as I exhaled it made the air from my nose disperse in light little clouds. The space seemed impossible to warm up. I sat next to the radiator, wrapped in a blanket.

Although I lived alone, I could feel the presence of others: every word of the neighbors' arguments reached me through the porous walls, and in the evening when they made up and fucked, I could tell who came first by their muffled or piercing screams.

■ ■ ■

Through the poorly ventilated underpass, gleaming with neon signs and small shop windows, working people and students hurried downtown, gushing, unstoppable, like viruses. At the station, by the entrance to the underpass, the rattling buses that had brought them here from the suburbs gathered their strength for another ride. Homeless people with red noses dragged around with their plastic bottles and hauled their heavy stench behind them. Loudspeakers whined advertisements for contests, perfumes, and meat product sales in the supermarket on the underground level.

That winter, life spun around in circles of drunkenness, hangover, and sleep. Despite the no-crossing sign, I crossed the railroad next to the switchman's box. I tugged up the legs of my pants so as not to get them dirty with black grease that covered the rails—and jumped across looking left and right. I stayed at the Railroader's until closing. When I stumbled home drunk, I paid less attention to the grime on the rails: after a few weeks in the new neighborhood, the legs of all of my pants were soiled with that black goo, which wouldn't come off in washing.

■ ■ ■

I met Zlatka on that day when DJ Scrap played at the Railroader's. I wanted to see the concert; not so much because I craved "Balkan Drum & Bass," but because I feared the loneliness that would almost certainly have skinned me to my shuddering, sad core had I stayed home that evening, alone with myself, with all my sober thoughts, and those moans from the apartment next door.

Again there was no warm water. My hair had been greasy for days. I walked into the first hairdresser's I ran into: this was actually just a big glass kiosk, leaning up against the Engineer—Society for Culture and the Arts. The salon was called Rin Tin Tin and it serviced both men and women at discount prices.

Zlatka was alone in the salon. When I came in, she crushed her cigarette against the side of an ashtray and put down the magazine she was leafing through. "How can I help you?" she asked. The beauty of her face—prominent cheekbones and large, dark eyes, her nose and lips, eyebrows, bangs, chin—didn't fit the Rin Tin Tin's interior. In a nearby cabinet, which looked like someone had stolen it from a landfill, there were plastic boxes containing curlers, scissors, and shampoo; two little dried-up rose bouquets; a frame with the price list; and a photo of a laughing dog. Washed-out posters of women with puffed-up hairdos decorated the glass walls of the salon.

I was embarrassed because my hair was dirty and I felt sorry for Zlatka's fingers slowly making their way through my greasy curls under the stream of warm water.

She told me my tips were cracked and needed to be trimmed. I told her to go ahead and do it; their prices were sensationally low anyhow.

■ ■ ■

An early, gentle winter evening doesn't mean much at the Railroader's: the light of day doesn't make its way through the windows darkened by painted canvases; the booths always feel like they're deep inside some catacombs. I twirled a lock of my hair, shiny and squeaky from washing, around my finger and let the waitress pour mulled wine from a large pot into my cup; she did it using a ladle, as though it was soup. Behind my back, DJ Scrap was pushing a metal box from one end of a small stage to another, dragging the cables that came along with the box, and every now and then stopping by the microphone, tapping it lightly, and saying, "Check, check, one-two, one-two."

Someone was throwing a birthday party; drinks started flowing faster, the atmosphere loosened slowly, talk became witty. Someone complimented me on my hairdo; it was strange to take a compliment, maybe I even blushed a little. Time rushed ahead like first love: the next time I looked behind my back, the club was already full to the brim, strobe lights pierced the darkness, and the voice of DJ Scrap, who had finally arranged all his props around the stage, took hold of the microphone confidently and released a salvo of loud kisses at the crowd. He promised them in a thick Serbian accent, "Tonight, we party!" and this made the front rows scream like they were getting bikini waxes. And when the too-loud music started, the grunting of the DJ's fans got all the more intense, and gyrating limbs were suddenly scattered all over the dance floor. Soon the Railroader's ventilation problem again made itself obvious: the fervor of DJ Scrap's admirers, condensed into drops of sweat, gathered on the ceiling and slimed down the windows.

I downed yet another shot that someone, when I wasn't looking, had placed in front of me.

She sprung out of the crowd and elbowed her way next to me at the bar. She waved at the waitress with a crumbled bill and yelled in a raspy voice, "A beer! Large!" I recognized her immediately, though she didn't look the same as she had earlier that afternoon: wild hair, her mascara beautifully smeared under her eyes. I couldn't take my own eyes off of her.

"Hey, ciao!" I howled in greeting, trying to outshout the noise. She stared at me as though she was nearsighted, but that lasted only a second; the next moment she was offering me a wide smile, leaning toward me, and in a cracked voice asking what I was drinking. I pointed at the steaming caldron and she got me a cup of mulled wine and sat next to me. "You're alone?" she asked, and that was enough to start with, to fill the silence with trivialities. She was alone; she'd come to the concert straight from work. She didn't care much about DJ Scrap, had never heard any of his songs, she only felt like going out. She told me that there had been a competition on the radio and that she had made the call, given the wrong answer to the trivia question, but had won two tickets anyhow. She couldn't get anyone to come out with her, because it was the middle of the week, her friends had children, worked, didn't feel like it . . . she had almost given up. Still, she was glad she was here. By the way, her name was Zlatka. "That's such a nice name," I said, and it sounded sweeter than I wanted.

Some awful guy in a leather jacket approached us when the fuse blew. There must have been a short circuit or something, the lights went out, the music stopped, the crowd got restless. The problem was solved in a couple of minutes, Scrap screamed into the microphone a little, fondled with his cables, and as soon as he got his bearings, again cranked up the volume to the max. Whipped by strobe lights, the dancers screamed gratefully.

The guy in the leather jacket, as soon as the power came back again, leaned over us; he wanted badly to stand at the bar right between Zlatka and me. He wanted to catch us by surprise; he came up from behind and put his arms around us as if wanting to share his deepest thoughts and fears. I took my drink and stepped away. I expected Zlatka to do the same.

But Zlatka didn't move. She let him sit next to her, on my stool, and she even moved closer to him. The greasy leather jacket was screening her from me. Still, I could see her smiling flirtatiously, enjoying his flattery. A sluggish wave of disappointment washed out the fascination I had until a moment ago felt with my new hairdresser.

Standing alone behind her back, I felt rejected and insecure. I approached the edge of the dance floor and danced a bit with my drink, then I downed it to get it out of my way and let the crowd suck me in. In a moment I was jumping all over the place and screaming into my clenched fist meaningless chunks of verse that kept repeating into infinity, like a skipping CD.

My bangs soon went limp from moisture, the heat felt like a heart attack. At just the right moment, pushing away the young shirtless dancers in front of her, Zlatka appeared in front of me with a smile on her face and two pints of beer in her hands.

"The DJ rocks!" she yelled into my ear and started coiling around me like a snake in some sort of a parody of a dance. It made me laugh. She swung her hair as though she were at a death metal concert, flexed her neck to the rhythm of the music, and at the end of every song screamed so hard that the veins on her neck popped up and her cheeks turned red. Everything was good again, all at once, as if that guy had never come around.

The people around us were just a moving background, extras in a movie starring Zlatka and me. I got carried away. At moments I felt a sort of joy, thick and saturated, clotting in me, somewhere in my lungs, in my esophagus—I had to open my mouth wide and yell into the noise, anything, just to let it, this something, come out. When some bouncy song started playing, the half-naked boys started jumping all over the place and shoved Zlatka and me together. I grabbed her forearm, slippery from sweat. Then she kissed me on the cheek, just for the hell of it. I felt absolute delight, so much that I was ashamed. She was smiling.

After the concert the crowd dispersed toward the bathroom and the bar. The dive's regular musical repertoire was now being piped in, so we stayed at the dance floor and danced a bit more and kicked around plastic cups with our feet.

"I hate it when the party's over," Zlatka said dejectedly. She was slurring. "I sober up immediately in horror when they turn off the music and switch on the lights. And when I see these bottles and cups all over the place . . . it's like the apocalypse."

I couldn't agree more. Everything is somehow more bearable in the dark.

When we got out, our bodies steamed. The cold forced us to huddle our necks in our shoulders like turkeys. We stood at the door and watched the darkness around us. In the distance, down the tracks, the train station glowed.

"What do you wanna do now?" she asked. I didn't feel like going home. The very thought that this night, so opulent and alive, could wither in the loneliness of my cold hole, on that limp red futon, to the tune of the muffled squealing of the water heater, made me draw my neck into my shoulders even more. And I couldn't even imagine taking Zlatka there. "Okay, let's go to my place," she said as if she could read my mind. She jangled her keys and pointed at an old, white Yugo parked at the entrance to the dive.

■   ■   ■

We took our time jumping on each other, we played the game of delayed pleasure, which—it was clear the moment we had gotten in the car, the moment we had stepped into the elevator—was as imminent as sobering up.

Her apartment was on the eighth floor of a skyscraper in Sopot, a shady part of Novi Zagreb.

"It may be small, but the welcome is big!" Zlatka echoed the slogan for Daewoo Tico, the smallest of small cars, as she let me in.

The hallway was also a kitchen; further in there was a larger room whose glass wall separated it from a narrow balcony with a concrete railing. We had to be quiet not to wake up Mila; the little girl slept in the other room. Framed photos of Zlatka and her daughter smiled from bookshelves. Not taking off my coat, I stepped out onto the balcony to get some fresh air. I felt a little dizzy; the vista of concrete lumps wobbled in front of me as gently as feather grass. Deep down below my feet Dubrovnik Avenue was cramped. The cars rushed maniacally through the traffic lights trying to catch the green. Behind me, back in the apartment, Zlatka put on a CD with covers of '60s hits.

"Why can't I stop and tell myself I'm wrong, I'm wrong, so wrong," softly sang some woman, possibly black? Zlatka came up to me and occupied her own piece of railing.

"See that skyscraper," she pointed her chin toward the building separated from ours by a plateau the size of a basketball court. "Some woman fell from her balcony yesterday, from the eighth floor, just like this one, across the way. She leaned over and fell," she said and stared down into the darkness. "I keep thinking about it. I wonder if she did it on purpose. I mean, these balcony railings are quite high, you can't just fall over by accident."

I lowered my eyes, looking into the abyss below. I imagined police and a forensic team crowding around a fat housewife's corpse and a huge bloody stain remaining on the pavement after the investigation.

"This morning I met a neighbor in the elevator and she told me a lot of the tenants didn't go to work yesterday so that they could see what was going on. They stood on their balconies like they were in a stadium somewhere, they spent the whole afternoon like that. Primitive bastards, see what people here are like?"

"Eh, it's the same everywhere," I said.

Down on the avenue a car ran a red light.

■ ■ ■

She offered me her toothbrush. I showered with her shower gel, I put her lotion on my body, and used her makeup remover and cotton pads to take off my makeup. When I was done, she tossed me a pink Mickey Mouse T-shirt. We opened the couch, put on the sheets, and turned off the light.

I started it. It was so natural to reach for Zlatka's breasts: it seemed they were shaped to fit the mold of my palms. My breasts are round in a perfectly normal kind of way; they're actually uninteresting. But hers are small, pyramid-shaped, and soft. I held them, my eyes closed, not breathing, until her hardened nipples pressed against my palm. I kissed them gently, as if kissing someone I love because they're unavailable to me. She held me tighter: I was hers. Her approval filled me with joy; I wanted to please her, as though she were some mythical goddess. I kissed her neck and slipped under the sheet like a worm under tree bark. I took off her panties. I paid attention to every movement of my head, to every twitch; I listened carefully to her breathing. She moaned. Just a quick touch of a soft curve of my tongue on her clitoris. She moaned again. Spread her legs wider, twisted and threw her head back.

■ ■ ■

It's morning, the blinds are up, the room is filled with light, and by my side Zlatka is still snoring like a man.

The first thing I see when I free myself from her embrace is the smiling face of a little girl maybe ten years old. Her brown hair reaches her shoulders, she kneels in front of me, and her sleepy eyes are so close to mine that I imagine that only a moment ago she must have kissed me or smelled me, like a dog. Then I realize this is Mila, she's already up, clanging cups in the kitchen, letting the water run in the sink, opening the cupboards.

"What kind of tea do you like?" she asks me as she materializes again. Embarrassed, I sit up in the bed and immediately pain invades my temples. I feel stupid in a wrinkled T-shirt with Mickey Mouse printed on it.

"Mint," I say in a voice that sounds squeaky and hoarse this morning. I'm confused and slow. I smile anxiously at Mila who, completely relaxed, begins to chatter away about having an early music class, about her listening quiz, which consists of the teacher playing a CD with parts of different compositions, for example of Mozart or Beethoven, which the students then have to identify on paper, Requiem or Pathétique. Her cheerfulness has a soothing effect on my sense of not belonging. It makes me feel soft.

Mila puts the tea on the nightstand by my side of the bed and then shakes Zlatka's forearm. "C'mon, Mom! I have an early class!" And then she goes to the bathroom. Zlatka slowly opens her eyes; when she sees me, her face gathers into a lazy smile and then she again buries her head in the pillow.

"An early class," she says and sighs, trying to get out of bed. When she realizes she's completely naked under the comforter, she wraps herself in it like a caterpillar. Without a word I lean toward the armchair and reach for the stretched-out T-shirt she removed so resolutely last night and threw into the darkness of the room.

We have cereal with yogurt for breakfast. A squirrel hunching over a large walnut like a fortune-teller over her crystal ball smiles at us from the cereal box. Zlatka and I share our hangover in silence, but that doesn't make it any more bearable. Only Mila seems genuinely happy: she talks about school, lists her favorite courses, and brags about her midterm grades.

In front of the building, we get into Zlatka's Yugo. She'll take Mila to school, drop me off at home, and then go to work.

The school is nearby. During the short drive over wet streets of Novi Zagreb I see a lot of right angles, heavy traffic, a few traffic lights, a tramline behind a neglected hedge. In a few minutes we're in front of a playground in which a couple of boys are hanging around the basketball court with a ball in their hands. Despite the cold, they've taken off their jackets and are jumping at each other excitedly, yelling. Mila adjusts her scarf and kisses Zlatka on the cheek; in return, Zlatka then kisses her on the forehead. "What a smart little forehead," she says. I say, "Good luck with your listening quiz!" Mila says, "Thanks!" and leaves. We watch her as she runs toward a group of smiling girls with a huge checkered bag on her back; one of the girls waves at her in a wide arc, like the guy at the airport who signals the planes. They fall into each other's arms with so much force that Mila's hair sticking out under her woolen hat shakes vigorously.

"They sit together in class," Zlatka says, then puts the car in gear and we move slowly on.

The rest of our drive is more or less horrible. We feel Mila's absence and have nothing to replace it with. As if everything that happened last night happened to someone else. On the bridge, the line of cars moves more and more slowly. The drive downtown seems like an impenetrable eternity. "It's always like this in the morning, every morning," says Zlatka. "You simply can't avoid it. I stopped worrying about it," she says. Still, her fingers are restless on the wheel, and when she puts one on the gearshift, there's a moist trace left behind.

I reach for the radio; I feel the need for a song, any song, to make the silence more bearable. Even the commercials for a weekend sale at Konzum Supermarket would do.

"It doesn't work," says Zlatka and glances compassionately at the radio. "It died on me."

"But didn't we listen to it last night, when we were driving to your place?"

"That was in our heads."

We drive on in the tense silence. Zlatka adjusts the heat, plays with the gearshift, looks down the river the color of chocolate pudding. I watch the cars stranded on the bridge. Today, they are mostly red.

She parks in front of Rin Tin Tin. I've told her she doesn't have to drive me all the way home, that I live really nearby, "just around the corner." Before we get out of the car, we sit there for a little while. We should say something; make our good-bye pleasant, normal. Still, we say nothing and everything is odd, unfinished, trembling from insecurity. Then, as if on cue, we reach for the doors at the same time, and get out. A smile, "Bye, see you!" and that's it. After a few steps Zlatka reaches the hair salon and disappears behind the glass door and its sticker saying, "Push!"

I'm left alone.

■ ■ ■

Instead of going to my apartment, I head downtown, across the railway. At eight in the morning the city looks foreign enough that it almost seems it might be possible to get lost in it. I can't remember the last time I was up this early. Everything is so interesting: teenagers with their doodle-covered backpacks and bloated, warm jackets running to catch the tram; women and men with circles under their eyes marching toward escalators and gluing their sluggish eyes to the newspaper in the hands of the fat news vendor waving around his wares and yelling out the headlines. A bit farther, retirees come out of the crowded tram carrying canvas bags. Everywhere, the smell of coffee.

I let the traffic lights set my course: I go wherever I see green. I walk along the botanical garden's fence: I glance at the sad, dried-up puddle that in May will become a small romantic lake, like on a tapestry. I walk over the asphalt strip of a grass-covered schoolyard, a path swelling over the chestnut-tree roots. The school's cafeteria oozes the smell of fried chicken into the morning—the smell of hot oil floating all over the place, sticking to rusty garbage bins and the benches on the far side of the hedge.

I walk into a coffee shop in a small plaza. I've been here before. I nod to a sinewy waiter with hairy arms who's fishing for dirty glasses in a foamy sink, sponging them vigorously. I say, "Espresso, please," and then take the wooden stairs to the gallery upstairs. There's no one there. I sit by the window and watch: a flower shop, a kiosk, a hot dog stand, a garbage man who's stopped his tricycle in front of a bakery to eat his bagel in peace. On the wall behind him someone spray-painted "IGOR" in red letters, put a frame around it, and pierced it with an arrow.

Then my eyes hit on a street clock. It stands above the monument of a war hero, himself standing on the tips of his toes with a machine gun in his hand and a wince on his face. The clock reads five to noon. But it can't be that late.

"Excuse me, what's the time?" I ask the waiter who's just brought me coffee. With his chin, he points to the clock on the wall across from me. It's just after nine.

I stare at the broken clock on the plaza and then at the brass soldier's face. That's my cue, it occurs to me, those frozen hands. I quickly finish my espresso, grab my scarf and my bag, and then go down, pay, and leave. The garbage man is no longer in front of the bakery, he pedaled away. The sky is gray, the air colder than it seems, and the plaza livelier than before.

"It might snow," I hear some woman say into her cell phone. I pass by her, head back toward the botanical garden, toward the train station, I walk quickly, rushing. Trams, people, cars. I rush through the city's images so quickly that they have no time stick to me. Later I'll remember nothing, not even the way I raised the legs of my pants as I crossed the rails and hopped across as if at a dress rehearsal for a folklore dance group, nor how I was already out of breath by the time I reached the switchman's box, but I'll remember how I went even faster because it was clearer to me than ever, than anything, that it was five to noon, it was high time—for anything.

■ ■ ■

At Rin Tin Tin, I saw through the window, there was no one but Zlatka. Trying to catch my breath, I watched her lean close to the mirror and trim her bangs using a small comb. She was so engrossed she didn't look outside even once, and perhaps she didn't even blink. When she was done, she stepped back and blew her hair away from her forehead. Then she disappeared behind a small door where the restroom had to be.

My heart was pounding in my ears as I fished for a lipstick at the bottom of my bag. I opened it and pressed it against the glass. My hands were shaking a little. My ears pounded. I hadn't planned it, the lipstick slid across the glass on its own: I wrote a large Z, shaky, the color of a rotten cherry. It felt like I'd been freed from something. Then I wrote L-A-T-K-A. Zlatka. She was still behind that door. My breath was shallow and irregular. I had a little lipstick left. I drew a heart around Zlatka's name and an arrow that pierced it. I put the lipstick back in my bag and went home.

■ ■ ■

On my way home I imagined her surprise as she approached the window, opened the door, and ran her fingers across the grains of lipstick stuck in the letters. I imagined a smile rising ticklishly at the corners of her mouth, making her face soft, those raylike wrinkles around her eyes. This made me laugh, at first silently, warily, but then I couldn't hold it anymore: I shrieked and laughed out loud, happily. In front of a small store the drunks looked at me in amazement, squeezing the bottles in their hands, frowning dully.

TRANSLATED FROM CROATIAN BY TOMISLAV KUZMANOVIĆ

AGUSTÍN FERNÁNDEZ PAZ

This Strange Lucidity

The time comes not to wait for anybody. Love goes by, silent and fleeting, like a train in the night. [J O A N M A R G A R I T , *F I R S T C O L D*]

Every night we return to the same place, like puppets directed by an invisible hand. He takes up position under the magnolia, except on rainy days; when it's damp, he seeks shelter in the doorway of the hardware store, as if still afraid of catching a cold or getting a migraine, as he always used to whenever he wet his feet or head. I'm not blaming him, routines end up sticking to the skin as if they were part of us. When I think about it, everything I do is a routine. If you could see me, you'd realize, after standing by his side for a few minutes, that I always grow impatient and start running up and down the pavement, without ever leaving the area between the corner shop and the greengrocer's. Sniffing here and there, at tree trunks, lampposts, garage corners, building walls . . . My snout permanently pressed up against things in an absurd attempt to pick up a scent, since I can't smell any more, odors have disappeared for good and all that's left of them is memory.

He stays on his feet all night, indifferent to the world going by. He only has eyes for the building opposite, more specifically for the windows on the sixth floor, which is where the Woman lives. We always arrive around dusk, so at least one of the windows is normally illuminated. If it's the right-hand one, I know she's in the lounge, possibly having dinner in front of the TV; if it's the middle one, I imagine her sitting at the desk in her study, staring at the computer screen; if it's the one on the left, which is always the last to go dark, I suppose she's in the bedroom, lying in bed and reading a novel, the way he used to.

Her lights go out early, they're rarely on any time after midnight. Some days, though, they stay on late and then he starts to get worried, you can see it in his expression. But that doesn't happen often, the lights are normally off at night. He never takes his eyes off them, as if the world were nothing more than those three dark rectangles. Meanwhile I pass the time wandering about, never going far, not that I have anywhere to go, anxiously pacing up and down the pavement, still unable to accept I can't pick up the wealth of scents that used to excite me so much. I know they're there, covering every inch of the ground, and I'm the one who's lost the capacity to detect them.

The first few days, I found it difficult to accept this change. I was vaguely aware of what was going on, but couldn't understand why the channels through which I received the sensations that made up my picture of the world were suddenly blocked, while another dimension I hadn't noticed before became open to me. This strange lucidity, this ability to fathom what was previously unfathomable, this way of relating things and drawing conclusions, this putting into words everything I experience. I didn't realize this would happen, I'd never even stopped to think about it. Perhaps it was better not to imagine anything before the time came, it would have been too terrible. It's better like this. Now that the end is coming and the final night is almost upon us, I can appreciate how the only good thing about this sentence is its expiration date, the fact it will all be over in a matter of hours.

This is how we've spent every night of the last year, the hours slipping slowly by until the darkness begins to disperse and the air fills with a clarity that obliges us to withdraw to this desolate spot where we pass our days. Him sitting on the sofa, me resting on the rug, both of us motionless, occasionally exchanging glances, possibly to confirm we're still there and not alone. A routine like that of some winter afternoons before my sentencing, except that now all we do is wait. We both know everything's changed and, while we may be surrounded by the same furniture and familiar objects, this is no longer our home, but a no-man's-land we occupy, waiting for the night to return, so we can take to the pavement again and renew our vigil opposite the Woman's building.

Sometimes, especially on dark winter evenings, we're lucky enough to witness her coming back home from work or one of her walks. These are the best moments, because his face lights up and he focuses all his attention on her every movement. I also get excited and try to attract her attention, though I know there's no point, since there's no sound coming out of my mouth. We both watch as she pauses in the doorway, searches for her keys, sometimes turns her head and stares in our direction, as if she could see us or otherwise detect our presence. Normally, though, she just puts the key in the lock, opens the door, and disappears inside the building. That's when I start counting slowly, not stopping until one of the windows becomes illuminated. I can reach 120 or 150, though sometimes she takes longer to go upstairs and, since I don't know how to count beyond two hundred, I end up getting bored; by the time I realize I'm bored, the lights have finally gone on.

I remember the first day we saw her, it was at the beach. She was sitting on a bench, reading a book with a yellow cover. I stopped beside her and she started stroking me. The truth is I hadn't stopped for her, but for the extraordinarily strong odor emanating from one of the bench legs. He was a little farther behind, at the beach he always liked to let me run free, and stopped when he reached us. They started talking about me and the book in her hands. After a while, she invited him to sit down and they stayed like that for ages, totally oblivious to me. Rarely had I seen my master so happy, he was positively radiant. I don't mean he was normally a bit sullen, it would be wrong to suggest such a thing. I just mean there was a special happiness about him that day which I'd never seen.

They talked and talked, until the sun was swallowed by the sea. Then, after they'd said good-bye and the two of us had returned to the car, he put on some livelier music than he generally listened to while driving and didn't stop singing all the way. Back home, having eaten dinner almost without noticing me, he took out a green notebook and started scribbling all over it. He must have carried on doing so for quite some time because that's the last image I have of that day, before going to bed and falling asleep.

After that, they started seeing each other almost daily. First they met at the beach, but we soon began to visit other places. She was very talkative and I quickly grew fond of her, since she treated me well and paid attention to me. And also because she made him happy and this put me in an excellent mood. Happy days! Most of the time, we went on long walks in places I'd never been to. I particularly remember a path between some oak trees, with the sun filtering through the leaves and lighting up small spots on the ground, so bright and warm I had to keep stopping at them. What a feast of unfamiliar fragrances! I was used to city smells, which while pleasant were always predictable, and was confused by these wilder, more piercing odors, traces of animals hiding not far away, in among all that silence. I remember another afternoon by the river, with the water bubbling along and me desperately trying to catch the butterflies that alighted on the flowers in the riverside meadows. It was the first time I'd seen so many, with such different colors, and I didn't know which one to chase. I spent half the afternoon wasting my time, since they always flew off just as I was about to reach them. I also remember from that day the hum of the crickets and grasshoppers that leaped away as I raced toward them through the tall grass. Meanwhile the two of them sat on a log, holding hands, smiling tenderly, as if they were alone in the world and nothing else mattered. I remember another morning, climbing a hillside along narrow paths between wild gorse and broom, the three of us panting from the effort. Then, at the top, my amazement at the vastness of the world stretching out over valleys in a patchwork of fields, woods, and farmland. Happy times! I would feel a twinge of nostalgia right now, if it were possible for me to feel such a thing under these conditions.

One day the Woman came to our house for lunch. From early that morning, our routine was smashed to smithereens. The only thing that didn't change was our brief walk around the neighborhood shortly after we got up. On our return, the tranquility we normally enjoyed on his days off simply vanished. The artificial flowers in the vase in the hallway disappeared to be replaced by a bunch of freshly cut white roses. The lounge was cleaner than it had ever been, and that included my favorite rug, where I often used to doze. The table was covered in a light blue cloth I'd never seen. Two places were set, plates and glasses carefully arranged, together with a small jar holding a yellow rose. The aromas emerging from the kitchen, the scent of meat that used to drive me so crazy, had me on edge the whole morning.

I wasn't expecting to go out again before lunchtime, but quickly recovered from my surprise once I was in the open air and realized we were heading for the park with the yellow benches. I always liked going, especially on days like this, when there were fewer cars and everyone seemed to have agreed to take their dogs for a walk. As we wandered between trees and bushes positioned to protect the flower beds, I kept an anxious eye out for the brown-haired bitch I liked so much. There were setters, spaniels, mastiffs, westies, but that morning she wasn't among them. I was very sorry, I rarely had a chance to sniff her and run around with her, but I soon got over it and started playing with every dog I came across, that's how spontaneous I was back then.

I was panting by the time we got back home, it had been a very long walk. We'd just come in when she arrived, with that happy expression that made her different, a happiness that always influenced my master. I soon discovered the treasure in the oven was not for me. Having placed the meat tray on the kitchen surface, he began to cut thin slices, which he put in a serving dish and proceeded to drape in thick, golden gravy. He then took the dish into the lounge, while I got meatballs as usual. I wolfed them down, I was that hungry, and, as happened most days, soon fell asleep.

When I woke up, the lounge was empty. The remains of the meal were still on the table and I had to resist the urge to jump up and take a piece of meat, I knew he wouldn't like it. Besides, my attention was drawn to the noise and muffled laughter coming from my master's bedroom. I ran toward it, but found the door closed. This surprised me, the doors in our house were never closed. "Off you go, Argos, back to the lounge." His order was obscured by the Woman's giggles. I left with my tail between my legs. I'd never felt so humiliated, he'd never done this to me before. It took them some time to emerge. When they did, they both had a strange glazed look on their faces and were clearly sharing something that didn't include me.

There were many days like this. On others, having taken me for a longer walk than usual, he would leave me alone at home. I shouldn't have minded, I was used to him doing this whenever he went to work, but I was sad it happened on precisely those days we used to spend together. It wasn't difficult to guess where he'd gone, the look on his face when he came back was the same he had when the two of them spent the afternoon shut up in his bedroom. So, although it hurt spending so many hours without his company, my pain was softened by the great joy in his eyes when he returned, a joy that drove him to play with me as when we were first together.

Now that I have a better understanding of things and can reflect on my previous life, I recall the many hours I spent alone at home. They struck me then as boring, I waited anxiously for my master to return, but now I realize they could have been just as interesting as the hours we spent out walking, despite the fact they all passed between the four walls of our home.

In the mornings, we always got up early, however dark it was in winter, and quickly headed outside. We'd go for a short walk in the neighboring streets, never going farther than the entrance to the park. I loved these walks. The streets would be crawling with dogs, since lots of other people took their dogs out at the same time. This was my chance to see the brown dog with the attractive scent. Some mornings, depending on whether they let us off the leash or not, we could sniff each other to our hearts' content and even race along the pavement. But these moments were fleeting, or so they seemed to me, as if happiness in life were always limited to small doses guaranteed never to satisfy our longing.

After that, we'd return home. He'd soon head for work and I'd be left alone. As the doors were normally never closed, I could come and go as I pleased through the different rooms. Some mornings, the cleaning lady would arrive and then, for a few hours, everything was much more fun, she was like a whirlwind and never stopped moving and singing. "Goddamn dog," she would complain at times, "your hair is all over the place!" But I knew she didn't really mind, you could tell from her tone of voice. I would run along behind her, from one room to the next, clinging to her skirt until I grew tired and flopped down on top of the rug. It calmed me, knowing she was there, dogs of my breed aren't used to loneliness. Maybe that's why I found the mornings the cleaning lady didn't come so hard to endure. Too many hours spent in silence, when time itself seemed to grind to a halt.

It occurs to me now how silly I was, there were plenty of things to occupy my attention. The house was silent, okay, but not the rest of the building. Noises came from other apartments, which I learned little by little to recognize. The child above us crying, the muffled sound of the television that was always on in the room next to our lounge, the trills of the canary downstairs, the music coming from one of the interior windows . . . I could hear these things clearly if I went into the kitchen or spare bedroom, both of which looked out onto the light well at the back. Light well! That's ironic. Light was the last thing to reach this confined space, which may have been why I preferred to stay in the lounge, listening to the monotonous sounds of the street outside. The cars, their horns, sudden braking. The rumble of a machine, the hustle and bustle of people. Noises that in winter would sometimes be silenced by the raging wind and rain beating against the windows.

The noises in the building were made by people who, like me, had stayed at home while others went to work. They were almost always women, who insisted on cooking when the sun was high in the sky, creating a stream of odors that reached my nostrils even when the windows were closed and kept me on tenterhooks until my master's return. Now that I think about it, I feel nostalgic for those days. If I could relive them, I would pay attention to the sounds of life I previously ignored.

One day, my master returned home in a pool of sadness. It's the only time I remember him walking straight past me and shutting himself in his room. He didn't come out for ages. This had me worried and confused, I didn't know what to do. It was obvious something serious had happened, but I had no idea what it was. I ended up howling next to the door of his bedroom, I couldn't bear it. He opened the door and finally acknowledged my presence, holding me close and bursting into tears.

The days that followed were terrible. I never found out what had happened, but understood he'd broken it off with the Woman. She wouldn't be coming around anymore, and we wouldn't be going around to her place either. There would be no more walks along the beach or in the country. Sadness became a permanent fixture in our home, music was silenced, walks were shorter and duller. Such bitterness! He again paid attention to me, I could spend all the hours I liked at his side, but this didn't make me feel any better, his sadness was like a cloud over our lives.

As the weeks went by, his sadness decreased. Perhaps there's truth in the saying "time heals all wounds." One afternoon, the music went back on, though only sad, melancholy songs. Our walks got longer and I suspect at the time he was happy to have me around and so feel obliged to take me out every day.

Over the following months, three women came into his life. One of them was very nice, whenever she entered the house it was as if an earthquake was making even the tiniest object vibrate. How I longed for my master to shut himself in his room with her as well! I wanted to hear that laughter again, see the same sparks of happiness in his eyes. But it never happened and none of these women lasted very long. Soon it was just the two of us again.

After the last of these relationships, he renewed his habit of leaving town from time to time, as we had done when I was young. I enjoyed traveling in the car, though I didn't like being confined to the back seat. It was pleasant watching the world go by, understanding how much more there was to discover. Our destination was always the house of his mother, a white-haired woman who treated me well and handed me treats. It was impossible not to love her. We would return home in the evening, happy at the good time we'd had.

I remember the last of those days, how could I forget it? It was autumn now and the morning was magnificent. We walked beside the river and then went to his mother's for lunch. Later, on the way back, he decided to leave the main road and take a detour in search of a place he used to visit as a child. When we got out of the car, I discovered it was an old chestnut grove. The ground was covered in dry leaves and a large number of burs. Burs I was seeing for the first time and had to be wary of, their spikes were very painful. Some of them were half open and revealed the chestnuts held inside. My master went to the car to get a plastic bag, where he placed the chestnuts he had collected. I hadn't seen him so enthusiastic in a long time, as if this childhood activity were returning the smile he'd lost due to the absence of the Woman he continued to love. I also let myself go and didn't stop jumping up around him, I've already said I was easily influenced by the happiness of others.

Dusk was falling when we got back in the car. The sky that had been blue in the morning was now covered by thick, black clouds. Lightning flashed in the distance, illuminating the heavens with its disturbing glare. And then came the sound of thunder, a long rumble drawing gradually closer, which made my heart sink. It started raining, more and more persistently. The windshield wipers couldn't get all the water off the glass. The road was unmarked and it was difficult to know which way to go, my master kept complaining he couldn't see a thing. That was when two strong lights appeared in front of us, flooding the inside of the car. I only had time to hear a terrible noise and then I fell into a darkness that swallowed up the lights, the car, the rain, and everything around me. That blackness devoured everything, including him.

The dawn is coming. The bedroom light has just gone on. She is waking up to another day, though today is special. I wonder if she'll remember what the date is, it's been a year since he and I abandoned this world. Though I should say "started to abandon this world," since there's this delay neither of us was expecting, these 365 days of the strange life we've been given to bid farewell to our loved ones before we vanish.

I watch my master standing motionless like a statue, eyes fixed on the rectangle of light. As I watch him moving his lips, I know he's speaking his final words, possibly some of those verses he liked so much and used to recite to me:

> Thanks I would like to give
> for the days you share with me,
> for caresses and kisses.

I see something like a tear sliding slowly down his cheek, which accentuates the expression of infinite sadness on his face.

An older woman approaches on the pavement, accompanied by her dog, a black fox terrier. On reaching us, the animal stops and sniffs around the area where I am. I notice the confusion on his face. He's obviously aware of my presence, but can't see me or smell me. This is a sign that something of me, however small, is left in the world. I want to bark, reward his attention, but no sound comes out, we ghosts can't bark. Our presence, I realize now, is a terrible punishment, reminding us of the things we've lost.

The fox terrier continues on his way. The tugging on his leash gets stronger and forces him to leave. I look in the direction of my master, who has become a hazy figure, as if his body were disintegrating. I watch as he turns into filaments of strange mist that merge with the morning air. He still has time to look away from the window and glance at me for a split second, long enough for our eyes to meet for the last time.

Then I notice he's not the only one disappearing. Everything around me is turning into a gray, uniform mist that makes it more and more difficult to discern things. Trees, houses, lampposts, cars, clouds, everything is falling apart. Finally, reaching the end of that strange lucidity that has accompanied me for the past year, I understand what's really happening is that my body's beginning to fade, dissolving in a succession of threads that loosen the knots tying them together and disperse as the light of day grows stronger. I realize this year of a strange life is coming to an end for me as well, never again shall I be present in this world I loved so much. My head is being emptied of words, I can't string together enough sentences to express how grateful I am for the days I've lived. The only sentences I retain are those of the poem my master liked to recite:

> Thanks for youth and senses.
> Thanks for the wind that makes us strangers to ourselves.
> Thanks for the sea, absolute and powerful.
> Thanks for silence and verses.[1]

TRANSLATED FROM GALICIAN BY JONATHAN DUNNE

---

1   These lines are from a poem by Xulio López Valcárcel, "Another Poem of Gifts," from *August Memories*.

desire

JANUSZ RUDNICKI

The Sorrows of Idiot Augustus

My life is motionless, *motionless like a glove from which a hand had been withdrawn*, as Bruno Schulz put it. I am, as of recently, a teacher of Polish, though have now been given early retirement. Middle school. I live in a city of medium size, I am of medium build, I have a medium-sized pension, a medium-sized apartment, and I am middle-aged. Deeply middle-aged.

I am, as of a long time ago, a father, and as of recently, a grandfather, although I see my grandson only rarely. My daughter emigrated, she lives in a big city and has a big belly—she's giving birth again soon. I am, as of ten years ago, a widower. I once translated a poem for my late wife's benefit, it was by some German poet, I can't remember his name, but I remember the poem, it went something like this: *Die before me, a little bit before. So you don't have to go back home by yourself. I had to go by myself.* The funeral was purely symbolic, she'd been coming back from visiting our daughter, all that was left of the plane was the black box. I look at every one that flies over me, and each greets me with a tilt of its wing flaps. I've looked at every single one, for ten years now.

Today I went to the cemetery. I sat down by her, on the little bench, as usual, and as usual I read. Schulz, as usual. My Schulz. I am like his "Old-Age Pensioner," I live because death has passed me by. I am of no consequence, so that the *mere sound of the barrel organ launches me upward*, and as soon as there is a wind, I am like a leaf *gliding along through yellow autumnal expanses*. I could become chairman of the Schulz Club, if such a thing were to be founded.

Today I decided to leave town. For the first time, after all these years.

What's more, today I decided to start a diary. For the first time ever, outside of school. I decided to leave because . . . I decided to leave because . . . Hmm. I realized that it was the thirtieth anniversary of my wedding. Yes. Today. Thirtieth altogether, although in essence the twentieth. That was the first thing. I wanted to leave, to go where we'd gone back then, after our wedding. To Sicily. To Taormina. I hesitated because of my blood pressure, but I'd really already made my mind up. Because of our anniversary, but that wasn't the only reason. Because of this couple, too, today at the cemetery, that was the other reason. At the very edge of the cemetery, they were sitting on a bench, they thought that nobody could see them, and what do you know, that nobody just happened to be me. They were sitting next to each other, unrepentantly young, kissing and touching each other, hurriedly, nervously, *the serpentine movements of their limbs*, as though they had more than four hands, in order to get there faster, she spread her legs, his hand slid underneath her dress like a ser- pent, she moaned, with his other hand he undid his fly, and now his Count of Monte Cristo, kept imprisoned till now, finally peeked out through this window onto the world, which must have made her shy, because instead of leaning over his fate pointing now at nothing, she turned away, which didn't mean that she left him at the mercy of his fate, no, she took it, that fate, in her hand, and that was it, after a couple of vertical movements, that was it, a soundless explosion from a cannon aimed at the sky. He started to search through his pockets for something, one-handed, because she, irritated, was holding onto the other, and he took out a tissue, with which he started to wipe off his pants, while I retreated in silence, giving up my role as witness, and I went home, alone as usual.

And as usual I sat down alone on the balcony, then in front of the TV, then again on the balcony, and as usual I called up the whorehouse, as usual only when I really have to, and the whore came over, as usual with a condom, and I came, as usual in her mouth, because it's not like I could do it there, in the other place, that would be too intimate for me, too close, embarrassing, but here is distant, functional, you can stay a little detached. Then, as usual, I threw out the fact that had flowed out of me, into the trash, with ambivalence, and as usual I felt embarrassed by the fact that a rubber with my ejaculate in it was in the trash, so I went and took it out. As usual.

And then, in bed, I thought again of Powązki Cemetery. Our first trip together out of our medium-sized city and into the capital. She was wearing yellow shorts, much to the outrage of the elderly ladies passing by. We sat down on a bench and kissed, there was none of what people might call *heavy petting* today, even in Polish, though we might have been doing it in our heads, without using our hands.

Powązki Cemetery then and that couple at the cemetery today. And our thirtieth anniversary, which is basically our twentieth. And maybe also because I've never gone anywhere else, since then. Those are the reasons I decided to leave. To leave! I was so excited about my decision that I couldn't fall asleep. I just started thinking about what to take; what's more, I actually got up to start a little list, so as not to forget anything. I wrote: *Camera, Schulz, charger, don't forget!*

And when I'd written that, I added up at the top: *Taormina*, but then I crossed this out and wrote: *Trip to Sicily*, but then I crossed that out and wrote: *I am, as of recently, a teacher of Polish*, though have now been given *early retirement*. And that's how this diary got started.

I've arrived. I'm at the airport in Messina. I was flying with her, all the time. I was holding her hand, so much so that the armrests turned my fingers white (I won't write about her anymore). An hour's bus ride (*To travel the clear ribbon of the highways*, I sang under my breath) and there it is, Taormina, my love. Two bays, islets, beaches, and from there it's all uphill, the little streets, the houses, the tiny houses, squares, tiny squares, churches, tiny churches, castles, tiny castles, all the way up to the amphitheater, all strung by the hand of God along the precipitous slope of Mount Tauro, all of it suspended over that slope like a tablecloth, and above that, further up, up, that smoky oil lamp of cosmic proportions, Her Highness, Mount Etna.

I'd booked an exquisite hotel, the aristocratic Villa Ducale. Fifteen minutes to the historic town center going in one direction, and going in the other, three seconds to the sea, flinging yourself off the cliffs. I'd booked for three days, the Junior Suite, cheaper because it's the end of September, two hundred and fifty euros a night, goodbye savings. The Suite takes your breath away, the magnificent bed in the bedroom, the entresol, and the rest of it all made me want to put on my felt slippers first thing. The view from the balcony: the sea and the bay. The view from the terrace: Taormina, and above it, Mount Etna. Breakfast is included in the price of the hotel, but I got there too late and missed it, went to the veranda, sat down, and ate my sandwiches along with the paper they were wrapped in, because it had been soaked all the way through along the way from the Medium-Sized City.

I'm sitting at the Teatro Greco, the amphitheater. I walked down Corso Umberto, through Piazza IX Aprile, near the San Giuseppe Cathedral and a bar called Wunderbar, where there are a lot of people waiting, hoping to see some star. One of the earthly ones, not one of the ones in the sky. (I was walking with her, I'm not going to write about her anymore.)

I'm sitting in the very back row, the stage is down below, and I'm surrounded by walls that predate Christ. I feel like I'm sitting astride the very pinnacle of history. Is there a girl on the stage? A young woman? Too far, I can't see. She's practicing her cartwheels, some of them successful, some of them not. The successful ones look like spinning stars.

I'm at the hotel. I was in the shower, and now, on the balcony, I sit and wonder. Because, at the amphitheater, I went down to see her from up close. Because I was speechless when I sat down and saw her from up close. Because she looked like Salma Hayek with her legs in the air. Because she was doing a handstand, and her blouse had ridden up to her chin and revealed two peaches with these two little pinpoints. She saw me looking, she saw that I saw, she very clearly saw me looking, because she stayed like that, even though she knew that her blouse had ridden up and exposed her. On the floor, black hair all wound up, above that her face, over her mouth and neck a red shirt, above that—look higher!—above them a stomach, dark from the sun, like it's sculpted, trembling, glistening with her sweat, and then at the very top a pair of sneakers. I leaned over so we could see each other from the same angle. She said, *ciao, signore,* which pained me a little, it made me feel like a senior citizen, being called *signore.* I said, *ciao signorina,* gave a little wave, and got up to leave, but then I caved in, I turned around, by then she was standing, she was on her legs again, she looked the same, only reversed.

I'm going to bed . . .

I got up, it's one in the morning, I can't sleep. Underneath my eyelids are curlicues that insist on merging into a single shape, into her shape. And surrounding her, the walls of the amphitheater, and behind them the Ionian Sea, and Mount Etna.

Have you lost your mind? Go to sleep! Come to your senses! Take a look at yourself and go to sleep! Sleep, sleep, sleep!

I can't believe this! This can't be happening, it's like a movie, not like life! I went down to breakfast earlier, even though I hadn't slept enough at all, I was one of the first, so that I could fill up once and then come back before noon to eat one more time and save money on lunch that way, and maybe even dinner, so I went down, and I was eating off the buffet of Sicilian specialties, on the terrace with the panorama view, I was eating, I was drinking, drinking, eating, and at some point I saw her! She was holding a tray and refilling the seafood at the buffet, in a waitress uniform! At my hotel! It was like I had been struck by a bolt of . . . well, what, exactly? I went back up, to my room, I stood in front of the mirror and slapped myself. Then I walked around, from the balcony to the terrace, from the terrace to the balcony. I opened up Schulz, just to escape from myself. In the story "Mr. Charles," Mr. Charles can't even get into his own apartment's good graces, which is why he treads so lightly in it, to not occasion any other intruder *in the guise of the echo of his steps.*

Soon I went downstairs, for my second breakfast, I sat down with my back to the buffet, facing the sea, and then I caved in, and I got up and sat down again with my back to the sea, facing the buffet, and there she was! She was standing there by the buffet, again, polishing the silverware, the forks, blowing on them and wiping them down with a cloth, I observed her *with a mixture of apprehension and pleasurable excitement,* she looked at me, I nodded my head, I raised my hand, and with my other hand I set my glass of juice back down on the table, and she smiled and kept wiping off the forks, slowly, up and down, up and down, that scamp, that scamp! If Saint Anthony had ever been tempted like this, he wouldn't have become a saint. Back to my room, back to the mirror, back to slapping my own face, onto the balcony, from the balcony onto the terrace, from the terrace onto the balcony and then back down, noon, breakfast over, it's empty.

I went out, I walked along Corso Umberto again, I saw the public library, I wanted to go in, I was actually going in, but just then an invisible hand seized me by the collar . . . but whose hand? And pushed me out onto the street, and pushed me on toward the amphitheater.

I'm sitting up at the top of it, she's not here.

She's here, she's here, she's very much here! I'm at the hotel, so much has happened that . . . where to . . . well, I went to the beach, from the amphitheater I went to the beach, down those narrow, winding streets, there weren't that many people on the beach, it's the end of September after all, I didn't have a bathing suit, I didn't have anything to sit down on, I was the only one sitting there fully dressed, my shoes sitting next to me, I must have looked like I'd come straight out of the People's Republic of Poland, on some delegation, all that was missing was the handkerchief on top of my head, with its four tied corners. I sat, and I waited, and she came! With a helmet in her hand, with people, with a whole group of people, like a loud, laughing ball rolling along and dropping right into the water and flying off into a thousand individual, movable parts. Slapped savagely in the face by youth, I felt.

She floated all the way out, her friends went to the bar, I didn't take my eyes off her, she came out of the water slowly, so slowly she looked like she was standing in place while the sea retreated. When it had retreated down to about her knees, she waved at me, and in that instant she stumbled over a rock, she stumbled, and she started limping, so I stood up, rolled up my pant legs, got a glimpse of my skinny, white calves, rolled them back down, and I went into the water with my pants on, the water went up to my own knees, I offered her my hand, which she took, eagerly, and I felt like she was caressing my very heart, and we walked up to the shore, slower and slower, and who invented shores? Or this one, specifically, in Taormina? It should recede a little bit. If it has to be there at all, it could at least recede. The people on the beach gave me a round of applause as we walked up, for my chivalry, I took a little bow, we sat down, and then the moment I had been dreading finally came, conversation, a little bit in German, a little bit in English, *parole, parole, parole,* I felt like showing off, calling attention to myself, I said, isn't it interesting that in English they use *butter* as a verb meaning *to ingratiate,* so imagine what it must sound like to them when they say *butterfly,* while in Polish, isn't it interesting, we use the word for "bread" in the same way, *chleb,* so we say, for example, "don't bread me up," *nie pochlebaj mnie,* when in English they say "don't butter me up," and she said she did find that interesting, and she told me she earned her living as a waitress and performed in the evenings with the people that had gone to the bar, they'd sing something, recite something, and she had that gymnastic show of sorts, I didn't understand exactly, and me? I am a journalist, I said, a reporter, I was sent here by a newspaper in Poland to write something about Taormina, and I had just about two days left, and then I was going back. Just two? That's how she said it, just two? Looking at me in such a way that the word "just" meant fewer and shorter than it ever had before.

They came back from the bar, she introduced them to me, they were young, with no clothes on, bad enough that I could've been everyone's father, on top of that I was wearing these old ragged clothes.

As though they'd just been introduced to the guy whose job is to collect fees for using the beach.

I couldn't understand what they were saying or what they were laughing at, I slapped something resembling a smile onto my face, just in case, and that was how I sat there, looking like the textbook definition of an eager-to-please idiot. Finally I stood up, started to say my good-byes, and she stood up too, asked if I wanted to go for a drive, I deduced based on her helmet that she meant on a motor scooter, the others made some comment or other, shouted out something to her as we were walking up off the beach, but it didn't matter, only this ride mattered, on a scooter, around Taormina. On either side of us there were vineyards and citrus trees, and ahead of me there were her thighs coming out from under her black dress, I was altogether struck *by the accuracy of their argument*, and her hair in my face. And the *vista sul mare*, from every spot, and craters overhead, and portals, and cornices of lava. I wanted for us to get frozen like that. In the middle of Taormina. On the Piazza IX Aprile, for example. For us to stay like that, on that scooter, cast in lava. As a monument, to the last love of her passenger. Out of lava, her hair, flying back. Out of lava, her dress, lifted up by the wind. The wind out of lava, his tears out of lava.

She dropped me off at the hotel. She told me where to go in the evening for their performance. I'm going . . .

Night. Pacing up and down my room. I have to go home tomorrow. I have to go home tomorrow.

I sat at the performers' table, clapping, not knowing what was going on. Some sort of juggling thing, they gave some kind of recital, played some music, sang, and her? She came on and did her cartwheels, like spinning stars, and in front of the microphone she did her handstand, and standing on her hands she started to sing "Ich bin von Kopf bis Fuß auf Liebe eingestellt," or "Head to toe, I'm ready to love," a kind of parody, in Polish for some reason it gets translated into "I'm made just to be loved," nobody would ever figure out what was really going on. She started singing, standing on her hands, and only then did she sit down on that barrel from *The Blue Angel* . . .

I have to go home tomorrow. I have to go home tomorrow.

And then, when we were all sitting around the table and drinking, she told me to stay, I said I had no reason to stay, she said I could perform with them, of course I knew immediately what my role would be. She said I would have dinner every day and a few euros, and where would I sleep, I asked, joking, because I thought that she was joking, too, and she said, well, where she—where they all—slept, in a big apartment, everyone had his own little nook, and I would stay with them, with her, in Taormina. I said that that would be nice, but that I had to go home, for work, she said, it would be nice, it's a shame you can't do it, and she asked if I wanted for her to take me back to the hotel, she felt like having a little walk anyway, because she had drunk too much, and when we were walking out, she ran her fingers through the hair of one of the guys, and then we got into a paddle boat that was sitting on the beach, by ourselves, the city above us, the sea before us, I took her hand and kissed it, she said we should push the boat into the water, the tether was long and we could float out a little, so we floated out, and she sat down on top of me, for the first time in over ten years I found myself there, a kind of cosmic relief on entering the gates of that wet heaven. Little by little I pedaled, little by little she rose and little by little she fell, we glided like a royal swan, almost soundlessly, noiselessly, waves came, from a ship crossing up ahead of us, and then, on those waves, the sea rocked us until it was over. And immediately I was surprised that there would be a ship so close to the shore. She told me to turn around, I turned around, the beach was far away, we had floated all the way out, I hadn't realized, I was facing the other way, she'd let the tether out, it had come undone, we were dragging it behind us, we were like a kite loosed from grasp by the land.

I have to go home tomorrow.

I'm at the airport in Messina. On the terrace. I saw it start up, take off, and disappear. They'd called my name out, a couple of times. What do I have to go home for?

I have my little nook. Mattress on the veranda, not enough space in the apartment, there's always someone sleeping somewhere. But I like to be alone, anyway. She sleeps in a room with a girlfriend, she can always come out to see me. But she doesn't. The starry night above me, mixed feelings inside me. Because she doesn't. And because she seemed confused when I came back and sat down at their table while she was singing. She swayed a little on her hands, I thought out of emotion, but then when she came up she acted like an embarrassed student greeting the teacher who had surprised her with an unannounced visit to her apartment.

During the day, while she works at the hotel, I'm at the beach, or walking around Taormina, or sitting at the public library. I know what Jarosław Iwaszkiewicz said about Taormina, the high heights, the silken sea, Mount Etna dissolving in the glow of the sun like a crystal, and the magical scenery of the Greco-Roman amphitheater, the only one like that in the whole world. I didn't know that Goethe had written about it too, had written it was *the greatest work of art and nature*.

At night I perform. My performance consists of going up on stage dressed like a clown and made up like a clown, my face looks out-of-date, I go on and carry her broken, heavy barrel for her, I can barely walk with it, I put it down in the middle there and want to get off, but the other clown shouts out at me (Idiot Augustus! Idiot Augustus!), he's smarter than I am, he's the one whose hair she ran her fingers through, he tells me to lift the barrel up and take it back to where it came from, and then he comes up to me, knocks it over, and shows me you can roll it, and then I, pleased that I won't have to carry it, roll the barrel. At the end of the program, though, I carry it off the stage the same way I carried it on, in my arms.

I wait for her at night, but she never comes, during the day she works at the hotel, fine, but only in the mornings, and there are fewer and fewer guests, and where does she go off to in the afternoons? I wait for her at the beach, I wait at the amphitheater . . . I only see her in the evenings, when I'm a clown, and then for a little bit at the table. It's hard for me, it's like I'm carrying that barrel in my arms all the time. I wrote before: *ambivalence*. Why don't I just be honest with myself here? Ambivalence? I'm in agony. This is torment. Pure torment.

I waited by the hotel, she came out, I wanted to go up to her and then thought better of it, so I hid, I thought I'd follow her, secretly, but I forgot about the scooter, she got on and went off, up, into town, I took the tram up, I can't walk so much anymore, can't exactly hop around and frolic in the hills, I saw her scooter, at the Wunderbar Bar, she was sitting with the other clown, they were fighting about something, I was standing behind a tree, she was crying, she jumped up from her seat, she left.

I'm waiting, I'm lying on the veranda, stars above me. I wait in spite of everything.

I was in the bathroom and heard her, in the other clown's room, I heard her whisper.

Mount Etna.

It kills and nourishes. The eruptions destroy, burn houses, kill people, but from a bed of deadly lava there grow orchards and groves. In the fertile, volcanic soil vineyards are born, whole plantations of trees.

Love is Mount Etna. Its heart is the crater the lava flows out of. It's a curse and a blessing. It's an active volcano, albeit dormant, in the best-case scenario, but it's never altogether out.

Fewer and fewer spectators, fewer and fewer tourists. A suspiciously large number of them departs, and a suspiciously small number of them arrives. Although it's still warm. The beach is almost totally empty, I watched them put the paddleboats up in their hangars. In the sand, next to me, I saw a dead dove. Apart from the fact that it is a symbol of peace and the Holy Ghost, it is also a symbol of love, or, of course, the irony of fate. And the next day I saw it again, in the paper. Me and the dove! That was the first time my picture had been in the paper! Which is nice for me. A souvenir of sorts. I brought my camera but haven't taken a single shot. The dove in the foreground and me, a lone tourist, expressionless, in the background. Underneath the headline, and the article, which the paper vendor explained to me using his hands and a couple of different languages:

Bird flu in Sicily. Swans have tested positive for the H5N1 virus. Minister of Health Francesco Storace warns: "Do not touch dead birds." Public outcry has intensified due to the delay in this information being released, as well as the subsequent warnings concerning this epidemic. A crisis crew has been called up to Rome. In danger zones, special safety sectors have been established with greatly heightened hygiene methods, particularly for places with a wet climate. A special problem is posed by birds in captivity, which must be either isolated or eliminated . . .

The paper vendor pointed out that people in the area tended just to have a couple of chickens and turkeys, for themselves, so what use would they have for a henhouse? Nobody has one, so where could you isolate the birds? And that now the Sicilians are petrified of anything with wings. They look at their poultry just like the civilian populace looked at the Germans. That's why there's been such a panic among the tourists, and that's why they've been leaving. And now this dove, right here, yesterday . . .

We said our good-byes, but then he caught up with me and asked me if I wanted a Polish paper, because he had one. I read it like Sienkiewicz's Lighthouse Keeper read *Pan Tadeusz*. And suddenly, for the second time that day and the second time in my life, I saw myself! My picture! In a "Missing" column. With a request for immediate contact with my daughter. She'd had to come back to Poland, and I hadn't told her about my trip, I hadn't told anybody. And she had no way to contact me, because, out of *Reisefieber*, I hadn't brought my cell phone, even though I'd put it on the list. I'd brought my charger but not my phone. Typical me. On a bicycle trip in school, I once forgot my bicycle, I showed up with just the pump.

Night, sitting at the amphitheater. I jumped the fence. I'm all made up, I'm wearing my clown costume. I ran offstage. After rolling that barrel up, the one I just caved in. I walked up to the microphone and made the announcement, I said, now ladies and gentlemen you'll meet a woman who's like Chernobyl, and I am her victim. She came out to laughter and applause but she didn't do her cartwheels, she came on but she didn't do her handstand, she just sat straight down on the barrel.

On my second and final entrance I rolled in the barrel instead of carrying it. I spoiled their punch line, it's true. But I just couldn't lift the thing any longer, so the smarter clown came up on stage quick, unexpectedly, and started improvising. Or acting like he was improvising. He talked to the audience rapidly, and for me to understand, he illustrated his words with mimicry and pantomime. He pointed to her, to her belly, indicating with a motion of his hand that she was pregnant. He pointed to himself, to show that it was his, he repeated this once more, he pointed to me with his finger, mocking me, he made fun of how I went back and forth with the barrel, repeated the phrases *stupido Polacco*, meanwhile, he showed us, him and her, behind the scenes, making thrusting movements with his hips, he pointed to her and to me, he came up to me from behind and played me like I was a double bass. I was an instrument, a tool, she'd been trying to make him jealous, she'd played me, and him? He doesn't want her, he mimed not wanting with his hands, he doesn't want her, no, no, let her live with this *stupido Polacco, stupido Polacco*, so I lifted up that damned barrel and threw it, I meant to throw it down by his side, but he moved, right in the wrong direction, and it hit him, he fell over, there was a yell, I flew out onto the street, I ran away, on the street there were children pointing their fingers at me, I bowed, they asked me to pose for pictures. I posed. And then to the amphitheater, over the fence, because it was closed, and I'm sitting . . .

I'm getting sleepy . . .

Should I lie down here, on the bench?

Did I break any of his bones? Either way, the police will be after me . . .

If the police find me, they'll arrest me. And maybe then they'll deport me back to Poland, or I'll be extradited . . . If so, then perhaps there was a method in this madness . . .

On the beach. It's . . . indescribable! It's . . . But from the beginning, from the beginning! At dawn at the amphitheater I was awakened by shots, individual shots from a firearm. Their echo went through the hills. And there were more and more of them. On the stage of the amphitheater something fell, I went up closer, it was a bird. Shot dead. I left the amphitheater, there were more and more shots. No one was on the street. Dreadful cackling of hens, gaggling of geese, quacking of ducks, and more shots. A turkey on the street, crazy with fear, spinning around its own axis. Cages with parrots, some of them lying on the bottoms, some of them repeating phrases in Italian. And birds falling, one after the next. I made it to empty beach, no, not empty, full of birds that had been shot. A carpet of bird carcasses. The paper vendor showed up, he was walking along the waterline, he had a little parasol over his head. I frightened him, done up as a clown, early on the beach, he didn't recognize me, I asked him about the shots, where did people get all those weapons from, he said they'd brought in the Mafia, from Palermo, and that I ought to go back to the circus, it'd be safer there, nothing would fall on my head.

I'm sitting on a little boat, the shots haven't died down, in fact, there are so many of them now that you can't tell between them and their echoes. Birds are falling like big drops of blood, some of them straight into my . . .

One of them fell right onto my head! I'm shocked, I actually even passed out for a moment. My face is covered in blood. It's lying in front of me, it's pretty big, pretty heavy, is it an eagle? I don't know what kind of bird it is, I can't tell, I know that Sicily has around seventy species and that some of them fly off to Africa. It's good it wasn't a swan, I would have ended up the first human victim of the bird flu in Taormina . . .

I don't know why, but a minute ago, I cackled. I was walking down the shore, and I raised my elbows, and I cackled. And I crowed. Maybe because I've gone crazy, or else so that I don't go crazy.

Aha. I can see them, out of the corner of my eye. The police. I'm sitting with my back to the sea, facing Taormina. They're coming my way, from my right-hand side.

Aha. I can see them, out of the corner of my eye. Nurses, and an ambulance behind them. They're coming my way, from my left-hand side. What else . . . Hurry, hurry.

In spite of it all, in spite of it all I would like for her, when I die, to come to my grave. For her to stand over it, look to the right, look to the left, get on top of me, slowly take off her underwear, lift up her skirt, open up her legs, and pee on me, right around where my head would be. Well. I'm an idiot, aren't I? After which she would walk off, holding her underpants in her hand and spinning them around like a purse. Isn't he an idiot? While the men sitting around watching would applaud. One of them could be whistling the whole time.

Oh no, one of them . . . anything but that! One of them is holding a straitjacket. No, no, anything but a straitjacket, hurry, isn't it just, oh my brothers of a certain age, that love, that fickle thing, always hangs us out to dry? That it's only when looking in the mirror that we realize it's not a hat we're wearing, but a dunce cap?

Not a straitjacket! In a straitjacket I won't be able to write even a single wo—

TRANSLATED FROM POLISH BY JENNIFER CROFT

GABRIEL ROSENSTOCK

" . . . *everything emptying into white*"

She herself was from Lipica. Lipica of the countless caves and sou-
terrains. Snobbish white horses. If one may put it like that. Not so.
They have airs and graces only when they perform. Leave them to
their own devices and they are perfectly fine.

"Born black, I understand?"

She nodded. Tired of answering the same old questions, was she?
I made a mental note not to ask too many questions. She responded
nonetheless.

"As black as your Aesop! Can't say I'm terribly interested in them.
They are so clichéd, aren't they? Like yourselves and the leprechauns."

I let it pass. Lipizzaners and leprechauns. Tenuous. Good word
that. A word to describe much of what we had heard during the
conference.

It was my first time in Slovenia. Miljana—that was her name—
was my minder. I would have been happy enough to be alone (I
think) but we lecturers were each assigned a personal assistant.
Some of them more of a nuisance than an assistance, possibly.
Mentioning the horses was just passing the time. Small talk. Talk
for the sake of talk. For someone who earns his living by talking,

I'm not much good at it, am I? Not unless I'm rattling on about folkloric motifs. The water nymph and the veil. Greek legend. Compare to similar myths and legends concerning mermaids and kelpies in Ireland and Scotland. Compare and contrast the sexual tropes in Greek myths and Irish tales concerning mermaids and nymphs.

> Yes, yes! Yes, you will give me back my veil, yes you will, but not before you have learned to love me more than any man has ever loved before. Then, and not until then, will you give me back my veil so that I may join my sisters again, nymphs immortal as the rivers.

"If you'd like, of course, we can go and have a look at them after the conference."

Nymphs? Oh, horses.

"I'm quite content to see them from my window. They fill me with calm."

That was true. To an extent. When they grazed I felt quite unruf-fled. But when one or two of them decided to trot around the field, flicking their tails for no obvious reason, only to return more or less to the same spot, sometimes rubbing one neck against the other; then I was no longer calm. No.

She looked at me curiously, not knowing what to make of me. Her long, golden hair. Manelike. Her white body, whiter than the Lipizzaners.

"And strength," I added. "They fill me with strength."

True. And yet sometimes they drain me of everything.

"Strength? Might it not be all in your imagination?" Hard to de-tect from her tone, her inflexion, if the observation contained irony or not. Myths and legends, their origins, that's my field, yes, but that doesn't mean I believe in fairy horses. Like most scholars, I'm a rationalist. I don't know if I ever met a colleague who—that's not quite correct. Finlay, from Edinburgh. He went a bit funny in the end, didn't he?

She kicked some leaves that had gathered together on the gravel path. Idly. Without any force or malice. But not quite playfully either.

"Going by the paper you read yesterday, you must have some imagination!"

I was slowly beginning to warm to her. She was trying to be friendly. Informal. That was her function after all.

"Know something about ancient Greek fables then, do we?" I asked, teasingly.

"Well, thanks to your paper, I do now. I had forgotten—if I knew it at all—that Aesop was black. Is your room okay?"

"Fine." I didn't know what else to say. The bed is a bit lumpy? Sheets slightly damp? Wallpaper so old-fashioned. The prints on the wall. Those romantic sunsets. But the view from the window compensates for any defects. Something like that? But I wasn't fast enough. I rarely am. Scholars think slowly. I kicked some leaves as if by repeating her action earlier we would, somehow, no longer be strangers to one another. They were already turning black and mushy.

We were taking the air. Literally. I was trying to scoop as much of it as I could into my lungs. A little break before lunch. A stroll. Stretching of the limbs. I would have preferred to have been by myself (as I have indicated) but she had a job to do. To be my shadow. Not to let me out of her sight until I'd been shovelled onto the plane in Trieste. They had "lost" a lecturer at the last conference and it wasn't going to happen again. His wife rang the day after the conference had ended. Where was Roberto? Why hadn't he come home?

A heart attack? Gone off with the fairies? (He was a world authority on Persian fairy tales.)

Some distance away a cyclist dismounted. In full racing regalia, he stepped toward a fig tree, reached up and gently dislodged a fig, ate it slowly, but with relish, wiped the juice from his mouth, mounted his bike, and cycled away. As though he owned the world. He was all in blue. A modern, athletic version of *The Blue Boy*.

I breathed in deeply.

"The air is good here," I remarked.

"You don't have good air in Ireland?"

I looked at her. I wanted to say that the air was drier here but I just smiled, a little sheepishly. Some fifty yards from us I noticed a small apple that had been squashed underfoot. A crow was gorging itself on it, looking around every so often at a magpie who had also eyed the juicy prize. The crow, the blackbird, and the raven in Irish and Welsh folklore. Discuss.

"You remind me of someone," she said.

I do?

"France Prešeren, our national poet."

In what way? I would have liked to ask, but didn't. I knew next to nothing about Prešeren but one thing I did know is that no portrait existed, not even a vague likeness. She should have known that this information was in all the guidebooks. Was she teasing me? Maybe she was thinking of something other than physical characteristics?

The gong. She had appeared again, like some innkeeper from a Hammer horror film, or a supervisor in a concentration camp. Eight times the harridan gonged unflinchingly. Twice would have been more than enough. We made our way toward the dining hall. Miljana, my shadow, preceding me. For a minute, I felt we were prisoners.

Gabriel Rosenstock 69

I had hoped our little stroll would have done something for my appetite. It hadn't. Time to open the communication lines again. For the sake of good manners if nothing else. I glanced at her left breast and her name tag: Miljana Mahkota. I already knew her name. Why did I need to double check? Just in case. In case of what? In case she had changed her name overnight?

It takes me a day or two to adjust to new surroundings, new accents. The air. The bedroom. The light. Everything, really. How some people make such transitions effortlessly is a wonder to me. How do they do it? Six weeks ago I had given up smoking and that had made me a little fidgety, I suppose, not quite knowing what to do with my right hand. The loss of the familiar cigarette was, I felt, something akin to the phantom limb of an amputee.

No, there was something else amiss. I couldn't put a finger on it.

"Well, Miljana. Do you do this often?"

"What, eat lunch?"

I attempted a little laugh.

"Actually, you're my first!" she grinned, lifting a grey napkin and shaking it, like one might shake a sheet, and reverently covering her lap with it. At least, it struck me as an act of reverence. Self-reverence.

"It's a part-time job. I used to work for a film club in Ljubljana. For about four and a half years. Then the founder died and things were never the same again. Something was lost forever. A vision. Know what I mean?"

"I suppose," I said, lamely.

"It's hard to explain. The vision died with him." She looked into the distance, searching for a word, I thought, a word in her own language, with no exact equivalent to be found in the somewhat formal

English we were speaking. Somehow I knew that I would never hear that word from her lips.

"I understand," I said. I tested the bread roll for freshness.

"Are you interested in film?" I asked.

"I was for a while," she replied.

She must have loved that person. That's it, I said to myself, pleased with my discovery. Soup was served. Vegetable soup. Bland. Nondescript. It needed salt. But I had been told to cut back on salt. The bread roll was limp.

"We were living on air in those days," she remarked as she tasted the soup.

I had no idea what she meant and she quickly picked up on this.

"We were a new nation then. We wanted to taste everything, everything that was forbidden. Books, music, film . . ." She sprinkled some salt on her soup.

"Of course," I said. "One forgets about such things . . . I read something recently, a newspaper report. The film censor in Sweden said that they should get rid of his job. Adults should be allowed to look at anything they want."

"I—"

Her response was interrupted by an announcement that the final session would commence at two o'clock. Why announce it? We all had the programme and everything was running like clockwork so far. But she babbled on nonetheless. I lifted a spoon, mindlessly, and saw myself in it, distorted, a monster from Tibetan folklore. Maybe this is me. Or maybe it's Prešeren? The elusive France Prešeren, tracked down at last. I returned the magic spoon to its place. There was something about this dining space that unnerved me. It might have suited soldiers once. Or monks even. Wherever one looked, there was no sign of a feminine touch. How grey the napkins were and how uninviting to the touch. I thought, maybe there are some places left in Slovenia that are still looking back, people for whom the great leap to freedom was a leap too far.

Main course was a choice of pork or fish. We both had the fish. She seemed to be concerned about the bones. Afraid of choking? She handled the dish as one might defuse a bomb. I asked what kind of fish it was. She couldn't think of the English word. Was it caught locally? She didn't know.

We spoke little during the rest of the meal. I couldn't get last night's dream out of my head. I was in a coach. On my own. It was the time of the Austro-Hungarian Empire. I was somebody of some minor importance. The horses were Lipizzaners. I was reading Heinrich Heine. I turned a page, casually looked out, and saw that the horses had sprouted wings. We were flying.

"You didn't like?" she asked.

I had only eaten half of my lunch and what remained was cold, shapeless, desolate.

"It was fine," I answered. "Not very hungry."

"I suspect you spend too much time stuck in books? You should get out more often."

"So my doctor tells me."

It was then that I noticed how astonishingly healthy she looked. All over. Hair. Eyes. Limbs. Eyes. Mouth. Teeth. Gums. Everything. Breath. Fingernails.

"Coffee?"

I said yes.

Neither of us bothered with dessert. She alluded again to my lecture.

"So, Alexander's soldiers brought dozens of tales back with them from India, tales which would influence European storytelling for centuries. You may not have noticed, but your theories annoyed a few people."

"Goodness, why?" I hadn't noticed. I'm slow to pick up on such things.

"Well, some of my fellow Slovenians in particular, I have to say." She glanced briefly to her left and then to her right.

"Go on." I was curious. I couldn't recall a previous occasion in which a paper of mine had been a source of annoyance. Boredom, yes. But annoyance?

She licked some foam from her lower lip.

"You see, we're not in Yugoslavia anymore. We're all Europeans now and—purely on an unconscious level, you understand—some of us don't like anything that might diminish our sense of the importance of Europe. If Aesop is more Indian than Greek, as you claim, well that's one small chipping away at the foundations of European culture and we won't buy it. I buy it but right-wing bastards are on the move again. Had you said Aesop was influenced by the Irish, that would have been tolerable enough. The Irish are white. But India? A horse of a different colour."

I exhaled deeply. Bastards? Hadn't expected that word from her lips.

"I didn't intend that people should take my lecture personally."

She lifted an eyebrow. How well she did that. What films did they show in that film club of hers? Had she studied them? *Casablanca?*

"Isn't everything personal?"

Is it?

I shrugged. That was the extent of my response.

The eyebrow was still raised, suggesting she needed a better answer than that.

"This conversation is personal, isn't it?"

I thought about this for a second or two.

"No it's not . . ."

She's confident almost to the point of cockiness. Well, she's of a different generation. What is she, twenty, twenty-five years younger than I am?

"Am I in love with my wife? Now," I exclaimed, "had you asked me that, our conversation would have been personal."

"Are you?" she shot back.

People had begun to disperse, the noise of chairs, laughter, conversation in German, Croatian, French, English, Slovene; lecturers, minders, administrators all making their way by circuitous routes back to the lecture hall. My name tag was askew. I straightened it and stood up. I closed the middle button of my jacket. My weight had been fluctuating a lot in the past six months but the jacket closed easily. I sat down again. A sudden dizziness. Had I taken the blood pressure tablets?

"Feeling okay?" Her voice was somewhat distant.

I took a swig of water and felt revived. After a little while I stood up. She offered me her arm.

"What happened to your man?" I asked.

"Who?"

"The lecturer who never made it home."

"Oh! Roberto. The trouble he caused! They found him in that big cave, the one in Vilenica, you've been there. Three days and three nights he spent underground. Poor fellow didn't know if he was coming or going."

I tried to imagine his ordeal.

"We needn't go back to the lecture hall," she suggested.

We were the last two in the refectory, apart from the staff.

It was my turn to raise an eyebrow.

"We could go and look at the Lipizzaners. If you like."

That was four years ago. I never saw her again. I was briefly reminded of her by an item on television about the Lipizzaners. Don't ask me what it was all about. I didn't hear the commentary, transfixed as I was by the horses. Dancing. Prancing. Leaping out of their skins.

TRANSLATED FROM IRISH BY THE AUTHOR

elsewhere

ZSÓFIA BÁN

When There Were Only Animals

Why. Why take a picture of this too, why take one of everything. Will
it make you feel better to have a picture of her looking like this, a picture that won't even be of your mother, but of a stranger camouflaged
as a corpse? Whose nose is this, whose mouth, and what are those
tubes? Where the hell does that get you? No, it did no good shoving
this obsession down my throat, all this organizing of everything in
albums. You tried, but it did no good, gluing it all nice and neat into
a book but leaving out life, sticky, gooey, running-all-over-the-place
life, shaping it instead into a compact little story, a cock-and-bull
story, if you ask me, because who's going to believe that it happened
like this and *only* like this, that it all played out high above the sordid
world below, like some mountain climber who lives on the summit,
but that didn't keep you from acting cute and ignoring the asthma
attacks, the bouts of fever, those numbing moments of humiliation,
the lies, the smugness, the murderous impulses, and the fear. No,
sweetheart (it's time you tried on the word for size), enough already
of always getting what you want, thought Anna, smiling faintly, for
even these were her mother's words, you can't always get what you
want, because you're the kid and I'm the mother, and not vice versa.
These words had always set Anna laughing, which in turn only sent

her mother into more of a rage. Now what are you sniggering about, she'd say, cut it out, act normal, but this made Anna roar with laughter so much that she just couldn't stuff it back into herself; sure, she took a little stab at shutting up, but that only made her gasp for breath, whereupon her mother turned beet red, ran out of the room, and slammed the door shut behind her, yes, this was their usual scene, one they'd played so many times before, indeed they'd refined it to such a degree of perfection that it would have hurt not to perform it on occasion, like taking a breath, like saying pass me the salt or run down to the store for some butter. They each needed the other to play their part; after all, in who else's presence could they have stoked such well-oiled, raging, quavering passions? We only ever have one greatest adversary.

■ ■ ■

Most people don't even know Antarctica is round, why, it's unbelievable how little is known about the place, not even the most basic facts, griped Gina, who for her part knew everything about the lives of penguins, and it seemed that once again someone had posted a comment on her blog. Dear Gina, most people don't even know what makes them happy, much less what Antarctica looks like. That was from Alan, who would normally comment only on his own area of specialty, oceans. For a moment everyone looked up. But they imagine they know what it's like, continued Gina, unperturbed, just because they saw a few pictures, and here Gina raised both her hands and, in characteristically American fashion, curving her index and middle fingers just a tad, formed quotation marks in the air, "dramatic" pictures of icebergs and of one or two cute penguins, but don't take it too hard, Anna, dear, I'm not blaming photographers, it's not your fault, or at least it's not just your fault. How comforting you are, dear Gina, I was practically starting to feel uncomfortable, and though her words came off sounding ironic, Anna really was feeling uncomfortable, *uncomfortable* was nothing less than the most suitable word to describe what she was feeling, indeed this feeling hadn't left her in days. So what is it for example that makes you happy, Julie asked Alan at this unexpected opportunity, Julie who, as she was apt to put it, had been taken into the project as a "landscape worker" to beef up the art department, and who for days now had been seeking the right moment to strike up a little chitchat with the soft-spoken oceanographer. Oceans do it for me, said Alan without so much as stopping to think, at which they all started laughing. Alan, a New Zealander of Maori descent, cast an awkward, apologetic smile as he ran his fingers through his lustrous black hair. The snow and the ice suited him well: he was a black king on a white chessboard.

■ ■ ■

The light green tile on the wall behind the bed. The floor covered with light green linoleum washed respectably every day but still hopelessly stained. The suffocating heat of the room. The motionless leaves on the trees in the park beyond the window. Her mother covered only by a thin sheet, and even that only half over her as she lay completely naked underneath. Believe me, said the nurse, it's better for her like this, there's no other way to bear the heat, and as if to prove her point, Anna presently discovered two tiny beads of sweat between her mother's breasts as they formed a little stream and trickled downward onto her belly. Not as if she had never seen her mother's naked body, no, the sight of a body was not taboo to them, but then again, the *sight* was everything, said Anna aloud, as if speaking to the green tiles, to the grouted gaps between the tiles; the sight without touch, smell, sound, speech, just the sight of the body showering onto the retinas again and again: the now sagging breasts still somehow beautiful in their autumnal repose, the nipples with their enormous brown areolas resembling little yards, *dvor* in Russian, *na dvare* came the words from a long-ago Russian class, yes, *na dvare* full of tiny little bumps, especially when she was cold; and on the lower parts of the belly, the horizontal, *state-of-the-art* bikini cut superimposed by the striated marks of stitches, as if carved in stone by some ancient centipedal creature, a paleontological trace of a world before human beings, a world *when there were only animals*, as Anna had put it at the age of three, in words that, to her, meant simply *a long time ago*, yesterday included. And when this came to her mind as she watched her mother's blue-veined hands resting upon that wrinkled bedsheet, hands speckled with faint brown spots, it seemed to her that all of this—childhood, the past, and even this present, suffocating moment—had indeed happened in some strange, distant space and time.

■ ■ ■

That's why those Buckminster Fuller maps are so good, Gina rattled on as if nothing had happened. You know, those maps sprawled out like squashed frogs, maps that finally do justice to Antarctica by showing it like it is. Traditional mapmaking is pretty screwed up, ain't it? It pretends to be scientific, though you know that's not true, that it's just a bad convention, and a dangerous one at that, seeing as how it drips ideology right into your brain without you ever noticing. Sure, it's clever how it works, but that doesn't make it likeable. Just look at those maps that don't have Europe in the center, for once, but, say, Australia. Sure puts things in a different light, huh? While talking, Gina was busy carving her section of the ice bench. She'd learned this and many other things in training camp: how to carve benches, chairs, and tables out of ice, as well as how to make an igloo, not to mention a bed—everything needed for survival when survival is at stake. They were almost finished making three benches and a table to have their lunches at, since it would have been a shame not to take advantage of that day's searing sunlight, even if the unusual warmth was also an ill omen. While the effects of global warming on the lives of penguins was among Gina's favorite subjects, it was nonetheless possible to talk with her about other things. Human relationships, for example. Not long before, she'd been dumped by her girlfriend, a climatologist who, in a turn of events that surprised even herself, had fallen for one of the helicopter pilots stationed here. Now and then Gina flirted with Anna, if only to stay in practice. But she could see it wasn't worth her time. The two-dimensional take on mapmaking really does screw things up, she jabbered on. When I was little, I too thought the South Pole was a sort of big white blotch spilling all over the place at the bottom of the map, but it seems there have been a few interesting developments since then. Remember that Australian dude the other day who told us about a project using sonar-equipped planes and other machines to measure gravitation and magnetic fields that give you a topographic picture of the land lying under the ice? Really something, huh? Like a murder mystery. A slippery business, representation. What do you say, Anna, you big white woman? You're the authority, after all. Like some everlasting solar cell, Gina's endless supply of working-class Italian-American spunk regularly filled up the team's depleting energy reserves; had Gina not been on hand, Anna might already have lain right down on a bed of ice and not gotten up for a good long time. She hadn't taken a single picture in two days, and Gina, as usual, in her no-nonsense, free and easy style, had once again cut right to the heart of things. Sometimes, said Anna evasively, it seems you don't need special devices to figure out what's under the ice. A few days ago I saw the carcass of a dog that belonged to the Scott expedition. Just imagine, the ice melted right off it in this insane heat, and even the chain is still around its neck. Anna now recalled that apt little idiom from her native tongue that had come to her mind on encountering the dog, *Here's where the dog is buried*, but as she'd seen little sense in saying it aloud to the others, and then having to either explain or not explain that what she was really saying was, *That's the root of it*, Anna had simply said nothing.

■ ■ ■

At the foot of the bed there was a card that read, *3 part. mat.*, gave birth three times, *partus maturus*, which Anna read again and again as if immersed in a masterpiece of world literature, one that contained everything, like the great classics, but even better, for who could have put things more concisely than this? Maybe the minimalists. Not that they wrote great, epic novels. No, doing so would have run counter to their ars poetica, mused Anna. *Only the tip of the iceberg, that alone must be visible.* That's no way to go about writing an epic novel. Or was it? The words on the card suggested to Anna that maybe, just maybe, it was. And whoever had written those words—a born genius of a nurse or, perhaps, some doctor—had obviously chosen the wrong career, yes, they would be well advised to hide away somewhere and write till they drop, because anyone with such a vein, a poetic one, that is, shouldn't be fiddling with medical instruments, wallowing in blood and mucus, pressing pus-filled wounds, or groping about among tumors. No, there are plenty of people to deal with all that, but few can say so much in such little space. But then again, thought Anna, what was so good about brevity after all? What was there to like about it? Wasn't it better if words were spoken properly—not swept under some rug, not clipped, but given all the time in the world? To Anna, it pretty much looked like her mother was the greatest minimalist of all, and unconquerable at that, considering that before having Anna, she had already given birth twice—as Anna discovered only by chance while rummaging through some of her mother's old medical papers and photos. One picture, which looked like it was from around the early forties, was of a little boy: blond, around two years old, playing in a striped sun-suit among the hens in a dusty farmyard. Who is this kid, Anna asked, to which her mother replied, don't you see I've got things to do, and coming from her this was somewhat surprising. After all, she'd always wanted to document everything, to carve all of life into a neat little story, to use picture books and albums to recount that *this happened like this*, and *that like that*: marriage, pregnancy, little baby Anna, little Anna going to nursery school and then to school, little Anna at a poetry recital competition, wedding anniversaries, Father with his arm around Mother's bare shoulders as they sat in a lantern-adorned garden restaurant, award ceremonies, Outstanding Worker Medal, Workers' Gold Medal, little Anna's marriage (but not her little divorce), summer on Lake Balaton, friends and colleagues and relatives (not that too many of them were still around after *all that*), but grandparents and great-grandparents nonetheless pasted in meticulously along with Great-granddad's beloved colleagues: Miksa Weisz's furniture factory in the city of Szeged, 1905, Great-grandma in rustling silk dresses and colossal, crazy hats. What a look! How could Miksa have gone to work every morn-ing in that dumb furniture factory, leaving that voluptuous woman in bed, letting her lie fallow all day long? Who gives a damn about furniture? Let people live in tents and lie on straw! Yes, that's what Great-granddad should have said, I'm not letting go of Kamilla for an instant now that I've got her, I'll hold her and clutch at her and tear her and knead her till the day I die. But that's not what hap-pened, because die they did—of hunger, in the Budapest Ghetto, one day before the liberation. Not like that was in the album either, *part. mat.*, checkmate. Later on, Anna couldn't find the child's photograph again.

■ ■ ■

This constant shower of light, this endless day, seemed bent on exhorting her to see, to finally see what must be seen rather than to be peering always into her camera's viewfinder, fiddling about, waiting for suitable light and form. Not that she'd done much of that for days now. No, Anna would have much preferred to sleep all day and all night in that perpetual flood of light. Never in her life had she slept as well, as deeply, and with as much devotion as here, of all places; here in the snow, ice, and light. There's no getting around it, said Gina, chattering away, they were at the penguin colony Anna had grumpily accompanied her to, where Gina proceeded to record the precise weight of each tagged penguin before the creatures swam off in search of food, and then did so once more after they returned to the ice floe. Everyone here's got a screw loose, isn't that so, my loveliness? You know, who else would want to come here, of all places, for weeks or months on end—here, to the ice and into this freezing air? Not that there's all that much ice or cold, nowadays. But let's face it, you're a little odd yourself, what with this iceberg obsession of yours, and your mantra that icebergs are like people and that you're not taking landscape photos but portraits. What kind of crazy idea is that? I mean, an iceberg is an iceberg is an iceberg. Who was it that said that? Whatever. But imagine if I ran around telling everyone that penguins aren't really penguins, but little penguin-shaped philosophies? Anyway, as I see it, the best take on life is *not* to try doing what you do as if you're doing something other than what you're doing, if you catch my drift. Once again Gina had mercilessly dug right into Anna, as into some open festering wound, because Anna,

when she went rock collecting earlier with Robert, the half-Indian
ship builder from Alaska, had been pondering precisely this, of
all things, *this*, as her back began to hurt from the weight of her
rock-filled knapsack, and as a skua, that heavy-bodied gull, raptor
of the south, kept swooping down on them with sustained aggres-
sion as if trying to drive them away, even though there couldn't
have been any skua nests around there, no, it seemed the bird was
also trying to tell Anna something, that indeed the entire landscape
wanted to lead her to something or other, so as to finally give some
meaning to her having come here in the first place, *here*, to the
end of the world, to give some meaning to the whole question of
her having applied for this project and having been selected, yes,
there must have been some reason more compelling than photographing icebergs, which all at once struck Anna as an inadequate
and ludicrous endeavor, but she'd wanted to somehow make up for
what now she believed was more than mere negligence, the fact
that she hadn't taken a picture of her mother *then*, and that she'd
somehow thought that *here*, down here, she'd find one, an image
capable of conveying what Anna had felt when her mother, waking
up in the steaming hot ward after several days in a coma, suddenly
said, in a hushed, measured tone of voice, my feet are cold, put
on a pair of socks, at which Anna, startled, frantically rummaged
through the nightstand until she finally found a homely pair of orange terry-cloth socks and slipped them slowly, carefully onto her
mother's feet, whereupon her mother sighed with satisfaction and
died, Anna turning her head toward the patient in the neighboring
bed, giving the woman a look as though to ask if she too had seen
what Anna had seen, and the old lady stared back at Anna with
frightened beady eyes as if to seal their mutual secret, the thin con-
gealed surface of the cold stewed spinach sparkling on the nightstand all the while. Did you know, continued Gina rhapsodically,

that the Antarctic is the only place on Earth where places can be named after living people, that you can nominate people to name places after, and then a committee convenes and names the lucky person, and you won't believe this, but even I have a little island, a whole island, named after me. I've been coming here for almost twenty years, after all, and when I found out, I went to that island, pulled down my pants and panties and, swoosh, I pissed on it. I'm a motherfucking biologist, after all.

■ ■ ■

Mother in her hat, her ribboned, summer, girl's hat. A colored hat, it seems, but on this jagged-edged, miniature photo even it is black and white, yes and no, everything still so simple. Mother smiling into the camera, not suspecting a thing. Mother in a stilted, confectioner's apprentice cap, its blinding white enhancing the creamy white of the pastries lined up with pride on the tray in her hands. Mother with her tweed trekker cap cocked jauntily over her ear, standing proudly on a cliff, looking off into the distance as one should: *Souvenir from Transylvania*. Mother in a jockey cap, promenading buoyantly across the city's main square, arm in arm with her girlfriends: *Miklós Seidler, street photographer, Szeged*. Mother in her festive lace shawl standing under an ornamented tent, with a dapper, trustworthy-looking young man beside her who is wearing an embroidered yarmulke. Mother in a peasant's kerchief, as if it isn't even Mother but someone just living her own life in Mother's image, and her bewildered stare seems to suggest that this is exactly how it felt, too. Mother wearing her stenographer's hat, in a gray costume and with a black purse, even the brim of the hat seeming to tell of her ready-and-willing resolve to get to work, of a belief that life is now starting anew, that the nation has a second chance, and that she, for one, will seize this opportunity by the throat. Mother in a restrained, rather plain-looking bridal hat recommended especially for workers, and yet her eyes sparkle underneath it all the same, eyes that say, with wonder, *After all.* Mother at a company event in her proper, lady worker's hat. And now, all at once, Mother in a wide-brimmed, *otherworldly* summer hat, and although her eyes are covered by giant, butterfly-shaped sunglasses as she stands there with a coffee plantation in the background, the way she's holding her head reveals the unhoped-for sense of relief that has come with freedom. Mother in a colorful, parrot-adorned shawl, her head down, gazing at her bulging belly. Here, with an uncovered head, hair drawn back in a tight bun as it never was later on, a newborn on her interlocked knees, Mother not holding, not protecting, and not even touching the baby, her two palms instead turned upward on her thighs, resting there helplessly or, it seems, calling for help, as if she can't understand how this little bundle got there in the first place and what she's now supposed to do with it. Mother in a straw hat, her eyes scanning the foaming, billowing sea, like one time when she took Anna down to the sea coast near their flat, where they often went, perhaps it was a weekend, there was a huge crowd, not that this stretch of coast was sparsely populated even during the week, but Mother must have let her attention drift, for Anna, who was six or seven, suddenly realized while roaming about that she was lost, her mother nowhere to be seen, and Anna immediately despaired, bawling infernally as she made her way down the seaside and well-meaning adults stopped regularly to ask her what her mother looked like and where she'd seen her last, and then all at once Anna saw her mother, standing with her back toward her. Barely able to catch her breath from the joy and relief, Anna approached without making a sound, and as she did so she heard her sobbing mother, who hadn't yet noticed her, say repeatedly, "My God, here too, even here?" but what these words referred to, Anna hadn't a clue. And now her mother's head is covered with a black mantilla, as if at the funeral of a Spanish don, Don Ernő, otherwise known as Dad, Mother standing in a tiny cemetery on a late-autumn hillside north of Budapest in the Danube Bend, chestnuts showering down upon the gravestones, he'll like the view from here, said Mother, *buena vista*, she spoke seven languages, she did, not that she ever said a thing, and *hasta la vista*, but Mother said this—*see you later*—in Hungarian, *viszontlátásra*, throwing a handful of dirt on the coffin, at which Anna looked at Mother with surprise, thinking she must have said this by mistake, for they didn't believe in the afterlife, insofar as they believed at all, for they'd long ago let that God loose in the wind who'd allowed *all that* to happen. Mother, in a tasseled knit cap, shrunk to half her size, on the tree-shaded grounds of a mountainside sanatorium, the pants of her warm-up suit hanging loosely on her thighs, as if she was wearing someone else's hand-me-downs, one of her knees bent beneath her in a well-practiced pose, like she used to do back when she went to receptions in her low-cut evening dress, posing on the marble floor of their living room, palm trees out beyond the windows, her thick glasses weirdly enlarging her pupils underneath her cap, making her look as if she'd seen a ghost, and who knows, maybe that's how it was, maybe by then she knew and she had seen what was to come, her rougeless mouth a bit agape, as if she was wondering whether she was really seeing what she was seeing, and then for a moment Anna was left wondering too: What exactly was Mother's mouth like? Mothers' mouths come in many varieties, after all: soft, full, fleshy, tender, sensual; lips pressed tight in anguish until they're almost white; purple from cold; stern and slender as a blade; rouged or rougeless, but even within this category a mother's mouth can be many things, depending on *how* it's rouged or *how* it's not; festively rouged; rouged for a reception, a dinner, the theater, or a soirée; rouged for flirtation or seduction; rouged in so many splendid shades of red, perhaps for official business, such as asking someone to pull some strings for you, discreetly or not so discreetly rouged for a working lunch, rouged while on the way to pick up important laboratory results, or rouged just to counter anxiety. And, if rougeless, a mother's mouth might be sporty, as when having just emerged from a swimming pool, or having recently leapt with abandon into the sea; it can be rougeless in a disheveled, sleepy, or early-morning sort of way; rougeless when a mother finally shows her real face; rougeless in a hospital, while ill, or while just running down to the store for bread. But a mother's mouth might even be defiantly or vengefully rougeless, as if to say, as hers surely did, *no way am I going to spruce myself up for some commies.* In a word, it's all but impossible to take into account all the myriad states of rougedness and rougelessness that might characterize a mother's mouth, to exhaustively map this complex and endlessly refined language. And yet one thing seemed certain all the same, as Anna stared at that picture of Mother on the sanatorium grounds: she could no longer conjure up her mother's mouth; why, she had trouble even remembering how it looked, much less its texture.

■ ■ ■

A helicopter was due to set out the next day for Cape Evans, so Robert told Anna he'd take her along to see Scott's Hut, left behind from the Terra Nova Expedition. Until then Anna had only seen the hut from Shackleton's Nimrod Expedition. During the flight, Robert told Anna that he'd studied veterinary medicine in Texas, but that when his marriage failed he'd wanted to get as far as possible from his original home, and so he wound up in Alaska. His only regret, he added, was that he so rarely saw his daughter, who by now was grown-up and living in California with her husband and two little kids. Unbelievable, he said, lost in thought, that I've got grandchildren, and you, he asked Anna, do you have a family, my last relative died a year ago, and the ease with which Anna pronounced that bleak, neutral word, *relative*, surprised even her. It seems everyone around here has a fragmented family, mused Robert, if they still have a family at all. Come on, take a look at the stables, and here, he said while clambering onto a knoll of ice, here I always get goose bumps at the thought that I'm standing where Mawson was standing in that picture. Stepping into the hut, Anna was surprised at how different it was from Shackleton's, how much bigger and, on account of the many objects left behind and the sundry traces of life literally frozen in time, far ghostlier. The spacious kitchen was still stocked with myriad supplies, and then there was a science lab, not to mention Herbert Ponting's darkroom, in which the photographer evidently slept as well. A stuffed penguin even stood atop a desk, and the entire hut was well endowed with shelves, recesses, boxes, and more, as if only waiting for someone to come along and put everything to use once again. Anna lingered in front of a wall mirror, one whose silvering was so deteriorated that the mirror reflected practically nothing, but this nothing wouldn't let Anna go, for all at once she felt that it had something to do with what Gina had said the previous day, that she shouldn't always try reading anything into things, but instead to see them as they are, and that's what she was pondering when Robert now pointed to an out-of-the-way little section of wall, by a bed, on which one of the men had written the names of those who had already died. You'd never think this was here, said Robert, unless someone showed you. All at once it struck them that it was getting late, and that if they didn't hurry they would miss the helicopter back, along with that evening's presentation on base. Stepping out the door, Anna and Robert saw that they saw nothing. The sky had turned overcast while they'd been inside the hut, and the diffused light that filtered out from behind the thick clouds perfectly concealed the surface of the snow and the ice, rendering it impossible to gauge any distance whatsoever. The entire landscape had become an exquisite splotch of grayish white that swam about in the glimmering light. The horizon had disappeared. There was no up, there was no down. Knolls and inclines alike had vanished into thin air, and all surfaces of snow and ice seemed irretrievably lost in alternating tones of white, the foreground being a shade grayer, the background brighter. They stared goggle-eyed out into the Antarctic summer night and saw nothing, nothing but light and space. Somewhere off in the distance was smoldering Mount Erebus, and somewhere, the frozen, endless plain of the Ross Sea, but all Anna and Robert could see were so many sparkling crystals of ice blown about by the storm clouds. *Whiteout*, Robert announced, at which Anna nodded, for they'd drilled the word into her at training camp, the same as they'd drilled into her the things you had to do if this exceptional, terrifying natural phenomenon struck when you were out on the ice. Now, though, it had hit when they happened to be at Scott's Hut, so they were not in any immediate danger. But they did have to wait until it stopped before they could head back to McMurdo Station. Come on, said Robert, let's go in, what's the sense of us freezing out here, but Anna just kept standing motionless by the door. She'd travelled here for this, for this moment alone; nothing that she'd seen and experienced up until then counted, neither the icebergs nor the people; neither Captain Scott nor any of the other legendary figures mattered one bit, not even the region's fauna, and suddenly everything else, her pictures included, seemed an insignificant little sideshow. Without once taking her eyes off the swirling light, Anna unzippered her bag, pulled out the camera that she'd carried around untouched for days, popped off the lens cap, raised the machine to her eyes, and took the picture that was finally capable of conveying the serene and enveloping whiteness of the moment that had transpired in the hospital a year before, a moment when colors, smells, sounds, and space itself had disappeared, a moment in which they and everything else had dropped back into that singular, uncanny stratum of time, the time when there were only animals.

TRANSLATED FROM HUNGARIAN BY PAUL OLCHVÁRY

ARNO CAMENISCH

Sez Ner

The dairyman's hanging from a paraglider, in the red firs below the hut on the alp at the foot of Sez Ner. You can hear him cursing from the hut. He has his back to the mountain, is facing the range across the valley where, shoulder to shoulder, peak after peak rises, Piz Tumpiv at the center, all 3,101 meters of it, that amazing presence it has, outdoing the other—snowless—peaks. He'll come down when he's ready, his farmhand says. Let him wriggle for another while, just. That'll teach him not to clear the trees.

The cheese is swelling. During the night, the stone weights crash to the floor, wakening everyone. The swineherd and the cowherd carry the over-ripened cheeses through the clear night, across the square, through the cowshed, to behind the cowshed, and dump them in the slurry. Neither the dairyman nor his farmhand budges to help. They stay where they are in the doorway, their hands in their pockets.

The farmhand has eight fingers, five on his left hand, and three on his right. His right he keeps mostly in his pocket, or resting on his thigh beneath the table. When he lies in the grass outside the hut, next to the pigpen, fast asleep with his boots off, and socks off as well, the swineherd counts his toes. The farmhand sleeps in the afternoons because, by night, he's out and about. He vanishes when everyone's gone to bed, comes back at some point during the night. He takes the dogs with him, to stop them barking.

The swineherd has a bad conscience. A pig's lying in the pen and won't get up. Its cold snout, the swineherd knows, means the pig's a goner, but he pokes the lump of ham with his steel-toed boots anyway. It could still get up, sure. *Quel ei futsch, ti tgutg,* the dairyman says. Just nineteen pigs now. Twenty, counting you, the swineherd thinks. The dairyman returns to the cowshed, his one-legged milking stool around his waist, and the swineherd takes the pigs back up to the pigsty, willing that stool to collapse. In the pigsty, he counts the pigs, makes it eighteen standing and one lying down. That one's a goner, too. That's how quick it can be, the swineherd thinks. Keep going at this rate, and there'll be none left in the morning and I can take myself home. The evening sun's already sinking behind the mountains, Piz Tumpiv dark yellow in the dusk, when the vet arrives, your man Tscharner with his beard, fat stomach, and fat son, who doesn't acknowledge the swineherd, just the dairyman. They've eaten too much, the vet says to the dairyman, their insides have burst.

Clemens's cow, the dark one, head-butts the fence-post, knocking it over. Clemens's cow gets out, and his other five cows trot after her. The vet says cows are bright, much brighter than horses. With horses, it's all about status, he says. They might look elegant, but, basically, they're thick. Cows may well be more intelligent. Right now, though, the cowherd's scouring the forest, hoping to find Clemens's cows before the sun goes right down.

Later in the evening, the cowherd from the alp bordering with Stavonas comes by in the car. She's just back from Glion, apparently, where she had her dog neutered. It all went smoothly, it seems, but the thing's totally dazed, still. She opens the rear door of the red car— where the dog's been allowed to lie, just this once. Whimpering and whining, it is. He doesn't seem to want out, she says, and the dog lies where it is, just. It'll be fine, the farmhand says. Takes a bit of time, that's all. The cowherd says to come with her, to help her carry the dog in, up at the alp. The farmhand does so, takes his own dogs too. They run along behind, there's no space in the car. He whistles out the window to make them keep up. Make sure they don't turn back.

In the morning, on the bench outside the hut, the dairyman's out for the count with a half-empty bottle of schnapps in his hand, while the goat's up on the divan, up in his room, admiring the view of Piz Tumpiv, maybe; peeing on the bed, for sure.

Every day, the pigs get out of their pen, down from the hut. They dig beneath the electric fence and head across the pastures, down to the trees where the dairyman was hanging. The swineherd doesn't care, knows—come the evening—they'll be back. The dairyman does care. Show them who's boss, he says, thrusting the rod with the rings into the swineherd's hand, and packing the farmhand off with him. In the pigsty, the farmhand takes the rod and the rings, and the swineherd picks a pig, grabs it by the ears, and jumps on its back, making it squeal even louder. He pulls back its ears and digs his knees in its ribs, to help the farmhand get the rod in its snout, and press. Once the ring is on, the pig bolts to the opposite corner, to hide behind the other pigs who lick the blood from its snout.

Tourists arrive on the dirt road, improved last spring, stop their beautiful cars at the fence outside the hut, and toot the horn. Seeing Cowherd and Swineherd sprawled on the grass on the slope above the hut, they toot again. They keep tooting until—finally—they give up, get out of their beautiful cars, open the gate themselves, and drive on. Twenty minutes later, they're reversing back down as the road doesn't go much further and doesn't have a big enough turning place. They have to stop at the gate again, the gate they left open, but is now shut again, to reopen it. This time, the herdsmen, sprawling on the grass still, wave to them.

You hear him before you see him: the priest rounds the corner on his moped, sending dust flying everywhere. He's wearing a helmet in the afternoon sun, and his cassock flutters in the wind he's creating. Seeing this, the dogs bark and leap at the priest, send him spinning down the slope, nearly, and into the roses. The priest parks his moped beside the hut and is given a coffee before he asks them all to gather in front of the hut that looks onto the mountains; gives the dog jumping up and licking him a slap; then invites them to pray to God Almighty, Lord of all they see before them, for the summer they've not yet had. A wind comes up, and the herd moves down in front of the cowshed as the priest, now with a stole around his neck, hands out prayer books from among the cows and beasts. He announces which page it is, then reads it to them. The pigs have got out too, and come up to the priest and snatch at his cassock. The parishioners repeat whatever the priest says, like parrots. A good half hour it is before the final *Amen*, before everything's been blessed that needed blessing, and, a wheel of cheese and five kilos of butter richer, the priest gets back on his moped, pushes his way through the waiting, already grumpy herd, and—in the last of the light—vanishes.

The black ram with the white patch on its head is bang in the middle of the cowshed when the cows come crashing in and break its legs. Both front legs end up in plaster. The black ram is anything but tame. Normally, he wouldn't let you pet him. In plaster, he does: he can't get away. One time before, when he was tied to the cowshed—his legs, at that point, were still in one piece—he snapped the rope in two when the swineherd tried to go up to him, and ran away. There's no need to be afraid of the swineherd, the farmhand says.

The rooster isn't afraid, it doesn't run away, is one aggressive bastard, the farmhand says. When the farmhand gets too close, it jumps up at him. Your man's steel-toed boots it takes, to shoo it away. The rooster, a handsome beast, guards its hens, covers them constantly. Any time, any place, anywhere.

Kneeling at his bed, the cowherd shows the swineherd the projectiles he found among the edelweiss and roses. The length of your lower arm, the projectiles are, all twisted and bent, some with, some without heads. The swineherd turns them all the way around, throws them in the air, and catches them. They end up back under the bed, with the cloth over them. On one occasion, when the dairyman—for once—goes into the pastures, he finds a projectile too. He orders the two herdsmen to put a fence up round it right away, a good distance away, then puts the cowherd on sentry duty, and drives down to the village in his Subaru Justy. Early that afternoon, a military convoy rounds the corner, three huge vehicles with specialists in them, wearing gloves and special uniforms. They're careful not to touch the projectile, crawl up to it from different angles, have instruments they note down readings from. Finally, they dispose of the projectile, and walk, in step, back down the pasture to outside the hut again, the officer out in front. Not a word is spoken as they climb into the camouflage vehicles. And disappear, in a cloud of dust.

The dog's jumping up, and licking away at the cowherd, the other dog, the older one, is trotting ahead, in front. The young dog jumps and sinks its teeth in the cows' tails, gets a free ride until the cow gives it a kick, and the dog, with a whimper, lets go. Its tail between its legs, it gives the cows a wide berth on its way back to its master. They get on well, the young dog and the old gray one. They only ever fight over food.

The one with the limp doesn't want to move, the one with the limp trots behind the others, stopping time and again. The cowherd takes his stick to her, beats her on the back till the stick breaks. The herd's vanished, long since, into the trees.

Late in the evening, at the side of the hut, the dairyman's at the wheel of his gray Subaru Justy, the bottle of plum brandy in his hand. His farmhand's beside him, in the passenger seat. The cowherd and the swineherd and the dogs are behind him, in the back. The car's the safest place, the dairyman says. Each time the lightning strikes, ruins the cowherd's fences, or sets the firs at the edge of the forest alight, he winces. The rain sweeps across the alp, giving both it and the filthy Subaru a good clean.

TRANSLATED FROM RHAETO-ROMANIC AND GERMAN
BY DONAL MCLAUGHLIN

RUI ZINK

Tourist Destination

He arrived in the morning on the night flight. There were no problems at the airport. Or, rather, he was expecting more problems, but
since he experienced none of these expected problems, there were
no problems.

His visa was in order, his passport valid until Methuselah's next
birthday. There weren't many people on the plane. Nowadays, the
only people who landed there were either fools, suicides, soldiers of
fortune, arms dealers, or else journalists without much in the way of
brains but with a great desire for glory. Nevertheless, it took a while
to cross the border. A passenger with the look of an experienced traveler, possibly a businessman, murmured: Damn bureaucrats.

And he was right. It was a known fact that the country was just a
fragment, that it wasn't even a country, only a zone, a zone of death,
a savage, brutal hunting ground, so what were they up to, pretending
to be great defenders of order? That was the impression given by the
entrance to the frontier: a grandiloquent gateway, full of arabesques
and curlicues, that opened onto nowhere, pretending not to know
that the palace it served as entrance to had been wiped from the face
of the earth. In a way, though, the frontier was an accurate forecast
of what lay ahead. Farewell, outside world. Hello, hell.

When customs officials found a semiautomatic weapon in the businessman's suitcase, he got angry:

"What do you mean, I can't go into the country with a gun? You're joking, aren't you?"

The weary, knowing, cynical guards replied:

"Security measures, sir."

"Security measures? That's like banning high heels from a night-club!"

"Those are the rules, sir."

"Look, I have a license to carry a weapon. I've even got a license to kill. You must be kidding me."

"We're just carrying out orders, sir."

"Damn bureaucrats!"

"That's rather uncalled for, sir."

"Uncalled for? Why, you monkey, I'll give you unca . . ."

"Would you mind coming with us, sir?"

What would they do to the man when there were no witnesses? Beat him up and show him that he couldn't insult the authorities with impunity? Or simply make life uncomfortable for him and give him the boredom treatment, stick him in a locked room without even a toilet, and then put him on the first plane back to civilization? The most likely outcome was that they would simply confiscate the gun and let him go. The country needed foreign currency, and not even a band of uniformed psychopaths would kill the goose that laid the golden eggs.

When he leaves the airport, he's greeted by a whitish light, by dust and bare earth, the dried-up remains of what had probably once been pools of mud or else craters left behind by the feet of some giant reptile. And that, while improbable, was not impossible: in the brochure they referred to the zone's picturesque history and local folklore. Apparently, there were stories (though it was hard to say how reliable they were) of the existence, a few years ago, of just such a monster. Unexplained attacks, people disappearing, mysterious footprints. True or false (or, rather, *false* or false), it made a good story. There were two theories: one, that a race of extinct dinosaurs had been resurrected by mutation, the fruit of years and years of an endless cocktail of radiation and chemicals; the other, rather more poetic, that the monster had *always* been there and had simply been hibernating for a season or so, about sixty-five million years, a mere nothing.

From a logical point of view, the fact that no one had confirmed the existence of this creature certainly wasn't proof that it didn't exist. The same reasoning that had been applied, elsewhere, to the existence (or not) of weapons of mass destruction was applicable here— or was this zone somehow inferior to other hotspots? It would be a terrible injustice to make hierarchical distinctions between the world's various paradises of chaos.

Then again, life has never been fair.

He found a taxi easily enough. He didn't even haggle, on the principle that only a very stupid driver would propose a price that was much higher than that of his competitors. Not that this mattered, he had money enough. Even if you were going somewhere in order to die, you still needed money. Besides, money was for spending, especially given the continuing rise in the cost of living, unless you invested in such surefire things as fuel, food, or nanotechnology.

Inflation was a worldwide scourge. Even stable countries were dying on their feet, and so it would be interesting to find out how much death cost here in the zone. The moralizers never tired of repeating that the zone was a microcosm in which all the usual values had been turned upside down, although they said this in resigned tones, more resigned than moralistic. If life was worth little or nothing, perhaps death was worth more than it usually was. And he was prepared to pay whatever was necessary.

Two lines of tanks, one on either side of the street, 120mm guns set at the diagonal (like scimitars), ensuring that the one road between the airport and the city would not be taken by rebels.

"You see how our government prizes security, sir."

It was impossible to gauge whether there was any mockery in the driver's voice.

"Yes," the passenger said.

"Not that the nationalist rebels would try anything," the driver went on. "It's not in their interest."

And he explained something that the passenger perhaps already knew, that many of the rebel gangs made their living from kidnapping foreigners. If the airport ceased to function, they would lose one of their main sources of income.

The passenger had no idea if he was in an official, regulated taxi or not. He didn't yet know what the taxis there were like, the color, the smell, the signs, if they had a meter or haggled a price per kilometer. It was likely to be a pirate taxi—a private car transformed by some enterprising individual by a simple act of baptism. On the other hand, experience had taught him that the weaker the government, the more it tries to control everything.

"If you like, I can be your driver for the next few days. Cheap, boss, cheap. I can take you wherever you want. To see our beautiful country."

"I'll think about it," answered the passenger.

The driver eyed him in his rearview mirror.

"Are you American, sir?"

"No."

The driver fell silent and waited, as if that one question had exhausted all possibilities.

After a few moments, the passenger gave a sigh and lied:

"I'm Swiss."

The driver seemed relieved. "Ah, Switzerland. A beautiful country. Not that I've been there. But from what I've heard, a beautiful country. Mountains and tunnels and snow, eh? And neutral too, eh?"

The passenger agreed, "Yes, neutral."

The driver said approvingly, "That's good. Neutral is good. And do you have a name, sir?"

The passenger looked out of the window. They were crossing a kind of grubby brown desert interrupted by occasional houses, mostly shacks, a few bodies walking through the void with bundles on their heads, and others just standing, watching the world pass by. A shepherd, tall, thin, and almost naked, crook in hand, leading his scrawny flock. And the carcasses, lots of them, of what had once been vehicles. The burned-out bodywork of tanks, jeeps, SUVs, vans, ordinary cars, even helicopters. A cemetery of carbonized metal bones, except that it seemed unlikely that any diamonds would emerge from that particular mine.

What did it matter if he told him his name? What difference did a name make in a conversation between strangers? He could simply tell the truth. On the other hand, he could continue to lie. Like that Greek hero, Odysseus. A consummate liar was our Odysseus. When the Cyclops asked him his name, he said: Nobody. And when the monster complained to his father about what the Greek had done to him—put out his one eye—and the angry god asked who had done that vile deed, the foolish ogre replied: Nobody, Papa, Nobody did it. Yes, "Nobody" and "Odysseus" were both good names. But what other name could he give himself?

"Greg," he lied. "My name is Greg."

"Guereg?"

"No, just Greg."

"Guereg. A good name. I'm Amadu, at your service."

"Nice to meet you, Amadu."

"Nice to meet you, Mr. Guereg. The pleasure is all mine."

Amadu spoke English, which was good. The agency had told him that everyone spoke English there. It was like a second language, or sometimes a third or fourth language, but they spoke English.

It seemed that poor people had a way with languages. A genetic thing perhaps. English wasn't Greg's first language either, but it shocked him, really shocked him, when no one spoke English or at least Hindi or Mandarin. There, thank God, it wasn't a problem. Some people would be sure to speak English. Thank you, God, Greg felt almost compelled to say, *sukran, gracias, xie xie, vielen Dank, dhaniavaad, spassiba, djecui, samalat po, barak brigadu,* for having someone in this godforsaken place who speaks English.

"Soldier of fortune, Mr. Guereg?"

Amadu might not have been a great driver, but he was nothing if not persistent. Perhaps it would be worth hiring him for a few days. Like a marriage of convenience. Until death us do part.

"No."

"Businessman?"

"No."

Amadu had one eye on the road and the other on his passenger. His left eye was fixed on the dusty whiteness that was the world outside the car; his right eye kept watch on the rearview mirror. He seemed to have given up, poor man, unable to guess the profession of his illustrious passenger.

No, one last try:

"UN?"

Greg decided to lift the veil on the mystery which *was* no mystery: "Tourist."

"Ah." It would be no exaggeration to say that Amadu's eyes lit up.

Greg, however, didn't seem to understand that look, because he felt it necessary to repeat:

"Yes, a tourist."

Amadu laughed, and the passenger was somewhat surprised to see that he still had all his teeth. He must be younger than he appeared. In fact, now that Greg looked at him properly, he really was *much* younger than he appeared. Not in his forties or even thirties, but in his twenties. Maybe even the moustache was fake. A good sign. A very good sign.

Amadu nodded, still laughing, and said:

"Tourist? Yes, I understand. Tourist. Welcome to our humble country, Guereg the tourist!"

Greg didn't know if the taxi driver—amateur or professional— had overcharged him or not. Nor did he care. He didn't know how much time he would be spending in the zone, although he hoped it wouldn't be long. He had reserved a room for a week, half-board. However, if all went well, his stay would last only two or three days. That's why he had come, because this country had a reputation (deserved, he hoped) for being a place where one didn't have to wait too long to get the particular product he was after.

They were entering the city now. Battered, dilapidated, charred buildings; it was hard to tell whether they were half built or half destroyed. Many had no roof, others only half a roof, still others were mere ruins or else bare structures, nothing but concrete and steel, and the occasional brick building. The streets were nothing but dust, with rubbish and plastic cluttering the ground and the air.

And all around a blinding light. The expression "blinding light" should be a contradiction in terms, but it wasn't, not there. Far from helping you to see, the light was so bright you could hardly see anything.

During the journey, Greg could make out (rather than see) a few squares, a few shops, some people wandering the streets. Here and there, in a black crater, he thought he could recognize the ghost of a café or a pizzeria, even though it was besmeared with soot, a sudden blackness in violent contrast with the whiteness of the light. Besmeared or besmirched? Let the devil come and decide.

What was he saying? The devil didn't have to come, he was already there. The devil was, if not the owner, certainly an inhabitant *honoris causa* of the zone. That was the reason (precisely because it was a hell) that Greg had chosen that place, what remained of it, because the devil of that former paradise had made his home there.

Let's be clear. Greg had come there to die. And filled by a sense of euphoria, he almost offered a toast: he had a feeling in his bones, an intuition, a hunch, he felt that he had chosen the right Scaramouche, Scaramouche, will you do the fandango, for me, for me, for me?

After living life more or less on a God-will-provide basis, only to end up with the brutal knowledge that God had signally failed to provide, his death would at least make some sense, because he had sought it out, pursued it, had been the one to choose the place, if not the hour, for his last (or first—opinions on this differed) meeting with the creator—or creatoress.

The hotel had a swimming pool. Greg didn't know whether to laugh or cry. The hotel had a swimming pool.

Even though the rooms weren't all occupied, there was still quite a racket in the reception area. A lot of businessmen, some looking overburdened with work, were talking on their mobile phones or sitting on the sofas, leaning earnestly forward, embroiled in some passionate discussion.

A man with his hair slicked back, as if with brilliantine, was gesticulating wildly. A tall woman, wearing a khaki waistcoat with a lot of pockets, and a pair of high boots, somewhat reminiscent of Lara Croft (the actress who plays her in the movies, not the one in the video game), was issuing instructions to a hairy man with a camera resting on his knees. A group of Filipinos were following what appeared to be a local woman (pretty in her way) who was holding aloft a circular fan, looking like a traffic policeman. Now there were Filipinos everywhere. Always in a group—worse than the Japanese.

Amadu was unable to help Greg carry his suitcase, for which he apologized; unfortunately, taxi drivers were not allowed into the hotel. There had been a few problems some time back, perhaps Mr. Guereg had heard about it. Apparently, the management thought that it damaged a hotel's reputation for their guests to be blown up in the foyer. It wasn't so much inconvenient as inelegant. After all, that was what the zone outside was for, wasn't it? The hotel foyer was a place for relaxation and repose, as safe and sophisticated, given the circumstances, as was humanly possible.

Greg kept Amadu's card, but made no firm arrangements. He would see what transpired. A porter accompanied him to reception, where he gave his name, showed his passport, and left his credit card details. Greg assumed that, as usual, this was so that they could charge him later for anything taken from the minibar or for any telephone calls, or even for using the gym, but the receptionist peered at him over the top of his glasses as a librarian might look at a reader who was late returning a book.

"We thought you knew. We charge a week in advance for any expenses incurred for hospital treatment, emergency transport, personal services, detox, prosthesis, casino bills . . ."

"In advance?"

A slight, almost imperceptible grimace appeared on the receptionist's face, which could have meant (a) that he deeply regretted this state of affairs or (b) that he regretted the guest was so slow on the uptake.

"As I'm sure you know, sir, it's impossible to get travel insurance to visit the zone. For the same reasons, although much to our regret, we have no option but to charge in advance."

"Oh, so you charge for services I haven't even had . . ."

"But you can be sure that, at the end of your stay, if the balance is in your favor, it will be our pleasure—although it is, alas, a rather rare pleasure—to reimburse the difference."

Greg thought it best to let the matter drop. Why get into a fight he couldn't win?

"Fine. If those are the house rules . . ."

"And the good news is that access to the swimming pool and the Turkish bath is free. If you've forgotten anything, bathing trunks or tennis shoes or swimming goggles or any other piece of sports equipment, we will be happy to provide you with them for a modest charge."

"You're not telling me there's a tennis court in the hotel?"

"I'm pleased to say that there is. Naturally, the use of the courts depends on the waiting list or on the need to sweep up any bits of mortar shell, but that's relatively rare now."

"Your hotel is full of surprises."

"Pleasant ones we hope, sir. We may not be the largest hotel in the zone, and we're certainly not the oldest, but we try to provide our worthy guests with the best possible service. We live by the motto: In the midst of barbarism, civilization."

Greg was intending to take a stroll around the area as soon as he had unpacked his case. He lay down on the bed to rest for a minute, but found himself admiring the high old ceiling, which was impressive both for its height and for the relief arabesques, motifs drawn from the plant or perhaps the marine world, fish or eels, eels being halfway between snakes and fish, with the difference, in relation to snakes, that they were less disgusting to eat. Sea creatures coiled about each other in a circular movement that went (in a spiral? like a Rorschach ink blot?) from the candelabra in the middle to the four corners of the ceiling . . .

When he woke, he felt slightly irritated, as happens when a person's sleep patterns are disturbed. He shouldn't, he realized, have under-estimated the effects of jet lag and, then, when he felt for the light switch, he almost knocked over the bedside lamp.

He hadn't dreamed at all; at least, when he woke up, he had no memory of having dreamed, which, to all intents and purposes, came to the same thing. So he hadn't dreamed.

He tried to turn on the light—nothing happened. He got up and flicked all the other switches too, even in the bathroom. Nothing. He lay down again on the bed, feeling a headache coming on. After a long moment, he remembered that the receptionist had warned him that there might be power outages. He had even told him where to find the matches. Of course. In the chest of drawers.

Greg discovered that there were candleholders on the walls complete with candles, rather like the torches you see in medieval castles in movies about medieval castles. It was the same in the bathroom. The power outages must be a daily irritant.

Bent over the sink, he splashed his face with water and didn't like what he saw in the mirror: a full, rather plump face, its brown eyes already dull, and with suspicious marks on its somewhat flaccid cheeks—liver spots probably. The face of a man who was already more on that side than this in the balance of human time.

He opened the curtains. Everything lay in darkness. It was still night. He was about to go back to bed in order to try and sleep when an orange flare lit up the sky, followed by another and another. It was hard to tell how far away it was—although it clearly wasn't very close—because had there been any noise from the bombardments, it would have been muffled by the double glazing.

Hm. Interesting.

His good mood restored, Greg lay down. Contrary to his expectations, he soon fell asleep again.

This time he did dream. He dreamed about an enormous dinosaur, possibly a tyrannosaurus, grinning broadly, with a flattering, reptilian smile; it had vast back legs, pure muscle, that contrasted with its comically feeble arms, with which the tyrannosaurus was doing . . . crochet! Crocheting with the bones of its victims? Making a pair of bone bootees for a baby that was on the way?

It was the very definition of a comforting dream.

By the second day, he was beginning to get acclimatized. He still couldn't make out the names of the streets, most of which, as far as he could see, were more like goat tracks than streets, and used by shepherds with goats and sheep and by carts drawn by donkeys or mules. A woman had walked past him only minutes before, barefoot, carrying her child in her arms, its head and arms hanging limply, and leaving a trail of blood on the ground. Where was she going? Was there a hospital nearby? Why didn't anyone help her? Was it normal for a woman to walk down the street holding her dying child, so normal that no one offered to help? And who was there to take her to the hospital? The few cars on the streets must have other things to do than go out of their way for someone else. Fuel was expensive. And, of course, only those involved in the war would have access to it.

Besides, memorizing street names would take up time and willpower he no longer felt he had; yes, he was lacking in both items, time and/or willpower. However, he felt that he could safely explore the streets within a radius of five blocks from the hotel without getting lost. If, that is, they would leave him alone. They wouldn't. His short morning walk was taken under escort from the hotel security guards. He tried to shoo them away, but to no avail: "Those are our orders, sir."

Even this failed to dent his good humor. On an impulse, he took his cell phone out of his pocket, checked that there was a signal—there was—and called his wife. The answering machine responded, of course, but he spoke to it as if he were speaking to her:

"It's really nice here. Yes, you're right. It is dirty and chaotic, but even the dirt and the chaos are nice. A little while ago, a woman walked past me holding her child in her arms. It looked like the child had been hit by a cluster bomb, you know, those bombs that explode before they hit the ground and which don't kill, but maim."

The signal died. He didn't try to phone again, even though he felt like talking, with an enthusiasm that was only partly feigned. He imagined the rest of the conversation: Did she understand the beauty of the cluster bomb concept? Yes, exactly, to do as much damage as possible to human flesh, by spraying out thousands of nails, an instantaneous zap-zap-zapping. Like a harpooner, not of whales, but of sardines, who, when he throws his harpoon (it doesn't matter in which direction), releases a thousand mini-harpoons, each going off in search of its sardine or its baby. Anyway, I'd better go. Lots of love. Yes, I'll wrap up warm, don't you worry.

TRANSLATED FROM PORTUGUESE BY MARGARET JULL COSTA

war

DAVID DEPHY

Before the End

The soldiers are standing in a line. I am pressed against the wall and they are aiming at me. The moment is dragging on. The order of the chief is heard: "Fire!"

They fire.

In this interminable moment, the flight of the bullets slow after they emerge lazily from the guns. The guns stink with the smell of gunpowder. The bullets are slowly, lazily floating. Turning around and around. The soldiers' livid faces look like masks in the mist. They stare at me in rage. The spinning bullets are approaching me. Impudently and steadily moving forward. Their determined advance is ruthless. Don't you see that time doesn't exist? I can run away before the bullets enter me, can't I? But my body doesn't listen to reason. I am standing, pressing against the wall with my back. The bullets are halfway between the soldiers and myself. The soldiers are still aiming. At this moment, they don't exist; they're stuck back in the second before my idea cropped up and got hung on this dragged-out moment. The smoke from their guns is swaying. It's not dispersing yet. The bullets are swirling, moving forward. Three of them in front of the other two.

I feel hot.

I see my childhood behind the soldiers. I'm playing in the yard. A cockroach is on my palm. I pet it with my finger. My mother is calling me from the balcony. I hear music. I hear the melody of "Strawberry Fields" from a distance. My favorite, "Strawberry Fields Forever."

The bullets are two paces away from me. They approach lazily. On my left I notice a familiar face.

"It's incredible, isn't it?" it's saying to me.

"What?" I ask.

"The thing you're feeling and seeing."

"Is death like this?"

"Like this as well."

"I'm not a deserter!"

"I know."

"Nor a traitor . . . Why are they shooting me like a traitor?"

"It's wartime now. Nobody is responsible."

"That doesn't matter. The tribunal made a mistake. I don't deserve to be shot."

"It's wartime now. Maybe they mistook you for somebody else? . . . But there's no point worrying anymore."

"Are you my death?"

"Yes."

He goes quiet. He is looking in the direction of the soldiers. They're still standing in the same position, with guns aimed. The smoke has drifted farther up, the bullets have come nearer. They are turning around steadily, slowing down even more.

"And now?" I ask.

"Nothing," he answered. "Now what usually happens, happens. It's quiet."

"Stop making fun of me, stop tormenting me."

"I'm not laughing at you or tormenting you. War justifies everybody's death."

"War?"

"Yes. It doesn't end, it doesn't begin, it always exists. No matter whether you win or lose, it exists and nobody can avoid it. How tired I am . . ."

"Why are you tired?"

"You are not responsible for death in war. War itself absolves you of that responsibility. That's why I'm tired. Immortality, too. That's another enemy, and it never dies. Enough, your time is up. Don't be afraid."

"Why should I be afraid? I'm a soldier."

"I know."

"And I'm not going to give up so easily."

"I'm not going to argue with you. You are standing with your back pressed against the wall. The bullets are already flying. So don't speak to me like that. I'm your fellow soldier, and I love you like my brother."

"What have I done to deserve your love?"

"You aren't alone in this."

"Who else is there?"

"Everyone. I stand by everyone. I can't leave anyone."

"What do you mean?"

"It's always the same. I keep myself at this distance." He extends his hand, touching me on my shoulder. I feel hot and cold and hot. The bullets have almost reached my chest. I look down at them, they are spinning. One of the soldiers has raised his gun, the rest are standing in the same old positions. Everybody is motionless. The smoke seems to have dispersed.

"I am a brother to every one of you, I fight only because Death exists and because we can be enemies, but to fight you should be able to do the most important thing . . ."

"What?"

"Enmity," he looks into my eyes. "How beautiful and how terrible it is. If you want to love, you should be able to hate at first sight, yet fight for the one you hate as well. But nobody fights by this rule: only myself. This is why I am the end of everybody, because I have enough courage to love you and still be your enemy, yours and everybody else's . . . I am the last enemy and I am looking forward to the day when my eternity ends. But now your time is up, come along with me."

He embraces me.

"Be strong, you'll be amazed when you see and understand everything," I hear him say as the bullets enter me, two into my chest and one into my head. My body, covered with bullet wounds, falls down to the ground, sliding down the blood-stained wall. As if time has been switched on again. The soldiers hang their guns over their shoulders and disperse quickly; my childhood disappears. Over there heavy machine guns can be seen. There is more smoke all around. The wounded are being placed in the trucks. Far away, lines of soldiers are rushing off somewhere. The music has stopped. There are trumpets instead of "Strawberry Fields." The war is continuing. The tanks are rattling. The helicopters are flying in the sky. There is smoke everywhere, heavy smoke rising up.

TRANSLATED FROM GEORGIAN BY TSISANA GABUNIA

DESMOND HOGAN

Kennedy

A nineteen-year-old youth is made to dig a shallow grave in waste ground beside railway tracks near Limerick bus station and then shot with an automatic pistol.

Eyes blue-green, brown-speckled, of blackbird's eggs.

He wears a hoodie jacket patterned with attack helicopters.

Murdered because he was going to snitch—go to the guards about a murder he'd witnessed—his friend Cuzzy had fired the shot. The victim had features like a Western stone wall. The murder vehicle—a stolen cobalt Ford Kuga—set on fire at Ballyneety near Lough Gur.

The hesitant moment by Lough Gur when blackthorn blossom and hawthorn blossom are unrecognizable from one another, the one expiring, the other coming into blossom.

Creeping willow grows in the waste ground near Limerick bus station—as it was April male catkins yellow, with pollen, on separate tree small greenish female stamens. In April also whitlow grass which Kennedy's grandmother Evie used to cure inflammation near fingernails and toenails.

In summer creeping cinquefoil grows in the waste ground.

He was called Kennedy by Michaela, his mother, after John F. Kennedy, and Edward Kennedy, both of whom visited this city, the latter with a silver dollar haircut and tie with small knot and square ends. He must have bought a large jar of Brylcreem with him, Kennedy's father, Bongo, remarked about him.

"When I was young and comely,

Sure, good fortune on me shone,

My parents loved me tenderly."

A pious woman found Saint Sebastian's body in a sewer and had a dream he told her to bury him in the catacombs.

Catacumbas. Late Latin word. Latin of Julian the Apostate who studied the Gospels and then returned to the Greek gods.

The Catacombs. A place to take refuge in. A place to scratch prayers on the wall in. A place to paint in.

Cut into porous tufa rock, they featured wall paintings such as one of the three officials whom Nebuchadnezzar flung in the furnace for not bowing before a golden image of him in the plain of Dura in Babylon but who were spared.

Three officials, arms outstretched, in pistachio-green jester's apparel amid flames of maple red.

The body of Sebastian the Archer refused death by arrows and he had to be beaten to death. Some have surmised the arrows were symbolic and he was raped.

As the crime boss brought Kennedy to be murdered he told a story:

"I shook hands with Bulldog who is as big as a Holstein Friesian and who has fat cheeks.

It was Christmas and we got a crate and had a joint.

He says, 'I have the stiffness.'

He slept in the same bed as me in the place I have in Ballysimon.

In the morning he says, 'Me chain is gone and it was a good chain. I got it in Port Mandel near Manchester.'

He pulled up all the bedclothes.

He says 'I'll come back later and if I don't get me chain, your Lexus with the wind-down roof will be gone.'

He came back later but he saw the squad car—'the scumbags,' he said—and he went away.

A week later I saw Cocka, a hardy young fellow, with Bulldog's chain, in Sullivan's Lane."

The crime boss, who is descended from the Black and Tans, himself wears a white-gold chain from Crete, an American gold ring large as a Spanish grandee's ring, a silver bomber jacket, and pointy shoes of true white.

He has a stack of *Nude* magazines in his house in Ballysimon, offers you a custard and creams from a plate with John Paul II's—Karol Wojtyła's—head on it, plays Country and Western a lot:

Sean Wilson—"Blue Hills of Breffni," "Westmeath Bachelor."

Sean Moore—"Dun Laoghaire Can Be Such a Lonely Place."

Johnny Cash—"I Walk the Line."

Ballysimon is famed for a legitimate dumping site but some people are given money to dump rubbish in alternative ways.

"Millionaires from dumping rubbish," it is said of them.

By turning to violence, to murder, they create a history, they create a style for themselves. They become ikons as ancient as Calvary.

Matthew tells us his Roman soldier torturers put a scarlet robe on Christ, Mark and John a robe of purple.

Emerging from a garda car Kennedy's companion and accomplice Cuzzy, in a grey pinstripe jersey, is surprised into history.

Centurion's facial features. A flick of hair to the right above his turf cut makes him a little like a crested grebe.

South Hill boys like Cuzzy are like the man-eating mares of King Diomedes of the Bistones that Hercules was entrusted to capture—one of the twelve labours King Eurystheus imposed on him.

"If I had to choose between Auschwitz and here," he says of his cell, "I'd choose Auschwitz."

As Kennedy's body is brought to Janesboro Church some of his brothers clasp their hands in an attitude of prayer. Others simply drop their heads in grief.

Youths in suits with chest hammer pleats and cigarette-rolled shoulders. Mock-snake skin shoes. With revolver cufflinks.

One of the brothers has a prison tattoo—three Chinese letters in biro and ink—on the side of his right ear.

The youngest brother, who is the only one to demur jacket and tie, has his white shirt hanging over his trousers and wears a silver chain with boxing gloves.

Michaela's—Kennedy's mother—hair is pêle-mêle blanche-blonde, she wears horn-toed, fleur-de-lys patterned, lace-up black high heels, mandorla—oval—ring, ruby and gold diamante on fingernails against her black.

Her businessman boyfriend wears a Savile Row-style suit chosen from his wardrobe of dark lilac suits, grey and black lounge suits, suits with black collars, wine suits, plum jackets, claret red velvet one-button jackets.

Kennedy's father Bongo had been a man with kettle-black eyebrows, who was familiar with the juniper berries and the rowan berries and the scarlet berries of the bittersweet—the woody nightshade—sequestered his foal with magpie face and Talmud scholar's beard where these berries, some healing, some poisonous, were abundant. He knew how to challenge the witch's broom.

John Joe Criggs, the umbrella mender in Killeely, used to send boys who looked like potoroos—rat kangaroos with prehensile tails—to Weston where they lived, looking for spare copper.

"You're as well hung as a stallion like your father," Bongo would say to Kennedy. "Get a partner."

In Clare for the summer he once turned to Michaela in the night in Kilrush during a fight.

"Go into the Kincora Hotel and get a knife so I can kill this fellow."

He always took Kennedy to Ballyheigue at Marymass—September 8—where people in bare feet took water in bottles from the Holy Well, left scapulars, names, and photographs of people who were dead, children who'd been killed.

He fell in a pub fight. Never woke up.

His mother Evie had hung herself when they settled her.

Hair ivory grey at edges, then sienna, in a ponytail tied by a velvet ribbon, usually in tattersal coat, maxie skirt, heelless sandals.

On the road she'd loved to watch the mistle thrush who came to Ireland with the Act of Union of 1801, the Wee Willie Wagtail—blue tit—with black eyestripe and lemon breast, the chaffinch with pink lightings on its breast who would come up close to you, in winter in fraochán—ring ouzel, white crescent around its breast, bird of river, of crags.

On the footbridge at Doonass near Clondara she told Kennedy of the two Jehovah's Witnesses who were assaulted in Clondara, their bibles burned, the crowd cheered on by the Parish Priest, and then the Jehovah's Witnesses bound to the peace in court for blasphemy.

Michaela's father Billser had been in Glin Industrial School.

The Christian Brothers, with Abbey School of Acting voices, used to get them to strip naked and lash them with the cat of the nine tails. Boys with smidgen penises. A dust, a protest of pubic hair. Boys with pubes as red as the fox who came to steal the sickly chickens, orange as the beak of an Aylesbury duck, brown of the tawny owl.

Then bring them to the Shannon when the tide was in and force them to immerse in salt water.

The Shannon food—haws, dulse, barnacles—they ate them. They robbed mangels, turnips. They even robbed the pig's and bonham's—piglet's—food.

"You have eyes like the blackbird's eggs. You have eyes like the *céirseach*'s eggs. You have eyes like the merie's eggs," a Brother, nicknamed the Seabhac—hawk—used to tell Billser.

Blue-green, brown speckled.

He was called Seabhac because he used to ravage boys the way the hawk makes a sandwich of autumn brood pigeons or meadow pipits, leaving a flush of feathers.

He had ginger-beer hirsute like the rufous-barred sparrowhawk that quickly gives up when it misses a target, lays eggs in abandoned crow's nests.

A second reason for his nickname was because he was an expert in Irish and the paper-covered Irish dictionary was penned by *an Seabhac*—the Hawk.

Father Edward J. Flanagan from Ballymoe, North Galway, who founded Boys Town in Omaha and was played by Spencer Tracy, came to Ireland in 1946 and visited Glin Industrial School.

The Seabhac gave him a patent hen's egg, tea in a cup with blackbirds on it, Dundee cake on a plate with the same pattern.

Billser used to cry salty tears when he remembered Glin.

Michaela's grandfather Torrie had been in the British Army and the old British names for places in Limerick City kept breaking into his conversation—Lax Weir, Patrick Punch Corner, Saint George's Street.

Cuzzy and Kennedy met at a Palaestra—boxing club.

Cuzzy was half-Brazilian.

"My father was Brazilian. He knocked my mother and went away."

"Are you riding any woman now?" he asked Kennedy, who had rabbit-coloured pubes, in the showers.

"You have nipples like monkey fingers," Kennedy said to Cuzzy, who had palomino-coloured pubes, in the showers.

The coach, who looked like a pickled onion with tattoos in the nude, was impugned for messing with the teenage boxers. HIV Lips was his nickname.

"Used to box for CIE Boxing Club," he said to himself, "would go around the country. They used to wear pink-lined vests, and I says no way am I going to wear that."

"He sniffed my jocks. And there were no stains on them," a shaven headed boxer who looked like a defurred monkey or a peeled banana reported in denunciation of him.

A man who had a grudge against him used to scourge a statue of the Greek boxer Theagenes of Thasos until it fell on him, killing him.

The statue was thrown in the sea and fished up by fishermen.

Barrenness came on the country which the Delphic Oracle said wouldn't be removed until the statue was restored.

In the Palaestra was a poster of John Cena with leather wrappings on his forearm like the Terme Boxer—Pugile delle Terme—a first-century BC copy of a second-century BC statue which depicted Theagenes of Thasos.

John Cena in black baseball cap, briefs showing above trousers beside a lingering poster for Circus Vegas at Two Mile Inn—a kick-boxer in mini-bikini briefs and mock-crocodile boots.

Kennedy and Cuzzy were brought to the Garda Station one night when they were walking home from the Boxing Club.

"They'll take anyone in tracksuits."

Cuzzy, aged sixteen, was thrown in the girls' cell.

Kennedy was thumped with a mag lamp, a telephone book used to prevent his body from being bruised.

Cuzzy was thumped with a baton through a towel with soap in it.

A black guard put his tongue in Kennedy's ear. A Polish guard felt his genitals.

Kennedy punched the Polish guard and was jailed.

Solicitors bought parcels of heroin and cocaine into jail.

Youths on parole would swallow one eight heroin and €50 bags of heroin, thus sneak them in.

One youth put three hundred diazepam, three hundred steroids, three ounces of citric in a bottle, three needles up his anus.

Túr Cant for anus.

Ríspún Cant for jail.

Slop out in mornings.

Not even granule coffee for breakfast. Something worse.

Locked up most of the day.

One youth with a golf-ball face, skin-coloured lips of the young Dickie Rock, when his baseball cap was removed a pronounced bald patch on his blond head, had a parakeet in his cell.

Cuzzy would bring an adolescent Alsatian to the Unemployment Office.

Then he and Kennedy got a job laying slabs near the cement factory at Raheen.

Apart from work, Limerick routine.

Drugs in cling-foil or condoms put up their anuses, guards stopping them—fingers up their anuses.

Tired of the routine they both went to Donegal to train with AC Armalite rifles and machine guns in fields turned salmon-colour by ragged robin.

The instructor had a Vietnam veteran pepper-and-salt beard and wore Stars and Stripes plimsolls.

The farmer who used to own the house they stayed in would have a boy come for one month in the summer from an Industrial School, by arrangement with the Brothers.

The boy used to sleep in the same bed as him and the farmer made him wear girl's knickers.

In Kennedy's room was a Metallica poster—fuschine bikini top, mini-bikini, skull locket on forehead, fuschine mouth, belly button that looked like deep cleavage of buttocks, skeleton's arms about her.

"It was on Bermuda's island
That I met Captain Moore . . ."

"It's like the Albanians. They give you a bit of rope with a knot at the top.

Bessa they call it.

They will kill you or one of your family.

You know the Albanians by the ears. Their ears are taped back at birth.

And they have dark eyebrows.

I was raised on the island.

You could leave your doors open. They were the nicest people.

Drugs spoiled people."

Weston where Kennedy grew up was like Bedford-Stuyvesant or Brownsville, New York, where Mike Tyson grew up, his mother, who died when he was sixteen, regularly observing him with clothes he didn't pay for.

Kennedy once took a €150 tag off a golf club in a Limerick store, replaced it with a €20 tag, and paid for it.

As a small boy he had a Staffordshire terrier called Daisy.

Eyes a blue-coast watch, face a sea of freckles, he let the man from Janesboro who sucked little boys' knobs buy him 99s—ice cream cones with chocolate flakes stuck in them, syrup on top—or traffic-light cakes—cakes with scarlet and green jellies on the icing.

He'd play *knocker gawlai*—knock at doors in Weston and run away.

He'd throw eggs at taxis.

Once a taxi driver chased him with a baseball bat.

"I smoked twenty cigarettes a day since I was eleven.

Used to work as a mechanic part time then.

I cut it down to ten and then to five recently. My doctor told me my lungs were black and I'd be on an oxygen mask by the time I was twenty.

I'm nineteen."

The youth in the petrol-blue jacket spoke against the Island on which someone on a bicycle was driving horses.

A lighted motorbike was going up and down Island Field.

We were on the Metal Bridge side of the Shannon.

It was late afternoon, mid-December.

"They put barbed wire under the Metal Bridge to catch the bodies that float down. A boy jumped off the bridge, got caught in the barbed wire and was drowned.

They brought seventeen stolen cars here one day and burned all of them."

There were three cars in the water now, one upside down, with the wheels above the tide.

"When I was a child my mother used to always be saying, 'I promised Our Lady of Lourdes. I promised Our Lady of Lourdes.'

There's a pub in Heuwagen in Basel and I promised a friend I'd meet him there.

You can get accommodation in Paddington on the way for £20 a night. Share with someone else."

He turned to me. "Are you a Traveller? Do you light fires?"

He asked me where I was from and when I told him he said, "I stood there with seventeen Connemara ponies once and sold none of them."

On his fingers rings with horses' heads, saddles, hash plant.

His bumster trousers showed John Galliano briefs.

Two stygian hounds approached the tide followed by an owner with warfare orange hair, in a rainbow hoodie jacket, who called "Mack" after one of them.

He pulled up his jacket and underlying layers to show a tattoo MAKAVELI on his butter-mahogany abdomen.

"I got interested in Machiavelli because 2Pac was interested in him. Learnt all about him. An Italian philosopher. Nikolo is his first name. Put his tattoo all over my body. Spelt it Makaveli. Called my Rottweiler-Staffordshire terrier cross breed after him. Mack.

Modge is the long-haired black terrier.

Do you know that 2Pac was renamed Tupac Amaru Shakur by his mother after an Inca sentenced to death by the Spaniards?

In Inca language, Shining Serpent.

Do you know that when the Florentines were trying to recapture Pisa Machiavelli was begged because he was a philosopher to stay at headquarters but he answered," and the youth thrust out his chest like Arnold Schwarzenegger for this bit, "that he must be with his soldiers because he'd die of sadness behind the lines?

They say 2Pac was shot dead in Las Vegas. There was no funeral. He's as alive as you or me.

I'm reading a book about the Kray Twins now.

Beware of sneak attacks."

And then he went off with Mack and Modge singing the song 2Pac wrote about his mother, "Dear Mama."

"When I was a child my father used to take me to Ballyheigue every year.

There's a well there.

The priest was saying mass beside it during the Penal Days and the Red Coats turned up with hounds.

Three wethers jumped up from the well, ran towards the sea.

The hounds chased them, devoured them and were drowned.

The priest's life was spared."

They were of Thomond, neither of Munster nor Connaught, Thomond bodies, Thomond pectorals.

The other occasion I met Kennedy was on a warm February Saturday.

He was sitting in a Ford Focus on Hyde Road in red silky football shorts with youths in similar attire.

He introduced me to one of them, Razz, who had an arm tattoo of a centurion in a G-string.

"I was in Cloverhill. Remand prison near a courthouse in Dublin. Then Mountjoy. You'd want to see the bleeding place. It was filthy. The warden stuck his head in the cell door one day and said, 'You're for Portlaoise.' They treat you well in Portlaoise."

"What were you in jail for?"

"A copper wouldn't ask me that."

A flank of girls in acid-pink and acid-green tops was hovering near this portmanteau of manhood like coprophagous—dung-eating—gulls near cows for the slugs in their dung.

A little girl in sunglasses with mint green frontal frames, flamingo wings, standing outside her house nearby, said to a little girl in a lemon and peach top who was passing:

"There are three birthday cards inside for you, Tiffany."

"It's not my birthday."

"It is your fucking birthday."

And then she began chasing the other girl like a skua down Hyde Road, in the direction of the bus station, screaming, "Happy Birthday to you. Happy Birthday to you."

Flowers of the magnolia come first in Pery Square Park near the Bus Station, tender yellow-green leaf later.

A Traveller boy cycled by the sweet chestnut blossoms of Pery Square Park the day they found Kennedy's body, firing heaped on his handlebars.

I am forced to live in a city of Russian tattooists, murderously shaven heads, Rumanian accordionists, the young in pallbearers' clothes— this is the hemlock they've given me to drink.

The Maigue in West Limerick, as I crossed it, was like the old kettles Kennedy's ancestors used to mend.

Travellers used to make rings from old teaspoons and sometimes I wondered if they could make rings from the discarded Hackenberg lager cans or Mr. Sheen All-Surface Polish cans beside the Metal Bridge.

I am living in the city for a year when a man who looks as if his face has been kicked in by a stallion approaches me on the street.

"I'm from Limerick city and you're from Limerick city. I know a Limerick city face. I haven't seen you there for a while. How many months did you get?"

DANILA DAVYDOV

The Telescope

Ippelman was extremely lucky. The explosion killed everybody on the bus, the driver, the passengers, everybody except him. His good fortune must have been due to the fact that he was standing by the rear doors intending to get off in a few minutes' time, and the bomb (if it was a bomb, rather than something else, something even more improbable) was at the front of the bus. Just at the moment Ippelman was thinking about the spirit of competition, there was a sound too loud to be heard, a blinding blaze of light, and the bus evidently toppled over. Ippelman saw green and orange ellipses, felt a stinging pain in his eyes, and fell but did not lose consciousness; instead he submitted to an instinctive craving for survival, his hands found an escape hatch that appeared to have opened specially for him and which flung itself into his arms. Ippelman still had little idea what had happened as he crawled out but, when there was a second explosion behind him (the fire had reached the fuel tank), he saw with extraordinary clarity that he was blind. Most likely slivers of glass had cut his eyes a moment after the explosion, although he wouldn't have argued if told that his blindness was simply a symptom of concussion; he wasn't clear about the effect of the blast. I may just be in shock, he told himself, and when I get over it my sight will come back. It wasn't long, however, before he realized that this wasn't going to happen. He tried to find out if anybody else had survived, although he was all but certain they were dead; he called out three or four times but there was no response. It was cold. It occurred to Ippelman that he shouldn't stay there. He should get away. The town limit was about two kilometers away, but without visual clues, walking there wouldn't be easy. The simplest thing would be to keep to the road, but when he crawled out of the burning bus Ippelman had no idea which side of the road it was laying on. I just need to walk, Ippelman thought, and either I'll reach the town or a village along the road in the other direction. The main thing was to move, because otherwise he might die. Ippelman had no idea what he might die of, but suddenly thought of blood poisoning and decided that that was what he had to worry about. He tried to stand up, swayed, lost his balance, and sat down; he tried again, got up, took one step and then another. Apart from his eyes the rest of him was in one piece. I've got to go, he said out loud to himself. He liked the sound of that and repeated it, as if responding to applause from an imaginary audience which had taken its seats in twilit bushes he could no longer see. He walked for half an hour or so in total silence until he found he was exhausted. He sat down in the middle of the road in the hope of getting a lift from a passing car, but no car passed, there was only an owl looking for prey hooting in the darkness. Not surprising, Ippelman thought, you won't get a lot of passing cars at two in the morning on a weekday in the middle of the countryside. Now there were two owls, they'd discovered each other and started arguing. Ippelman wasn't sure whether owls ate human flesh. He knew crows did, but owls didn't seem to have much in common with crows, and besides, they only came out at night. It got colder. Suddenly he heard a vehicle approaching. It stopped, a door slammed, and the driver crossed to Ippelman, grunted, and gave him a hefty kick that sent him rolling into a ditch, then the driver got back in the car and drove off. Ippelman dragged himself back onto the road and staggered on without knowing which direction he was going in. He walked for a long time, a very long time. On several occasions he collapsed helplessly on the asphalt before resolving again to go on. To his surprise the pain in his eyes was not unbearable, but neither could it be ignored. Ippelman reckoned it would be daybreak soon and, even if he was walking in the wrong direction, a passing car would stop sooner or later not to taunt an injured man but to help him. The thought came to him that news about the explosion on the bus must already have reached the forces of law and order, they would certainly be searching for survivors, and he would shortly be found. For some reason, however, he could hear no cars, only small animals squeaking or whimpering in the grass by the side of the road. Ippelman now relaxed and felt an inner calm. Like getting your second wind, he thought. The freshness of the morning, if, of course, it was already morning, seemed paradoxically in harmony with the stinging sensation in his sightless eyes, which, predictably, showed no sign of stopping. He heard a cock crow far away, so it was morning and there must be a village nearby. He felt no joy, only emptiness, of which there was so much that Ippelman overflowed with it and lost consciousness without even noticing. He didn't notice waking up either, only why—a wet hand touched his forehead. What's happened to you, a thin voice asked, seeming neither surprised nor scared. Where am I, Ippelman asked, or didn't so much ask as just say. Here. Ippelman tried to get up but realized he no longer had the strength, and in any case the hay under his back was very comfortable. Lie there, the voice laughed, I'll bring you some milk. The person ran off. Ippelman heard it clearly, the person was soon back. Drink it. The cold milk was just what Ippelman wanted. You need a bandage, you're covered in blood. What's your name? What's yours?

Ippelman, said Ippelman, for some reason very proud that his memory had so clearly registered that he was indeed Ippelman and not anybody else, and then, a moment or two later, he realized he had been thinking aloud and had exultantly shouted out his name and been behaving like a lunatic, a complete lunatic. You think I'm a lunatic, don't you? I'm Lyokha, the voice said, laughing again. No, do you hear what I'm saying, Ippelman was embarrassed at his loud, unrestrained self-naming. It hurts, that's why I'm a bit odd. It's okay, everything's fine. The boy called Lyokha suddenly put his arms round Ippelman, hugged him, and laughed again. How old are you, Ippelman asked? Granny went off to town yesterday, and then something like this happens. Something like what? You should answer when a grown-up asks you a question. Ippelman's voice didn't sound menacing, it wasn't, you couldn't have found a hint of schoolmasterishness in it. There was some gauze, I'll see if I can find it. He ran off again. His grandmother went off to town yesterday, Ippelman thought, and then something like this happened. What does he mean, something like this? He began picturing all kinds of horrors, perhaps even an alien invasion, but not really, lazily, the way he might think back over the latest episode of some low-budget soap opera in bed, just to get bored and fall asleep. Hold your head up a bit, Ippelman hadn't noticed the boy coming back, I'll bandage it for you, oh, I forgot the iodine. Have you got iodine? Well, maybe just herbal disinfectant, I'll go and look—he ran off again, and very soon, unnaturally soon somehow, he was back and lavished a stinging liquid on Ippelman's eyes. Ippelman swore, but why, he immediately wondered, something stinging on something stinging should have been like a double negative. Do you know what two minuses make? he asked Lyokha. 'Course I do, the boy said, offended by this doubting, and began wrapping a bandage round Ippelman's head, but without saying it made a plus. What are you doing here? Well, I took a bus to do some stargazing. Why couldn't you do it in the town, aren't there any stars there? Ippelman thought for a moment. Well, how can I explain. You can see them there, of course, but there's a lot of light around, even at night, streetlights, light from windows, that sort of thing, and quite near here there's a mound with open fields all round it, no trees, no houses, you can see to the horizon in every direction, it's a good place for looking. What do you want to look at the stars for? The boy's question might have seemed stupid but Ippelman didn't think so, quite the opposite. He thought for another moment. You see, I've got a telescope, at least I did before the explosion. Do you listen to the radio? Ippelman asked, suddenly anxious, Granny's got a television. Lyokha stroked Ippelman's head: how is it, sore? No. It was sore but Ippelman preferred to pretend it was just the iodine stinging and not him demonstrating manly stoicism. What do you need a telescope for? It's a hobby, something I enjoy doing, I like looking through the telescope, on Saturdays I go into the countryside and look at the stars all night, it makes you feel very peaceful. I've discovered a planet, he added proudly. You did! I did. Really? Yes, really. Lyokha pressed up against him once more and kissed him on the forehead. It's only a little one, of course, five kilometers across, just a large rock in space, but I was the first, so that's why they called it Ippelman. You know what? Lyokha said, there's something going on out there, it was on the television, and then you turned up. Space invaders? No, the boy's voice was very serious, a war, I think. He kissed Ippelman hard and started pulling his pants off. What are you doing, stop it, it's okay, it's okay. When they woke, Lyokha said, you lie here in the barn—Ippelman was pleased, he had been sure it was a barn—because Granny may have come back, if she didn't get hurt like you, or something worse. He ran off. Ippelman decided to think about the stars. The information about a war didn't upset him, he felt like someone who's fallen on the field of battle and could now afford

to let his thoughts be detached and unworldly, dealing with astronomical magnitudes, but his reflections on astronomy immediately
ran off in the wrong direction and Ippelman unintentionally found
himself picturing an armada of space invaders, the armada rather
than the invaders themselves, because now he was thinking even big
individual aliens seemed insignificant compared to a whole galactic
flotilla. Granny's done for, Lyokha said, coming into the barn, want
some sausage before they get here? Before who get here? You know,
them. What do you mean them? The enemies. Come on, tell me
what you heard. Well, they said it was a war. You know, Ippelman
struggled to lift his back from the hay, I was just thinking and realized there's something behind all this. What? The war, the explosions, your grandmother not being back yet, me lying here. What? I
think, Ippelman said, getting into his stride, it's not just a war, it's a
special kind of war. Why? Nothing is ever that simple. Let me change
your bandage. Wait will you, there's time for that later. Ippelman was
carried away by the image of global cataclysm and talking with his
mouth full of sausage: it's a takeover, you see, a takeover from space,
it's a very simple plan, nobody will believe it's happening until they're
here as large as life, taking over everything, and it's only then people
will start coming to their senses, but by then it will be too late. He
swallowed the last of the sausage. I think they've grabbed everything
already, I mean, all the major urban centers, they've taken everything
into their control. The boy burst out laughing and leaped on top of
Ippelman. Hey, take it easy. Helping Ippelman to dress, Lyokha kept
saying, you're weird, you're really weird, what do you mean aliens,
it's enemies, what are you going on about, there's nobody in space, I
heard it on the television, I bet it's the Chinese. Yes, Ippelman
thought aloud, maybe it's the Chinese. But, and this he thought just
to himself, aliens would make me feel more heroic, so let's stick with
that, and anyway who cares, I'm blind anyway, if they kill me I won't

see it. Lyokha, are you afraid of dying? What, yes, of course. Me too, only I don't care anymore. He started crying, in spite of the bandage, in spite of his hurt eyes, and it only struck him an hour later or maybe more that crying must mean his eyes were still where they should be, just not working, so there was hope, although, of course, he was no ophthalmologist, he didn't know the first thing about these things, and he doubted aliens would have field hospitals for treating earthlings. Lyokha pulled his bandage off, licked his tears away, and then the aliens came and took him by the arms and legs and carried him off and put him down somewhere, Ippelman was a bit surprised they just laid him down, very carefully really, and didn't throw him like food for their extraterrestrial dogs, and then drove away with him, because the place they had taken him was a vehicle, it smelled of fuel, it bumped over the unevenness in the asphalt and then Ippelman started crying again and wanted to know where the boy was, Lyokha, where are you? I love you, don't you know, I love you. Take it easy, the voice was unexpectedly human, be brave. They were Chinese, Ippelman thought, feeling humiliated because if they had been aliens there was nothing to be embarrassed about but if they were Chinese it was a different matter altogether, they were like us, not cosmic. What, have you conquered us? Ippelman wailed. This guy's not right in the head, the voice said. In shock from the pain, said another. No problem, we'll take him to the district hospital, they'll sort it out. You bastards, Ippelman wept, you bastards, usurpers, rats. The boy had hidden from the orderlies behind the barn until the ambulance disappeared around the bend and now ran home. Granny, what's a telescope? You should be given a good beating, that's what. No, it's true. Well, I'm sure I don't know. Granny, is there going to be a war? You'll get your answer sooner than you think. Granny! Go milk the cow. Granny, who's stronger, us or the Chinese? Us, of course, what do you think, and if you're going to be bad I'll tell your dad and when he comes back he'll give you a good beating. Granny! But seeing the expression on his grandmother's face, Lyokha fled from the hut and headed, needless to say, not for the cowshed but to the barn where, hidden under the hay, was that thing that looked like he didn't know what.

TRANSLATED FROM RUSSIAN BY ARCH TAIT

thought

JIŘÍ KRATOCHVIL

I, Loshad'

From Ivančice we made for Brno. Our cavalry was part of the First Guard equestrian and mechanized division under the command of General Pliyev; after Podivín it was accompanied by the remnants of the 41st tank brigade, which after the fall of Captain Chepukh in an engagement near Dolní Kounice was led by Lieutenant Mutkin. All this I remember exactly—I may be a horse, but I have a memory like an elephant. We had been the best Cossack cavalry detachment, the elite *konarmiya* of a Cossack general whose dream it was (yes, I even remember the chevaliers' dreams) to enter Berlin in glory on my saddle. But then and there, we were merely a part of Marshal Malinovsky's Second Ukrainian Front, whose victory promenade had the character of a long, all-devouring gut. I saw horses die, I saw men die. Horses by the dozen, men by the hundreds. The horses either dropped to their knees, slowly tipped onto their sides, and lay that way with their bellies twitching, or else they fell to shells, blasted into two or three pieces—red flags that were too heavy for their poles, and so flopped into the mud or settled on the heads of horrified soldiers like enormous, bloody uhlan shakos. We horses also served as meat that the soldiers called "live bully"; it was expected that those who fell would end up in the field kitchen. But sometimes there was no time in which to prepare horsemeat and it was simpler to plunder a house in some village; when that was the case, our bodies would lie at the wayside bejeweled with flies, who were the true victors in this vile war.

The boy who was assigned to care for me—though a mere *malchiska* from some insignificant *dyerevni* by the Dniester, he had a great understanding of horses—died in a minefield; he was torn to hundreds of small pieces that the great jewel box of the heavens sent back to earth as rubies with the first rays of morning. I despaired then for the touch of a hand that was gone forever—a hand that groomed me so well, stroked me with tenderness along the long, strange, white bump that starts between my ears and ends at my nostrils, which distinguishes Arabian horses from all other members of the horse family. Nor, I hope, will I ever forget how he would crouch down to my belly and with deft fingers pick out the military lice there, which were as big as the cherries in Dmitri Ivanovich's garden. (We shall speak of Dmitri Ivanovich a little later.) The boy who cared for me had the ordinary name of Volodya. There are millions of Volodyas in the land that stretches from Lake Ladoga to Okhotsk, but only one among them knew that I understand not just a few human instructions and commands but the whole of human speech, so that while he was grooming me or collecting my lice he could tell me (provided there was no one within earshot) how he had bidden farewell to his girl in the village on the Dniester and confide his words of love to me. And the bloody rubies that later spangled the heavens beyond Ivančice, this was his last brilliant bouquet, his last words of love for his girl, which I firmly believe she then read in her dreams. If she did not, then nothing in this world could make sense ever again.

We took Brno after endless days and nights that were indistinguishable from one another—the same cascades of explosions, rumble of steel tracks, machine-gun chatter, screams, and dying. The city survived, more or less—only every fifth building was wrecked; some Germans, too, survived—savage, suicidal striplings from the *Hitlerjugend*, snipers in attics, a few barricaded remnants of German units whom *Starshiy Leytenant* Andrei Tolstoy discovered to be holding Schörner Street under orders to ensure that the Red Army advanced no further than Brno. For the liquidation of these militant remnants a special group was set up. It proved possible to save a number of prisoners who were still awaiting execution at the Kounic Dormitory, but not to apprehend their executioners. Nor was it always possible to control the soldiers of the Red Army who yielded to the usual victors' frenzy, which is always taken out on the conquered territory, in particular its cows, pigs, hens, and also its women. And in Brno, cows, pigs, and hens were not plentiful.

General Issa Alexandrovich Pliyev didn't want to give up on the idea of his passing through the Brandenburg Gate on an Arabian thoroughbred. As he was a favorite of Marshal Malinovsky, he was granted permission to stable me and several horses of our cavalry in a residential quarter of Brno. A little later I discovered that our stable was known as the Tugendhat Villa.

So that we might make further progress in our story, I now owe you an explanation. I belonged originally to a translator from French and German, one Dmitri Ivanovich Khlomakov. His love of the poetry of Mallarmé and Valéry was wedded to his love of the Arabian thoroughbred. As a translator of some importance (he had translated the work of Marx and Engels), he was permitted to live at the Peredelkino writers' colony, and it was here, with the fee for his new translation of *The Three Musketeers*, that he acquired me. By lucky chance he learned that an Arabian—and a very rare specimen at that—was for sale at a certain *kolkhoz* by the Volga. Without hesitation he went off to the place in question, where he noted right away that apart from my possessing the qualities of a true Arabian—a bold, fiery temperament guided by a noble character—I was a specimen with a particularly well-developed second signal system, as conceived by Pavlov and his disciples. I showed him the workings of something I had kept hidden from the *kolkhozniks* for fear they would take me straight to the slaughterhouse—my intellectual apparatus. With a hoof I drew in the sand a sketch of Euclid's theorem. As a result, Dmitri and I cultivated a deep intellectual friendship founded on the understanding that although my highly developed second signal system would be of great interest to the Pavlov Institute, we would not entrust it to the shifty sort of people who worked there. Dmitri's apartment had two rooms; I was accommodated in the library. We carried on our conversations in the garden, under a magnificent spreading pear whose crown gave these conversations such shade that not a word of them got through to Dmitri's neighbors. But speech caused me considerable difficulties—in the process of phonation my vocal cords move toward and away from each other in a manner completely different from that by which humans articulate. Furthermore, before now I had considered it a good idea to understand human speech but very dangerous to use it myself. Dmitri and I came to spend whole evenings talking together under the pear tree. He gave me my initiation into the conquests of world culture, and he seemed to regret I lacked his enthusiasm for experimental poetry. I was keener on philosophy—classical and modern—and was quite interested in the history of metaphysics. Still, I was allowed to delve into his library, where a thinker of my stripe could find whatever his heart desired. Things quickly went to rack and ruin, sadly. Dmitri Ivanovich rashly expressed his admiration for the poetry of Osip Mandelstam in public; to my horror he was sent to the Gulag. But by this time Hitler's tanks were rolling toward Moscow and again I was requisitioned. I was assigned to the First Guard equestrian and mechanized division under the command of General Pliyev. But the general's Cossack heart spared me the worst, and I was sent to the lines only after the victory at Stalingrad, once the front had been re-drawn, and we were on course for Berlin. I traveled a large stretch of the front in an armored vehicle, because it was the general's dearest hope—as I shall repeat ad nauseum—that he should live to make the triumphal entry into Berlin on my back.

When we were put in the Tugendhat Villa, the place had already been pillaged, if not entirely cleared out; we weren't its first plunderers, that's for sure. Of those of us billeted there, I was the only one who knew anything about modern architecture: in Dmitri Ivanovich's extensive library there had been a book about Le Corbusier, which I had read with great pleasure. Although the villa was in a dreadful state—its glass walls had caved in to the pressure waves delivered by nearby bombardments, and its "dematerialized space" had been violated—I understood immediately that what we had here was a true wonder of functionalist architecture. All the others, from the general down to the lowest orderly, saw the villa as nothing more than a military installation with a good location that made it an ideal stable. The city was in full view; the villa sat on an urban promontory, which enabled us to see where the fighting was still going on and also the wide ring of American Shermans from Marshal Malinovsky's arsenal that were protecting the city center like so many steel-plated battlements. I was stabled in the great hall of the ground floor, where there was enough space for us studs to horse about and to couple with the mares, when our hooves would press down on the cork linoleum in a kind of choreographed equine ballet.

Even though the dear soldiers made fires on which they roasted pieces of meat, and the smoke then trailed about the room before withdrawing through the broken glass wall, and even though the cream-white floor was beset with bundles of stinking horse dung, every evening at dusk the onyx wall (which had seen out the plunder with a

Moroccan calm) conjured with the setting sun a light that took one's breath away, and for a moment we horses appeared to be cast in stone or bronze; and if this moment caught us rearing up, we would afterward hold this position, our hooves in the air, and the ocher puddles of light would turn brown and perhaps even red and be reflected in our flanks and backs like deep, bloody gashes, or blows from a broadax, or burning stigmata, and the *soldatiks* would stare captivated at the onyx wall as if it were an iconostasis, and one of them would whisper *Gospodi pomilui!* and make the sign of a large Orthodox cross.

As I think I mentioned already, by now we were part of the Second Ukrainian Front, and we were waiting—that is, General Pliyev was waiting—to see what Marshal Malinovsky would decide to do next. But dear soldiers impelled onward and onward and then, all at once, rendered marooned and motionless, don't know what to do with their urges. To begin with they found entertainment in inciting the stallions to couple with the mares, which requires a certain knowhow, and all the soldiers here were grooms who had lived among horses since they could walk. But me they left in peace: they were well aware that I was the general's protégé. Anyway, had they tried to involve me, they would have failed: I had no intention of playing the fool in their sex games.

Then, at the end of April, the news came through that Hitler was kaput. These were tidings both glad and grim. There were many among the generals who had been looking forward to taking Hitler prisoner themselves: Stalin had promised half of the Volga-Don Canal and the hand in marriage of his daughter Svetlana to whomever delivered Hitler to him alive. There would never, they knew, be another such opportunity.

General Pliyev granted permission for a small party in celebration of Hitler's death. There was no danger here of what happened in Ořechov, where a totally soused regiment was routed during a lightning attack by the Germans. None of the dear soldiers needed to lift a finger—somehow the news of a forthcoming party at the Tugendhat Villa went around of its own accord. The residents of the fancy villas nearby gave voice to the full range their throats permitted, some in fear that these throats might soon be slit, particularly as the *Krasnaya Armiya* had in the course of its mine clearance through the city done other things besides; it did not pay to rely too heavily on the dovish Slav character.

And in addition to the booze and provisions, kept until then in secret cellars, the most assiduous soldiers brought back a certain Hilda Hänchen, a teacher at the school on Merhaut Street. They carried rather than led her because she did everything in her power to resist them—like Marie Antoinette on the tumbrel, she knew what fate had in store for her. Please excuse my persistence in placing before you the seeds of my meager learning, which I owe to those late afternoons and evenings under Dmitri's pear tree, where we would wind together strands from history, paleontology, archaeology, entomology, and etymology, to say nothing of Darwinism and behaviorism. There's no doubt too that my stay in Dmitri's library contributed much to my understanding. Of course, no other *loshad'* will ever acquire such encyclopedic knowledge: I am one of a kind, if you like. Those who view me with favor perhaps consider me an equine Socrates or Spinoza. And I'm happy to raise my proverbial hat and nod in acknowledgement of such accolades; but make no mistake, what I am telling you now is just a screen intended to block your view of what the dear soldiers were engaged in with the German teacher on the cork linoleum. So all you will learn is that while my equine colleagues looked on with disinterest, I, as much an initiate in human delights and woes as Meister Eckhart in Neo-Platonist emanationism—no, no, I take that back, it was a foolish comparison, more like a Scandinavian fisherman in the sorrows of the Greenland whale; anyway, I, the initiate, watched what the dear soldiers were doing with Hilda Hänchen—there was no screen to keep it from me—with loathing and disgust and, regrettably, a little curiosity and a trace of something to which I'd rather not give a name. But you should know when at last I turned away, it was too late, and I bore away with me a feeling of guilt. Did I really have to take the same journey as every Russian intellectual, struggling through the most sophisticated philosophies only to fall face-first into the most squalid shit?

Once the unspeakable act on the cork linoleum had been played out, the dear soldiers lifted the lady teacher and carried rather than led her to the floor above, where they intended to transfer their attentions to their hip flasks and the large glass demijohns in woven baskets. But here their *politruk* raised his hands and clapped for quiet. He made haste to remind them of the Cossacks' first commandment: provide for the horses before taking care of one's own stomach and throat.

The matter was subjected to brief discussion before the decision was taken to lead the horses out to the dandelion-filled meadow. Soon all the horses were outside—two tethered to a nearby weeping willow, the rest to trees that shielded the meadow around both its open sides. I stood on my own, the only one of our society whose rider was not present. This rider, as we know, was a Cossack commander, whom I now imagined keeping company with Marshal Malinovsky in a hotel down in the city. This hotel was hit in an air raid; a wall has fallen away to reveal a lounge with a shattered table and armchairs with charred upholstery. But just beyond another wall, one that is still standing, is another lounge, and here Malinovsky is placing on a table a splendid shagreen valise; this he opens with a click before pulling out a framed picture and nodding to General Pliyev. Pliyev, who has pushed a stool against the wall, now hammers in a hook. Then the marshal hands him the picture and two of them stand back to admire the effect. They salute Generalissimo Stalin and propose a toast. *To the family! To Stalin!* A pretty scene for a horse to think up, don't you think? But anyway, back to me.

As we know, I did not have my own rider. After the *malchiska* assigned to me was ripped to pieces by a shell, my care became the responsibility of all the grooms. In the garden they would first tether their own horses, but before they took them their pails of water they would hurry to attend to my needs. As they approached me that day I could hear them discussing whether or not it would be better to leave me where I was: I might be better protected inside (there was still the occasional gunshot, and it could come from any side), and, after all, wasn't being there just like being outside? The great room was like an extension of the garden, the garden an extension of the room, so fluidly did the interior merge with the exterior. They brought me an armful of fragrant hay and a pail of fresh water, and they stroked my silken coat. (Perhaps I haven't mentioned yet that I am a fine, well-proportioned bay whose neck and high, broad crest are in perfect harmony.) When tethered by a long rein to a chromium-plated column, I could move freely about the room, and, should I wish, put my front hooves down in the garden.

It was the late morning of a beautiful April day. The dear soldiers were lying in the grass with their hip flasks, and there was birdsong. It was as though the war had really ended, despite the burning house I could still see, somewhere in the city center. Nevertheless, this was probably what the human world calls an idyll. In the distance (and no great distance at that) people were still dying, but at the same time here was pastoral birdsong and a sun rising slowly to its zenith; and the dear soldiers in the garden were falling asleep. The only ones moving around the meadow were two men with machine guns, guarding the villa. By their gait it was obvious that they, too, had been drinking. Then one of them got an idea. I turned my ears in their direction—it's always a pleasure for me to listen to people talking, particularly as I'm safe in the knowledge that they have no inkling I can understand their every word.

Hang on. What would the general say? the second of the men asked. But the first—the one who had had the idea—just snapped his fingers and laughed. It was apparent immediately that he had the devil in him.

He'd like it. Compliment us on the idea.

You think so?

Whatever pleases the general's stallion, pleases the general. Then he'll please us.

They gave each other a wink; then they got to work.

One of them untethered me from the column while the other ran his hand along my bump before putting it to my mane, which he tousled tenderly. They led me upstairs. I was perfectly calm—not only did I know that the "invisible hand" of General Pliyev was watching over me, I knew, too, that these two were among the best grooms, that they loved horses more than anything else in the world, that the scale of values by which true grooms live their lives places horses above wife and children, and, with some of them, even a bottle of vodka. Of course, I didn't know what their plan was—they were using the crudest military slang (as I could tell from their gesticulations)—but what these boys had thought up was a source of curiosity to me, not dread.

But I was taken aback when they opened a door and led me into the room beyond, in which I saw again the lady German teacher. I presume this room was once the bedroom of one of the villa's original residents. The teacher was naked and bound in chains, and thus always prepared for coupling. Only now did it dawn on me what the boys had been talking about, what the gift was that they were offering me. By the expressions they wore as they departed the room, I knew they were thinking of themselves as Santa Claus. I would have plenty of time to play with my present.

The door clicked shut behind them, and I was left alone with the teacher. I knew above all that she was an extremely proud creature. When they did it to her on the cork linoleum, she didn't let out a single cry, not even a groan. Even now she wasn't letting on that she was afraid of what was to follow. In this she reminded me of Dmitri Ivanovich when the two men came to arrest him, and he knew, of course, that he would end up in Siberia; all he said to them was: *I've been waiting for you all my life. What kept you, for goodness's sake?*

The teacher did no more than close her eyes. German does not come as easily to me as Russian, or even French, in which Dmitri Ivanovich gave me a thorough grounding. So I did my best in my halting German, although my labials rebelled against my attempts to articulate. *Ich habe viel auf dem Herzen und ich versuche Ihnen das langsam sagen,* I managed to say. And I knew that once I'd warmed up a little, I would produce the German with much less trouble. She opened her eyes in surprise. There was no trace of fear in them, just amazement, which was understandable. Anyone else confronted by a horse jabbering in German would be horrified, but what she had experienced was far more horrific than this; I was for her something in the nature of a fairy-tale apparition. And she was quick to realize that I did not have aggressive designs upon her. I am the kindest among the Arabian thoroughbreds, noble in body and soul—this is something else Dmitri Ivanovich gave me to understand. On top of everything, I was still suffering from the guilt of having stood by and watched as they were doing what they did to her. Let us consider as well that this was an extraordinarily proud creature who, in a very unpleasant situation—several times raped, now bound in chains, practically crucified—had succeeded in retaining her dignity and even developed a remarkable analytical intelligence that enabled her to see straight through to my soul, to what remained there of love and peace. I asked her to close her eyes again for a moment. And then I caught in my linguistic labia, if you'll pardon the expression, a headscarf that was lying over the back of an armchair; I laid this carefully, like a fig leaf on *eto krokhotnoye mesto, diese winzigkleine Stelle* if you will, thus sparing us both further embarrassment. She opened her eyes and smiled at me. We realized quickly we were going to be good friends. I gave some thought to how I might rid her of her chains, but they were held in great steel locks; I might have risked kicking these away, but I decided not to try, because I couldn't be sure I wouldn't injure her in the process.

The situation was less than ideal for a sociable conversation, but soon we found a topic by which we had both long been excited. Once, I'd touched on this topic with Dmitri Ivanovich, but he viewed our relationship in terms of patron and protégé; he would initiate me in the deeper reaches of knowledge and secrets of existence so that I was always aware of his superiority—as debates go, this is not a desirable state of affairs. Besides, his interests tended to literature rather than philosophy, and an appreciation of common ground and interdisciplinarity did not come naturally to him. Of course, I am somewhat ashamed to be speaking now so openly and disrespectfully of my beloved teacher, but, after all, it was Dmitri who taught me that the truth must always be supreme. Anyway, it was with the lady German teacher that I first had the opportunity to discuss Immanuel Kant in depth.

The first time I read Kant's *Critique of Pure Reason*, Hilda Hänchen told me, his expositions and system of categories left me very confused.

Yes, indeed, I said, delighted: I, too, had known this confusion. But today I understand pretty well that from the category of quantity is derived the principle of opinion: all phenomena are extensive properties in space and in time.

Exactly! the lady teacher rejoiced. And the principle derives from the category of quality that phenomena are intensive properties too.

And let us not forget, I rejoined, that analogies of experience are derived from the category of relation, which is to say that with every change there remains an immutable substance.

How glorious! Hilda moaned with delight. What pleases me most is that the exigencies of empirical knowledge are derived from the category of modality, because only then can the object of our experience be called real.

For, as we know, I said, thus closing this particular chapter, objects adapt themselves to categories!

And here we moved on from Kant's categories to his bringing together of inner and outer experience.

Two things! Hilda exclaimed as she rattled her chains. Two things have for a long time filled my mind persistently with a growing sense of wonder and respect—

—and they are, I cried, my exhausted lips smacking together, and they are the starry heavens above and the moral code within!

That's right! she continued. The coming together of inner and outer experience, and not only of the starry sky and human ethics! What is deepest inside man, the sensations and phenomena man attains, in Kant merge smoothly with an apparition of universal law. Is Kant not the founder of modern cosmology, convinced that man by his very substance is compelled to abandon himself to knowledge and step outside and above himself?

Not only man, I said, unable to restrain myself. In certain rare cases, horse too. But I wanted to say how fortunate we are to find ourselves in a villa that provides a model of Kant's philosophy, a clear demonstration of this coming together, this *fusion* of the inner and the outer. The living room is an example of an open architectural space that radiates beyond the borders of architectural composition and connects it with its surroundings. Although regrettably, I thought it apt to add, these relations have for the time being been somewhat obliterated . . .

But here I fell silent. I heard footsteps on the staircase, and then those who had brought me here were back inside the room. And they were in a dreadful hurry. They didn't even look around, just asked me if I'd poked the *chuvikh* yet. Of course, I didn't reply, even though there were all kinds of things I might have said. They took hold of my bridle and led me rapidly away. I didn't even have time for a backward glance.

Twenty minutes later our cavalry was mobilized. The dream of our Cossack commander was realized: Marshal Malinovsky sent us to the very heart of Hitler's Reich. As we were leaving, I saw them lead Hilda Hänchen out on to the pavement in front of the villa. I called out, but I don't believe she so much as noticed me. Standing between us was *Starshiy Leytenant* Andrei Tolstoy, writing in whitewash on the Tugendhat Villa: *Kvartal proveren min nyet!* And with that we left for Berlin.

The Arabian thoroughbred—named Orlando by Dmitri Ivanovich—was shot near Leipzig, and used as "live bully." The German teacher was forcibly removed from her home during the "wild evacuation" and murdered. But Orlando and Hilda were among the final victims of the war. At last the country has awoken to a life of freedom and happiness, in which noble horses will never again serve as "live bully," and in which no proud, brave women will ever again be executed.

TRANSLATED FROM CZECH BY ANDREW OAKLAND

ARMIN KÕOMÄGI

Logisticians Anonymous

It began four years ago, when I suddenly found myself taking a basic course in logistics. The job I had at the time was driving me crazy, and hoping to make some sense out of my life, I was signing up for all sorts of courses. I remember my excitement when the straight-backed lecturer, with a calculating look, glided diagonally across the room and said:

"Hello."

Impossible to think of a simpler greeting, more precise, more brilliant. "Hello." Ten out of ten. The previous course, where I had spent just a week before Logistics, began with some aimless twaddle from a shaggy chap in a cardigan about how whether it was now morning or daytime or night was, in a sense, of no importance, and therefore he wasn't going to greet us with any reference to a particular time of day, and taking an even wider view, why use greetings at all—do such formalities make anyone happier, or, for that matter, unhappier? Oh, I remember that from that first sentence alone I got such a headache that it made concentration on the subject at hand impossible. A basic course in philosophy. What's the use of a class whose only benefits are complete confusion plus a two-hour headache? I left as soon as I politely could.

But I'll never forget the lecturer in basic logistics. The way he took the shortest route from the door to his desk; the very rational movements with which he organized his class materials on its left-hand corner, whence it would later be convenient to lift them up to the lectern; the skilled gesture with which he opened the two buttons of his jacket, whereupon it landed most dynamically on the back of his chair without even crumpling . . . Then, when he stepped up to the dais, he would charm us with a half-second long chuckle, and begin. I remember feeling a wet drop of spit land on the back of my hand. Only then did I remember to shut my mouth, which had been open in awe throughout his well-argued introduction.

Today, four years later, I myself could of course give that lecturer dozens of suggestions as to how to improve his life. That's how far I've gotten. And I have to admit that, in a sense, it's a problem.

Now that I've had enough time to think it over, I realize that it all actually began much earlier than when I started that class. I remember my summer in that youth camp. It was my second stint there. A crazy, funny group: cool, resourceful guys; cheerful, beautiful girls. By the second half of the summer, when all our friendships had developed far enough, we boys were in the habit of going over in the evenings to kiss the girls goodnight. Then, one night, when we trooped into the girls' room in our underpants, and, in the excitement of the full moon of a late July night, we hungrily eyed the girls and worked out who would be fondling whom, I found myself heading for the nearest bed. Since the girls in our group were all just about equally pretty, it didn't matter who you kissed. So I chose the shortest route. From that night on, the nearest girl always got a kiss from me. It wasn't always one and the same girl. No. They switched beds from time to time. I don't know why. The reason for all this moving around didn't occur to me. And if some girl by the campfire showed an interest in my night-time geographical tactics, then I would explain that it was simply the shortest way to a kiss. Everyone would guffaw, and I became well liked. But for me it was no joke.

I can't remember the last time I was kissed. I have no time for such absurdities. I deal only in the necessary: I move only the necessary parts of the body, I exercise only the necessary muscles, I think only necessary thoughts. At the right time, in the right place, in the right amount. Always. But one thing troubles me. I don't understand my own feelings. Sometimes I find myself getting irritated, annoyed, angry, desperate. If it were in my power I would do away with the genes that make all that possible. Emotions are a waste of time. And I'm not just talking about negative emotions. For example, what's the use of a sense of triumph? Hurrah! Why hurrah? What for? What does it give us? What is a victory, exactly, that people want to crow about it so much? There's an outcome, a result, a score, a provisional summary of accounts. These are the ordinary parts of any process. So what is there to crow about?

I've admired my grandfather since childhood. At the age of ninety he still used to sit behind his desk, quick-witted as ever. Behind him was a bookshelf graced, in jumbled profusion, by the masterpieces of the world of technical engineering and architecture, along with the travelogues of famous explorers. Only useful information. No fictional absurdities. When I'd grown old enough, Grandfather initiated me into the world of profit and loss. He had a notebook for every calendar year since 1938, containing a complete account of income accumulated and expenses incurred. We played a sort of game where I would name a year and month, and Grandfather would read from the notebook in question what had happened during that period.

Down to the last cent. Sometimes information as to Grandfather's height and weight during that year were also included. He would stare right at me with a triumphant look and I felt I was the grand-child of a genius.

I remember that my grandfather once took me to church with him. I hadn't been in that church before. At that time I hadn't been in a church at all. When Grandfather invited me along with him, I was actually very surprised. Grandfather and the church? I did know that occasionally Grandfather liked to listen to soothing organ music, but as a rational person he usually relied on the classical-music station while sitting at his desk. Anyway, off we went. The church was odd, somehow. At first I didn't understand what was different about it, but gradually I saw that the church lacked the flamboyant atmosphere and symbolism that I figured one might expect in a house of God. This church was simple. Simple pews, simple windows, a simple altar, simple paintings on the walls, a simple ceiling. Grandfather looked around for a long time, knocking on the walls, trying out the doors and the rows of seats, inspecting the beams. Then he nodded approvingly and we left. On the way home Grandfather talked to me about his work. He had designed many bridges, apartment blocks, and factories. And he had also designed one church. And that was the church we'd just seen.

On the last curve of Grandfather's life, when he was run over by a car, broke both tibiae, and got his feet crushed, it was clear to all of us, as he lay in bed, that he didn't intend to continue living. And that's what happened: before Christmas Grandfather announced to us all that he wasn't expecting any gifts from Father Christmas that year. Luckily we all understood the situation, so we spared him the senseless piles of woolen socks, rulers, and accounting books. On "the Day" we all gathered around Grandfather's deathbed and each of us said something by way of farewell. My turn came. I looked at the stumps of Grandfather's legs, which because of the accident had shortened his height by nearly twenty centimeters, and I asked him how he would like it if we fitted him into a somewhat smaller coffin. Now that there was no longer any need for a full-sized coffin, we could manage with a considerably shorter and cheaper one. I remember how everyone looked at me in astonishment. In Grandfather's eyes, however, there glowed a shimmer of economic pragmatism, and a squeeze of his cool hand gratefully approved my idea. And so it came to pass.

You see, then, that a rational view of the world is in my genes. As with my grandfather, who built such a matter-of-fact church that a mystical godly aura had no place in it, and my father, who bought four pairs of ski boots at the same time, because they were ridiculously cheap, so it is with me, as I weigh myself before and after eating a kiwi, and then subtract the weight of the kiwi fruit to the nearest gram, and with my son, who always gives a two-second warning before he shits his pants. And so on. But I'm not proud of it. At least not so much anymore.

During my not very long, but pretty eventful and successful career, I've transformed six companies into such perfectly functioning corporate entities that, if they were global businesses, every single one of the six billion inhabitants of the world would feel pure pleasure that they exist. Just think: only necessary things, and what's more, absolutely no advertising or any other marketing bullshit. At my last job I took optimization so far that in the end I had to fire myself. Before that, I told the board that the managing director and the marketing manager would be redundant if we carried out one hundred percent of the reorganization I had suggested. Being greedy people, they agreed to my suggestion, after some hesitation. As an honest person I took their agreement to mean that I myself would be dismissed twenty-six days later. That was how long my planned reorganization took.

While I lived in a one-room apartment, everything was simple. I minimized my life logistically to such a degree of perfection that it could easily have won the Nobel Prize for Engineering Achievements in the Development of Domestic Conditions. My dear little fully automated paradise. Things started to change when I decided to take a wife. The family line has to be continued, after all. Especially if the blood of generations of absolute rationalists is flowing in your veins. And so a woman came into my life. And although I knew that women are anything but rational beings—I remembered my grandmother's collections of poetry and my mother's long telephone calls—my wife presented me with a real challenge. The order in which I laid down my clothes on my chair before going to bed, the precision with which I portioned out the toothpaste onto my brush each morning, likewise how precisely I could fold toilet paper into the right shape for wiping my bottom, in what order I placed groceries in my refrigerator, and the logical means by which I conjured the last drop out of the ketchup bottle—none of this earned me the faintest esteem in my wife's eyes. But esteemed or not, devoid of emotion. I felt that my wife simply didn't understand me: she who puts enough washing powder in the machine to scrub clean three football teams' uniforms; she whose hairs are clogging up our sink and bathtub drains because she can't be bothered to comb by the garbage; she who throws away potato peelings, enough to feed all four of our neighbors' children; she who hauls back from the shops a whole ton of creams and gels, only to petulantly throw half of them away; she who flicks the remote control on the television so frequently that I can't follow what the Teletubbies are doing on Urmas Ott's talk show and which rally team Marje Aunaste will be driving in next week. She doesn't understand me. *Mamma mia!*

So be it. I could have lived with this silent misunderstanding, but one evening things went too far. I was sitting on the sofa watching a show on television that showed how stuntmen prepare their tricks. They work to a pretty high standard, but every now and then a screw or a bolt gets loose and then they have pretty memorable stunt funerals. I was sitting there, I had to piss and I was thirsty. I waited for a commercial, got up, grabbed a less than half-full beer glass from the table with my left hand, and went to the toilet. The kitchen was a meter or so from the bathroom. On the way to I opened my fly with my right hand and pulled my member out. Since the door was open, I saw that the seat had been lifted. This gave me a noticeable time advantage while I got my external urinary sphincter relaxed, a couple of steps before standing in front of the bowl. So it was. I should add that all this time I was drinking the beer glass empty along the way. Naturally my calculations were precisely correct. The cascade of urine that burst from my member during the final step reached its target at just the right time, without the least careless splash on the sides of the bowl. When I left the toilet contentedly, I met my wife standing at the kitchen door. Her mouth was agape and her eyes were bleary. I went past her to award myself a new beer from the refrigerator. My wife stood frozen, her back to me. I poured the beer skillfully into the glass, such that the depth of the head would be no more than two to two and a half centimeters. And then she started to speak. She said that she had seen me as if in a slow-motion replay. She had seen me coming, my nose in the mug, at the same time as my watchful eye had sized up the toilet; I had fished my member out of my trousers, and, Lord save us, a yellow cascade of wee-wee had spilled out of me, making her afraid that I would cover the floor, the wall, and even herself with it, but at the last moment the full arc of the cascade had plopped into the bowl. She was so shaken that she couldn't get another word out all evening.

I took her reaction as a compliment and congratulated myself that at last my sufferings were bearing fruit. That night I climbed decisively onto my wife's back and celebrated our little achievement with some rapid and attentive screwing. To my great surprise, the next morning, my wife packed her bags and left. Impregnated, fortunately. The next time I heard from her was about nine months later. A son had been born to us, and I'm allowed to see him every Sunday. I was very pleased with that, because to the prospect of embarking upon a new adventure with yet another representative of the irrational female sex for the purpose of spawning offspring didn't seem very inspiring.

Now, though, I'm sitting here. It's an odd place. We're sitting in a circle, there are five of us, four of us patients. At least that's what the fifth person thinks—in her own estimation, she is healthy.

I don't remember how I ended up here, but I do remember the first time I attended. The group was supposed to meet "at about six in the evening," it said in the flyer. That specification drove us all mad. At 18:00 precisely there were four mutually unacquainted men in the room, and our faces betrayed the fact that the one who had summoned us was not present. The room was repulsive: cheerily colored curtains, chairs of different designs laid out chaotically on the floor, in one corner a pile of different-hued mattresses, and then a shelf with all sorts of bric-a-brac and stacks of stupid magazines. The ceiling was lit ridiculously bright, with electricity being consumed by the most uneconomic bulbs I've seen in my life. We all felt uncomfortable. We shifted from one foot to another, not daring to sit down or touch anything. Finally a fifth person entered the room. A woman. She smiled guilelessly at us and told us she was Katrin. By way of response we looked at our watches. The time was 18:18.

In the course of time we've gotten to know each other. I've come into contact with some very exciting personalities here, and I feel good around them. Arved, for example. Arved always sits to my left. Every morning and evening he measures and weighs his wife, his two adolescent children, and himself. He has compiled a collection of statistical data on his family going back eighteen years, on the basis of which he does dynamic future projections of his family members' body measurements. At three-year intervals. Calculating trends based on world markets, consumer-price indices, and prognoses of central bank rates, he has constructed a mathematical model for his family budget, which makes it possible for him to estimate, for example, how much will be spent on clothes and food in 2014. With 98.5 percent accuracy. We all appreciate Arved's work a great deal. Except one of us: Katrin.

Or Martin, for example. Martin is a wonderful guy. As a result of thorough calculations, he's discovered some very interesting things. Martin actually found that eighty percent of the movements of his family in their home occur over twenty percent of the floor surface area. Adding the area covered by furniture to that needed for movement, he designed a new house for his family. With a surface area nearly four times smaller, the family was able to maintain more or less that same standard of living. But what a saving on building costs! What economy of execution! To say nothing of the fact that Martin's house stands on a thirty-eight square-meter plot that he bought from a man for the price of a sandwich when his guard dog died of old age and he couldn't do anything else with the kennel. We think Martin is a genius. But again, Katrin doesn't think so.

And then of course there's Ott. Ott was already a smart operator when he took a new name for himself: Ott Kott. His parents had provided him with the name Otto Gottlieb. Well, listen. Ott Kott, with the initials O.K., is the dream name of any logical person. Ott was a taxi driver. He honed his skills so as to construct a minimal taxi and yet offer maximum service. He removed two of the car's four cylinders, since, having estimated the average speed of travel in the city as twenty-seven kilometers an hour, he simply had no need for so many cylinders. Ott sold the cylinders at Kadaka car market, put the money he got for them in an envelope and posted it to the management of the taxi company. Ott used very little petrol. In addition to the savings from the reduced cubic volume of the engine, in his own garage Ott mixed petrol with cheap kerosene in a barrel reserved for the purpose, reducing the cost of fuel by a third. In choosing his routes, Ott always proceeded from a calculation of optimal mileage, without disdaining side roads, always overlooking some of the less-important traffic signs, and cutting right through any green spaces. Always with the aim of getting the passenger to their destination by the most direct route. On his dashboard, Ott replaced all the unnecessary gauges with cardboard fakes, and paid the proceeds from the sale of the original items, to the last cent, into the company's bank account. That's the kind of inventive man Ott was.

So here we are: Arved, Martin, Ott, and myself. Four great men. And we pretend that we're listening to Katrin, who thinks she's curing us of a terrible disease. She calls our group Logisticians Anonymous. Actually we feel surreptitiously proud of that. Logisticians—a word to be proud of. Logistics—that is the greatest thing. It is what makes people human. Separates us from the animals. We're able to compile all rational knowledge, calculate, measure, and then draw the right conclusions. We don't tolerate waste. We recycle life—we who are each the result of a single, efficient pregnancy. Though, if you start to think about it, even that's a bit of a waste. Wait a minute. How many spermatozoa are there in a single ejaculation? I'll do a study of that at home. I'm sure that it's possible to economize on that and solve our country's overpopulation problem at the same time. You see—we're full of good ideas! So it can't be an illness.

TRANSLATED FROM ESTONIAN BY CHRISTOPHER MOSELEY

art

RÓBERT GÁL

Agnomia

"It seems undignified," says Jan, "to accept congratulations for the past, as if the context of that past, not worth remembering, is totally irrelevant. This isn't a criticism of heroism, but a criticism of the need to hang your heroism out for adulation, as if every heroic act is equal. You can't just equate an act of socially defined heroism with an act of highly individual—and therefore socially indefinable—heroism. Where is the boundary between the social need for heroes and the accidental hero, a partaker in a heroic deed, who doesn't feel the need for a social proclamation of his heroism?" Jan is the hero of an invisible terror. Every opportunity for rebellion is punished. And because each rebellion is already punished while still in a state of potentiality, it's never able to reach actuality in any other way but wounded. This is true for all Jan's relationships, which never have happy endings. We're talking about the hidden side of Jan, something one-sided, which is by definition already invisible, because it's in the shadow of our hero. What occurs in the shadow can be only seen from inside the shadow—which means that we only learn about it when the shadow begins to speak. And then it's necessary to differentiate what the shadow says from the fact that it's being said by a shadow. Character isn't built on the soft horizon of a sob, says Father, based on his beliefs, which he forces into my head by simply rejecting all of my objections. And this forces me to start up my defense mechanisms, so that *inward screams*, piled one on top of the other, gradually prevent my exterior from having its own face, a face that might reveal the character of my interior. This is how the need arises to compare one's inner state with the exterior world of this or that environment. Errors posed as truth command the truth. Is a proof of belief confirmed by intransigence? And then there are all those unexplored areas of an incorrectly posed question. Standardized obsessions that fit the scheme of some *ism*, or others gulping down their breath in attacks of clairvoyance. The stirring of tensions between the two brings up a third type of obsession, the search for and discovery of order in chaos, which it shatters by following a single line of thought toward one final outcome. To reveal one's color to others means to multiply the contrast, to bestow sweaty T-shirts to the backs of generations that will silently tag us as our own perpetrators. A circle is always one-sided and that side always depends on the direction of its spin. Spinning it faster means, in practice, that a glimpse of its end naturally blends with the vision of its beginning. To push oneself off from any point on a circle is possible, though it never happens entirely at random. Transformation of form through content is not a linguistic game. It has to do with the inevitability of sustaining form and thus displaying its content. As in music, here it's not about thoughts, but about the permanent tension caused by the need to think, about belonging to this or that content to the point of accepting it in the form of parasitism. Because the scalpel of intellect isn't able to adequately discern between operation and autopsy, the object of its incision is abstract at first and only during the act itself does it emerge from the fog of unconsciousness into the sphere of understanding to gradually acquire the face of a conscious reality. A reality whose essence is deadened by autopsy, but is not actually dead, because it still exists. When Blevin showed up in Jerusalem with a huge suitcase, I was there by accident. I recall the burning heat in his eyes. It grabbed me at once because it contrasted whatever fragility marked his personality—just as Blevin's smallish figure was in such stark opposition to the size of his luggage. Felix and I sit in a small pizzeria, waiting for him, and as soon as he shows up we order some pizza for everyone. Felix is very happy to see his friend after so many years and, right away, he starts explaining something to him. It has to do with the fact that the two of them actually have no place to stay, but "that doesn't matter, the important thing is that you're here." I also remember my second meeting with Blevin rather well. It was in a small house in the leafy and lush Jerusalem district called Ein Karem. I went there invited by Felix one spring day shortly after noon, and after a series of forceful knocks on the door (and some silent communication with the dog tied to its doghouse next door), a wooden gate opened and Blevin, with a sleepy look, invited me in, as if he didn't recognize me at all. His heavy eyes looked bleary from sleeping, but I was soon told how tired he was from hours and hours of meditating in the dark of his windowless room—specially built for just this purpose—in the attic of his house. On a wooden secretary near a wall, dozens of labels were glued with various maxims, imperatives, and simple advice for living. Carefully spaced, yet somewhat limiting the use of the desk, they were arranged in compartments—a regular structure of *neurotic order*. The labels were supposed to repeatedly remind Blevin of the strict differences between the desirable and the undesirable, as if some authority before him had engraved them into words and thus made them eternal in these very formulations. In a monastery park in the middle of Prague, a family of peacocks walks about freely. The majesty of the much-admired father peacock is suddenly disturbed when one of the park visitors opens a bag of birdseed, just like the old lady last time, who first frightened the peacock, then ostentatiously fed him her crumbs, and then finally, as if all that wasn't enough, exclaimed in surprise: "Geez, he shat on me!" But let's get back to Jan. Jan is a terrorist without a cause. He's a hundred times brighter than most mortals, yet still missing that *something* which would make him wise. He's like a lion with caged eyes, beaming his stare into eyes that are equally caged. This system of cages upon cages is a manifold product of his own caged brain. It is the language he opens with every word, so he can repeatedly lock it down into one and the same thought. Jan shaped his little missy in his own image, "to have her gain value," but then she wanted to *breed* and so she married a tractor driver. Yes, anyone seeing Czechs and Slovaks abroad in the world has the tendency to think: What did these people come here to represent? And then a second question immediately follows: Can a Slovak comfortably experience democracy anywhere but in Slovakia? And soon other sequential questions stem from these, in which one can ask himself and immediately answer; understanding now why most citizens of small, meaningless countries remain stuck in those countries as though there were no other options. It's precisely in small and meaningless countries that one finds writers who naturally think of themselves as "reproducers of reality," but why this reality needs to be amplified in their writing, they don't say. If we claim—and we *do* claim precisely this—that such reality must be *produced* in an artistic way, not simply *re-produced*, then we need to separate the *work of art* from *art*. Someone like Eli Roth shows up, a controversial Jewish film director, and simply shoots his *chainsaw massacres* in tiny Slovakia, to which Slovaks react first with rage, before realizing that this is a perfect way to get Slovakia some publicity. Roth, a *young Tarantino*, accomplishes in a single moment what dozens of elite intellectuals have attempted. Yes, people sense what other people are feeling and act toward them accordingly. They can be malicious that way. And in this sense, those of us whose destinies are to struggle in the waters of our own restlessness will always find ourselves at a disadvantage. Jan introduced me, one by one, to all his hostages. He drew me into his cunning conversational maneuvers, the results of which were more and more frightened looks from his girl, one of six current girlfriends. He liked to situate me between him and whichever of his girls as part actor and part observer, thus indirectly imitating my own situation of being unable to reach one because of the other, which may have something to do with the famous complex named for old King Oedipus. In this sense Jan functioned as my psychologist, yet more subconsciously than consciously, because that's not how sadists think. Jan always has six girls, with one of the six receiving special attention, and who's then rotated out. That is, so to speak, one is always manifest and the other five latent. They're all so devoted to him that none of them dares to have another boyfriend. Jan would only find out about it anyway, they tell themselves, and spend their evenings masturbating, thinking of Jan. Meanwhile, my father, who simply thinks that Czechoslovakia should never have been divided, tells some anonymous person in a political discussion on the Internet what a wonderful person I am. My father, the most wonderful of all people, who for years has based his beliefs exclusively on his *exertions* within the need for their own *implementation*. This is the definition of a man of action, though how could such a term ever be defined when the result of an action is precisely a change of definition? Unless it's the other way around, actions taken precisely to *prevent* some other action and thus sustaining the original definition (such as the political unit called Czechoslovakia). But if ideals are abstract, the actions corresponding to such ideals must be equally abstract. Thus, any previously defined words, around which the aforementioned process of recycling an action revolves, must gradually turn into memes, and thus lose their definitional substance. What's left are dead-end streets, those snakes of well-meant, calculated reality, which always, for whatever reason, unseen by the scientist's eye, manage to defy calculation. Yes, we all want to be oh-so understood! And yet we know very well that some of the things we try to understand are simply incomprehensible, and this precisely because of their essence. Why do we so stubbornly look for locks in every door—even the ones that are already open? This is also one of the questions regarding Buñuel and *The Exterminating Angel*. Mightn't the existence of a lock on an opened door change the status of its openness? And so on. To create a culture necessarily means in most cases to be acultural. For why should a creator need to know what others create, for the purposes of his own creation? A widespread and blind groping about is sufficient for a creator, since as he knows very well that no groping can be without limits or else it would spill into something else. The role of the creator is to sustain the spill within one's own character, preventing it from ever spilling into something else. As such, we're dealing with the permanent maintenance of the desired flow, which for this reason becomes a flow of thought in the sense of a tautology—that is indisputable. A flow of thought in the sense of a realization of the act of thought, the flow of what's being thought continually melting into the flow of thinking. This isn't philosophy, just the gradual process of a creative undertaking—with jackhammer in hand. A creator is always more of a worker than an intellectual. A man forced to observe is learning to observe; a circle inside a circle, repeatedly burst like a bubble. The lure of traps—traps that even traps fall into. *I say: only people who are perverse in their body and soul can perform great deeds!* claims František Drtikol in one of his letters, adding: *But it must be a pure, beautiful, original, free-spirited perversion, bubbling up from the man's own depth! It may not be a plagiarism, an imitated thing* . . . One thing has a name, another is looking for a name. And it's discovered that the name doesn't belong to the named, but to the designation. The leap into the identity of that name, which is legitimate, because it's already legitimized. The leap into the illusion of a break—for it is an illusory break—it never ceases appearing as a fault-line. Like a thought that isn't thinking about itself, but about what it doesn't want to think about, and from which it tries to separate itself. The mental process of the unfinished intention of desire. Shouts of an unknown nature. The claustrophobia of concerning oneself with them as a certain type of limit. Is this a sense of humor about the humorless? But jokes must come with humor, no? I'm sitting on a bench, a little before midnight, thinking; I settle down. And suddenly a girl sits next to me. I think intensely of lighting a cigarette and in the end I actually do it. The tension between us didn't last long. I wanted to give her a chance, but she was impatient. She leaped up in a rage (I only then noticed her delicate nose and glasses with elegantly thin rims), just so that she could turn on her heel in front of my eyes and stamp out the cigarette butt of her desire with a disdainful gesture. But I survived it. And a day later she appeared again in the form of a different woman. An equally intemperate intellectual with tortoise-shell glasses and good skin. After a few days of getting to know each other, she informs me by cell phone that *I* need someone more refined. Laughter, like a dog barking, is a reply, an outburst, a response to my feeling for her; let's call that feeling "resignation." Response as a designation, a marking. Response— Narcissus's echo to the silent companion of his doubled desire. My relationship to women is monomagical. To enter every situation unprepared, as though in the remnants of a dream. Building up the vibrations of what's already been lived through, the tension generated by the possibility of survival. To find a window of a moment. To fail a test, an indicative sentence of contradiction. A human gets a taste for another human—cannibal. Images of fertility, geysers exorcizing ghosts. The sun winding through empty deposits of anxiety. A cohort of useless resolutions meeting behind enemy lines. The order-loving movement of a tumor of the spirit toward healing, away from one's own body. And from every pain a question mark jumps out: Is this pain the right one? Defocusing the invisible toward greater and greater visibility. An escape manipulation, the coordinates of a spiderweb thrown into space. The insatiable cameras of untalented people, who float wherever they walk. Only to open their beaklike mouths, from which seeds of hatred are propelled by pressure. A guy with three mobile phones like three cocks and across from him a big-breasted babe who's trying with all her might to look serious, as if it were possible in her case. Two toughs behind her back react to a remark by the aforementioned macho man who gets up for a moment to enact the screen-test of a gunslinger without a gun, *because now he's having a good time.* His chick has been in the restroom for the last ten minutes. A fat boy from the next table sits in her place. The mirror of a window, through which I'm observing all this, is slowly fogged by the unexpected course of the evening. Spurred by nothing I can see—one, two, three—they all wink at me in succession. I'm in the groove. I'm tapping this nonsense into my head and don't pay attention to the people I'm talking about. In one of the illustrations—self-portrait photos of naked L., depicting herself searching and in some places even in spasms, finding the right form of her corporeality—there are two spots on her neck, photographed from behind her back, which seems in this photo even more androgenic than it does in reality. The spots were of course painted on for effect, the photo wasn't meant to be a document and yet for me they are always a memento, a visual meme, triggering an entire sequence of chain reactions: accusations and self-accusations. (To what degree must we provoke change in a human being while they are already being changed?) To bring out feelings as if internally hiding something. Controlled denial of wanting, which isn't based on anything, nor is it justified by anything. The emptiness, which frightens us immediately, is barred by the structure of the net and breathing in it. Empty cans of what's been drunk rattle through a street of static sculptures of the just restored. The looks of tourist children, their chirping cameras capture what was, angels included, and transform it into other materials. Time shifts between expectations and disappointments—unsteady, almost invisible. This is an annihilation of the sun and other such hermits. This is a tautology of every moment, as if every moment was necessarily a tautology. "If I knew she was so mentally unstable, I definitely wouldn't have married her," Ben says. And the vision of Ben's interest in my work surpasses the consequences of my expectation. I need to reintroduce myself, years later, for he no longer walks around my place with a funnel in his ear to eavesdrop on me. What do Jan and Ben have in common? Nothing and much. Jan thinks of himself as a gourmet of life, to the point of having the need to lecture others about how to live. Jan still hasn't lost his belief in reproduction, although preferring to constantly produce new things himself. Ben doesn't talk about reproduction yet, but he's also as an author, almost unproductive. Despite that, one can feel in him the need to change this state of affairs. Ben is insured against obvious loneliness through his paper marriage, though this evidently never much suited him. The illusory security of this status, which he imposed on himself and his wife, is primarily intended to hide something. But even Ben doesn't believe in the irreversibility of his fate—and yet his actions, which all seem to haunt him, don't support this confidence. We might point to the fact that he's the younger of the two by a bit, because even Jan, when he was Ben's age, perceived things similarly. Jan ran away from a childless marriage, stating that he was good enough to deserve other women. Ben probably thinks the same. At a certain stage of their lives, both could be seen walking around Prague in long black coats, cloaking the solidity of their pose even when walking. One flirted with artistic inclinations, the other only theorized over them. They both liked cats, but neither knew why. Both carefully maintained their daily bachelor rituals during relationships. One is convinced that women are supposed to tyrannize him; the other believes the opposite, a belief he practices fearlessly in private. They each have rock-hard reasoning behind their convictions, as demonstrated when push comes to shove. At that moment, they pay attention, focus their senses and, giving out the refined screams of intellectuals, recklessly disown themselves as well as anyone close. For every secret is generated by the revelation of something similar. Is there an urge to create the similar? But the similar thing is always equidistant to its original. It is the movement of illusion that displays the patterns to images, by which they are perceived. This is overstepping the boundary of necessity to return to the form, which the noise of contrast shed of its color.

TRANSLATED FROM SLOVAK BY MICHAELA FREEMAN

MARIE DARRIEUSSECQ

Juergen the Perfect Son-in-Law

My mother calls me on my cell phone all the time, she's retired. The sound of a Bavarian fanfare alerts me to her call. I can't always pick up, but usually I manage to call her back the same day. I'll be in London, in Los Angeles, or in Paris, in a parade or in the middle of a shoot, and my mother will tell me the latest about her neighbor, her cat, or her geraniums. I do like it, really.

My mother is a widow, I've always known her as a widow, I have no memory of my father. I'm the only thing she's got aside from her cat. She absolutely supported my decision to live in London and then, after that, places farther away. But she visits us a few times a year, and we have the flight times memorized. London-Munich-London. It's so nice that she gets on well with my husband, Juergen. And, just like him, she goes along with my artistic projects. I think they talk about them and try to figure them out together, but they never complain in front of me.

I'm a photographer, I began in fashion, and then I started doing more and more portraits. I like pregnant women, fruits, animals, caves. Whatever I shoot has to be lighthearted, and at the same time, I'd like to capture the other side of these things, I don't know, their fragility. I'm always conscious of the fact that all the people I photograph will die. That gives a sort of melancholic patina, pale and green, to my images. The people who like my pictures appreciate that, and they should, but these last few times I wondered if this patina wasn't, rather, a sort of glaze, a sort of glass pane that I hadn't yet broken. I'd like to get past that barrier, but something holds me back. And sometimes—maybe it's a crazy idea—I tell myself that fate or something else has made a mistake, and that it's Juergen and not I who should be a photographer.

I met Juergen in Bavaria, we were teenagers. I was already taking pictures, he was absolutely crazy about soccer. He let off some steam, played around, even if he didn't really know how to do that except with a ball or a mug of beer.

It did us both good to leave Bavaria. From the beginning, in London, I earned enough money for the two of us, and Juergen kept busy with our children. Juergen in particular has an incredible talent for making friends, for talking about different things, so that everything's more exciting when he's around. He's also got an incredible memory for things people have told him, and he can always tell when someone's sad or not feeling well.

When that Bavarian fanfare trilled in my bag during the three days of vacation we'd finally managed to take, and my mother sobbed to me that her cat had disappeared, it was Juergen who insisted that we take the first flight to Munich. I was underestimating the importance of the cat to my mother, he told me. She lives alone, that cat is what she lives for. We had to stand by her during this ordeal, help her to find the cat again. Juergen was quite serious. We juggled planes and managed to get our children taken care of for a little longer, and here we are now at my mother's place, a small chalet thirty kilometers from Munich. All this to ascertain, effectively, that the cat isn't here. It's been three days since he disappeared. A ginger male with white stripes, rather ugly if I remember correctly. "Cats wander away, Mom," I tried to put it in perspective. "He'll be back, all mussed up, and he'll be starving."

I can't bring myself to care about this business of the cat. I took a few pictures around the house, of little winter flowers, yellow and nearly dried out, of everlastings, of the moss. All in all, I felt uncomfortable. My mother cried, and I had never seen her cry except a bit when my father had died. Those memories are rather blurred. I was three years old. I only remember that, my mother's tears, as if she had poured herself out all at once so as never to cry again. My mother is a woman who keeps to herself. Had to be, to get through it. She always tried to raise me without burdening me with her grief. To see her crying for a cat really did bother me.

But Juergen understood my mother and tried to comfort her. Really, he didn't say anything more than I had, but he said it *right*, I don't know how he did it; and somehow he managed to make her laugh. His absolute attention to others exasperated me sometimes. Well, it wasn't really about the attention, I'm getting it mixed up; it was just that when he paid attention to someone, when he understood my mother, he seemed to take off from where he was and touch down in the other person's place, forgetting where he'd come from. I did admire him for that as well. And if he wanted to handle my mother's sobbing, so much the better. I watched them both and I had the impression that Juergen had hands, eyes, a mouth, made differently from mine, and that he knew how to pass through the bell jar that I myself saw around every human being.

It was this sort of barrier that I wanted to pierce with my art. Juergen tells me that it's idiotic to separate my work and my art, he's right, there's no need for a divide between the two. I don't know. I'm trying to get to the other person, that's all I know, and can I really do that by taking pictures of shoes? You don't take pictures of shoes, Juergen says, you take pictures of people in shoes. That's all. At one point I began to take photographs of myself, but I saw the bell jar everywhere. I saw it as I took the picture, and I saw it as I looked at the picture. I saw it around me and I saw its reflections on me. Passing through it became an obsession. Then I took nude photos of myself. At first, these self-portraits were successful. But even in my nudity, my skin was a barricade, and my face as well: I always had the impression, looking at the picture, that my eyes were veiled, as if covered by cataracts, or blurriness, like a zombie's. I began to photograph parts of my body while avoiding my face, and I realized that I had to go for my orifices, for the interior of my body. People protested, cried obscenity. I made diptychs, and on one side would be my genitals, perineum, anus, and on the other would be rocky formations at the bottom of caves, calcareous clitorises, vulvas in rocky folds shining with humidity.

Juergen and my mother courageously supported that, but people spoke of trash, of misunderstood feminism, and always about pornography. I didn't understand how there could be pornography down there. It was a work about myself. If I managed to get closer to myself, I would finally get closer to others. Instead of being a thief of souls, photography would become an offering. Why should others unveil themselves if I held myself back? I wanted to suggest an exchange— give everything, show everything, and only then dare to ask the other person to offer me his face. Then the bell jar would be broken open.

Juergen reproached me for my aestheticism. And he was right. He was wearing me down. "Why diptychs?" he asked me. "If you want to photograph your pussy, do it, if you see clitorises in rocks, take pictures, but don't justify one by the other. Just show, that's all. You don't have to excuse yourself for anything." And I told myself, once again, that it's Juergen who ought to be a photographer instead of me. This unemployed man. That talent.

It was around then that I convinced Dirk Bogarde to do a series of photographs with me. I like his enigmatic style, and the sadness at the heart of his gaze. Dirk, who knew about my photos and liked them, told me that he was fine with it all, except for the nudity. We set up shop in a large hotel room with French Rococo furniture. I played around completely naked, Dirk cuddled me, babied me, all the while impeccably dignified and elegant in a silk peignoir. Out of that whole series there's one really striking photo: Dirk is hieratic at the piano, his gaze distant, and I'm on the piano, and I'm spreading my cheeks with both of my hands. Juergen thinks this photo is quite strong, but I wonder if he's saying that to be nice. Looking at this series, which I entitled "Pompadour," I started to have my earliest doubts: was I really the only one to find these pictures funny? Why did people talk about trash and pornography? Could I ever really dismantle the stereotypes, the clichés about women? If Juergen, for example, had fooled around in front of the lens, his butt sticking out and his finger on the shutter release with an iconic woman at the piano, would they have said of him what they'd said about me, that he had lost his dignity? Men who have fun at their own expense are irresistible, and Juergen had that talent. As for me, when I have fun at my own expense, everyone else is disgusted, is it because I'm a woman or because I'm a bad photographer? After this series, the glass of the bell jar seemed to grow thicker, and the faces around me, even the most familiar ones, became blurred.

The cat never came back. Juergen had scanned a photo of the cat, made two hundred copies, and we put up LOST signs here and there all around the area, up to Munich. They said that cats could travel hundreds of kilometers and return months later. I repeated that to my mother. In any case, we had to go back to London. The children were waiting for us, and I had work to do.

"At least come say hello to your father," said my mother, and to make her happy, considering the state she was in, we went to put a chrysanthemum on his grave. I took pictures of mold on the marble, and lichens on the surrounding walls. I was in a gray period, and yellow, and brown. Someone had scrawled "LIEBE" on a wall, like he'd dipped his finger in blood or shit, maybe mud, and I took a photo of that as well. If I was becoming, well, more sentimental, losing something, touching on some crude form of love, I didn't know. I always hope that my images speak for me, tell me things that I otherwise wouldn't know. Juergen would take, I'm sure, an incredibly Romantic picture, deeply Romantic, as powerful as anything by Goethe or Schiller, but modern, cutting-edge. In any case, that's what I really wanted to strive for.

"Your problem is you're married," my mother often told me—she was one to talk, considering she was a widow. "You always believe that Juergen can do everything better than you, and that's holding you back. Free yourself, my daughter!" That was what my mother, who absolutely loved Juergen, had to say. I couldn't see how to free myself in any better way than to show what I had been showing. But that didn't really show anything, it seemed. Everybody had an opinion about my photographs, all the time, and that annoyed me. I would have liked to take pictures that could shut them all up.

I should have paid more attention to what happened with the cat. It really would have made my mother shut up if I'd brought her cat back. And that would have saved us from everything that happened afterward. We'd only just gotten back to London when the Bavarian fanfare came: my mother had found her cat. Dead, two steps from the house, flattened on the side of the road. Tears all over again. I take another plane, visit for the day. My mother had wrapped the cat in a small white flag, and set it in her basket while waiting. "Waiting for what?" I ask. For someone to make a decision. "The trash can," I suggest, and immediately regret my cruelty: my mother is weeping. "We could bury him in the garden," I say. I already see myself with a pickaxe, -10°C outside, in this glacial winter of my Munich childhood, attacking the hard earth in rage.

"We could have him stuffed," sniffles my mother. I know what she's thinking: her neighbor is a taxidermist, and I had often wondered if there wasn't something going on between them, or if my mother, at least, hadn't thought about it. But the neighbor is strict: no more then three days, the skin only lasts so long, and it's already been ten days, no point in thinking about it. The cat isn't so poorly preserved, thanks to the cold, but it's completely flat, with a faint tire tread on its coarse coat, and there isn't much left of its face. We're not keeping it here, in any case. And my mother is against incineration. At least, that's what I believe to be true. I pass the time watching her hold back her tears or mumbling to herself.

Juergen is the one to come up with the idea, over the phone: a pet cemetery. I extend my stay. We have coffee at the taxidermist's next door. He has Internet access, he looks for information. He has a few beautiful pieces at his place, especially a brown bear standing upright, paws in the air, like a huge beast sleepwalking that then follows me in a nightmare.

I wonder what I'm doing there instead of being in London. But it's as if my center of gravity has been thrown off kilter, as if an old weight has finally caught up with me and anchored me here, thirty kilometers north of Munich, in the subdivision where my mother lives. Where do the dead go when they die? They come here, to this subdivision, and they drink coffee at my mother's neighbor's. And the neighbor himself is dead, as dead as the bear, and he doesn't know it, like the bystanders peering through their blinds. More violently than ever, I have the impression of seeing everything, like them, through a pane of glass. My mother's head rests on the doily covering the back of the flower-patterned couch. On the windowsill, porcelain deer surround a grassy plant that looks like algae. It's like we're under the sea, waiting for I don't know what, for the past to come back, for us to be judged right there and executed. This torpor is familiar to me, and these objects frozen in time: the seventies of my childhood, the silence, the rustic but soft furniture, upholstered, in varnished wood. And everything seems strange and far away, I'm at my place but a sort of mute terror dwells in the objects, a frenetic sadness, and I tell myself that I've been tricked: I should not be a photographer, I should stay here, near Munich, in the former FRG, go from village to village as a carny, run a shooting gallery where someone could win stuffed animals or porcelain deer. That would be more sensible, yes, more logical . . . I thought I recognized people in the window, I gave them a slight nod of my head, and the reflections of my mother, her neighbor, and the bear shone in front of the other faces on the glass.

"You've got your head in the clouds," my mother reproaches. But she's the one who starts murmuring again. We take more time off. All the formalities can be handled over the phone. We have to buy a small coffin the right size for the cat. I place the order after having measured the cadaver. The neighbor would have gladly made us one in his studio, but the *purchase* of a coffin is required. On the phone they don't say "coffin," they say "funeral receptacle," so as not to offend our sensibilities, I imagine; we might want to bury the cat, we can make a distinction between humans and animals, but in the end, we're all buried in catholic earth. I'd never envisioned my mother as caring about a cat, but I can see that she's changed, or maybe simply grown older. At her request I also ordered a tombstone, and a plaque with the cat's name.

Juergen and the children came to Bavaria for the weekend. I didn't ask for the children to be there, but it was more practical that way, and it may have cheered their grandmother up a bit to see them; it was as a family that we buried the cat. I'd never set foot in a pet cemetery before, and after the carefully chosen words of the employee on the phone, I had expected it to be rather somber, but since decorations are left to the discretion of the families, I saw more crosses, cherubs, memorial plaques, and garlands than in any human cemetery. Everything is simply smaller. The graves come in rapid succession, in rows by species: dogs, cats, rodents, or birds. There are monuments and even vaults, but with the dimensions of dollhouses—with exception of the canine sector, where the graves are almost as big as those of men, for the larger species such as Great Danes or German shepherds.

My mother gave a short speech; I had asked her to restrain herself, out of respect for the children. Do animals have souls? We would have argued about it if Juergen hadn't been there. He put up the plaque with the cat's name and dates, with an estimate of three days, more or less, for the day of its death. My mother planted a box hedge and a small rose bush. And we were done.

All this made me very uncomfortable and London was soothing by comparison, the normalcy of London, its rhythms, its activity, the routines of children, and the materiality of our lives. Nothing for three days, as if my mother could tell that I'd had enough. And then a Bavarian fanfare: the cat had come back.

My mother didn't say "resurrected." But she believed it so thoroughly that Juergen and I decided that we should take the initiative and go see her: it was her mind, her age, her loneliness. We talked to her several times and discussed what we should do. Did we need to put her somewhere? My mother and I, we were still rather young. To think so early about such a future upset me.

But the following weekend, at my mother's, we could not help but notice that the cat was indeed back. He was a bit thinner, but it was him, he had found his food, his window, and his usual spot on the sill. We had buried the wrong cat.

"Mother, you picked up a carcass on the side of the road. We thought it was your cat, but it wasn't your cat. It was just something squashed flat." It cost two thousand euros for the burial plot, the coffin, the marble tombstone, and the plaque. That's quite a lot that shouldn't have happened. But my mother is just amazed. She silently thanks God. I see her large pale face flush with delight. She hums as she thinks about the cat, she hardly dares to touch him. "It's enough to make you religious," she whispers. She speaks with an air of revelation. I had always known my mother to be an atheist, even rather anticlerical, and now she's a holy fool because of this cat.

We don't lock up people for little things like this, Juergen chastises me. He's fine with my mother. She had found her cat, and the neighbor seems to be keeping her company: now we're headed *zurück nach London*, back to London.

Life took on a regular pace for a while. The only thing that had changed was the regularity of my mother's phone calls. Just once a week, and to talk about nothing, to give me news about the weather. At the beginning, I wasn't worried. It was actually a relief. I didn't dare ask about the cat or the neighbor. Even over the phone, I didn't want to remember the subdivision, the bear, the blurred faces, the strange forms of moss on walls. The photographs of lichen and moss, the photos of that winter, I looked at them with a feeling of immense melancholy; and after a while I had to close my eyes, I had the impression that these walls and this frost covered an unnameable silence, something that made me want to scream, to curse everything that brought me back to my father, to my mother, and to Bavarian subdivisions.

One evening, as if nothing was wrong, my mother called me to tell me that the lease on the burial plot for my father's vault was about to expire. I didn't know the details; it had been thirty-five years exactly, and after this time, we either had to pay for the plot again or proceed to incineration.

"To what?"

"To incineration. They empty the grave and collect the remains in an urn, they have professionals do that."

By the tone of her voice, I could tell that she had already organized it all; she talked about it as if it were nothing more than changing the drum of a washing machine. By tacit agreement, everything that had to do with my father was my mother's responsibility, and so I let her do it.

That wasn't the end of it, though. Whenever I called, her phone kept going to the answering machine. I felt like I was always waiting for the Bavarian fanfare and I kept hearing it everywhere, in my children's games, in the noise of the street, in the other chimes of London life, in normal life, in my own life.

I didn't know that the desecration of graves in a pet cemetery was a criminal offense. My mother had been caught sacking the cat's grave, the tomb of the flattened carcass. It was the taxidermist next door who told me when I called him, unnerved after an especially long silence. My mother had planned a nocturnal expedition with all the necessary equipment: shovel, pickax, flashlight. Among the things they'd found on her body, there was also the urn containing my father's remains. From what they were able to figure out, it seems that she was planning to put it in the small tomb. So that my father might come back, just like the cat. Since she'd had my father incinerated, she hadn't bothered seeing the taxidermist first. When he went over to see her, he found her sitting and murmuring—it seemed—with the urn between her knees.

I had to put my mother in a clinic close to London for her to rest. I wanted to confiscate the urn, but Juergen was opposed to it. "Where will you put it?" he asked me. "On the mantel?" I, who'd believed that I knew dead people—I had underestimated the cumbersomeness of their presence.

My mother stayed with the urn, first in the clinic near London, then at her place again, when she was able to go back to Bavaria. At her place in Bavaria, all the prettiest things were on the windowsill, and the urn had pride of place there, as if my father needed the view.

The cat kept it company. And my mother never quite forgot the idea she'd had about the pet cemetery. My mother never took no for an answer. She never admitted defeat, hadn't even been cured, if we went by the clinic's criteria.

I went to Bavaria for the fifteen days following her stay at the clinic. The final weekend, the urn wasn't on the windowsill, but there was a man my mother's age sitting next to her on the sofa. She introduced him to me as my father. He had grown older, but I recognized him immediately, like a veil being torn away. I finally saw a face amid all these blurred faces. And it was shocking how much he resembled Juergen.

TRANSLATED FROM FRENCH BY JEFFREY ZUCKERMAN

I occasionally write for artists. I'll look for a verbal equivalent to their physical work, rather than criticizing or illustrating it. As if the artist had to use words for his own materials.

"Juergen the Perfect Son-in-Law" was inspired by the photos of Juergen Teller, especially his Nürnberg book, and his "Louis XV" series with Charlotte Rampling. This story was published in the exhibition catalog for "Do You Know What I Mean," which took place at the Cartier Foundation from March 3 to May 21, 2006.

Juergen Teller has a certain propensity for photographing himself in the nude. He likes soccer and bears, and he seems to have been born in Bavaria.

—MARIE DARRIEUSSECQ

BJARTE BREITEIG

Down There They Don't Mourn

The other boys in the class are swimming around the pool fighting for the ball, while the girls stand at the shallow end shivering,
their skin pale. I'm sitting on the bench together with Karsten
watching. It's the first lesson of the day and sleep is still deep
in my body, like some kind of glue. I've handed over the note to
be excused because of my cold, but Karsten doesn't have a note.
He doesn't need a note; he's excused from swimming lessons because he's got a fear of water. That's what they say anyway, there's
a story about how he nearly drowned once, that he was dead for
seven minutes and that he was brought back to life. Maybe that's
why he's the way he is. Maybe he should actually have died.

He turns to me and yawns, says he couldn't be bothered with this.
His eyes stare in opposite directions behind his thick glasses the way
they always do when he's talking to you. All the same, you know it's
you he's looking at.

What do you say we sneak out of here? he asks.

Okay, I say.

There are a lot of things that are weird about Karsten. For starters,
there are those boots he always wears, no matter what the weather,

green lace-up rain boots. No one else wears boots like that. And then there's that thing with staircases, he always has to take one step with one foot and two steps with the other. Ask him why and he'll tell you that the steps are just a bit too low to take one at a time and just a bit too high to take two at a time, but if you alternate they're just right.

That's probably the kind of thing he thinks about when he's shuffling around the playing field on his own at recess, his hands squeezed down into the pockets of those tight jeans of his. But I hardly know him. I don't really know anyone at the school, and even though I'll have been here almost a year soon, they still call me the new guy. He's new, they say, every time there's something I don't understand.

We stroll past the toilets and on down toward the arts and crafts rooms. Karsten's boots scraping along the floor at every step. He tries the handle on each of the doors as we go past them: home economics, textiles, and the woodwork room. Everything is locked, and behind the doors it's quiet, no one has arts and crafts classes this early. But the door to the ceramics room at the end of the corridor is open, and Karsten turns to me and grins:

They forgot to lock it, the idiots.

There are no windows in the ceramics room, and as the door slides shut behind us, it's almost completely dark. The only light is from the emergency exit sign; it casts a greenish glow over the shelving along the wall, which is full of small, newly made pots. Karsten looks up at them and says there sure isn't much to look at here. Several of the pots are cracked; they mustn't have been able to take the heat in the kiln. He takes down a lopsided, pear-shaped vase and holds it up to the light.

Look at the state of that, he says.

And he's right, it's ugly. Its thin, wrinkly neck has sagged to one side and hardened.

Let's smash it to pieces, I say.

Karsten grins. And without a word he raises his hand and smashes the vase on the floor. Then he picks out two more, holds them high up in the air and lets them go, the two of them at once.

They're so fucking ugly, he says, kicking the shards across the dark floor. I don't know how anyone could screw them up so badly. All you have to do is slap a block down on the wheel and sit there holding it.

He walks slowly down along the shelf, looking up. He's the best in the class at arts and crafts. The rest of us just make the things that Engebret suggests we make, but Karsten comes up with projects himself. While we all sat shaping those stupid ashtrays, he made a spherical, hollowed-out candleholder, and then carved a lattice pattern in it. It's only been a week since Engebret turned out the light and held the newly fired sphere up in front of us. A tea candle gleamed through the slits and we all saw the pattern outlined across the walls and on the ceiling.

Almost like being in a tomb, says Karsten, as he stops by the massive kiln in the corner. Here's the cremator and everything.

A red light comes on as he turns a knob.

Do you know how they do it in Nepal? he asks.

Do what?

When someone dies. They burn them on a bonfire.

Why? I ask.

To get rid of them, of course. The family stands in a ring around the bonfire, watching, but they're not sad, because down there they don't mourn. They don't even know what it means to mourn. They have a party instead, they clap and sing and bang on drums.

Behind him the kiln has started ticking. The warning light gives his hair a reddish tinge and makes his glasses glimmer. Then he starts talking about the corpse. He says that when it catches fire, it changes position; it sits up in the middle of the bonfire.

It's the gut drawing itself together in the heat, he says. The lips are burned off, and then the guy just sits there grinning at his wife and kids.

Sometimes the skull explodes as well, he adds. Boom!

He slaps his hand against the kiln door and laughs when he sees me jump. He gropes his way along the far wall, opens the supplies cabinet, and shoves something aside. Then he climbs up onto the shelf. The door creaks shut after him, and for a few seconds I hear him rummage around in there, but then it goes quiet. I figure he's just sitting there waiting for me to open the cabinet, and when I do, he's going to let out a roar or throw something at me.

Karsten, I say. Cut it out.

But nothing happens. The kiln starts to make crackling sounds and I go over to try and turn off the heat but I can't manage it. First I turn one knob, then another, but the light doesn't go out, and I feel the heat from the kiln door on my face. In the end I creep over to the cabinet and fling the door open. Karsten isn't there. Then between the bags of clay I see that the cabinet is open on the other side, it's brighter through there, and I can make out part of a row of carpentry benches. I climb in and creep across the springy shelf, between boxes and tins of paint. When I climb out, I'm in the woodwork room.

Karsten is standing by a bench and he doesn't look up as I come in. He's placed a half-finished plywood and rattan pizza tray in the vise at the back, and now he's about to tighten it.

I can't manage to turn that kiln off, I say.

He doesn't answer. He puts his weight against the vise handle. The iron jaws eat into the circular tray and the screws in the vise creak. Suddenly the tension is too much for the tray; it cracks and bends until it buckles gently.

That's the way it goes, says Karsten.

He sits calmly up on the bench beside the broken tray.

I tell him that the firing oven in there is just ticking and ticking, and ask if there isn't a danger the walls will explode if we don't turn it off. But it's like he doesn't hear me. He puts his toe against his heel, pulls his boot halfway off, and lets it dangle at the end of his foot. Then he starts asking me things.

Where did you live before you came here?

I've lived lots of places.

Is it a pain starting in a new class?

I shrug my shoulders. Then I say that maybe it's a bit of a pain before you get to know people and stuff, and that for the first few days you just stand there hoping that someone will come over and talk to you.

You don't have that many friends, says Karsten.

I don't answer. I look out through the rectangular windows along the top of one wall. A yellow plastic bag blows by in the morning light.

There aren't many people who like you, he says.

I shrug my shoulders.

Is that a pain?

No, I say.

Karsten lets a sticky clot of spit drop to the floor. I imagine what he'd look like without lips. I picture him with empty eye sockets behind cracked, soot-blackened lenses.

There aren't that many people that like *you* either, I say. Weren't you even dead once?

He lets out a new clot of spit. It lands right on top of the last one.

Seven and a half minutes, he says. I hyperventilated. Do you know what happens when you hyperventilate?

I shake my head.

You empty the blood of carbon dioxide, he says, and then you can't feel it when you run out of air. Nothing hurts.

Then he tells me how it happened. He'd decided to swim straight down as deep as he could. The mask pressed against his face and he could feel the water get colder the deeper he went. It was murky and hard to see, and in the end it started to get dark. When he reached the bottom, he grabbed hold of a huge clump of seaweed and decided not to let go. He was hanging like that for a long time, upside down from the clump of seaweed, but in the end he let go all the same, and it was then, as he floated up, that he blacked out.

But it didn't hurt, he says. Not until later. Being dead was beautiful.

Beautiful? I ask.

He nods. He looks at the floor.

But when they brought me back to life, it was fucking awful. I should have just held onto that seaweed a little longer. Just a little longer. You know?

I nod.

No, he says, jumping down from the carpentry bench. You don't know shit.

He walks over toward the wall and starts opening the cabinets. He takes an angular spatula out from one of them.

Ugly, he says, breaking it over his knee.

He throws the pieces at me, and I can see that something's gotten into him now, that his eyes are darting from side to side behind his glasses. He takes out a turned lampstand from another cabinet and slams it against a carpentry bench. The base of the lamp snaps off but the two pieces stay joined together by the fibers; he tears them apart and flings them across the room. Then he opens our own class's cabinet, where the half-finished bird feeders are stacked on top of each other on the shelves. He takes one out that has walls on it but no roof yet. He runs his fingers along the edge and shakes his head. And then he does something. He walks over, turns on the circular saw, and lifts off the safety guard. Within the space of a few seconds the noise rises to a shrill screech, making it impossible to think of anything else. He pushes the bird feeder toward the rotating wheel and shouts something, but I can't hear what. As the wood meets the blade, the screech becomes a scream. I stand motionless staring at Karsten's hands, which begin to vibrate, and all of a sudden I notice how good it feels to see the spinning metal eat its way into the flimsy woodwork, first through the border that's supposed to keep the breadcrumbs and oatmeal in place, and then, with a slightly more rasping sound, through the plywood panel itself. The sawdust is blown across the steel plate in tiny waves. When the two pieces come apart, I'm the one who gets a new bird feeder from the cabinet. My hands are shaking as I lay it down, but it's a good shaking, that only gets better as the vibration of the blade spreads upward to my elbows.

This is what happens when they can't make anything better! Karsten shouts over the din.

I notice I'm laughing out loud. I don't shift my gaze from the blade, from the grayish area where the teeth fly around. It's like the cut is eating its own way inward, as if it's always a few millimeters in front of the blade. When the pieces come apart, I toss them at the wall, get a new one from the cabinet, and continue sawing. Karsten has found a hammer in the tool cabinet, and he's letting loose with it on the flimsy cabinet doors so that they split open and swing back and forth on their hinges. I saw up table after table, feel how the wood resists but gives way in the end. It's beautiful, and I can see that Karsten feels the same, he's roaring and laughing. He empties the cabinets, throws everything out onto the floor, first the tools: saws, hammers, chisels, and screwdrivers, big rolls of sandpaper that he kicks across the floor. He tears folding rules apart and smashes levels against carpentry benches. Then he gets started on the students' work: magazine racks, key holders, spice racks, and toilet-roll holders, bentwood boxes and milk carton holders, all these pathetic things we've stood hammering and whittling, now Karsten is smashing them to pieces, and the sweet scream of the saw blade is hanging over everything.

I don't know how many tables I've destroyed when I turn to see Karsten dragging along the kennel he's been working on for the last few weeks. It's made of small wooden beams that he's notched together and jointed with wood glue, and I remember how I've seen him plane and sand the beams so the dog won't get a splinter. He's designed it himself, brought in drawings and explained it all to Engebret, and Engebret has been checking on him all the time to see how he's getting along. This is going to turn out well, Karsten, Engebret kept saying. This is going to turn out well.

Karsten tries to heave it up on top of the saw.

Move! he shouts.

But I don't move. I can't move, and when he tries to shove me out of the way, I cling onto the saw plate. He screams something in my ear, but I can't make out the words, only notice the smell of his breath.

You made that yourself! I shout.

For a few seconds he stands there in front of me as if he doesn't know what to do, but then he gets hold of me, twists my arm behind my back, and grabs hold of the back of my neck. At that moment I go limp. I can't offer any resistance, and as he bends me down toward the saw blade, I just close my eyes and give in. I come so close that I can feel the breeze of the blade on my lips. Everything caves in inside me, and I become vaguely aware of a warm and wet sensation spreading down over my thigh. Then I think: I'm pissing myself, and that's all I manage to think, that now I'm pissing myself.

After that I'm lying on the floor, sawdust and broken bird feeders around me, while Karsten stands by a workbench chopping away at it with an ax. The beams of the kennel lie scattered around. Karsten isn't laughing or yelling anymore, his face is as stiff as a mask, and he puts everything he's got into every blow. It hasn't left him. It won't let go of Karsten. He chops away as if blind, the ax veering off to the side, but he raises it again and again. He doesn't even notice Engebret coming in, that he's standing in the doorway looking dumbfounded, holding his thermos flask and that green attendance book of his. Not even when Engebret turns off the saw and the noise abates does Karsten stop chopping. The ax slams into the bench and the solid wood splinters under the blade. He doesn't let up until Engebret grabs him from behind and forces the ax from his hands. Only then does he collapse to the ground and allow himself to be hauled across the floor. Engebret doesn't say anything as he catches sight of me, and I can see that he's terrified, that he actually has no idea what to do with Karsten.

Out of the way! he yells at some pupils who've gathered in the doorway.

They move aside, but crowd together again as soon as he's gone. A little farther away in the corridor I hear Karsten begin to bellow. Lengthy, hoarse roars that grow fainter the farther away he gets. The pupils stand in the doorway talking quietly to one another.

It's that new guy, I hear one girl say.

I slowly get to my feet. The only thing I'm aware of is that I don't care. I couldn't care less that I'm standing here in front of these idiots with piss all over my pants. I couldn't care less if I'm the new moron who's demolished the woodwork room. I couldn't give a shit about what's going to happen to me and Karsten, if we have to pay for the damage, if we're expelled, if we have to go see a psychologist or if it makes the local paper. I don't care about anything at all, and I saunter across the floor, kick a piece of wood from the kennel out of the way, and then I climb in the cabinet door, while everyone's watching, wriggle my way back to the warm, dark ceramics room, and once in there I close the cabinet door behind me, sit down on a stool and lean my head against the wall. Even though the kiln has stopped ticking, I can feel the heat radiating from the door. Up on the shelves the pots stand in irregular rows, each representing a student, boys and girls I don't know. And there, on one of the top, dark shelves I catch sight of Karsten's candleholder, which Engebret must have put aside in order to show to other classes. I push the stool over, climb up, and take the sphere between my hands. It's heavy. Heavier than it looks. Now that I'm looking at it close up, it's even nicer looking than I'd thought. The surface is smooth and shiny, and the colors in the glazing twinkle in the dim light from the emergency exit. A faint tremble passes through me, a remnant of what I felt a little while ago. I lower the sphere slowly down by the chain and let it swing back and forth, like an ancient weapon.

TRANSLATED FROM NORWEGIAN BY SEÁN KINSELLA

music

MUHAREM BAZDULJ

Magic AND *Sarajevo*

MAGIC

In the beginning of the 1990s, the social life of my town centered on a triangle, the corners of which were a dance spot club called the Gaj, the café La Mirage, and the row of benches alongside the old Ottoman graveyard on which people would sit all night long in the summer, right up till dawn, like at the ocean. The Gaj was situated exactly halfway between the Jesuit high school and the Orthodox church with its graveyard, while the Mirage was on the ground floor of the building containing the city's main theater, below the hill where the Catholic, Jewish, and Muslim cemeteries stood, one beside the other. In the midst of this imaginary triangle was the little café known as the Konak. It was built on the ruins of the old vizier's residence.

Back then I was an elementary-school twerp, familiar with the above-named places only as the immediate neighbors of our sporting venues. That is, our basketball court and soccer field were both next to the high school, and when we played there at night we could hear the music from the Gaj. The handball courts were over behind La Mirage, and we'd pass through the area with the benches when we were heading home, all tired, red-faced, and sweaty.

We were all waiting eagerly to take the state exams and register for middle school, because that was considered a kind of informal initiation into the grown-ups' paradise. As a junior high-schooler I'd be able to hang out at Gaj and La Mirage and the benches and nobody would look twice. We longed for our first cups of coffee accompanied by cigarettes, for beer and long conversations on those warm nights when you weren't cold in your short-sleeve shirt even at three in the morning. But alas, we were not fated to have such a lighthearted adolescence. The war started.

It was in the very spring of 1992 that I finished the eighth grade. In the decades-long history of the school, my class was probably the first to go without formal final exams and a public graduation ceremony complete with inexpertly knotted first neckties. By the same token, that was the first year that school in my town didn't begin in September. The school year 1992–1993 simply did not exist. There were more important things.

So there were no classes—and the famous triangle also perished. The Gaj closed down, and one of the artists' service organizations, a military unit dedicated to recreation and morale-boosting, moved into the theater building; in the old graveyard alongside the row of benches new graves began sprouting, and an NGO called the Children's Embassy was quartered in the Café Konak. We were simply abandoned in the streets, at least until dark, up till the curfew that we had at that time and that people who claimed to speak English would call *the police hour*. They took the night from us, and it's in the nighttime that the fountains burble. Only the *fešte* remained to us.

All of wartime Bosnia had the same experience. In the center of the country we called them *fešte*, fiestas, while to people in Sarajevo they were *derneci*; in Mostar the Herzegovinians drawled about *paaaartis*, and in Tuzla I once heard a term for them that I knew only from

Andrić's prose—*gide*. But the principle was the same in every case: a throng of young people gathers in an apartment, whereupon they drink themselves into unconsciousness. Our social life consisted exclusively of these *fešte*, and the passage of time was measured by their occurrence. In the first years of the war I frequently caught myself wasting my time cursing my bad historical and metaphysical luck. Of course I would be the one spending the best years of his life in wartime monotony! The guys my age five or six years earlier spent their time camping at the seashore, screwing Czech girls, crisscrossing Europe, and partying like crazy, while our destiny was to vegetate like a bunch of old men. And this was the kind of mood I was in as I waited for the *fešta* at Vildana's place.

Vildana's party, in an ideal world, would be the hands-down favorite to represent a true *fešta*, its perfect embodiment and shining paradigm. There were twenty of us in a three-room apartment on the sixth floor, men and women, roughly fifty-fifty. In a porn movie an orgy would have ensued, but in Bosnia, in that spring of 1993, there was just silliness and ennui. People were drinking "bamboos," the stupidest drink ever, consisting of a mixture of red wine and Coca Cola. You don't feel it going down your throat but then it kicks you in the head. And in the stomach. At some point a group of four or five of us ended up on the narrow balcony, where we started a drunken conversation complete with armchair philosophizing. It was three or three fifteen in the morning when I was seized by an unshakeable sensation of anxiety. I bolted without saying good-bye. I went all the way out of the building . . . The night was warm. A day or two earlier the rumor had gone around that men who were caught out after curfew were being sent out to Meokrnje to dig trenches. But I wasn't thinking about that. The night air was intoxicating.

I walked all over the deserted city. There were no streetlights; the only things shining were the stars and the white minarets. Everything was lovely and unreal. I walked around slowly, like a sleepwalker, and then headed, for whatever reason, toward the steps below the Gaj.

This winding flight of broad steps was the place where we usually smoked our weed in the days before the war. I sat down on the cool stone, and the night, drawing to a close, seemed to grow cooler. Everything was quiet and dark, and then from above I suddenly heard—from the building where the club had once been—the soft, familiar chords of a piano. I knew this song. It was by Springsteen. It was the one that starts off from this little germ of melancholic intimacy and progresses by way of loud guitar riffs to an emphatic, hymnal ending. And I was cut to the quick, there in that lonely cool before dawn, by the Boss's voice as he sang: *Show a little faith. There's magic in the night.*

Yes, the night held magic, and the cracked asphalt lanes of Školska Street were linked to all the streets and roads from Amsterdam to Vladivostok. The scent of linden flowers clung to the air, the river gurgled noisily, and my anxiety passed. My night was no less magical than any other night, anywhere, from any epoch. I'm running from the cops, just like in the movies, I thought; and I'm listening to Springsteen on a pitch-black night relieved only by light from the stars.

When I got home I fell asleep right away. And at six thirty A.M. I was awakened by the explosion of a shell. Later I was to learn that it hit in the cluster of trees about fifty meters above the steps where I'd been sitting. Crazy shit.

SARAJEVO

Sarajevo, made of mud and snow.

He told his mother he was going to Smederevo to say hello to Milica. The old lady was still happy about that. She was sad when they split up. America doesn't mean what it used to mean, she said; there's this Internet thing, and in a year she can follow us. He didn't have the heart to tell his mother that the departure for America wasn't actually what had caused Milica and him to break up.

With a backpack on his shoulder, he went down Zeleni Venac. He pulled out his wallet and looked at the bus ticket one more time. On the thick blue paper the word "Centrotrans" was printed in large Cyrillic characters. Underneath that the letters were smaller and fainter: "Belgrade – Serbian Sarajevo – Belgrade." Three days ago he had asked the women behind the counter if there was any bus that just went to Sarajevo. As many as you want, the woman said, munching on a pita of some sort. I mean to the city itself, he added, and not to Lukavica. Her mouth full, the woman responded that she didn't deal in tickets for the Federation. Then just give me this one, whatever you have, he said appeasingly. With her grease-covered fingers the woman clacked away at the keyboard and looked him in the eye for the first time. You can get local transportation or a taxi to the city. That's what everybody does, she said, as she handed him the ticket.

It was cold outside, but too hot in the bus. The vehicle was full, the heating was ratcheted up to the maximum, and the air was heavy and stale. The majority of his fellow travelers were prematurely aged people who were loud and messy. The driver proudly played a cassette of *gusle* music. Stefan popped his headphones on and turned up the volume on his Walkman.

He hadn't been in Sarajevo for exactly ten years now. His father had sent him and his mother to Grandma's in Belgrade in March of 1992, right after the barricades went up. Until things calmed down, as his father said. For the first month or two, they anticipated returning to Sarajevo. Then they waited several months for his father to meet them in Belgrade. They got nothing they waited for.

Bridge. Border. He wasn't sure, but he thought they had come out over the same bridge ten years ago. At that time there were no border guards, and no one asked him for his documents.

On the other side of the bridge, everything seemed different. Bosnia. Narrow streets, burnt-out houses, dark forests, rough landscapes. He had never seen a more depressing place in his life than the drab little town called Vlasenica. And then just past Vlasenica: Romanija. His ears were hurting already, so he took off his headphones. It was quiet in the bus. There were no conversations.

Now the road turns and goes downhill. They stop briefly at the bus station in Pale. He feels his chest tighten. Lukavica isn't far off, surely not. A road sign reads:

YOU ARE LEAVING THE REPUBLIKA SRPSKA—HAVE A NICE TRIP.

It's already dusk. The bus enters a tunnel. After the tunnel he looks for the Romanija forest, but it's no longer there. Down below is Sarajevo. Here is Sarajevo, then, the real Sarajevo. An image from out of his dreams: red roofs, violet sunset, white minarets. He calls up to the driver, "Can I get out here?" The bus stops, and he gets out. Here I am above Bistrik, he thinks; here I am above Bistrik. He walks slowly downhill. There isn't much traffic, and most of it is made up of taxis. He takes out a cigarette, lights it. I've never smoked in Sarajevo, he thinks.

Darkness descends onto the city with him. He finds himself in front of the church at Bistrik. He used to love this church because of the color of its façade. It was similar to the outfits worn by the Sarajevo soccer team. Way back when, in primary school, Stefan had been a fan of theirs.

His legs steer him by themselves to Papagajka. In one of the third-floor windows, the window to his room, a light is visible. A lamp is on. He sees a shadow: somebody is walking from the bed toward the table. In a horror film, he thinks, he'd now catch sight of his own face.

All their relatives tried to convince his mother to request that the family's apartment be returned to them, but she didn't want to listen. It's a routine thing, they said. It's yours, they said. Reclaim it and then sell it right away, they said. An apartment in the city center! they said. Take the money for your child, they said. His mother was usually silent and kept her thoughts to herself. But just once she said: Fuck your apartment. They took my husband.

He won't ever forget it. Never ever. On the twelfth of November, 1992, he was awakened by his mother's sobbing. Đorđe is dead, she repeated over and over through her tears; Đorđe is dead.

They took him away, that was all the neighbor said. Fikra. She called from Germany, just after she had arrived there from Sarajevo. They led him away one day, to dig trenches, and he didn't come back. And the very next day some other people moved in. That's what she said.

His grandmother was still hoping he was alive, and Stefan was still hoping he was alive, but his mother just cried. Over the following months, the story gradually became clear. A detachment of soldiers took Đorđe, Stefan's father, away. Fikra had said it was to dig trenches, but his mother kept repeating, amid her nearly hysterical sobbing, that they'd led him off to the slaughter, to the slaughter.

His body was never found. Father's name remains on the list of missing persons. His mother seemed to reconcile herself to this. She told him once, not long ago, how the two of them, before Stefan was born, took a trip to Skopje. Along the side of the road somewhere in Serbia, she remembered, they had seen stones. Đorđe explained to me, she said, that these were wayside grave markers, memorials, put up by families for soldiers who'd perished abroad. My Đorđe wasn't a soldier, she said, but I want to put up one of those for him. That's what she said.

For a time Stefan hated Sarajevo. He hated it with a passion, the same way he had loved it in his childhood, and to the same degree that he had yearned for it during his first eight months as a refugee. He didn't hate Muslims. He couldn't hate them—footballers Husref Musemić and Safet Sušić were his idols. He just hated Sarajevo. He didn't hate the football team, nor his school and his friends, nor his memories, nor the nearly twelve years he spent there. He only hated the city. Let the whole thing be razed, he thought. Let all of Sarajevo go up in flames. That kind of hatred, though, did not last long. It was painful for him even to think about Sarajevo. He said to himself, I will not think about Sarajevo anymore. Then the city came back to him over and over, but he repudiated it, and these thoughts faded. He was preoccupied with chess, preoccupied with mathematics, and, ultimately, with Milica too. Then his mother got a green card for America in that immigration lottery, and since he still hadn't turned twenty-one, he had the right to go with her.

He wouldn't have come here if it hadn't been for the song. He wouldn't have lied to his mother. He could have told her: I'm going to say good-bye to the city. But he'd barely had the strength to admit to himself that his dreams were still rooted in Sarajevo. In these dreams he saw his Belgrade friends, the Belgrade streets, and the boy who'd grown up in Belgrade—himself, Stefan as he now was. And there was Milica. But the setting was always Sarajevo. How could he tell her: on account of the song . . .

He heard it three months ago on the radio. For the first time— he would have sworn that he was hearing it for the first time. He'd never been a rocker; techno was his music. He found it on the radio by accident, but he then immediately went and bought the cassette. The group was called EKV, "Ekaterina Velika," a Belgrade band. They weren't a Sarajevo group, so that's probably why the song hit home. *Sarajevo, made of mud and snow*, went the song, and that view from the bus in March, 1992, suddenly came alive for him again. He sees his father standing in the dirty snow on the platform, standing and waving to his wife and son while the bus moves in reverse. Stefan waves at him and sees him for the final time.

It's midnight. Stefan is in Marin Dvor, going toward Pofalići. From there he'll take a cab to Lukavica. The bus will be heading back to Belgrade tomorrow morning. Snow starts to fall. *Wipe the frost from my eyes and brow*, goes the song. *Leave me*, goes the song. Stefan walks along slowly, smoking and looking at the few windows that are lit up. He can hear the bells ringing.

> *Let my eyes see, one more time*
> *Let my ears hear, just one more time*
> *Sarajevo.*

TRANSLATED FROM BOSNIAN BY JOHN K. COX

GERÐUR KRISTNÝ

The Ice People

I never figured out how Olga knew that girl. She wasn't from our neighborhood. One possible explanation was that their parents knew each other. Olga's mom and dad were commies who were famous for buying their daughter liquor and who didn't seem to care that she refused to be confirmed. On a wall in their home was a poster honoring the proletariat, those people who sustain the bourgeoisie who in turn support the elites who in turn validate the aristocracy who in turn sponsor the royal courts who ultimately prop up the emperor. Most likely our visit to this girl was instilled with the values of communism, which, as everyone knows, springs from the notion that there really is no such thing as class and, consequently, nobody should be above cheering someone else up by visiting them. Following this line of thinking, the elite shouldn't be above dropping in on the bourgeoisie, who in turn would have a cup of coffee with the working class.

We three used to hang out—Olga, Steina, and I. Our get-togethers were a great diversion from the typical weekend routines. We met regularly at one another's homes to eat candy, trade candy, and talk about candy. Whether it was better to drink Tab or Fresca with this or that kind of candy or whether it was better to consume cream cake or chocolate malted balls with soda. Once all the ingredients began foaming strangely inside our mouths, we often wondered whether it wouldn't have been a better idea to simply eat Mars bars. And later we'd contemplate whether a person got more for their money if she bought the assortment bag.

Most of the time, we hung out at Steina's house. Her parents weren't commies, and they had just finished building a house up in Ártúnsholt. It would never have occurred to them to buy liquor for their kids. They never had time to do something like that. They owned a business and were always working. My dad and mom were even less likely to buy me liquor, even if I wanted them to, because they were dead set against it. They talked regularly about how this or that person was an unbelievable drunk. All the same, there was never a shortage of liquor in our home, so in all likelihood someone was going to the liquor store. Dad used to have a drink at night. The first couple of mouthfuls made him so happy that he'd sing while watching the fishing report. By the time the nature programs began, he'd have a heavy frown, and finally, when the spotted leopard hooked its claws into an antelope, Dad would start an argument. Then Mom would announce that it was time for everyone to go to bed. She wished me goodnight, but he wouldn't. He didn't seem to notice me as he leaned against the wall, looming over me as I made my way to my bedroom. It was like he was a specter in a darkened passageway and I was an invisible, tattered spirit.

My parents' bedroom was next to mine and I would sit in front of the television late into the night so I wouldn't have to listen to them through the wall. He quibbled and hissed. She whimpered. One night I started a garage band in my mind. The band was made up of happy boys who practiced in the storage area in the garage. They were all great friends of mine and sometimes we just jammed together. I played keyboards. The band was nothing without me and sometimes I felt that I wasn't anything without them either. When I knew the guys in the band were out in the garage, I felt that life was tolerable. My friends cared about me. They would intervene if my parents' arguing got out of hand.

But there we were, daughters of communists, homebuilders, and teetotalers, setting off to find a girl that Olga didn't even know very well. In any case, we were unable to get Olga to give us any more information as we fought our way through a blizzard—like the three wise men trying to find the baby Jesus. "She gets teased a lot at school," Olga finally said and sniffed. "She actually doesn't have any friends."

No friends! That was like not having any arms but still having to carry on. I always had friends—they weren't always interesting but they were friends just the same. We three—Steina and Olga and me—had been in class together since we were six years old but our friendship didn't really start up until last winter, when we were in seventh grade. Both of them played handball in the winters and soccer in the summers. I had no interest in sports and wasted most of my time coming up with songs on my keyboard, songs that I forgot immediately. It was good to be able to shut out my home life with headphones and imagine that the boys were waiting for me in the garage just to hear my latest composition. Sometimes I removed one of my headphones so I could listen absentmindedly to my dad's and mom's voices and come up with a song to accompany them. I let the bass mumble and curse, the volume rising and then suddenly falling into a stunning silence— until it all began again.

I knew that some of the kids thought I was strange, and because of that I felt like I was very lucky to have Steina and Olga as friends. The thought of having none was unbearable. Now I couldn't wait to meet this friendless girl.

She lived in a three-story house like the ones built at Hlíðar. Those lavish homes sparkled from war profiteering in shell sand, and their inhabitants undoubtedly were indebted to Hitler's arrogance for their arched living-room windows. Olga rang the doorbell and the friendless girl answered the door—alone, of course. She stared at us with serious, gray-colored eyes from under a mop of thick hair; on each cheek a large red spot. It was as if she was ashamed of herself, but at first look it was impossible to figure out why. She was a very ordinary-looking girl who lived in a very ordinary house and had very ordinary parents. They appeared briefly to throw a hello our way.

Instead of inviting us into her bedroom—where we could have spun around on the desk chair and lay down on the sofa bed—the girl showed us into the living room. The room was furnished with those ever-present decorative wall plates, deep sofas, a glass cocktail table, and embroidery-upholstered chairs. It looked just like my home. My parents would have liked to know that I was visiting such a home. A good home. Smarties candy had been poured into a crystal bowl. We sat up straight, just like we were waiting for boys to ask us to dance. We felt so grown-up. I was really shy and wished I was outside again in the calm winter night. The snow fell gently outside the windows.

What were her parents up to, I wondered, listening for them. I could hear endless, muffled chatter coming out of the kitchen. In the living room, though, our conversation was barely moving. At first our host listened on in silence as we girlfriends discussed whether pink Smarties were better than the yellow ones or if any of the other ones might, in general, be better. Olga recalled a worldwide research study to determine what the new Smarties color should be and that most people chose blue. "Wasn't that about M&Ms?" asked Steina as she wolfed down the treats.

"Was it?" Olga looked at me questioningly and I shrugged. I had missed that bit of news. Really, I had completely forgotten why I was there. The guys in the garage band were probably wondering where I was. The friendless girl looked at each of us in turn, serious-looking as ever. She seemed, at the very least, not overly thrilled that we had suddenly appeared out of the bad weather to entertain her in her solitude. Maybe she was just now beginning to understand what it was like to have girlfriends, what they really talked about together. She undoubtedly missed being alone, playing solitaire in her bedroom. Why hadn't she invited us in there?

All of a sudden Olga set the tone of our visit: we must show this girl some small interest. Olga sniffed powerfully and began asking our host questions about school, about her teachers, and about her favorite subjects. The answers were incredibly short, like each syllable cost as much as individual characters on a telegram: "I think math is fine," or "The biology teacher is okay." Her bashful glances continued to wander between each of us and the red within the spots on her cheeks seemed to deepen in color with each passing moment. Steina and I gave out the occasional question but the only thing I really wanted to know was: Why don't you have any friends? Why are you teased so much?

It wasn't long until all the appropriate questions that we could possibly think of had been exhausted. The silence spread out from around us on the sofa and consumed the remainders inside of the crystal candy bowl. The girl shot glances around the room like a searchlight and then out of nowhere she asked, "Have you ever fantasized about being someone other than yourself?" The words came out slowly, as if she didn't trust that they could survive in this cruel, friendless world.

My heart immediately began to pound wildly, like it had to free itself from its suffocating ribcage prison. "Yes," I wanted to say,

"Yes, I'm the keyboardist in a band that practices in the garage at home! All the guys are fantastic and maybe we'll even go on tour soon!"

But I decided to let Steina and Olga go first. Perhaps Steina wanted to be some Swedish handball star? And Olga could then, for example, be some kind of working-class hero, the type that her father used to tell her about. But, instead, Olga and Steina just looked puzzled. "Nooo," said Steina after a silence, and she squinted at our host. "So . . . what else do you like to do?"

"Nothing?" said the girl and drew her feet up beneath her on the easy chair. I could still detect a trace of hope in her voice. I looked over at Olga and she shook her head slowly and finally said, "No."

The girl's stare was fixated on a point in the air just above my head when she added: "Sometimes I'm one of the characters in *The Ice People*. The girl, Sunna."

Steina and Olga stared silently at the girl in hopes of some further explanation.

"Have you read *The Ice People*?" asked the girl haltingly.

I had tried reading one of the books in the series, but I found Sunna—a member of a dark cult—too strange of a character to finish reading the book. My girlfriends had clearly never been drawn to Norwegian sorcery because we shook our heads at the same time. My heart continued to race and I didn't add anything more to the conversation but instead allowed my girlfriends to do the talking. There was no way to pick up the thread again anyway. After a brief pause, we each made a show of checking our watches, said something about how late it was getting, and stood up. I was relieved but hoped that the other girls couldn't sense that.

"May we see your bedroom?" asked Steina on her way out.

The girl opened the door, saying, "It isn't very tidy in there." She had splotches all over her, more than before. We didn't have the courage to cross the threshold, but opted to look in through the doorway. In there was a desk with dictionaries on it, a record player with albums by Limahl and Level 42, and a bed covered with stuffed teddy bears, rabbits, dogs, and cats. Suspended above all these animals was a small, white-clad Pierrot. Despite its broad smile, tears dripped down each cheek of its porcelain face like some grotesque Virgin Mary statue weeping for the sins of mankind.

On the way home, I walked a few steps behind my girlfriends and entertained myself by taking each step in their ankle-deep tracks in the snow. The blizzard was over. The neighborhood was quiet and we didn't have anything to say.

"That girl is very strange. Who exactly are these Ice People she kept talking about?" I heard Steina say.

"They're just from some book series. Don't worry about it. We'll visit her again anyway," said Olga and added: ". . . some day."

Our way home happened to take us across the most dangerous intersection in the country, where Mikla and Kringlumýrar Avenues intersect. Shattered taillights were strewn around the roadside and yellow and red pieces glittered like jewels in the snow.

Olga and Steina continued in the direction of Háaleiti but I went on toward Álftamýri. I had yet to feel the excitement in my chest subside and it took me almost the whole way down to Safamýri for me to figure out why. I had met a girl who had a life that was almost like mine, except that I had friends and she didn't.

My parents slept the sleep of the exhausted and depressed that night—a much deeper sleep than the rest of us enjoy. Me, I didn't sleep a wink until morning. I heard drumming coming from the garage and my pillow vibrated from the bass. The guys were playing

"Dancing Barefoot." I knew what awaited me if I ran down there. Sunna dancing barefoot on the cold cement floor among the paint cans, bikes, skis, and ice skates. None of the guys could take their eyes off of her. She spins in circle after circle with a bright smile and rose-red, joyous spots on both her cheeks.

TRANSLATED FROM ICELANDIC BY CHRISTOPHER BURAWA

children

[SWITZERLAND: FRENCH]

NOËLLE REVAZ

The Children

We live in the blue house. It's not our house, but we're spending our childhood here. Our footsteps and voices ring out, the headmasters can't help but get annoyed and scold us, which is completely natural, even with very well-behaved children. Madame Morceau and her husband are in charge. The teachers come during the day. We have four cooks. The ivy is full of snails.

Here is what's happening now. Today we wake up and Madame Morceau says to us: this morning, children, I have something to tell you. She gathers us all in the yard, Monsieur Morceau pensive and silent behind her. The headmistress is kind, her words flow, she resumes: I've something to tell you. Her eyes pass over our heads. Even though there are a lot of us, she knows each of our names. She doesn't need to shout for silence, she only has to widen her eyes. Her voice is calm: children, I have to tell you, today is not an ordinary day.

A few children start to play, but Madame Morceau continues: there is a workers' strike and nobody will be coming to watch over you. As for us, as headmasters, we must go and negotiate with the faculty. I hope you understand. There is bread on the table. I'll get the butter out for you. Don't get any jam on your pajamas please.

Also, I'm requesting that the most responsible among you look after the little ones. You may play in the yard, but don't go past the gate. I will be back in time to make you some lovely mashed potatoes, we cooked the potatoes yesterday and all that has to be done is to mash them with butter the way you like it. Above all, don't be worried, there won't be any nutmeg, I know how much you hate it. If I don't get back in time, it's nothing to get alarmed about—please put yourselves to bed without causing any trouble. If, as is quite possible, I still haven't returned by suppertime, you'll find the cereals in their usual spot. I'm well aware that cereal isn't very nutritious and I fully intend in the future to cook you healthy meals, but should I be detained, pour some milk in your bowls and be careful if you please not to spill any in the refectory. The big children should tie the little ones' bibs on carefully. When you go to bed, lie quietly until you fall asleep, just because I'm not there doesn't mean you get to have a free-for-all. And a word about the TV. If some of you are tempted to watch it, I'll know immediately by checking whether it's warm or cold. I'll think about you a lot while I'm gone. It's possible that I won't be there to tuck you in, but I'll come to give you cuddles as soon as I get back, even if you're sleeping, I promise. In the event of any little accidents in your beds, you know where the wardrobes are, there are more than enough sheets, put the dirty ones in the wash, below in the laundry room.

One last important thing: I've left some numbers downstairs, you can always call if you're worried about something, yes if the slightest thing happens, you dial those numbers, you think you'll be able to read them? Of course you will, you're not babies, you're capable of dealing with this situation, I'm proud in advance of knowing how you kept yourselves amused and how quickly the time passed, how you looked after yourselves for once without your headmasters. I'm not forgetting anything, lots of love, remember that you're with me, everywhere I go I'm carrying you, everywhere I am you are too and my thoughts are always here.

You're afraid of being sad. All right, it's okay, I'll permit it: you can turn on the TV, but only for a quarter of an hour, is that agreed, children? Not a second more, and don't watch that awful show, you must promise me you'll only watch children's programs, and no anime please; I insist because I've noticed that you sleep badly afterward and that you all want to come into my bed, which is certainly a utopian sort of consolation.

I think I recall all of a sudden that there are perhaps some of you who don't like cereal, you should check in the fridge, there should be some leftover gratin, will you be able to heat it up, no I'd prefer you didn't do anything, it would be better to do nothing at all, a hotplate is very quickly lit, but putting it out is another story entirely, those things could hurt you, or worse, the fire brigade might have to come and then where would you children go, already without moms and dads, fortunately I'm here, I watch over you and I know each of your names, first, middle, and last, your dates of birth, the dates of the most important events in your young lives, it's only this evening, unfortunately on this one evening it's only sixty percent certain that I can be at my post, that I can tuck you in tonight and ask you if you've made sure to do a peepee, moreover it will be necessary for one or another of you to look after changing the young ones' diapers, and I forgot the babies' bottles, but children if I remember before I go I'll prepare the bottles, you'll only have to immerse them in the bain-marie for twelve minutes, but no, I won't have time my little ones, you'll have to heat them yourselves, the measurements are on the back of the box, don't make a mistake with the powder, the babies with allergies get a different mixture, the round box under the window, you use three spoons, at least three good spoonfuls, three and a half, it depends on the milk, see how it looks, not too much liquid, it shouldn't be gooey, it's easy, will you be able to?

My children, I'm abandoning you, I must say I feel guilty, I'm afraid I'll faint, you can't imagine what it's like, to be in charge of your children and suddenly to have to head off and not to be able to know what will happen at all, if only one could split in two, you imagine all sorts of things, my God, but this is impossible, I want one of you to telephone me every half hour or I'll never be able to relax, who wants to do it?

Yes, you're right of course, there's no need to panic, how important you are to me, I learn from you every day. We must suffer through these events with calm. Everything will go smoothly, I'll be back at seven o'clock, let's say more toward eight rather, and even if I come back let's say toward ten or eleven o'clock, I've left you instructions and you're big enough boys and girls that everything will go swimmingly. Above all, and I'd like this to be clear, don't wait for me before going to bed, I'd prefer for you to think that I'm not available and then get a nice surprise rather than believing I'm going to come and making a scene when I don't and getting yourselves too worked up to sleep, and who will bring you your glass of warm milk to calm you down, no, I won't hear of it, especially not at night, listen I forbid you from going near the hot plates at any time at all, whether for the babies' bottles, they'll just take their formula cold, or for your supper, or for your warm milk to help dispel your fears and so delay your going to bed, you'll eat cold food, you'll drink cold drinks, that's all I ask.

Have you any questions perhaps, my poor little orphans who I'm leaving to their fate, I see that you don't mind, all you think about is playing and the rest leaves you indifferent. And so you're right of course, you must enjoy yourselves, it's only later that you'll understand, go on I'll leave you to your things, but don't forget to study, and if the TV's hot, Monsieur Morceau will spank you one after the other, even if that would surely wear him out.

We continue to play and Madame Morceau climbs into the car beside her husband. The engine starts, they pass beyond the gate while waving good-bye, good-bye. Who had the idea to go and see what it's like, the headmasters' room, we can't go in there, the bed takes up the whole space, the children we push inside jump on the big mattress like a real trampoline, and the little ones dribble on the duvet, it's no big deal, quickly fold back the sheet, Madame Morceau is always at her wits' end in the evening, she's not going to notice.

In the refectory there are some kids who pretend not to see the bread that falls under their chairs, but we do think to wipe up the puddles of milk. We scold anybody who cries, we want the headmasters to be able to say that their children are the best behaved around. When we're not at our best Monsieur Morceau comes to talk to us personally, he tells how sad he is to see his children behaving as stupidly as young animals, becoming coarse, deceitful, petulant like any other kids. When Monsieur Morceau comes back we'll ask if he'll explain to us how it's possible that the classrooms feel so empty, even though we're all there. Because there are no teachers, or else because there's nobody to keep speaking? The words dissolve in our mouths, they crumble like piles of sand, while those of the professors, of Madame, or better of Monsieur Morceau, are set like solid objects. As a result of which we naturally end up wondering how many children it would take to make one adult, if, Monsieur Morceau, you could shed some light on the subject, there are a lot of us here, but it's as if there's only one of us.

The next day the telephone rings, it's Madame Morceau's voice, she asks us to connect her to the loudspeaker and to gather around to hear her. Her speech surrounds us:

My children, I'm sorry, you'll have been surprised and disoriented not to find us home when you awoke this morning. We have been detained far from our orphanage. All my thoughts are for you and my memory is with you minute by minute, hour by hour. You have brushed your teeth. You have eaten properly. Your thoughts are beyond reproach and you express yourselves without swearing. I don't want any of those scuffles you get into when you lose your tempers, nor the kind of behavior that lowers you to the rank of illiterates.

Madame Morceau allows a pause, our eyes are on the loudspeaker.

The big ones will help the little ones. The girls will help the boys. Always be united. Make sure to eat enough and not to make a racket that will attract the neighbors' attention. Show nothing to the outside world that might betray your isolation. When you go to do the shopping, be the first to say hello, just as I've taught you. People will ask for news, you'll have to say that everyone's well. There's no need to go into detail. Yes, when you go out on your minor errands you'll always be smiling, polite, sociable, and well brought-up. Don't let the absence you might feel show, don't say: nobody's watching me, don't say: nobody's looking after me, say simply: good day Ma'am, goodbye, thank you. Thank you very much.

I'm giving you these instructions because we have just found out, and I'm crushed by this, my children, that we won't be able to join you again for at least several weeks. I'll send you some money. Dress yourselves neatly. The instructions for the washing machine are somewhere in the basement, I hope that, even if the pages are stuck together because of the damp, you'll manage to read them, separate the colors first of all and put the detergent in the right compartment. In the kitchen, you'll find a recipe book, there's a measurement chart at the back, a spoon, if I recall correctly, must hold about fifteen, twenty grams, look in your science books, you can easily convert grams and centiliters. Farewell my little children, it pains me to leave you, I would like so much to be able to feed you, clothe you, and look after you, fate is a fickle thing. Sending you billions of kisses. My husband would also like to express himself now.

Without a break, Monsieur Morceau's voice: I hope you're sleeping well. I'm proud at the thought that you all know how to cope and that you will finally be able to live alone and without problems like grown-ups. You children really do help make your caretakers' lives so much simpler, I must thank you and I can only tell you to carry on. In this way you will make us happy and you'll remain very good children. Don't say bad words, don't do naughty things. Your hands must be clean, nails white. Take care of one another. Discipline is unique to humanity.

Here his voice breaks off and we carry on with our day. A question that bothers us: what use is an adult? They are always so remote, and we don't really care about them, but can we exist without them, how to manage it, dear headmasters, our windows remain closed, we don't feel at home, we can't sleep unless we light all the lamps, shame that you couldn't say how long we'd have to wait to finally be mature and complete, we don't want to be small any longer, there are too many things we lack. We believe we're all going to blow away without a grown-up to hold us, without anyone to tie us down, to ballast us, weight us, peg us, fasten us, guide us, screw us down, drive us in, nail us down, surround us, and contain us.

The postmen bring the mail and in the middle is a letter from the headmistress. On the envelope she has written: this letter will be read aloud by the oldest among you. And so our eldest deciphers the letter:

My children, she begins, how are you my little ones. I hope that you feel well and that you are taking the time to enjoy yourselves a little besides your studies. I don't dare imagine how much your appearance has changed nor how many centimeters of skin are now showing at the bottom of your trousers. Your ankles must be showing, it's certainly ugly, please don't delay going to a shop if you have the chance. I'm sending you cash. I'm thinking nonstop about the meals that you could make yourselves, I'm setting aside recipes for you, though one day I'll be back to indulge your digestive systems and give your bodies what they might be lacking. But I am absolutely certain that you can be self-sufficient, thankfully there are so many of you, whether or not Monsieur Morceau and myself are in charge of you doesn't really make much of a difference, you never want for anything, you budget for yourselves what's necessary, perhaps you don't even feel this absence which is crucifying me, yes my poor children, I am in tatters because I no longer have my chicks, I am out in winter with no coat, my mind is cold and shivering, I think endlessly of the happiness of bringing you into the refectory, it's good to make you obey, to hold you in my hands, to know that you are mine and that you live under my wing, your thoughts are open to me and you always give me everything, all that you are, completely, because you are my children and I am your headmistress who keeps you under her protection and who will no longer let you go, no, never, no matter what happens. I insist so much on that because the times are difficult, we are still detained and for the time being I don't see any possibility of returning to join you again. While waiting, do keep sitting up straight in your chairs, don't bring shame to those who gave their lives for yours, you aren't hunchbacks, you aren't rolled up like little snails, don't forget your backbones, hold yourselves up proudly. I send my thoughts to all of you, from the biggest to the least-developed of you, I care about every hair on your heads. Note that I've intentionally employed a complex vocabulary in order that you can doubly profit from my letter. Don't forget the postscript. More kisses than ever, your sorry headmistress, Madame Morceau.

Postscript: my children, you are the salt of the earth, you are the compost, the leaven, you are divine goodness. Grow and multiply and don't forget, before going to sleep at night, that Madame and Monsieur Morceau were your guides in childhood. Your beloved headmaster, Monsieur Morceau.

We know that we'll do what we have to. We still cry our eyes out of course, but our noses are blown and we'll soon be able to laugh without showing our glottis and tongue. At mealtimes we force ourselves to stay until every dish is empty. We know that the head-masters would like to see us at midday, all of us seated as we are, amid the tinkling of the dinner service, we never lick our knives, we swallow cauliflower and so on without fail, but my God if only Monsieur Morceau could come back soon to make conversation at the table, it's a desert between us and we're bored to death, and if Madame Morceau could only come back too to take responsibility for the never-ending choices we have to make, so we could have fun again, that she could decide for us where to go when we go out for a walk or in which place to take refuge when we get caught in a storm, which shirt it's better to wear, whether we should put on socks or not, if it's time for a bath, what time to set the alarm clock, and how to grow up, how to react, what to think, what temptations to avoid, and on what to model our lives.

Someone came by one Sunday, a fax arrived somewhere else, it seems there was an error, it's addressed to us. Here's what we read on the pages: my children, as we are well aware, you are living where we no longer do. Please believe that we think about it at least as much as you do. We have tried to do what we could in this world. Please behave like adults, you are becoming young people, the knowledge is comforting, continue to grow and mature without creating problems for us. Think carefully about it. Choose your job according to your abilities. Refrain from smoking and getting into drugs. The blood that stains your linen is a sign of creation. You needn't be concerned about it. The sap flooding you when you wake up is nothing to worry about either, your bodies have grown up, your faces have become fine and mobile, the skin at your armpits is curling. Learn how to shave well and fight against perspiration so as to be welcomed within society. Resolve your Oedipus complexes. Laugh and speak with caution. Instinct is a bad counselor. Discipline your minds. How is it that you aren't more confident? You ought to be able to solve an equation with three unknowns and to fill out a tax form. At your ages one forges ahead, one no longer lets oneself be led astray by hang-ups and anxieties. You are going to start families and carry children at your breast. Avoid if you can duplicating our mistakes, if you see them coming. We did our best, but perfection isn't human. My children, we must say it, this will be our last contact, we are going to lose sight of you permanently in a short while. We don't know what you are, we don't see what connects us, and you aren't far from speaking a language that is alien to us. We had planned on having children of a different caliber, ladies and gentlemen, it seems strange to us that you are sleeping in our rooms, to think of your lives surprises us, we are puzzled, in fact, you aren't acting according to our wishes, some among you are still sticking your fingers in your nose, at night you make use of your hands in a way that embarrasses us, and we don't approve of the paths you're following. For what are you using the blood we've kept in your veins for the past thousand years? How can you inhabit bodies that disconcert us so? You are kilometers away and your voices are unrecognizable to us. We are forced to say it, we feel no closer than to ghosts or specters. You have taken our time, we devoted ourselves to you, you are grain that blows away. From now on it makes no difference to us to know that you're alive. In conclusion, be aware that tomorrow we die, please come to our graves, water the plants with care, rake the earth as necessary. Keep your tears inside, you are in any case tied to us for all time.

The fax concludes with those words. We understand that this is the moment, we must leave today. In the street we move forward, tall but empty inside, we make our way, all of us together, one body, which must separate.

TRANSLATED FROM FRENCH BY URSULA MEANY SCOTT

DONAL McLAUGHLIN

enough to make your heart

SEASON 1971–72

1.

It felt like Christmas had come early. First Liam knew, his da was tugging his toe.

"Surprise, son!" he whispered. "Get up 'n' get on you quick! We're going to the football!"

"What, *Parkhead?*"

Liam could hear himself how excited he sounded.

"Naw, they're away this week in Dundee. C'mon, get up 'n' get on you like a good youngfella. We need to leave soon—"

Liam waited for the door to shut, then jumped out. Sean & wee Cahal, he could see, were out for the count still. Room was that cold, he was hugging himself as he hopped round, looking out his clothes. Even pulling them on, he was shivering.

He hoped to God his mum had the fire lit.

Sure enough: she was kneeling in front of the fire, a big double-page out of the paper up against it, when Liam got downstairs. *The British Army is smaller than it used to be*, the huge big advert read, *but so is the world.*

There was a hint of a heat if ye went close.

"Mornin, Mum."

"Mornin, son."

The trick wi the paper was a good one. Liam loved the way it turned gold as the flame started to take. You'd to watch it didn't catch just. Soldier wi the helmet was in big trouble if that happened.

His mum & dad were talking bout how come he was going to see Celtic.

"Bring your boy," Mr. McCool had said, his da was saying. "He'll be company for my boy, sure—"

"It's not fair taking one 'n' not the other but, Liam," his mum objected.

"I can take Sean another time," his da said just.

"See 'n' enjoy yourself anyway, son!" his mum said as they left. She slipped him a new 5p.

It felt strange: heading out wi none of the rest of them up yet. Felt great but too: him & his da, the two Liams, heading off together.

They took the big green Zephyr and parked behind the Hibs.

Liam—wee Liam—had never been in a bar before. It was mainly empty tables, wi empty & half-full tumblers & ashtrays in front of people but, where there was people. One or two seemed to know his da.

"Pint of cordial, Liam?"

"Aye, John, please!"

Barman'd started to make it before he'd even asked.

Orange went in first. Liam watched the colour change as blackcurrant was added.

"Lemonade for the boy, maybe?"

"Aye, give him a bottle of mineral, John, thanks. What do you say to Mr. Higgins, son?"

"*Thank you.*"

The bar was beginning to fill. Some of the other men had Irish accents too. His da & him weren't the only ones. Some of the other men said aye, they were going to the football, they weren't all but. Ye could see themmins that weren't wished they were.

Was a good while before anyone Liam's age appeared. When they did, they crowded round a table across the room.

"Gaun over 'n' join them," his da kept saying. Liam wouldn't but. Not when he didn't know a single one.

He played wi his tooth that was coming out instead. Was still playing wi it, his tongue footering away, when the McCools turned up. That youngfella was over to the others like a shot.

Suddenly they were bundling onto the bus. One minute his da was going to the toilet & not wanting to be on his own, Liam went with him; the next, they were bundling on.

"Come on, O'Donnell! Trust you—always bloody last! Can ye no hurry up thon father o yours, son? What kinda example's thon to set the boy, O'D?"

There was a buzz about the bus as they left. Liam recognised the *obvious* bits of where they lived in Scotland, but not much more but. He asked his da how long it would be. His da didn't know. The man across the aisle didn't either. He leant across, all kind: "We've left in plenty of time anyhow, son. Don't be frettin." The man laughed. "Yir daddy here might even have time for a pint!"

"What—you don't *drink*? Pioneer, are you?" Liam heard as he drifted off in his own imagination.

"That you playing wi that tooth again?"

Liam nodded.

"Want me to pull it?"

He nodded again.

His da's finger & thumb went into his mouth. Liam ignored the yellow colour—tried to, anyhow—'n' the taste 'n' smell of it. His da rocked the tooth. Liam could feel it resisting.

"It's not ready to come out yet, son, 'n' I don't want to force it. I'll try again later."

Liam sat there just 'n' wriggled 'n' wriggled it, his face against the cold of the window sometimes. It got to the point the poem he'd learned in St. Eugene's wouldn't give him peace. The wobbly-tooth one—

They were crossing a river when a man appeared. He stood over them wi a cap full of toty bits of paper, folded up tight. It was the *sweep*, the boy said.

"Final score, is it?" his da asked.

"Naw, first goal-scorer for a change—"

"You choose, Liam. Let you choose—"

"That your boy?"

"Aye—my eldest. He's Liam, too."

"Pleased to meet you, son. What age are you?"

"Ten!"

"Ten?"

"Eleven in March, he'll be. For secondary in the autumn."

"Many others ye got?"

"Six. Another two weeboys and four weegirls."

"Jaysus, man!"

His da opened his ticket 'n' humphed.

The man laughed. "Who've ye got?"

"Evan Williams!"

"The goalie! Ah well—ye never know. Maybe it'll be an o.g. D'ye want another one to be in wi a chance?"

"Not wi luck like that I don't!"

We HATE Ran-gers 'n' we HATE Ran-gers

Singing had started already.

"Don't know what's brought that on!" his da said. Then but, he spotted the boys at the lights.

We are the Ran-gers HAT-ERS!

The Wranglers ones leapt out of their seats. Charged across the aisle to give the Proddies the vicky. Scary, it was. Specially when them other boys laid into the glass wi their fists. Least, over in Derry, the soldiers waved back if you waved nice.

Soon, the singing was that loud ye'd've thought the match had started.

"Mon the Cellic!"

Most of them said the name lik it had no T in it.

Before long, they were giving it all the *grand-old-team-to-play-fors.* For once, they kept up wi each other.

WHEN—ye KNOW—the HIStorY—

Liam knew the words 'n' all. Was too shy to join in but.

enough to make your heart go oh OH oh OH

His da wasn't. Looked at him as if to say, Wha's wrong wi ye?

ANimals SAY
WHAAAT the HELL do we CAARE

His da fancied himself as a singer.

a SHOW
'n' the GLASgow CELlic will be THERRR.

Singing was frightnin enough now, would be worse still at the ground but. Ye'd to wonder why the other team showed up even—

The roars o' them—

Liam always thought it felt lik, sounded lik, they could kill someone.

Eventually, they gave their so-called singing a rest, thank God. Kinda roads they were on, there was no one to taunt anyhow. At most, they brandished their flags 'n' scarves at other supporters' buses. All the ORANGE BASTARDS got shouted, whether it was Rangers buses or not.

"Aye, they're not the only ones, sure," his da explained. "Some of them wee teams are just as bad—"

Mr. McCool came up to speak to his da.

"Have ye met my Kevin yet, son?"

His da said he hadn't.

"Away up 'n' introduce yourself. He'll be delighted to meet you."

When Liam wasn't for moving, his da said his tooth was bothering him.

"Never mind—the Tic'll take your mind off it. We're goney stuff these boys theday, son! Where's your scarf anyway?"

"Not got one."

"Not got one? Ye want to get yir daddy to get you one!" Mr. McCool turned to his da. "Ye should get him one, Liam. All the other young fellas have them—"

"Who d'ye think Big Jock'll pick theday, son?"

Liam panicked. How has *he* supposed to know?

His da said something for him again.

"Who's your favourite player then?"

That was easy. Lennox. Bobby Lennox. Ever since the double he got against Falkirk. Wee Jinky was a close second. The rings he dribbled round folk.

"And can ye name me your favourite eleven?"

Liam couldn't.

"That boy o' mine can. Obsessed, he is. Nothin appears in the papers he doesn't cut out. You should ask him to let you see his scrapbooks, son!" The man turned back to his da. "I get him the catalogues wi the wallpaper samples from my work 'n' he sticks in everything he finds. I'll get you one, too, son, 'n' give it to yir da here to give to ye."

"That's kind of you, Feargus. What do ye say to Mr. McCool, son?"

"*Thank you.*"

They got there *eventually*. Dundee was the furthest Liam'd been in Scotland. Wasn't as if he saw much of it but—two grounds on the one street 'n' that was it.

Was Tannadice they were going to, not Dens Park. His da joked about making sure they got the right one. "Ye wouldn't want the match to start to discover it wasn't!"

Mr. McCool laughed 'n' all. "Aye—magine ye were stood there wonderin was that a new away strip Celtic were in!"

A fair number of buses parked where they parked. Whereas *Irish* accents tumbled out of their bus, the Hibs bus, Scottish accents piled out of the other ones. It was all the didni-widni-kidni stuff Liam detested. All the effin bees 'n' all. It could've been Japanbloominese ye were hearing, at times. To listen to them, ye wouldn't've known these boys had any connection wi Ireland, that was for sure.

Most of the men descended on the pub. His da said the two of them wouldn't. They'd head on in 'n' choose their spot just.

The embarrassing bit came next: his da would never pay for him. Insisted on lifting him over. Always a struggle it was 'n' Liam always got stuck. Was worse still when Sean was there 'n' all 'n' their da needed help. Thon shivery feeling as a stranger's hands went in under your arms—

They got in 'n' climbed the steps.

He loved this bit, Liam: the anticipation as you headed up the steps. Then: the immaculate green below. Perfect, normally, till the match started.

What was noticeable this time was: the atmosphere wasn't as good. Tannadice, compared to Parkhead, was a ghost town. At Celtic Park, they'd be playing records. "If You're Irish." Or "Hail, Hail."

"You'll Never Walk Alone" too, of course. Wi sixty thousand scarves held aloft.

His da lifted him onto a crush barrier 'n' stood behind him. Liam leaned back, knew not to cuddle in. If it stayed like this, he'd have a brilliant view. He knew from other games you could have a perfect view to start wi—then other folk would come but 'n' blot it out. It wasn't fair. By that time too, it was always too late to find another place.

The ground was filling up. United fans were getting their songs in while they could. Would be a different story later.

Teams were read out. The fans booed one lot, cheered the other.

"No surprises there!" his da & Mr. McCool agreed.

"Naw, nae surprises there, eh?" the guy next to them gave it.

A huge cheer went up. Drowned out whatever the guy said next. Players were running on.

"United haven't read the script, Liam," Mr. McCool was soon saying.

They'd the cheek to score first even.

His da 'n' Mr. McCool looked at each other. Was Partick Thistle goney be, the League Cup final all over again, looked lik. All the effin bees the men around them were giving it. Singling out the goalie they were. His da'd to call them to order.

"Mind the language, lads—there's boys present!"

"Aw—sorry, Jim. Aye, nae borra. Sorry, big man!"

They reached half-time without an equaliser. Liam couldn't believe it. There'd been a few near things in the goal-mouth below 'n' it was all he could do to remain on the barrier; the ball hadn't gone in but. United might even've scored a second.

It was a long cold wait at the interval.

"Don't worry, son," Mr. McCool said. "A different story in the second half it'll be—"

That didn't make Liam any warmer but, as he waited to be lifted again. Talking to someone about emigrating from Derry his da was. Scores from the other grounds didn't help either: Aberdeen were up there challenging still.

Second half started. All the action was at the far end now. It was all Celtic. Was hard to tell who was doing what but. Was the ball going in or not.

Crowd behind Liam was straining to see. There was so much leaning forward 'n' falling back, he wasn't safe on the barrier. His da'd to keep telling folk to spare a thought for the boy. It kept happening but. Soon the weeboy was so scared, he hadn't a hope of concentrating. Didn't help that the men round about him were baying for blood.

"United are hangin by a thread, Liam!" Mr. McCool said. "Like your tooth, son!"

Then Celtic equalised.

"CAESAR!"

Liam felt himself being swept off the barrier.

"*Big McNeill!*"

Took both his da 'n' Mr. McCool to catch him.

His da was livid—"Young fella could've cracked his skull open!" Fans were too busy celebrating but.

"*One each!*"

"*M'ON THE TIC!*"

No way was Liam getting up again after that. He stayed down even though he couldn't see. There was gaps between the men's bodies alright. They closed but, every time the ball went near the box.

Another four goals went in—Hood, Connolly, Murdoch, Hood again—Liam saw buck all but.

"Five-one!—Are you pleased wi the score at least, youngfella?"

Liam tried to say he was. Really but, for the last half hour, he'd been interested in nothing but his tooth.

They hit the road. Only stopped for fish 'n' chips. Perth was the name of the place. In the freezing cold, the steam off the food was something powerful. Heat made Liam's tooth scream wi agony.

"Eat wi the other side of your mouth then," his da said.

After that, the journey dragged 'n' dragged. There was nothing to look forward to. If he didn't see much on the way up, he now saw less in the dark, Liam.

He felt a sharp pain sometimes when he forced the tooth wi his tongue. When that happened, pressing against the window seemed to help. The cold would take his mind off it.

Two hours later nearly, he was still sitting there: poking 'n' wriggling. Felt lik a crunch sometimes, it did. Then, suddenly, it gave. His da hadn't to pull it.

Liam showed his tooth to Mr. McCool.

"Will ye be leavin it out for the Tooth Fairy?"

Was the first Liam'd heard of any fairy—though he knew about under the pillow.

"Don't know about that," his da said. "He's had enough—all he's getting—today."

Youngfella didn't care but. He was so browned off he wanted home just.

2.

Day it all happened, Liam'd been out wi a ball—ball he got for Christmas—up round the corner at the garages. No one else was out so he'd spent the afternoon, once twelve Mass 'n' the dinner were over, kicking the ball at the doors.

He knew himself he was getting better. It felt great when he got a rally going, the ball hitting the door, then dropping down the slope, falling for him. He could feel himself shaping up, posing nearly, as he shot 'n' shot 'n' shot 'n' shot at goal.

He kept going even when it started to get dark. Wi the streetlights on, it felt like a midweek game, sure. *Flood-lit.*

Felt so good, was only needing the toilet had taken him home.

"There's three dead in Derry," his mother said when she saw him.

"Is there?" he answered just.

He felt lousy. There was nothing he could say but. Was lik the times his mum would tell him, "Your granny was sayin Tony Devlin died yesterday." Or: "That's Bridie Breslin dead." He'd feel sad, sort-of. All he could ever say but was "Did he?" or "Is it?"

The names meant nothing to him, that's what the problem was. His mum, realising, sort-of, sometimes, would say, "You must mind

Tony Devlin? Man who ran the butcher's next to the newsagent's? Married onto your Aunty Mary's people?"

"Naw, maybe you wouldn't—" she'd end up saying.

Was only him she asked, too. She never asked the young ones.

Liam wished he *could* remember. Instead of being a dead loss.

"There's five dead now," his mum said when he came down again. "Did ye wash your hands?"

"Yeah," he said, racing out.

It was still bothering him but, as he looked to see who else was out. Ciara 'n' Annette were playing: them clacker things. Sean was nowhere to be seen. Boys next door were playing kerbie, so Liam sat 'n' watched.

The number went up to eight. Then eleven. Then thirteen.

The Derry ones were phoning Mrs. Henderson's. His da still wasn't in so his mum took the calls. Came out each time to tell them.

"The rumours are true," she announced at one point. "Bout the killings in Derry, I mean. There was even a bit on the news there."

"They haven't put a figure on it. Your Uncle Dermot says it's all round Derry but there's thirteen dead. Thirteen dead 'n' a whole lot injured."

Liam looked at her just. *None* of them knew what to say. He could see the shock too, sure, in the girls' faces.

At some point, later, his mum came out of the Hendersons' 'n' assured them the O'Donnells were all okay.

Jesus. It hadn't even occurred to him! Liam, when she said it, realised.

Her own family were all okay 'n' all. None of them had been on the march.

Some of their uncles 'n' cousins on the O'Donnell side *had been* but they were all home safe but, she told them. Their Uncle Dermot was just off the phone to say they were all home safe. Their daddy had got hold of Dermot 'n' all. Had phoned the Creggan from a phonebox.

When he got home from the Hibs, their da, you could tell from the look on his face it was really bad. You'd've thought, to look at him, someone in the family had died.

Now Liam felt even worse. Bout not realising how bad it was.

It was no time before Mrs. Henderson was at the door again. His da took the call this time, apologised for any inconvenience. Mrs. Henderson insisted but it was alright.

Turned out Dermot had phoned again 'n' John Hume had read out the names from a bit of paper. There was twelve names, thirteen dead but. Folk weren't sure who No. 13 was. Could be one of two people.

The weans were all in their beds, of course, when *News at 10* came on. They could hear Big Ben but up through the ceiling, your man Reginald Bosanquet doing the headlines.

For once, the weans had been good 'n' went up. Was as if they knew to. Sean was the only one to act up. Ciara & Annette were soon shooshin him but, urging him to be good for their mammy & daddy. Wasn't there thirteen dead, they said.

It was no time before they could hear their da 'n' all. Raging he was. Calling the soldiers for everything. Their mum they could hear trying to calm him.

When Liam went down for a drink, his da called him in.

"Mere 'n' see this, son—"

He didn't need to be told, Liam: the man on the TV, wi the balding head, was Eddie Daly. The Eddie Daly his da had gone to school wi. Father Daly now. He was waving a white hanky, Father, 'n' the boys behind him were carrying someone.

"Jackie Duddy, that is. Dermot told me on the phone. Seventeen years of age! Jackie Duddy's his name. And Father was shouting 'Don't shoot! Please don't shoot!' trying to get him to an ambulance—"

Jackie Duddy. Liam knew instantly it was a name he'd never forget. He remained sitting.

His mum & dad were *letting* him, he realised at some point. Were *letting* him stay up. He listened to the army boys being interviewed, his da blowing his top. Then listened to his da & his mum trying to take it all in. Trying to piece it together.

Thirteen dead. Six from the Creggan alone.

■

The next night, when their da came home, he was livid.

They all knew at work he wasn't long over, he said. Not a buckin one but had had the decency to ask was his family all okay? "For all they know, one of my brothers could've been shot!"

"They're all Catholics too. Each 'n' every one of them. Did they ask about Derry yesterday but? Did they buck! Not a single one!"

"That's the Scots for you—"

Their da stayed in that night, something he never ever done. Even wee Cahal commented.

Their mum & him were running through the names still. Trying to work out which Gilmore it was. Which Nash. Which McDaid. There were two by the name of McKinney.

It wasn't just grown men. There was seventeen- & nineteen- & twenty-one-year-olds, which made it even harder. Ye had to work out who they might be connected to. Whose youngfella it could be.

Liam listened to the names being repeated, over 'n' over. It was goney be another list you'd have to know by heart. He could tell already.

They'd a name for No. 13 now. Boy's family, God love them, had been told it wasn't him & it turned out it was.

Liam's mother & father kept coming back to Jackie Duddy. They never shut up about Jackie Duddy. Bout Father Daly carrying him. Trying to get him to an ambulance. Having to wave his hanky to stop them getting shot.

Fr. Daly who his da knew. From when they were schoolboys together.

3.

The first home game again, after that, was the following Saturday.

The funerals had taken place in the meantime. Dermot had described on the phone for them what people had felt: all them coffins, all laid out before the altar.

Their mum & dad hadn't given over—even here in Scotland, even—bout what everyone was calling Bloody Sunday. They went on 'n' on about Bernadette Devlin punching Reginald Maudling. Bout other ones setting fire to the British Embassy in Dublin.

It showed you how *serious* things were.

Things were *bad* gettin.

There was demonstrations in America 'n' all, sure.

Devlin was expected in Glasgow on Friday night. Woodhallside, or something.

They'd seen the letters to the papers too. One, in the *Scotsman*, insisted the Ulster Catholics in Londonderry lived no distance from the border. *So*, the boy asked, if they didn't go, didn't move across, if they preferred to be second-class citizens in Northern Ireland when they could be first-class citizens in Eire, *did that not tell you something?*

Their da flipped when he saw that. Was nearly writing in, himself.

The Saturday was a Cup game. Against Albion Rovers.

Sean was looking to go. Still hadn't been for when Liam had got to Tannadice. Their da wasn't having it but. Their mum didn't say nothing. However much she felt for the weeboy, it was a non-starter, she knew. He knew it was a bit twisted, Liam, something in him felt pleased but—specially when Sean got joined for asking once too often.

"I said NO, Sean, 'n' I'm not telling you again! It'll be a cuff round the ear ye'll be getting. Do ye not realise there could be aggro? It'll be no place for youngfellas—Parkhead—today."

Mr. McCool turned up at half one. When he saw Liam, he said his Kevin said hello. Didn't say much otherwise.

Then he minded the tooth. Liam'd forgotten, himself, until Mr. McCool mentioned it. His tongue felt for where the wound had been. Marshmallowy, it had been, really soft. *Coppery*-tasting. Now but, it had healed again.

"Are you satisfied, weeboy?" their da asked when he came back downstairs. Talking to Sean, he was. "Hasn't Mr. McCool left Kevin behind 'n' all? I hope you're satisfied now?"

He turned to Mr. McCool. "Do us a favour, Feargus, will ye, 'n' tell my two Parkhead's no place for youngfellas today!"

Liam drew him a look as if to say: He doesn't have to tell me! *Wasn't me was pestering ye!*

"That's right, boys," Mr. McCool confirmed. "Yir daddy's right. Yir better off at home theday, Sean, son. Ye never know what could happen, sure—"

"I hear there's an International Socialist march in Glasgow planned—" he said to their da. "Ye ever heard o them boys, Liam? The International Socialists?"

Their da said he hadn't. He'd heard about the sixteen arrests outside the Bernadette Devlin rally the night before but. An' about a boy called Pastor Glass who'd led a counter-demonstration. There was a photo in the paper. Liam'd seen it 'n' all. *The People's Democracy*, one placard read, *is a Marxist Plot.*

"Have ye got the petitions?" Mr. McCool asked as they headed out.

"Too right I've got them."

At quarter to four, Liam tuned in for the half-time scores, then listened to the second-half commentary. Sean joined him. It was okay: Celtic were two up, the Rovers weren't at the races.

The goals rolled in. Five-nil, it finished. Callaghan got two. Macari, Deans 'n' Murdoch, one each.

The boys couldn't wait for their da 'n' Mr. McCool. Would be great if Mr. McCool had time to come in. That way, they'd hear more. Would hear how Dalglish & Macari were doing.—The new boys.

When the two men did return, their faces were tripping them. Even Bridget commented.

"What's wrong wi yous? I thought yous would've been pleased. The two boys here were followin it on the wireless—"

Their da shook his head as if to say, *Don't ask.* He was browned off about something, ye could see it.

"They wouldn't sign our petitions, Bridget, love," Mr. McCool explained.

"Aye—they call themselves Celtic supporters!" their da just-about roared. "And the buggers wouldn't sign our bloody petitions—"

Mr. McCool was nodding away.

"They stand on them terracings, week in, week out, singing all the songs, *calling themselves Celtic supporters*—" their da continued, "calling themselves *Irish*—would they lift a pen but to put pen to paper? Would they buck!"

"Language, Liam!" Mr. McCool tried to say. "Cool it in front of the youngsters, mucker—"

Their da wasn't having it but.

He turned to their mum. "I tried to reason with them, didn't I, Feargus? Thirteen dead, I said. A whole lot more injured. Thirteen innocent people murdered—'n' you won't put pen to paper?"

"I tried to plead wi them. It's *true*, I said. The world press has got hold of it, sure. Like in October '68, I said. All them foreign journalists, cameramen, witnessed it, captured it, have put the English to shame . . . Wasting my breath but, I was, love—"

"Liam's right, Bridget. Hardly anyone signed. The boys at the Hibs did, but not the ones at the ground. For all their songs, for all they wave the tricolour, all ye got was: *naw, mate—ah widni want any bother wey the polis—*"

"Ye wouldn't've credited it, love," their da said. "Thirteen dead 'n' they were scared they'd get in trouble. Well, it's the last bloody time they'll see me. *If you're Irish*, ma arse! Green white 'n' gold, ma foot. That's the last buckin time *I'll* go anywhere near that friggin shower—I'm tellin ye!"

Way he said that last bit made Liam look at Sean.

Aye—

Sure enough—

Ye could tell from the look on his face: wee bruv knew he'd be a long time waiting, if he was waiting for their da to take him now.

SANNEKE VAN HASSEL

Pearl

Again I hold her tight. The water in the river—a plastic bag slips downstream. Weightless, it billows up. If I knew how, I'd offer a sacrifice. I stand on the embankment. So often thought about getting into the water myself. I clasp the rail, then I hold her tight, carefully slide her in. I spread my arms and then . . . nothing. She is not there.

We call her Pearl. J's keen on that. I don't like oysters but it reminds me of a photo of Nastassja Kinski: pearls in her ears, a damp, promising look. For a long time I copy her, the same wisps of hair at my temples, pearls for my birthday.

I get pregnant at a time when I can't get anything off the ground. Even the basil on the windowsill refuses to grow, no matter how much care and food I give it. I glide through the factory, crossing the warehouse with an order list in my hand, having boxes piled onto pallets and taken off again. J and I keep meeting as if by chance. He borrows coffee and stays the night. We have no plans, only encounters. And then I get pregnant; my body is pregnant, I follow.

The first month is staring out of the window together, his hand on my belly. Spring. Chestnut buds swell, the carillon chimes, seagulls shriek over the water. I enjoy the way the three of us lie together in bed, the endless Sunday mornings. On Queen's Day I buy blue children's rain boots.

J comes less often. I miss the drink, far more than I thought I would; it's not something my friends talk about, but I miss it. After two glasses of wine it's always been much easier to have J around, to tolerate his restiveness. At parties I'm tired, the conversation growing hazy and me top-heavy over an oven full of charred puff-pastry appetizers.

Sometimes J drops by to mop the floor, to whitewash walls. He puts up a hook in the hall for the stroller. One morning when I order apple tart with my coffee at Lindeman, he's furious: "For God's sake, Ka, you're not allowed cinnamon. It's bad for the fetus."

I take another bite to see that agitated look of his one more time.

The Maas flows away from me toward the Hook of Holland. Rippling water, in perpetual motion. What is the smallest particle? A molecule? Is it miles away already, swallowed by the sea? Or is it still around, does it split? Can water dissolve? Is it moving or being moved?

My belly is a balloon full of water. J detaches himself: now it's visible, now you can manage alone. No more sex—virtually incest, he says. My hand slides across his stomach, downward; he won't allow it. I want to feel his prick grow hard, his hands on me, to prove we're together. He abandons the bed. I let my hand slip between my legs, thinking of him, moist, making it last as long as I can. I'm getting better at sex with him without him, one hand stroking my breasts that have never been so full, the other descending. Longer and longer orgasms, fantastic but confined to one spot. He alone touches my whole body.

And in me grows Pearl, kicking me with the question: will I love her? J says hardly anything now, comes in, pours a drink, studies the contents of his wallet. At work I send cake boxes to a chicken-feed factory and fish-and-chip trays to a beer wholesaler.

The summer drags on into September. October is rain. As I walk my belly cramps up and I have to sit down. In November she washes out through my uterus. J arrives an hour after the birth and looks proudly into the aquarium, the plastic crib, where Pearl is lying. She sleeps a lot. The first few weeks of her life I have nightmares. I see myself dying in all the blood, dream I'm in terrible pain and no one believes me. Many have gone before you; it's good, it has a purpose, my dear, it's nature's way. Something causes you so much pain at the start that you can't help loving it—is that how it works?

The second week J drinks from my breasts. He sucks carefully, more carefully than Pearl. I provide, utterly dazed, wanting to die, turn to stone, like those statues by Rodin, or was it Camille Claudel? After that, J stays away for ten days.

I spend November in bed with Pearl. For a long time I feel torn open, don't dare push when I'm on the toilet. Tiles flash white. I see my feet, ask them if I'll ever be whole again. Some men prefer making love to a childless woman.

My first day back at work. J babysits and arrives late, he's got no jobs on the books, which makes him angry. After an hour of baby photos with colleagues the boss asks to see me. Restructuring makes me surplus to requirements; if I go without protest they'll give me a "settlement"—half a year's salary.

My winter with Pearl. The unwashed bedcover (there's only me to do everything) and the days that pass unnoticed. Single friends cheerfully cycle two toddlers to school in all weathers while I lie in bed, Pearl like a frog on tiny hands and feet, and imagine myself up to the elbows in suds with BBC News on TV. Sometimes I read. About Marina Tsvetaeva, who was alone with two children. Her lover went to the front lines, one child died of malnutrition and meanwhile she wrote astonishing poetry.

Again I stand by the river and hold her tight, stroking the doll in my arms. What have I done to deserve such a perfect doll? Such light blue eyes, such soft hair and pale-pink feet. I used to get dolls from the girls next door, but never this lifelike. "Children, time to come in . . . Dinner's ready." Play stops and you leave your doll lying there. Back the next day and she's still in one piece, the pouting lips, the hinged eyelashes.

J stays away all through February. I forget, I forget. First a bottle, then a diaper change. She hardly ever cries, just lies there in silence with a huge apple-juice stain on the sheet. Juice from three days ago. The first Sunday in March he's back: "You slob," he says and cleans the toilet. In the kitchen I cry, a pigeon takes a bath in the gutter, and I calm down.

He stays the night and I fantasize that he's my lover. Take Pearl out of the wicker basket and lay her on the big mattress where we made love shortly before. Briefly, unnoticed, we have sex. J, half asleep, comes and then goes on sleeping.

I hunt through my old college books for heroic role models from literary history, becoming absorbed in confessions by Anne Sexton and Sylvia Plath. The head in the oven, tea towels under the kitchen door. Poets of despair, stylizing for all they're worth. Sometimes I read a story by Colette; she perseveres in love, despite the ragged edges, the insoluble tensions.

By the door the mail piles up. I sit at the table leafing through a Praxis catalog: shiny kitchen taps, electric barbecues—things that don't feature in my life but needn't be at all expensive. Pearl lies on a mattress on the floor; J rolls a cigarette. He's come over for a cup of coffee, tells me about a job in South Rotterdam. He needs to put in a bid, recruit Poles, unearth batches of tiles. I'm so tired, I want to sleep by a garden lamp from Praxis that burns all night.

J jumps up: "Look at that child!"

In two strides he's at the mattress and he tugs the potato knife I was using to screw a candle into a candlestick yesterday out of her hands.

"Dammit, Ka, that's not a toy."

I look up from the garden lamps. Pearl cries. I stiffen. Shut my eyes for a journey through a mountainous landscape, fleeing in a carriage with a masked coachman.

Sometimes it seems as if the river is standing still, a mirror of the frozen moments in my head. In the cold, hard surface I see myself, changeless. After the morning with the potato knife J checks up on me, with unannounced inspections. I let him in; I don't want to disrupt the father-child relationship. Just seeing his hands on her is enough to recall his hands on me.

J counts how many diapers there are, how many jars are empty, makes shopping lists. He doesn't intervene; people ought to look at him first, since he's the father and from day one chiefly absent. I don't tell him that, and I do tell him by not letting anything go right.

A swan dives below the surface, swims three meters, its long neck outstretched. Comes up, shakes its head, paddles on, after the plastic bag. I stand by the river. Pearl is six months. I get no farther than our street. When I go shopping I buy as much as I can, stocking up in case J comes over. I manage to brave people's looks. I'm not afraid when they ask me how old she is. I calmly work it out, my smile a grimace, stuck to my face as if glued. Even when the greengrocer holds out an apple to her and she turns her head away. "She's tired," I say. I walk along the embankment with Pearl. People are moved. Such a pale young mother; such a fragile daughter. She has a deadly serious look. "An old soul," some say. My little Tibetan sage, an albino variant.

That Tuesday evening. Again I hold her tight. I've been sleeping badly lately because Pearl keeps waking up, with short, blood-curdling screams. I put her in the bath, so she turns rosy, gets in a good stretch tonight, leaves me in peace. I fill the bath with the thin jet from the shower, adding some oil that J has brought. It comes in a yellow bottle and it smells of babies, the way we want them to smell.

Pearl lies on the mattress in the living room. I check the water is the right temperature and then go downstairs to fetch her. She lies quietly waiting with wide-open eyes and looks at me calmly. Pearl can seem very resigned; I've sometimes looked into the bathroom mirror for an hour to see whether anything of that shows in my eyes. I lift her up, the small body of a young dog. She hardly moves, in some kind of half-sleep perhaps, or holding herself so much like a doll to avoid being a burden to me.

I let her slide from my arms into the bath, like a spoon in a soup plate, gradually, with dignity. Her head drops backward. Her hair spreads out, very light and fine. I step away and turn off the lights. A gentle evening sun shines through the top window onto the bathwater.

I close the bathroom door and take my raincoat from the hall-stand, although no rain is forecast. I pull the door shut behind me. Straight ahead, to the river—two streets to cross and I'm there.

TRANSLATED FROM DUTCH BY LIZ WATERS

family

MARITTA LINTUNEN

Passiontide

The first thing I saw was round, domed shapes: golden brown and pale yellow, smeared with egg whites and sprinkled with sanding sugar—dozens of little buns scattered before me.

My eyes then focused on the baking tray, which rested against a table leg, then on the egg mug, and finally on the rolling pin; the latter two lay on the floor in front of the oven. There was a discolored spot on the floorboards near my left shoulder: a shattered egg.

I took all of this in without understanding any of it, and then drifted off into a deep sleep once more. I woke up again, after an indeterminate period of time, to the same view.

I slowly inhaled and exhaled. It was rather drafty.

There was a crackling and buzzing sound from above my head, and then weak voices broke through the static.

A vein was throbbing at my temples. It produced, in short pulses, a blinding pain, which flooded first to the top and from there to the back of my head.

I raised and lowered my eyelids as if I were exercising.

I felt the floorboards against my bare stomach. I felt heat radiating from my left and a chill flowing past my right side.

Image by image, the scattered pieces were coming together.

Gradually, I recalled Miliza Korjus singing "Warum" just as I was about to put the second baking tray in the oven. They were taking requests on the radio. I liked to have it on in the background, more for the sound of people talking than for the music. The babbling portable radio on the kitchen table hailed back to the sixties, a little teak-cased companion.

It was good to have it in the kitchen: it produced human voices on demand, sweeping away the silence.

I recalled trying to hum along with it, when my hands suddenly went numb. The oven door opened on the wrong side, the dish cabinets flew for a moment against the opposite wall, and my back hit a sharp corner of the kitchen table.

I knew it had been Tuesday evening. The boy had called the day before and let me know that he would visit during the Easter break after all. He would come on Saturday, on the afternoon train.

Living alone, it was often difficult to start even small chores without someone else visiting. It was nice to clean, change the curtains, and for the first time in a long while bake for someone else, to plan meals for two. These days, the boy only rarely had time to visit.

My shoulders tensed with the cold. I must have left the living-room window open.

As I lay on my stomach, I realized that I could only move my right hand.

I could raise my head, turn it from side to side.

Feet—I could see that they were still there. That was all.

The crackle of static above me died away, and the voice of the radio announcer broke the silence in the kitchen:

The Maundy Thursday service will be broadcast from the Porvoo Cathedral.

Judging by the light, it was evening. Thursday evening. I counted out the hours, again and again, in disbelief. I felt like a fist was clenching around my heart.

Two days and nights had vanished into oblivion.

I moved my right hand, and felt it hit something rough, followed by a light blow to my shoulders. The broom. It had fallen out of the open cleaning closet to lie near me.

I seized the broom and strained with the last of my strength—the handle only just reached the power switch on the oven. I pushed as hard as I could: the switch moved, the light blinked off, and the overheated electrical appliance made a series of loud clicking sounds.

At least I wouldn't die in a fire. I might be able to get something to eat by dragging it in front of my face with the broom, but there was nothing to drink. Still, I might well survive until Saturday evening; I was in fairly good shape for a seventy-year-old. Unconsciousness would come before that, though.

My body shook with the cold. A wind was blowing in from the living room, and judging from the clatter of the roof tiles, it was storming outside. The oven had, until now, kept the kitchen warm, but now the chill from the living room spread throughout the entire house.

Take, eat; this is my body, which is given for you. Drink of it, all of you; this cup is the new testament in my blood, which is shed for you for the forgiveness of sins.

Each time, the priest emphasized the word "you."

I didn't go to church regularly, but now I fervently wished that what they taught there was true, and that I figured into the plan as well. That some invisible force knew what was happening on this street, in this small cottage, in this tiny, cooling kitchen.

The words of a hymn came from above me as I fell into a stupor.

The station broadcast classical music throughout the night.

Concertos, ballet, solo songs, arias.

I got sick of Beethoven's symphonies and the booming timpanis. I wished that the radio would get sick of them too, perhaps develop a malfunction. I would have preferred to lie there listening to the quiet hiss of static: the dead white noise of space.

Now it wasn't the cold that was making me shiver, but a fever. I only got thirstier after eating half of the closest bun.

The dry crumbs made me cough. It all felt unbearable: my shirt had rolled itself up into a ball under my chest, and my bare abdomen was soaking in the cooling urine that had spread under me. I'd gotten used to the acrid smell, but the fever chills continued unabated. They attacked without mercy—shook me awake every time I was drifting off to sleep. Disturbed dreams melded together into strange realities that threatened to ensnare my mind. The radio was my only compass: it dragged me back into the here and now, told me what time it was, and made me realize that I wasn't in a sunlit backyard pouring juice for a boy eating buns. It reminded me that the periodic screeching from above wasn't caused by swallows after all, but by my groaning tin gutter.

As dawn came, I struggled toward the spattered remnants of the egg. I stretched out my neck until I thought it would snap out of place. The tip of my tongue touched the egg white, and I lapped at it like a cat sampling desiccated jelly. I could only reach a few drops.

To pass the time, I read the only piece of writing that I could see from the floor: "Lemon Juice & Glycerin, citrus-scented hand lotion." I knew the ingredients by heart in both Finnish and Swedish. The words on that bottle of hand lotion drifted like a mantra through my muddled, fever-sick mind. Every now and then, I repeated them aloud.

Hearing my own voice, I knew I was still alive.

At some point I came to, startled from my sleep by the silence and the light streaming in from the window.

The music had stopped.

On the radio, the clock chimed noon, and I knew that I was in for the saying of the day. Someone read out a few aphorisms, but in my confused state of mind, they escaped comprehension. They seemed to form dichotomies: the first sentence stated something, and the next one refuted it.

What possible significance could they have? Thesis and antithesis.

A sea of speech and music washed relentlessly over me. It all sounded quite absurd. World news, domestic news, weather forecasts, traffic alerts—all the life of the world outside the cottage had become distant, unreal.

Had I really taken part in all that? What had been so important about it, I wondered, as I shivered in a cold pool of urine.

Had the life I'd been leading been, after all, someone else's?

The life of an immature person who was ignorant of all the essentials?

A shadow life directed by instructions delivered through radio broadcasts, magazines, letters?

Fear crept inside me, chilling my guts: I was growing numb, indifferent to my fate. Perhaps this was the apathy that preceded death. Was that why I had, after so many years, dreamed of Ilmari again?

I shifted my arm. It looked blue. Dead blood had started to spread from the elbow toward the wrist.

Ilmari died suddenly in the middle of lunch, after his fifth spoonful of cabbage soup. The man was gone so fast that he left his last sentence unfinished. I could see the rest of it in his eyes, while I waited for the ambulance. Ilmari escaped from our midst in such a hurry that it took the boy a week after his death to begin to understand that Dad would never again come to tell him goodnight.

Ilmari got lucky. Died without suffering.

That's what they kept on telling me over the years. I can't remember how many stories of slow human decay they've told me over the years to comfort me.

Necrotic tissue crawling with maggots, ventilators shorting out during blackouts, brain death, partial paralysis, paraplegia: endless stories of death by inches. All these they related to me in detail.

After telling their stories, they naturally expected me to nod and agree with them, to say that I was indeed relieved that Ilmari had been spared all that—relieved that I had been given the opportunity to wipe the cabbage soup off his chest and stare into his unblinking eyes and contorted mouth.

As for myself, a different fate had apparently been chosen for me. I would dry up faster than the bunch of tulips I had set in the vase. The tulips reminded me of the grave.

There was an empty stretch of grass next to Ilmari that I had reserved for myself. I hadn't quite brought myself to have my name engraved on the tombstone, though an acquaintance, a widow herself, had suggested I get it done right after Ilmari's funeral.

She was put out that I didn't, as I recall. I suppose I should have immediately crumbled into dust to join my husband. She even had the nerve to ask me whether I'd already found myself a new man, if a spot next to the old one wasn't good enough for me.

I told her that Ilmari's death hadn't robbed me of all my passions, particularly for life.

I just wanted to live for the boy, to raise him.

For years I sold handicrafts on the side. I knitted mittens, socks, hats, and woolen slippers, and deposited the money in the boy's bank account to accrue interest. I managed to accumulate several grand there, but the boy wouldn't take the money when he went off to school. There'll be time for that, he called out from the door. He even left a freshly baked loaf of bread on top of the coatrack in the foyer. He was a big man, ashamed to carry a sweet-smelling loaf in his bag.

I squinted my eyes. I suppose they would find all the papers, when the time came.

The will was in the bedroom, inside a drawer in the linen closet. The boy would inherit my savings, and the cottage along with its plot of land; the niece would get some memorabilia and the rose-patterned linen sheets I had made for her wedding. A wedding that never took place. A week before the wedding day, the girl found out that the groom already had two children and paid alimony for them from his small mason's salary.

Now there was a girl who lost her passion for life all in one go, and at the tender age of twenty at that. Dropped out of school, and settled down to become a dormouse for the rest of her life.

My vision was starting to go.

Anxiety weighed down on me, and compressed my lungs.

My heart beat like a drum in my ears. I gasped for breath, tried to gulp in as much life as I could. I wanted to last until Saturday, to see the boy one last time, to look peacefully at him for a moment, eye to eye.

I had to calm down, had to force myself to listen and stay conscious for as long as I could.

A middle-aged nutritionist, a young vegan girl, and an Orthodox monk from the monastery of Valamo were discussing the Lent fast in serious tones. After all, according to tradition, the fast was supposed to be at its most severe on Good Friday.

A time of quiet. Of avoiding travel. Of fasting. Asceticism. Abstaining from eating, drinking, and sexual intercourse.

The pit of my stomach started to twitch, and then my diaphragm. My larynx couldn't produce any words, merely a low gurgle that I realized was the sound of my own laughter. Urine trickled along my thighs in short, warm pulses.

I was being truer to the Passiontide than the inmates of even the most austere monasteries.

I had had no meat—not even a slice of pickled cucumber or a spoonful of sauerkraut.

Just half a dried-up bun, though even for that I had been punished with a painfully dry, parched throat.

No alcohol. What a joke—I would have given up my pension just to lick at the gall-wetted sponge that the soldiers had rubbed against Jesus' torn lips. I would have gladly lapped at any liquid: gall, vomit, even my own urine had I been able to reach it.

As for sexual intercourse . . . Who would even want to touch my half-paralyzed, stinking body?

I was observing the Passiontide, oh how well indeed I was observing it: I was having a real Passion of my own.

The urine stopped with my laughter.

I felt like crying out to Christ and Satan at the same time, felt like cursing the well-off know-it-alls philosophizing above my head, for whom life seemed to be full of options, full of choice.

My throat clenched shut, and then let loose a sob, releasing the stream.

Warm, salty liquid. A soothing rain from behind my own eyes.

I managed to lure a few tears into my mouth before they dropped to the ground: they tasted divine.

My mother's womb must have been full of tears when I floated there, safe in that warm sea, back toward which I was now starting to travel—sleeping, shivering, sleeping, shivering.

I heard the vegan girl raise her voice.

People should know the suffering of the caged fox, even if just for a moment. Know that cold, cramped space where the animal is forced to huddle until its death.

I sobbed, and was startled by the sound that tore itself from my throat. It sounded like the whine of a beast struggling to escape its prison.

The monk grew enthusiastic, and declared that the girl had just stated the meaning of Holy Week: how we should, through our own suffering, bear the pain of others.

I turned the other cheek to the floor and let loose another whine: a guttural sound that came deep from the pit of my stomach, as from a cave.

It was Sunday evening when they came.

They broke the lock, and immediately noted that the temperature was well below fifty degrees in every room.

They found my cold and unconscious body on the floor, but their first attempt to lift me fell through, because the youngest of the boys from the ambulance had to stop to vomit. He had noticed that the skin of my belly was peeling off, adhering to the floorboards. It looked like a pallid, urine-soaked scrap of dough.

Afterward, they all told me how clever I'd been, squeezing lotion into my mouth from the bottle of Lemon Juice & Glycerin that had fallen out of the cleaning closet.

That repulsive-tasting lotion and the minuscule amount of moisture in it had kept me alive.

But the tears, I stammered, but no one understood.

I woke from my long dream on Monday morning, and found myself in a hospital ward in the health center.

I whispered; that was all I was able to manage. The nurses couldn't make out what I was saying, and had to ask me several times. Finally they got it: please shut off the PA, which was blaring out an Easter hymn.

They soon had something to chatter about, as I told them, stiff-jawed, that the certainty of resurrection was all down to luck these days.

The light almost blinded me—the brilliant green and yellow tore at my pupils.

Ryegrass and daffodils.

There was an Easter bouquet from the boy on the nightstand.

Something had come up at work, and he'd been unable to make it. It wasn't the first time.

I stretched out my hand toward the flower arrangement. I closed my eyes.

The ryegrass stubble tickled the tips of my fingers. It reminded me of a boy, fresh from the barbershop. A little boy who always got a close trim, an easy haircut for the summer break.

TRANSLATED FROM FINNISH BY ARTTU AHAVA

DUNCAN BUSH

Bigamy

There was something in the paper this morning about this geezer, this lorry-driver, who had two wives, two houses, two domestic set-ups, and two batches of kids—six in all. One lot lived in Banbury and the other lot in Bedford. He'd kept this up for fourteen years, husband and father to two families, without either one knowing about the other and without anybody else knowing or suspecting what was going on.

Tony Pye started reading out the details for us.

"Christ," he said. "These bigamists. How do they manage it?"

It was our mid-morning break and we were sitting in the shed. He was reading Sunday's *News of the World*—someone must have brought in and it had been lying round the shed all week. Mike Buller usually brings in a *Mirror* or a *Western Mail,* and sometimes I buy an *Independent,* and they get passed around from hand to hand during our breaks over the day: eleven o'clock tea, lunch, and the cuppa we brew up in the afternoon in this cold weather, if we're working outside. But if nobody brings in a paper or today's is being read by somebody, and there isn't much talk going round, that old *News of the World* tends to get picked up. If only for another eyeful of that girl with big knockers and little knickers, giving you that panting look they have. Mouth open, eyes half-closed. As if you're just slipping it in.

Anyway, he was reading this piece about this geezer.

"See this?" he said. "About this bloke? Been running two wives? In two different places? Six kids? They reckon it had been going on for fourteen years. How the fuck do you keep two women fooled for fourteen years? I can't fool the one five fucking minutes."

He was sitting on the bench with his muddy wellingtons planted apart and his elbows planted on his knees and the paper open wide between his hands. He's a great man with a shovel, but there's something laborious about Tony Pye with a newspaper. You never see him double the pages back then fold them in half, to make it more manageable. Let alone fold them into a narrow strip of print like people standing in rush-hour trains. He holds it open like he's keeping it as flat as possible. Brings his hands together when he wants to turn a page. It doesn't even look as if he's reading it. More staring at it, furious blue eyes, like he's actually checking the layout and it's wrong.

But now obviously, on the fifth or sixth or dozenth time he'd picked this paper up, this one item had struck him.

"Six kids!" he said. "All his, it says. Four with one wife, two with the other. The oldest fifteen."

He looked up from the paper at us, one after the other.

"How the fuck do you manage to keep two households and six kids going?" he said. "On a lorry-driver's money?"

"Lorry-drivers earn bloody good dosh, these days," Mike Buller said. "Of course, you got to put the hours in."

He opened a corner of his sliced-bread sandwich, looked at the stained inside.

"Look at that," he said. "The slag. Call that a corned beef sandwich? More bloody Branston than corned beef."

He folded the sandwich into his mouth, chewed it, swallowed it in one.

Then he started talking about lorry-driving, how it was a job wouldn't suit him, stuck in a cab all day with all the stress of driving, because driving wasn't a pleasure, not with the traffic on the roads and motorways these days, he hated driving on motorways, especially in the rain, the other day he'd had to go up to Monmouth and he'd got on the M4 and it had started pissing it down, and all these big lorries, fucking juggernauts, throwing up all this spray, he couldn't get the wipers working fast enough see the fucking road ahead.

Tony Pye was still thinking about the bigamist. Looking at the story, anyway. Placid, but points of impatience stirring in his eyes. Waiting for Mike Buller to stop fucking talking. Which eventually he did.

Still, Tony said, picking it up again. Driving a lorry was the kind of job where you could get away with it. Having two women. In two different towns. Two households, even. Two gangs of kids. Because the fact was, as a lorry-driver you were always away from home. Being away from home *was* your fucking job. Simple as that. When you weren't with either one of the families, why would it occur to them you might be with the other? They'd think you were on the road. You could just say you had a trip to Spain coming up. Or Portugal. Or a run up to Dumfries. Whereas in fact you could be with your other family, and telling them you had the weekend off.

Mike Buller said *he* wouldn't mind having two women in two different towns. Or come to that, a dozen in a dozen. All about eighteen or twenty, like. But if you were *married* to them, like this guy in the paper, if you'd set up house and *home* with them, if you were the, like, *breadwinner*, you'd have to work every hour God sent to keep them households going. Just to get the rent paid and keep your kids fed and clothed and with shoes to go to school in. His kids were terrible on shoes.

"Nah," he said, "shagging two women sounds all very well. But you'd be too buggered from working overtime to manage it."

Tony Pye said he wasn't thinking about the shagging. What he was thinking about was, you know: say you were this lorry-driver. Wouldn't you get mixed up sometimes?

Mike Buller said, "What do you mean, mixed up?"

"Well," Tony Pye said, "what if you forget which house you're in, or which of your wives you're with? What if you call them by the wrong name? What if you get the kids mixed up? What if you start talking in your sleep?"

Mike Buller looked flabbergasted. "Why would you start talking in your sleep?"

"Well, you might," Tony Pye said. "And you'd never know you were doing it. Not if you're asleep. It's like snoring. You don't know whether you snore or not. Somebody's got to tell you."

But Mike Buller still wanted to know why having two wives and two families would make you more likely to talk in your sleep.

"I'm not saying it's *more* likely," Tony said, turning his eyes up as if to say, I'm talking to an idiot here. "Just that you might. You might call something out."

"Like what?"

"You might call out your wife's name. Only it's the wrong wife. It's the other one."

Mike Buller went dramatic, electrified like he'd been suddenly persuaded. Instant conversion.

"Hey, it might make you *walk* in your sleep too. You know, you get up in the middle of the night in your pyjamas"—he shut his eyes and held his arms out straight in front of him. "And you go downstairs. And open the front door"—he made out he was pulling a doorknob

with one outstretched hand. "And get in the lorry and start it up"—
eyes closed, lightly closed fists jiggling a steering wheel. "And drive
it all the way to Bedford. Or fucking *Banbury* of course. Depending,
you know, where you was to start with."

He laughed.

"You could end up *driving* in your sleep and all," he said. "You dull
fucker," he said to Tony. "Why should shagging two different women
make you talk in your sleep?"

Tony Pye ignored him. He looked at the yard through the bright
doorway, thinking it all out, all the details and permutations.

"You'd have to have two sets of clothes for a kickoff," he said. "Two
sets of shirts, vests, socks, underpants. One in each place. Two lots
of shoes. What if you wore the wrong clothes? Turned up in a shirt
or jacket your wife had never seen you in before?"

Mike Buller shrugged this off.

"You'd tell her it was new, you twat. You'd tell her you'd just bought
it."

"But what if she could see it wasn't new? What if it was an old
jacket you always kept in the other place, and you could see the wear
it'd had? What if it was an old pair of shoes she'd never seen before,
all cracked and scuffed and the heels worn down?"

Mike Buller shook his head, as if it wasn't even worth his while to
answer this.

"You just think about it," Tony Pye said. "My old lady knows more
about the state of my bloody clothes than I do. She could probably tell
you how many pairs of clean socks I got in my drawer. If a bloody sock
goes missing in the wash, she notices. God knows what she'd say if a
new one turned up. And what if one of these wives found something
in your pocket? Like an electricity bill for the other address? How
could you keep all them bills and paperwork from getting mixed up?
I can't keep up with one lot of fucking bills, let alone two."

"Yeah, but you're a fucking nincompoop," Mike Buller said.

But Tony Pye could see it all in front of him by now.

"And it's not just about paying two lots of bills," he said. He was getting excited, flecks of spit coming off his mouth. "Or having the money to. How could you keep all the other things separate? All those names and facts and all the things you've said and done? Over fourteen years? So you never once slipped up and said the wrong thing, or forgot which one of your families you were with or where you were? So you never forgot which kid had had mumps or a toothache or which set of kids you'd gone to Alton Towers with? So you never raised a whiff of a suspicion, in all that time? Never gave a clue to what was really going on?"

Tony Pye looked at Mike Buller, then at me, amazed blue eyes. He kept on looking at me. As if I was the fucking umpire. Because, well, I suppose, I was in charge and I'd been sitting there listening to all this and so far hadn't said a word. He took off the cap and scratched his head, his flattened white silk hair.

"It's hard to believe," he said. "That any man could be that bloody clever."

"Or any two women that fucking dull," Mike Buller said. He got up and stretched as if that was it, he'd had the last word.

Me, I looked as if I didn't know either way, and couldn't care. I looked at my watch.

"We'd better get back out there and do a bit," I said.

"Mike," I said when we got outside, "I think you'd better slip into JJ Williams's and get some more half-inch staples for that fencing. So we can get it finished off."

He probably thought it was favouritism. Cushy little trip in the van while the rest of us are working. But it was to get him off the job for an hour really. Because he's a tired bastard. And there's something about Mike Buller that grates on me. It always has. His manner, I suppose, and his big mouth.

Well, no: *who he is.*

Tony Pye went back to barrowing hardcore and I went to measure up in the old greenhouse. They say they're going to put a swimming pool there, once it's a health spa. It's a shame, the way the whole structure, all that Victorian ironwork, has just been left to rust, till the glass dropped out of the frames. A century of neglect. All it's good for now is scrap. Just bring a skip up and sling it in. With the old cast-iron guttering they stripped off the stables. All the crockets, or finials are they, along the roof. All the bars and hinged quadrants and winding mechanisms to open the top windows and air it. You'll never see ironwork like that again. *Made in Walsall, Staffs* stamped on it.

It was the First World War which changed everything in the up-keep of a big old place like this. I suppose for those four years there wasn't the labour. All the men and boys out in France and Belgium. Then a shortage of men for years after. And even for those who did come back in one piece, working on the big estate wasn't the same. Attitudes had changed.

Anyway, I paced out the distances. I didn't have my long tape. But three strides of mine are 2 metres 50 more or less exactly, so I knew I wouldn't be a lot out.

I was doing this, and putting the rough figures in my notebook, and thinking about the landscaping. But all the time I was thinking too about what Tony Pye had said. How a man could manage his life so as to not only marry two women, with all the complications *that* involved, but keep both of them without a clue of the existence of the other. For fourteen years. Whereas me, I'm not even married to An-drea, but I meet someone, I spend an hour sitting in a café with her, an hour nobody else knows ever happened. And Andrea senses it.

That something's changed. That I have.

Last night we were watching *Invasion of the Body Snatchers* on TV, the old black-and-white version. And it was that weird scene where the old feller, Uncle Ira, is mowing the lawn. By now most of the people in the village have been replaced by the aliens. Occupied's a better word. They look the same, sound the same, put on the same clothes, do the same things they've been doing every day of their lives. But they're different. It's not anything you can name or put your finger on. But they're not the same person. Something's died behind their eyes. The old feller goes on pushing the mower up and down, up and down, but you can sense he's an automaton. His eyes haven't exactly gone blank. It's not that obvious. But they're focused differently. What's blank's the brain behind them. It's waiting for instruction. He's not your grandfather any more, he's not a member of your family or even of the human race.

And perhaps that's how I looked to Andrea all weekend.

Distant. Different.

Lovesick.

And how I must have looked on Sunday when it stopped raining and we could get out. And we went for that walk, and the river was high and flat and the same colour as the mud in the puddles, this mass of water moving one way. And I stopped and I stood there staring at it falling over the lip of the weir like a long glassy fringe, and she must have been watching me. I don't know for how long, but she said:

"You've gone into it again."

I looked at her.

"Into what?"

"That trance."

"Have I? What trance is that?"

"The one you keep going off into."

"Oh," I said. "That one."

She was still staring at me.

"So what were you thinking about?"

There was a long moment. She was still watching me. I could see the flecks of her eyes. Then her pupils wobbled and widened, and I knew it was fear. And that's when I knew *she* knew. That second when she wished she hadn't asked, when she got scared that I was going to tell her.

BRANKO GRADIŠNIK

Memorinth

Soon after the Shangri-La episode I heard that Charley was at the old trauma ward. He had jumped out his bedroom window onto the green twenty feet below. His back was broken, but the spine remained miraculously intact. I went to visit him. He was tired but serene. He said: "I let Vitzliputzli out of his cage, because I felt sorry for him being behind bars all the time. He waited a bit and then he flew out of the window, so I followed." There was something tranquil and graceful about Charley's report, something surpassing the contentment of ordinary people. It wasn't suicidal oblivion that had sent him through his window; he hadn't been running away from figments of his imagination: his flight was just a metaphor, a substitute for all the angels that would hover in the golden windows of his icons if only he could afford the paint.

For no obvious reason, Mocca stopped using her litter box when she got older. My favorite librarian, Zdenka, was the only one who could offer an explanation: Mocca resented being inside all the time. So we started to let her out, hoping that nothing would happen to her in our apartment block consisting of several narrow interior courtyards. Zdenka was right: Mocca never took revenge on us again. But cats that stay at home all the time live an average of twelve years, while European alley cats usually die by the time they're three. Somebody out there gave her heavy-metal poisoning, and after three months of getting thinner and thinner, she passed away.

Charley's parents simply couldn't understand the rapture that began to shine through his writing. His father was an old-school policeman, his mother a simpleminded peasant picked up at some remote outpost of Yugoslavia where he had once served. Charley's idée fixe—that he could somehow make up for the absence of "The Absolute" in the world—made it impossible for him to hold down a steady job. His father procured various unassuming sinecures for him, but Charley was quick to declare each of these jobsites to be "Armageddon," and his fervor made him look quite aggressive, at times, even though he wouldn't harm a fly.

Crackle was the honorable descendant of many generations of white mice who had been trying in vain to flee from the labyrinths of the Department of Clinical Psychology at the University of Ljubljana. I was still pretty much a slacker—I'd been forced by Ivana's birth, two years earlier, to start earning my living as a translator, but I had no sense of discipline yet. That meant I had a lot of time to teach Crackle tricks. He'd run to me when I whistled, climb my trousers and jumper, and nibble a kiss on my earlobe. Then I'd get a kick out of scaring my drinking buddies— wannabe writers like myself—by pretending there was no mouse on my shoulder. I think that drinking, combined with my feeling of having been tricked into marriage, had a lot to do with me letting Crackle wander freely around the house. Once I went to take the plastic tub with Ivana's cotton diapers to dry out and so I had to open the bathroom door a bit. Ivana who was two at the time stood in the anteroom and was able to see Crackle at the doorpost. She shrieked: "No!" but I had already started to close the door. I pushed it open immediately. There was no blood. Crackle was able to pull himself out of the slit beneath the hinge. For a moment it seemed to me that everything would still be all right. But than he started spinning, once, twice, and then fell over, twitched, and became just as numb as me. Ivana was saying in the meantime—I hadn't even been aware that she could express thoughts like this, let alone that she could express them in a proper, temporal sequence, at only two years of age—"He is going to die . . . he is dying . . . he is dead . . ." It all happened just as fast as she was uttering those words.

After a few months of watching (we thought) a very forlorn Nibble, we decided to give it another shot and went and bought a new bride. We kept Linden (as Klemen called her) separated from Nibble for six months so she wouldn't get pregnant too soon—not really necessary, as it turned out, because we had been sold yet another male instead of a female. But they are still very much alive and reasonably fond of each other.

The only real difference, I think, between humans and animals, is that the latter will take their fate—whatever it might be—for granted. They share this naïveté—which humiliates and exalts at the same time—with small children. But animals (as well as children) are guided by the same free will that we humans claim was given solely to us—and which, when we perceive it in animals or in children, we disapprove of as nothing more than stubbornness. Aside from their usual, puerile faces, angels could as easily be given the faces of rats, fish, hedgehogs—the faces borne by Gothic gargoyles.

When Klemen and Ana were four years old, their much older half-sister Ivana got them an unannounced birthday present—a guinea pig. The twins showed it exemplary care, but the pet was weird, antisocial, and even prone to biting. As it turned out, this was because she was pregnant. She had a litter of three guinea piglets; we gave two to a friend of a friend and kept the third one as company for the mother, Chewy; but as it turned out, mother and daughter didn't care much for one another, and we had to separate them, giving each her own cage. Ana and Klemen started to cool off toward the animals pretty soon thereafter, and then I just kept looking for somebody, anybody, but nobody would take them. Once, I was on the brink of giving them away to the zoo, we even drove there, gave the cages to a caretaker who seemed really kind, but on our way out the cashier who knew me well enough asked if I was aware that there was no need for breeders just then. "Meaning what?" "Meaning they'll go to the, uh, *reptiliary*, sooner rather than later." Even the twins understood the implication, if not the word itself. We went back and took them home again. Three months later I persuaded the director of the same zoo to put our guinea pigs on display for a couple of weeks, and just when this period was almost up and we were getting desperate, another caretaker decided to take them both. From then on I kept on rejecting each new animal initiative with the unspoken sentiment that the twins could get a new pet when they were old enough to bury it themselves. Notwithstanding the fact that death of a pet endows a child with a sense of loss for which no amount of philosophical serenity can ever compensate.

If a man is doing nothing but sitting and typing, sitting and translating foreign words into his language, all those hundreds and thousands of pages are, after so many decades, liable to collapse at last into a single page, typed over and over so as to be illegible. When my father, a famous translator in our country, was over eighty-seven, his doctor prescribed him a gingko extract for his memory, but Dad had grown up during a time when it was seen as unmanly if you couldn't endure with as few fluids as possible, and so he was stubbornly declining to drink. Once, a year before he died, he expressed his regret that his beloved wife Katarina had been unable to find him a particular book he had been looking for. I'd had enough of this after a few repetitions and finally said to him, "Listen, Dad, why do you keep saying Katarina can't help? She's right here, standing in front of you, serving tea." And Katarina, who had preferred to remain discreetly silent in the face of Dad's mnemonic shortsightedness, mustered her courage and said: "Yes, Janez, here I am, don't you see me?" He eyed her carefully for some time and then shook his head: "Well, this sure is a puzzler. But you can talk it over with Katarina when she gets back." As he settled back, he inadvertently overturned the stack of books by his elbow, and the very one he'd been looking for was revealed. "Here it is! Open it at page seven, Branko!" "Okay, now what?" "Read it aloud!" "*The Master and Margarita.* So?" "What does it say below that?" "Translated by Janez Gradišnik." "You see? While everybody knows you did it . . ."

Where can a clever man hide what we now call religious mania and what used to be considered harmless zeal in the olden days? After five or six years apart—I had turned to other things, and wasn't really in contact with him; just sending, through a mutual acquaintance, some money on his birthdays—I ran into Charley on the street. He wasn't in good shape. His mother had died; his father, as an officer of the Yugoslav "occupational army," hadn't opted for Slovenian citizenship in 1991, and therefore became one of the "erased," losing his tenant's rights, his papers, his pension, his neighbors. He'd moved to Serbia and lost touch with Charley, who was thirty-five at the time.

Charley was living off his disability pension now. Since he'd been born in Slovenia, he didn't lose his tenant's rights. But living by himself was tough. He heard voices (one of them mine) and some of them were unpleasant. He couldn't write essays or even reviews anymore. I advised him to join the Franciscan order.

My oldest daughter Ivana was very attentive as a child. As a toddler of fourteen months, she'd started using a mysterious word: "moochi-goochi"—"Granny moochi-goochi not home," for example, and it took me a month before I grasped that this wasn't Japanese but an adaptation of the Slovenian word "mogoče"—meaning "maybe." Maybe! No wonder I was like an open book to her, even before she went to school—a feat I myself still struggle with at the age of sixty. Around 1976, my former wife and I had reached the stage where we argued openly, without even noticing Ivana's presence. At first, she tried to stop us, beseeching and crying, but later on she just retreated into drawing and painting in the corner. Once, we were fighting in front of some visiting friends. Ivana went out for a moment, and I remember wondering what for—she had never before separated willingly from us—and we called upon her to judge who was exploiting whom—was it me exploiting Mummy or Mummy exploiting me? Ivana just raised her little fist, clenched tight as if she had some candy hidden in there. But it was a carefully folded piece of paper and I read: "YU TWOO ARE XPLOYTIN ME NAU." She had only just learned how to make the letters, but she had me right there in the palm of her little hand. I would have cried if I'd been able to do so—but I wasn't, and I didn't, didn't, I didn't even give her a hug, upset as I was, I just carried on, and I never got her off her treadmill, and in spite of all her brightness, she kept treading and treading it until it got stuck.

There were many other animals that my family and I tried to keep, but ultimately failed with: Gigi, the gracious cat that followed Mitko to his bus stop every day and got hit by a reckless driver; Franko, my guinea pig that knew how to sing on my command and that my mother gave away while I was on my first holidays on my own; Huckly, my gerbil, who got so old—twenty-seven months!—that he finally went blind and became hemiplegic and had to be put to sleep, and then I met Charley, my high-school classmate, on my way home from the vet's, and because I couldn't speak I just showed him my receipt reading 1 GERBIL—EUTHANASIA—20 DINARS, and he said, "Why Branko, next time just tell your good pal here to help you out and I'll do it for ten!"; and when I was twelve, the moth with sodden wings, with burnt feelers, just because I was afraid of its markings, its glossy eyes, of fire, of wind and water, just because I was afraid, just because . . .

All of a sudden, the twins were ten. During the previous two or three years, they'd come along on visits—together with me and their mom—to our respective mothers at a home for disabled senior citizens, so I could no longer deny them the right to assume responsibility for a loved one. Preferably a cat, since they're suitably independent. Unfortunately, Klemen was allergic to cat hair. Okay, a small rodent then. I didn't want them to cry their hearts out after only a year or two, as would surely happen with mice or rats. The most long-lived rodents—up to nine years, I was told—would be degus, energetic but child-friendly squirrel-faced cousins of chinchillas. The twins loved the pair I bought them from the very start and cared for them wholeheartedly. But there were glitches. After two months, Klemen's Flickety died with absolutely no warning. In the morning he had been lively and happy; in the afternoon when they returned from school they found him cold and numb. After the initial shock and a suitable mourning period, we found a new mate for Ana's Nibble. She got pregnant. How proud Nibble was, fussing around the nest and bringing Figgy all kinds of seeds and rags to make it warmer! But after two days of agony Figgy died from exhaustion, in spite of all our efforts. Only later did I find a warning on the Internet saying: "Female degus can conceive frighteningly young, but get exhausted giving birth to large and rather developed litters, so it is advisable to keep them apart from males until they are at least six months old." Nobody had told us about this beforehand. The young ones, they died, still naked, still blind, but twittering long into their last night. I don't want to write about it.

The first kitten in our house was Mocca, brought by Mitko, my son from my first marriage, who was nine at that time. I suspect now that she was probably just a normal kitten, playful and naturally well disposed toward people, but our family had been living in such misery at the time that she was a constant ray of sunshine. I had just quit drinking, but kept on anesthetizing myself: whenever I wasn't translating or writing I was reading. Lying on the couch and holding a book with both hands, I wasn't able to play with Mocca—so she decided to teach me some tricks. She trained me, among other things, to fling a marble for her around the room. As a patient trainer, she ran after it every time, grabbed it with her teeth, and deposited it most considerately in my slipper so that my groping hand could find it there and throw it again. Oh, Mocca!

Then came the Shangri-La escapade: all at once, Charley went missing. His parents were so worried that they even went so far as to call me. But after a couple of days, there came word through diplomatic channels from India. Charley had flown there on borrowed money but was being detained at the Delhi airport because he didn't have a visa. It was then that his parents—who had to pay his fine and then repay his debt to a loan shark—decided he would be better off if he just stayed in the house. They employed a ruse at the beginning, asking him to record daily episodes of a soap opera (*Santa Barbara*, I think) while they were away at their respective jobs. I knew that half an hour's stroll would dispel Charley's swarming thoughts, at least until the next day, so I showed him how to set the VCR timer to record the show automatically every day. But as soon as Charley's father saw it, he couldn't stand the "timer set" icon flashing on the display. So while they were at work the next day I taped a small piece of black electrical tape over the icon—its surface area couldn't have been larger than a thumbtack. But Charley's father still couldn't stand the thought that there was an icon blinking invisibly underneath. And Charley's mother started to believe that I was somehow provoking her son (she never could admit to herself it was a disease). She accused me of stealing Charley's ID card in order to use it for some undisclosed, black-magic purpose. Next time she called she cursed my twins and I decided that I had to step aside, at least temporarily. As a parting gift, I bought Charley a dieffenbachia plant named Offenbach and a parrot named Vitzliputzli—let him have at least a bit of nature in his room, I thought.

I was terrified of dogs. I used to turn in any other direction as soon as I heard barking ahead. The last, the most humiliating panic came when my first wife was pregnant with Ivana: there was an Alsatian barging toward us over the neighboring Castle Hill slope, and I hid for a petrified moment behind her swollen belly. But with Ivana born, I mended my ways. I simply had to, for her sake, even if I was still a bit cautious. And when I started running, that was in 1986, even this vestige of fear went away for good. A few years after that, while visiting my mother to help her with groceries, she lagged behind as I entered the store. "What's the matter—aren't you coming?" She wouldn't say anything; just stood there like a child. I looked around—and there it was: the cutest Skye terrier possible, tethered to a radiator in the lobby, waiting patiently and peacefully for his master. And I saw, for the first time, even though it must have been obvious all those years: "It was you!" She'd always hid her fear behind mine. Grabbing the baby. Pulling it closer. Raising it into her arms. "It was our neighbor's dog," she explained at last. "It was on a chain, behind the courtyard fence, but so terrible that I had to run past it whenever I went by, and once I fell over and spilled all the milk!"

Labyrinths are good places to be, because you can so easily end up crossing your own path and finding yourself where you once were. A labyrinth might prove to be a giant lost luggage office. Like my dad used to say: "Things don't get lost. They just wait for us where we mislaid them." But there are no labyrinths in Slovenia. The one in the Chartres cathedral happened to be covered with congregational chairs when I was there in 1987, and now I can see on the Internet that it consists of a single, stony, straightforward path that, after having made some turns, ends at its center. It's a symbol of life, I read: nonsense—life can't be a yellow-brick road. It's more of a Cretan labyrinth, so complex, so secret that archaeologists still can't find it, despite having turned all of Crete upside down.

There was a brief period, even before the iconographic incident in school, when Charley tried his hand at writing. I'm sorry now that I didn't encourage him more. But his writing seemed too confused. You couldn't make head or tail of it. I repeated to him—paraphrasing Gardner, I think: "You'll have to switch to poetry. In fiction, one is as free as in poetry to erase one's tracks, so to speak, to offer one's truth as a puzzle, but after the reader has deciphered the clues and established a continuity—figuring out the causes and the consequences—there should be a story, and if this story isn't interesting, then no amount of juggling and smuggling will make it any better." But now I'm not so sure: if continuity means progression toward an end, what's the point of ever getting there?

"If you have an enemy, buy him a dog. I'm a businessman. I get up early in the morning in order to be the first to my office, but on my way out I always see my neighbor taking his dog for a walk on its leash, neither rain nor fog forestalling them. In the office, I pull some strings, make some arrangements, call some people, apply some grease here, some grit there, and lo and behold!—here I am, the proud holder of a controlling share in my neighbor's company. If he has a wife worth the effort I can even make love to her during my lunch hour—he'll be taking his dog for another stroll. In the evening, I lock up and go home—and I see my neighbor, the enemy, not knowing that his business isn't his anymore, that his wife is conquered, I see him huddling under his umbrella and trying to persuade his dog not to step into a puddle . . ."

Alcohol: it can brick up some passages and open up others. The last time I was drunk was at the general meeting of the Slovenian Writers' Association in the autumn of 1982. The New Year was closing in, there were some bottles of fine pinot . . . and all of a sudden, I found myself sitting next to my wife in the movie theater (the "Commune," as it was called in those days), wondering aloud, more and more horrified, why it was that nobody wanted to lend a helping hand to a man struck by lightning—it was a scene from the movie *Victor, Victoria*, and was supposed to be funny, except that I was too drunk not to take it seriously. I'd had a total blackout. Years later, a colleague of mine who collaborated with me on writing a comedy proposed that we put in my "famous 1982 Christmas meeting-of-the-SWA speech." "My what? I don't remember anything of the sort." "You gave us a very passionate and very funny ten-minute speech." "On what?" "On your late lamented white mouse—or maybe it was a rabbit, we couldn't tell." "At the SWA meeting? Why didn't you people stop me?" "We knew better. Yes, you kept on smiling and talking in a soft voice, but your eyes were on fire and we knew that you would lunge at whoever would try to take the floor, and tear his or her jugular out with your incisors . . ." What I tried to hide behind my laughter was the realization that, for so many years, poor Crackle had had no place in my thoughts—or, rather, that in order to let him resurface this once, I'd needed to let my mind go completely blank.

The Franciscans said Charley should present a "medical certificate" before they'd let him in. He was allergic to maneuvers of this kind because they had been used on him so many times before. (The civil authorities, for instance, had let him attend driving school, do all the work, take the paper part of the test, pay for the whole affair, and only then they'd ask for his "certificate.") I assumed this would be the last straw, so I suggested that he should wait at least until the end of the world—it would be stupid not to be present at such an occasion, I said. Armageddon got rescheduled, though: first into 2002, then into the next year, and so Charley carried on.

We have a dog now, a border collie by the name of Ferris. His owner is nominally Ana, who reminded me when she was nearing her thirteenth birthday—October 2009—that I had promised that the degus would only serve as a temporary test of her maturity in terms of caring for pets. I say nominally because Ferris doesn't recognize his ownership by anyone—he takes himself to be a family member with (at least) equal rights. His father was a blue-eyed, his mother a black-eyed bicolor. Ferris was number seven, the last of the litter. The first six were divided evenly, as far as eye color: three of them came out blue-eyed and three of them black-eyed. Since Ferris was the odd one out, one of his eyes is pitch-black, the other sea-blue. And this blue one used to upset me, because combined with its drooping eyelid, it gave Ferris an air of drowsiness, even of ennui—and yet he was never idle, never uninterested. A few days ago he came up—he's now eight months old, nearly grown-up—to my desk and laid his chin on my right elbow, as he does when he thinks it's high time for us to take a walk. But I just had to translate the sentence I was working on to the end—I always do that so I won't lose the thought, even when they tell me that lunch is being served or that a movie has just started—so Ferris flashed blue from under the drooping eyelid, snapped up a Russian book on the table, and ran off with it. And then it came to me as a bolt out of the blue: "This eye, this eye! I thought I knew it from somewhere, and now I see at last—it's my dad's eye, of course." It was my father, telling me not to repeat his sin of doing the same thing again and again. And even though border collies are a working breed, we get out every day and do nothing more strenuous than walk into the woods and through the fields, and chase away the occasional crow, and cross over the swollen brooks, me jumping over, he swimming, and run with wolves.

Charley was one of those accommodating children who keep on trying to meet their parents' expectations—until the last moment when, right in sight of a goal, they fail. During graduate exams in art history he had a terrible fight with his professor about the Immaculate Conception. The row escalated until Charley swept the good Professor M.'s iconographic diagrams out the window and walked away—forever, even though the university turned a blind eye toward this escapade. In a brilliant whim, he decided that he would be a painter (he had never painted before in his life) instead

of, as he put it, a "fart-history professor." This same sense of resent-
ment incited him to start writing art criticism too. As a critic he also
became a staff member on the arts magazine for which I worked a
few short years as an editor. But his critiques were becoming increasingly complicated, and through his progressions of abstract geni-
tives ("the impact of the plasticity of colors limited by the chasm of
the frame of the picture") one could discern more and more of something Charley called the Absolute.

I've been trying now for a few days to unsort these memories, give
them freedom, but they don't want it. However I toss them around,
they seem to have a tendency to get back in line. Early things told
late seem to bring revelation; late things told early seem to forebode.
It makes me think of Dad's theory of relativity: "Things that seem to
be difficult from afar prove to be not so difficult when you approach
them, and things that seem to be very simple from afar get much
more complicated close up."

I don't believe Charley was violent, ever, but they forced him to
check into a local psychiatric institution for a few weeks. Medication
straightened the flamboyancy of his thoughts somewhat, but still he
tended to—during some chance meeting—raise his voice in a tirade
against the moral decay of humanity, and he still used to visit the
Franciscan brothers and try in vain to engage them in discussions as
to why they'd renounced their former poverty. He still painted, but
his initial, uncertain *art informel* gave way to Orthodox-style icons.
His parents were upset, not only because of the Absolute, not only
as members of the Communist party, but because of the high costs
of the golden paint shining around the girlish faces of his angels,
divulging the faces' probable points of origin.

In 2006, in a cornfield near Villach in Austria, I finally stumbled upon a vast maze made as it should be, with unforeseeable deadends and trick passages that landed you back where you started. But people—as people do—had smashed passages through the wavering walls, and since the children making up our expedition were tired from their visit to Minimundus—the Klagenfurt park with miniscule models of various wonders of the world—I gave in to their demands and we snuck out through an illegal gap. It was there that I got the idea for a game. I had it all figured out. I even had a name: it was to be called *Memorinth*. You just write down fragments of your memories in paragraphs and number them according to a random sequence obtained from the family bingo spinner. Then you carry out the necessary textual switcheroo, following the numbered balls' instructions, and at last denumber the paragraphs. The resulting sequence should be both unexpected and obvious, just like dreams, or madness, or life.

Thank God—there must be a gene that makes people ascribe good luck to Providence—in 2005, Charley met some orthodox monks who were in Ljubljana for the Ecumenical Convention. They looked pretty much like him. When he approached them, they cheered him: "*Hristos voskres!*—Christ has arisen!" They had assumed that his long, disheveled beard was a sign of humbleness in the face of God, not the slackness one succumbs to after years and years of being fed with antipsychotics. And when he started to tell them about the Heavenly Jerusalem, the one who was from Ukraine pushed a pamphlet about his monastery into Charley's raised hand. A few months later Charley received the hegumen's summons and affidavit so that he could get the necessary visa—and now he's a monk. He sent me a letter: "Everybody here knows that the world is coming to an end. Nobody talks unless what he has to say is of the utmost importance to God. The monastery life is a very silent one. And this is good, because, you see, there's a *solovey*, a nightingale, singing in the garden." And out of the watercolor painting he had enclosed, an angel with outstretched wings sings to me through its beak.

When Crackle died, Mitko hadn't even been born yet, even though, following my premonition, the poor mouse took part in a short first-person story of mine, "Mouseday," about the author and his two kids who, while gathering chestnuts, discover the skeleton of a mouse. The children start to form simple animistic concepts as the narrator tries to placate them, arguing that "a mouse can't die because it has no consciousness—it's immortal, in a way." But the truth is that I had, in presence of desolate Ivana, who was too small to dig, buried Crackle under a poplar on the grassy embankment right in front of our bedroom window. There, not in the woods, is where his bones rest. There we can visit and mourn him almost every day while I'm hanging out Mitko's diapers to air on the manila rope stretched between the creaky trees.

TRANSLATED FROM SLOVENIAN BY THE AUTHOR

MARIJA KNEŽEVIĆ

Without Fear of Change

My name is Mariana. Though not always. I was actually christened
Mira. That's the name I got from my parents. Like the love that I'm
sure exists, and my religion too. Almost everything else is work.

In my working life I'm the heroine of the telenovela *Always and
Forever*. There I'm the daughter of a rich building contractor—
spoiled and difficult Mariana, as the producer described me. Even
as soon as Episode 3, people started calling me Mariana—family and
friends included. Now we're up to Episode 186, which will be broadcast tomorrow. I don't even think of the name Mira any more, except
today when I'm writing to you, and I'm writing because I'm feeling
down, I need to bitch about things. There's no "irrational" reason for
this confession. This is my story, remember—me writing about myself and how I see things. I don't care if anyone likes it or not. I feel
I've been obliging to others all my life. Now I want to do something
for myself. Or at least be obliging to myself. Like with this story. That
shouldn't be too difficult, I don't think.

My father's name—I mean my father on TV—is Max. Like I said,
he's a successful businessman. He runs several of the best-known
building firms in our small but wealthy republic, cooperates closely
with foreign partners, never comes home, makes heaps of money,

and enjoys himself. In addition to my mother, my brother, and me—that's starting with the knowns—he also has a lover, Juliana, which was revealed in Episode 28. We didn't know about her before that because the producer chops and changes things at random. Obviously a developer has to have a steady and reliable mistress, so that was decided on the spur of the moment, on the cusp of shooting that episode. You know how things work these days. They have to be done quickly, on the double. We know the next three episodes at the most. If you haven't acted in this kind of show before—never knowing what's going to happen at the end of the week—you just can't imagine how tense it is.

The producer only came up with Juliana in Episode 20. I didn't hear a word about her until the day we started shooting. My "real-life" father's name is Nenad. Until recently he worked as an engineer for a well-known firm that produced those huge pipe sections for oil pipelines—an export giant that paid high salaries. My mother, my elder sister, and I lived in the lap of luxury, as they say. At least that's how we see it now. Several years ago the company collapsed. I didn't understand why. Sure, Dad explained it to me, but I'm chronically exhausted from shooting the show and wasn't concentrating properly. Besides, his distress was so immediate that it distracted me from the details—it became the only focus.

The laid-off employees were paid a kind of "compensation" for a while—I remember that much from what he told me about the Crash. But after that there was nothing. They had the option of retraining or saying good-bye. The company was bought up by a guy who had immigrated to Australia and then come back (talk about crude and arrogant—I saw him once and once was enough) and turned it into a workshop for making tracksuits. Being fifty-two, my father decided to stay on at the factory. Now he works in the zipper department. The boss rarely speaks to his workers, and when he does it's in an uncouth mixture of rusty Serbian and bastardized English. The pay is terrible. That's how I came to be on TV, to cut a long story short—I was in the middle of my second year in Oriental Studies when my father got demoted to a zipper man.

All right. So why am I complaining? (I'm WHINING, to be honest, but you haven't heard anything yet because we're still at the beginning of the story.) I should say right away that I'm not sure. It's quite possible I simply can't express it—I rarely have to express things like this, all on my own. And perhaps I don't know exactly how I feel. I'm hardly one of those professional writers who can churn out a column a day. Nor have I ever written any letters to the editor, though I'd have a thing or two to say like everyone else—I just haven't got the time. I keep a diary that I write in when I get around to it, and once or twice a year I write a letter to someone or other. I'm not even an actress, really. I'm a CHARACTER. Are characters allowed to complain? I guess most things are allowed, these days.

I'll get right to the thick of things, I guess, because I can't keep track of where they begin and where they end. My life is a tangle. So let me start with the situation at home. I mean the home in the serial, which is mostly where I live. Way back in Episode 53—just to remind you, because I easily forget old episodes myself, and also for those who hate soap operas and have never seen the show—my TV-father was nominated for mayor. And was elected in Episode 55. Since then it's been impossible to talk to him. He's all wrapped up in being a politician. I can't tell you how much he gets on my nerves with his fake patience, persistent smile, and his constant squint when I'm telling him something. He says he understands EVERY-THING! Even without words—he's a master of empathy! What a superman! Not to mention that I now have to schedule any talk with him via you-know-who—Juliana. Though, to be fair, she's changed a lot, starting as early as Episode 70. That surprised us all. At first Juliana was just an ambitious secretary who used any means necessary to get herself more money, and through money, influence (or vice versa). But when she accomplished what she was striving for, something in her changed fundamentally, which you might have noticed in the famous scene where she talks to herself in the mirror. She began to reflect on the meaning of life! She reads a lot and has deep and meaningful thoughts. No one expected this change in the slightest, not even the producer. As it turns out, Juliana is the only character who's really able to listen. Rushed productions can be like that.

Where was I? Oh yes, my father—he rarely appears in scenes with his family. And when he does, he puts on that slick, mock-calm voice, always with the same intonation, and the first and almost only thing he says is: "So what seems to be the problem? We can sort it out, let's just be rational." Ugh, I really get furious when I hear that! My father drives me up the wall.

My brother and I still put ourselves through it, though, unlike Mother, who gave up long ago—she burns through money, has one boyfriend after another, a girl or two as well, and drinks more and more. Father assumes the pose of a patient listener (the preparations for this waste half an hour of shooting time!), then he just stares for an endless minute, or a minute and a half, mostly at my brother Mario and me, "listening" in silence the whole time until he's sure we've run out of steam, only to say, in the end, "I'll have a think. Don't worry, we'll get it sorted out." Always the same phrase over and over again!

It must drive the audience around the bend too. But the producer sticks to this phrase and won't allow anyone to do so much as complain, let alone rebel and demand a change. When we finally have the next "appointment" with our father he politely asks us to refresh his memory: "What were we talking about again last time?" And when we've told him, he says, "Sorry, I'm just a bit too busy. Of course I remember. Don't worry, we'll get it sorted out."

In Episode 71 my brother Mario got into an accident in his Porsche and for the next seven episodes kept us guessing as to whether or not he was going to wake up out of his coma. Before the crash he'd been up to everything you expect from someone with that mindset: he broke up with his girlfriend (who I knew from Oriental Studies; I helped her join the cast because her parents had also been ruined), got into a fight in a bar, and drank and snorted all the time. The shots of the speeding ambulance were intercut with three or four living-room and swimming-pool scenes. Mario survived, woke up in the best clinic in the world, and resolved to change his life radically. He saw the accident as a "sign from God," as he told the nurse, who he married in the next episode and now has two children with—a boy and a girl. I just want to say that I've realized how important symmetry is for this story. It looks like I'm learning to write after all. Who would have thought!

Anyway, Mario started work in one of Father's firms and, unsurprisingly, began easing himself into politics. All these things happened terribly quickly, I don't know exactly how long it took, but it was fifteen episodes at the most. Now, from today's perspective, it seems to me that my brother has always been like he is now. He's so taken up by himself and his business that we hardly ever see each other—except when he has to lecture me about a boyfriend who's "below our level" or will "ravage our finances," and when, once a week on average, he has to declare: "It's about time you grew up and decided what you're going to do with your life." Oh no, just like Dad! He keeps repeating the same phrase over and over.

Now back to me a bit. Mariana can't grow up and really decide what she's going to do with her life. If she did, the character of my brother would be seriously threatened. The producer keeps postponing my maturity because Mario, in so-called private life, is his boyfriend! He's madly in love. I overheard it when he confided in our stylist and told her he couldn't live without Mario, he'd kill himself if their relationship failed, etc. So here I am, it's almost Episode 180, I do all sorts of shit, get myself into crazy relationships, have one part of my body pierced after another—not to mention all the tattoos; I spend money like it's going out of style, go home less and less, and never before noon; then I sleep until evening, go out clubbing late at night, and that's it. In other words, my character is stuck in a rut just so that Mario can develop. As my father Nenad's boss said: "Life just ain't fair."

But changes can still happen when you do everything to prevent them. Life has its own script. You see, when our producer's wife found out about his affair with Mario she got over the "shock" with suspicious ease and immediately began blackmailing her husband: either he put *her* boyfriend into the show or she'd file for divorce and take the house! That sure kicked his ass into gear! It's amazing how quickly the tables can turn—everything is easy when it has to be.

It's obvious that if she initiated divorce proceedings she'd get more, much more out of her husband, given society's attitude toward gay couples, even though researchers claim that opposition is on the wane. Every society prides itself on being free of prejudice and holds aloft the banner of Justice, as tattered as it may be. But the unwritten laws are still there. The producer knows he'd be up shit creek—and penniless. So that's how the show suddenly got a new character in the person of Emil, who went on to become Mariana's great love, or rather mine. The producer had to see to it that Emil stayed in the show through till the end, otherwise—his wife put her foot down—it was good-bye to the houses, cars, and bank accounts.

Thanks to Emil I stayed too, I only just scraped by, because there were already whispers in the dressing room that I'd soon jump off the top of one of Father's buildings.

Emil and I love each other with a vengeance. Our love scenes last up to seven minutes! He doesn't have a family—or, to be exact, his parents divorced long ago and each emigrated to a distant country with a new partner. He hasn't been in touch with them for years, and his being an only child only strengthens our relationship further. My family went nuts in Episode 188 when I announced that I wanted to marry him.

"That's absolutely reckless and irresponsible! Can't you see he's just a lazy bum who wants to get his paws on our money?" my father Max said. "That's right!" Mario chimed in. "That guy of yours is a longhair—he's into music! What are you going to live on? Have you bothered to ask yourself that, or are you counting on our assets?" My mother Orleana, as usual, took a good swallow of whiskey and lit a long cigarette before saying anything. Then she launched into a long monologue about how she'd asked around about Emil and found out that before me he'd been seeing a rich girl who he jilted when her father went bankrupt. In the interim, she inhaled before continuing, he'd had one lover after another, so many that Emil lost track himself. She barely made it to her closing statement—"He's just a grubby little gold-digger!"—because twice during her monologue she had to pour herself some more whiskey. (Not juice or water with food coloring, but real whiskey.)

This scene of our broken family coming together will be in Episode 189. The producer wasted no time. He found a powerful backer in the upper circles of society—who knows how—there are all sorts of rumors but I don't want to talk about things I'm not sure about. Some say it cost him a lot of money, others claim he hooked up with a gay clique. Whatever really happened, he managed to arrange it so that he would be able to keep almost all his money if it came to a divorce. After having protected himself in this way he rushed down to tell his wife and Emil. He yelled and screamed so much that the audio engineer, who happened to be at their house at the time, heard it all. I think he was fixing the stereo in the massage room, perhaps six doors down from the living room. That same day the engineer passed on the gossip to the whole *Always and Forever* team, and since then—the day before yesterday—all us characters have been scared out of our minds.

If Mario's hired killer manages to weed Emil out of the serial, several of us are bound to end up without work. Because that sort of tragedy will probably drive me to the top of one of Dad's buildings—and you know the rest. Emil's former girlfriend, who used her connections to hound him throughout the storyline, will then no doubt drop out of the script. The big question is what will become of my mother Orleana, who happens to be best friends with the producer's wife. There are too many dramas in our show already for anyone to worry about her personal problems. She had to have her stomach pumped several times in a relatively short span of time—be it due to alcohol or pills or a mixture of both. The simple truth is that all the good suicide scenarios have been used up. My father Max even came out with a new phrase: "Damn it, if you don't change your attitude soon, I don't know what will become of you!"

Things are pretty desperate at my real home. You've probably re-alized by now that we're all living on just my pay. My father Nenad has completely withdrawn into himself—he comes home late, sometimes he skips a night and only comes back after two days, and our neighbor Goca once found him—entirely by accident— watching my show in a café near the zipper workshop. My mother's stopped leaving the house at all. Until now she at least went to her therapy sessions and largely cooperated in the treatment of her agoraphobia—or so her doctor said. She was able to go down to the store and to her friend's place, which is several streets from our building—albeit under medication, though the doctor said even that was an improvement. But then she had a total meltdown. Now she sits in front of the TV all day and only turns it off when it's time for the show with me, her daughter Mariana, to come on. My sister is still holding up pretty well, at least compared to the others. She took on a job at the Orlando School of Foreign Languages (I was about to say "of Executive Escorts"), which she initially declined when the lady manager pointed out that the pay wasn't much but she'd develop useful contacts with VIPs. She didn't have much choice. So now she's investing in her wardrobe for a few months—long enough so that the clients don't see her in the same clothes twice. She promised she'd support us later if we don't find a new character for me.

Let me get to the point.

I want to keep my story short, but you'll appreciate that I had to tell you all this so you could understand what I'm trying to say. It's so damn complicated that I can hardly get my head around it myself. When I settle down, and I guess that will happen one day, I'll write a whole book about it, like normal people do. But until then I want you to grasp at least the basics of the plot.

The gist of it is that instead of falling into some kind of depression myself when I found out about Emil's fate, I somehow calmed down. It's strange, terribly strange. I just can't explain it, and that's what worries me. It's not just that I felt this inner calm that I hadn't ever known before, but it gave me a real boost too—absolutely incredible! For the first time since I had to drop out of uni, the words "So what?" came out. My voice was flat. Finally things no longer depended on me. Not that they ever really did, if you've followed the story, but I had to live believing that I was important. Now I don't have to anymore.

I don't know where to go from here. I'm not used to this sort of serenity. Is it a health issue or a serious illness that might not manifest itself until later? Do you need pills for it? The problem is that I don't feel any problem. Can you live life like this? I don't know.

I keep on saying "I don't know," I realize, but I really and truly don't know. Nor do I understand why I've forced myself to tell you all this when I don't feel like it at all. I think I know what you're going to say, what everyone says these days: "Let's wait and see." No one has time for anyone, and everything gets put off into the indefinite future. That way no one can accuse you of having bad intentions. But honestly, I hope the story will go on. I don't know why—I just feel there will always be a "to be continued." Isn't that the way of the world?

In tomorrow's episode—I'm letting the cat out of the bag here—my father Max will say: "I've done all I could, and it's all been pointless. Now it's up to you to sort things out!" My brother Mario nods victoriously in approval. You can imagine the rest. But here I am, going out walking and enjoying the morning sun. It's September, I haven't mentioned that: the mornings are crisp—just right—the days not too hot, and the nights are pleasant for sitting in the garden. Shooting is in the afternoons, and afterward I go down to the quay. I've already met a few of the regulars out walking and we have a nice chat. Soon I'll be able to spend as much time there as I like. I wouldn't be surprised if I forget that the show ever existed.

The river is a marvel. Water, as such. When you look at it—it's enough just to look at it, you don't have to touch it—you sort of gather yourself and become one again without the slightest effort.

It's soothing. It's scary just how soothing it is. I'm afraid of being happy with such simple things. Then again, "afraid" isn't the right word. How could I be afraid in my words and in life? Anyway: let's wait and see.

TRANSLATED FROM SERBIAN BY WILL FIRTH

home

PATRICK BOLTSHAUSER

Tomorrow It's Deggendorf

The train stops and you get off. Nothing else you can do, end of the line. Your suitcase is heavy. *Sort of like back then*, you think to yourself, *when I went away*. The station has hardly changed since those days. Twenty-five years and nothing different worth talking about. Same scene every visit. A bar for lost souls, a kiosk that usually—like now—is of no help at all to passengers because it's never open during the hours it says it is, and a public john where the same—*even if they're not the same*, you think to yourself—the same pearls of wisdom are plastered on the once-white tiles over the urinals. Such as ANOTHER BRICK IN THE WALL, or I CAN'T GET NO SATISFACTION, or the ultimate in classic latrine humor, at least in the Men's, which leads directly to the question, what's on the wall in the Ladies', not this gem for sure: DON'T LOOK AT THE WORDS THAT BEFORE YOU STAND. BEHOLD THE JOKE THAT'S IN YOUR HAND!

Your suitcase isn't the same and you ask yourself, *How many suitcases have I ridden to death since then?* But it's a *suitcase* that contains basically everything you own, just like when you first headed out *into the big wide world*—you can't help letting your thoughts connect with what twists your mouth into a slight sneer, though that's something you can't see because there isn't any mirror, none over the sink you're washing your hands in, the same way you did back then and the routine's been the same ever since. You give in to that sneering smile for a moment, feel the abyss lurking behind it, and go out. You pop into the ladies' john, not really voyeurism on your mind but—as the current lingo puts it—"Gender Studies," comparative latrine linguistics, and you're blocked by a kid running at you to hug you, only half succeeding, at hip level, and so you discover to your embarrassment that your fly's open.

"Uncle, Uncle, we've come to pick you up! In our new car!" You're too taken by surprise to say anything or do anything, no affectionate gesture, no stroking the kid's curly, reddish blond hair, and you can't even pull your zipper up gracefully, so you just stand there, immobile, like a pillar of salt; then the kid takes your hand and shows you the way to your brother.

It's the first time Robert has picked you up at the station, and he hadn't prepared you for this premiere. And so the last time you talked to him on the phone you'd only given him the bus's approximate time of arrival, the bus that—as usual—was to bring you from the train station. He must have gone ahead and figured out which train hooked up with the bus you said you'd take, which isn't a problem thanks to the Web, but it was nevertheless a tricky move you wouldn't have expected from him. And so now here he is, arms folded, and with an expression on his face that's hard to read, and you ask yourself, *Do I detect a trace of brotherly pride there?* Your greeting is, as usual, a mutual nod of the head, as if there were no other way to do it, since of course your hands are occupied by your suitcase and the kid's hand, and your brother's hands aren't available because they're folded over his chest. You get no answer to your question, *What have you done to deserve this honor?* but instead you get a heads-up that your fly's open.

He doesn't waste words on the extent of your luggage, which might well seem suspicious to him—the big, heavy suitcase and the stuffed shoulder bag, though you're only spending one night at his place. *Maybe he's happy,* you think, *that I've got a lot of luggage because it shows off the huge size of the trunk* that he opens with an inviting gesture, *the first important thing to notice,* and you know you've got to say something about the car.

"Big," you say, "comfortable," you add, after sitting down on the black leather passenger's seat, and "amazingly quiet" after you've been moving along for some time. And it's actually true: the car *is* big, comfortable, and quiet, at least when you're in it, but it also belongs to the class of vehicles you wanted banned not so long ago when you signed that petition for a referendum about it.

"I've only had it a few days," your brother says and points out the factory-built features. "Special trim. Only in the States. Feel that power?" he asks, and pushes down on the gas pedal.

"Yes," you say, faking delight, your eyes glued to the dash and fixed on the fuel gauge because you're firmly convinced that the gas supply will noticeably sink with every increase in speed. The dash is trimmed in reddish brown wood, the same as part of the door covering, and you hope at least it's not mahogany.

"What CD do you want to listen to?" your brother asks, but he doesn't mean you, he means the kid.

"The one with the old man." the kid says.

"Which old man?" your brother asks.

"The one with all that wood," the kid explains, and your brother gets it.

"Oh, *this* old man," he says, pressing a button. "This works the CD changer in the trunk," he explains, and you fear the worst. Some god-awful, stupid comedian or Peter Maffay's kiddie kitsch. But from the very first note even you know which old man was meant.

"Good choice, my boy!" Your brother is so pleased. "That's real music!" And you concede the point, though you haven't heard this music for half a lifetime, not since one of your rituals was to smoke a joint on the stairway to heaven with Led Zeppelin ringing in your ears.

Back then you walked in your brother's footsteps. He was the model rebel for you; he'd bash his head against the wall in front of you just so you could imitate him. But when it was your turn to strut around chasing after freedom in a leather jacket, jeans, and cowboy boots, all in black of course, your hair long and stringy and your eyes red from smoking pot all the time, that's when he didn't believe you were serious; he even went so far as to think you were fucking with him. Still, you kept on acting like that for a while until you found another role and another and still another. And wound up making acting out different roles into your profession.

Rebellious brothers way back then, you think to yourself, *but today one of you drives a car the ad men say typifies independence and individualism, while the other is standing at the station with nothing in his hands but his suitcase. That's just the point!* you keep thinking, feeling a twinge of revolt. *But freedom's just another word for nothing left to lose, that's what Janis Joplin used to sing!* A second later you're thinking that freedom, if it's to deserve that name at all, should be spontaneous, and that's hardly going to be you in the near future.

"Tomorrow it's Deggendorf!" you say to yourself in a soft voice. "The community center in Deggendorf!" you mutter, but the leaden Zeppelin makes your words inaudible to the others.

Your mother beams when she sees you but stays seated. *Like she's already exhausted by late afternoon,* you think, *and too tired to get up right now, even though she's having a coffee.* You give her a hug and feel how emaciated her body is, how frighteningly thin, no, fragile she's become.

"How much did the train cost?" she asks you as soon as the hug's over and reaches for her purse. "Is a hundred enough?"

"Mom, I don't need any money for the train." You try to fend her off, but you've already got the bill in your hand.

"Then give it to the barber!" she counters in a friendly voice, and her smile renders you speechless. *I'm forty-three years old,* you think. *Can somebody please tell my mother that?* You'll slip the bill back into her purse surreptitiously as soon as she goes to the john.

Meanwhile your brother out on the patio has fired up the grill and is already having a beer.

"Come on, Uncle, I've got something to show you!" The kid grabs your hand and drags you into the garden. *Here's where I'd like to have grown up,* you think to yourself, and not for the first time. *A house with a large garden, surrounded by meadows and woods.* Your brother probably sees it the same way; after all, he's willing to work his butt off for this house, so much so he hardly has time on the weekends to enjoy this refuge.

"This is my snail collection. You can eat the big one! Daddy said so. I gotta watch out that he doesn't barbecue it. I think he's just kidding. And that's our new trampoline!" The kid orders you to take off your shoes and is already doing his warm-ups.

"Will you do your somersault for me, Uncle?"

When your brother's wife calls you to come to dinner, you breathe a sigh of relief. Not only because you've just wrecked your whole skeleton doing your first somersault in thirty years, but because you ended up falling right on your nephew, who stoically claimed it didn't hurt—though it really must have—probably to reward you for your effort.

"We'll play some more after dinner," he says in all seriousness, more than you've ever seen in an adult, then he dashes into the house.

Your brother has tied on a barbecue apron, THE BOSS IS COOKING, and fusses around masterfully with his tongs.

"How do you want your meat?" he asks, as if he hadn't known for years that you don't eat any.

"Alive!" is your answer, as always. He's got you a meat substitute, soybeans shaped like bratwurst. The brown stripes that appear when it's fried have been put onto the tofu by the meatpacker. *Probably made in China*, you think. *Child labor. A little girl's tiny little hands painting grilling stripes on sausage with a tiny little brush with carcinogenic paint in eighteen-hour shifts.* You have red wine with dinner and, as usual, when your brother conjures up a bottle from his well-stocked cellar, it tastes utterly fantastic. This doesn't escape your mother, who suddenly grabs the wine, too fast for anybody to react, and fills her glass to the brim, her water glass, because it's the only one she has.

"Mom, you don't like red wine!" Your brother nudges her memory along, as he takes her glass and the bottle away.

"There's no white wine, apparently," your mother gripes and looks around, offended.

"Hey, is there any ketchup in the house?" Your question is meant to change the subject to something innocuous—quite apart from the fact that the tofu sausage has zero taste and is as dry as a sandstorm—but it totally misses the mark and starts a marital spat instead. Only your nephew showed some understanding, backing you up enthusiastically.

"Ketchup! Me too! Ketchup!"

"Well done!" Now your brother looks offended too. "Won't you at least try for once to see how your meal tastes without a red apron on it?"

"Now leave him alone!" Your sister-in-law stands up. "Since we do have ketchup, he wants to have some, and you're the one who always buys it."

"For my fries, not for him to drown everything in!"

"Oh, yeah! I want some fries!"

"This is a nice kettle of fish!"

"There aren't any fries today and there's no ketchup either!"

"And I want a glass of white wine!"

After dinner you all sit in silence for a while, sipping wine, except the kid of course who's painting a picture in ketchup on the tablecloth.

"I'm going on tour again . . ." You try to get the conversation going. "Nothing special, Molière's *Misanthrope*, but the pay's pretty good." You don't get any farther. You can't understand why your brother's getting so worked up; you clearly hear him say, "Keep it up, Mom, and you'll wind up in a retirement home!"

An outing seems to be obligatory in this weather, so you soon start off—too soon, fortunately, for a second round of somersaults. Even five can fit comfortably into the new car. Your mother is in the front, you and your sister-in-law in the back—the kid in the middle—and your brother on the royal throne, steering wheel in hand, like the insignia of his power. The switchback road over the pass to the Bündner Herrschaft region provides him with ideal conditions to coax all he can from the car. It's too much for your mother, who keeps complaining and closes her eyes in protest near the end—and too much for a child's stomach as well. Just before the top of the pass your nephew pukes ketchup red into your lap and you think, *Lucky my suitcase is in the car.*

"Bravo, my boy!" your brother says when you get to your destination and he can check to see that the leather upholstery is unharmed. "It's a good thing you were sitting beside your uncle." There's not a word of praise for you, the recipient of the half-digested vomit. "It'll wash out," he says curtly and lights up.

The first walk I went on that I can remember, you think to yourself after a change of clothes, as you amble along beside your mom, *must have been here, on an autumn day like this, not quite forty years ago.* And because this involves a pleasant memory from a hidden corner of your childhood, it seems to you as though this stretch of the country were inculcated with an insatiable longing. A longing that overwhelms you all the more powerfully because the landscape appears to be more or less unchanged. *The same trees,* you think, *these wonderful lindens with the overhanging branches I used to swing on as a kid, they're a little older but they were already old back then. The gravel paths along the walls around the vineyards, walls to protect the vines from the night frost. And the old villages, hardly affected by the years, basically always true to themselves. Everything's relative,* you go on thinking, *especially the past. I found the train station horribly depressing, trumpeting how backward my homeland is, but here, the lack of progress makes me happy all of a sudden.*

And the gunshots are still there, from the gas-powered automatic guns scaring away the birds, banging on in a random rhythm in the Sunday morning calm; in the old days they didn't exactly keep you from pinching grapes off the vines by the bushel. They're apparently more efficient against birds. Starlings in particular pose a threat in the autumn, since that's when they're heading south in huge flocks and get so hungry from flying that they can strip a vineyard bare in minutes.

Your brother hardly chose your destination by chance, being a fan of the wines of the region, which is famous for its autumn grape harvest and where there's a *torkel,* a wine-press restaurant, always open on the weekend. As it was this Sunday too. Like many wine cellars they try to get you to come and eat by using folksy entertainment.

"Mom's had enough as it is, and the little guy's hungry," he says by way of justification and heads right for the first *torkel.* The patio tables are filled with cheerful guests and you're in luck because a party is leaving, or lurching, as if punning on *torkelnd*, tipsy, because they're literally staggering.

Your party orders a bottle of Grauburgunder, the local pinot grigio, and a platter of cold cuts and cheese. The kid gets some fizzy new wine and the promised piece of cake. You all have a toast with the regional salute of "Viva!"—your mother too—as you drink the wine from the vines around you. The sky overhead knows no bounds, its blue draws you upward into nothingness, a window on eternity, appealing in its offer of so much room for speculation but daunting for that very reason.

The sound of an accordion comes from the cellar up to the patio and envelops the world in gentleness—the customers' cheery gossip, the light so pure and clear that it almost hurts, and the air with a hint of the south—it's as if a filter lay over your senses, absorbing any sharp edges. Yours is the only table not caught up in this buoyant atmosphere. Arguments threaten to break out on all fronts, and you're glad your nephew has to go to the john right this minute and picks you to go with him, so you can escape from the tense situation for a moment. Your mother empties her glass in quick, long gulps, your brother watches the contents disappear and shows signs of stubborn opposition, under his wife's watchful eye. Their mutual, unspoken reproaches are palpable.

It's a little boy who's making that music in the cellar entranceway—his instrument is almost as big as himself—eyes closed and a smile on his face, as if seeing a glow from within, and you and your nephew both sit down on the cold stone at his feet and get lost in the music. The accordion tells of faraway lands, distant times, distant joy, and distant sorrow. In times past you used to like the nostalgia— these kinds of songs float you along—probably because they sound so naïve. But the sadness you sink into on hearing them again hides a little something that alarms you: *When did I stop feeling that being* on the road is an opportunity? you ask yourself. *Stop seeking out the unknown and all its potential and stop liking foreign countries because they were bewildering?* And you know that you've been left high and dry though you're always on the move. *Tomorrow it's Deggendorf,* you think, and wouldn't you know, *I'm the misanthrope again.* Your nephew's sitting quietly beside you and squeezes your hand, taking it so much for granted that it moves you. *What can he be hearing in these sounds?* you ask yourself. *How to figure out what the longing and melancholy in them mean?* You think back on your own childhood. The world of your different feelings back then don't seem alien to you; deep down they're connected to your feelings today, even though back then they'd have been less marked by hopelessness and more by wild, effervescent hopes, and full of dreams.

When the accordion boy takes a break, both of your legs have long been asleep, and you can get up only with great effort.

"Can I give him something?" your nephew asks quietly, and you press a few bills into his hand. He goes up to the music-maker very deliberately, but respectfully and with a certain circumspection, sort of as if he weren't seeing a child in him, a person of like mind, but an artist, a magician of sounds who had access to another world. *I love that boy,* you think, *and it was always like that, from the very beginning. Kinship is certainly a curious thing. It binds you, grounds you whether you want it or not.* As if your mother had heard his thought—she was sitting out in the sun and arguing with your brother—you now hear her voice quivering as she shouts against the noise of the guns driving off the crows:

"I am *not* going into a retirement home!"

And you know the outing is over.

On the way back to the parking lot you swing a bit to the accordion's rhythm in your head, a feeling as if the scenery is swaying, this place where everything revolves around wine-growing.

"Uncle, can you help me up?" You've stopped by the lindens, magically attracted by the golden yellow sheen of their leaves, and your nephew wants to climb a tree. You help him get to the lowest branches, watch him as he carefully goes higher—you *are* a little worried he might fall off—and you see yourself as a child in him, yourself as a five-year-old.

Once you're back home, you split up. *Time to take a breather,* you think, *to gather strength before the last act.* While your brother's wife is getting supper, your brother's smoking his cigarettes, and your mother's asleep on the sofa, you and your nephew go racing around. You're thankful he doesn't bring up somersaults again because you definitely feel how much it still hurts, and you know for sure it will be much worse tomorrow morning. *The community center in Deggendorf,* you think, *Alceste with aching leg muscles and a stiff lower back.*

After supper you and your brother take Mom home. She can hardly walk now and all of you practically carry her into bed. It doesn't smell particularly clean, nor does the rest of her apartment. As you turn to leave, she beckons you over again and takes your hand.

"It was nice that you could be here. Come back real soon! Do you have enough money for the train?"

"Yes, Mom, you gave me some," you say and tuck her in, and you can't decide which emotion is affecting you the most, because you're moved by all three: pity, disgust, and love.

In the car neither of you says a word, you and your brother rehearse your silence. *What grand words are there to say,* you think to yourself. *Words don't change a damn thing.* And when you notice that your brother's missed the intersection where he turns off to his house, family, and garden, you don't comment on it. He stops in front of a bar and gets out. You follow without delay or question. Two beers later you still haven't exchanged one word. You are the only customers, and the man behind the bar keeps quiet, like you two. And if it weren't for those songs in the room, that music especially for difficult and lonely times, you could hardly stand the silence. So you order a third round of beer and that breaks the silence.

"How's the acting business?" your brother asks and orders a schnapps.

"Show's on tour," you quickly answer and think, *Sore muscles won't be all that I'll hurt from tomorrow.* "We go from one hick town to the next, Molière's *Misanthrope.*"

"Always on the road! You know, I'm jealous."

"It's nothing to be jealous of."

"No, really! And I'm a teensy weensy bit proud of you. D'you know why?" Your brother drinks his schnapps. "You're living your dreams."

You almost choke on your drink when he says it. *A stranger,* you think, *is what my brother has become to me, and vice versa, the exact same thing.* But you're related, nevertheless, by your bloodline. It stretches between the two of you like an elastic band. You could free yourselves from each other and go your separate ways, but only for a certain distance. You only get so far apart and then the elastic pulls you back together, tighter than ever, just like this evening. And now the two of you are sitting in a bar, only a stool apart, and have nothing to say to each other. And yet it feels good.

TRANSLATED FROM GERMAN BY GERALD CHAPPLE

PEP PUIG

Clara Bou

This time I was It. I leaned on the mulberry tree, and hiding my head between my arms, I began to count one, two, three, four, five, six, seven, eight, nine, ten: first slowly and loud, to give everyone a chance to hide—and then faster and in a lower voice. From forty I jumped to fifty, from sixty to seventy and from seventy to eighty. When I turned around, nobody was there.

There was just the town's main drag. A street so quiet that for an instant I only heard the crickets chirping. And on the opposite sidewalk, the murmurs of the older folks washed away with the fresh evening air.

Without moving from my spot, I looked over my surroundings. Maybe one of the gang was too lazy to have run off very far and was hiding nearby, waiting for his chance behind one of the mulberry trees to the side, or laying under the baker's van or the Mestreprats' two-cylinder Citroën. Maybe that someone was Clara Bou, who's recently "become a woman" (as I'd been hearing lately from my grandmother Lola), each time playing the game with less enthusiasm and only waiting for us to call her name so she can sit on the bench and relax. But this night Clara Bou was nowhere to be found.

Looking continuously around me I crossed the street. But carefully: if someone decides to leave his hiding place, I have to have time to return to the mulberry tree and, knocking three times, call his name. For example: One, two, three, Pere Estevet!

That summer we were eleven, twelve, maybe thirteen years old. Even though adolescence was approaching, most of us still preferred to go out every night to the street to play our endless, familiar games. Of all the gang, I was the only out-of-towner. My dad had grown up around here, and he was the one who deposited me at my grandparents' house for a while at the end of every school year, so I wouldn't be a nuisance at home.

The street where we played was the Carrer de la Serra, a road so long and wide in comparison with the others that, as they say, it was in effect the only one in town. Like the banks of a river, there were two quite distinct sides. On one—which looked west, which is to say to Montserrat (for this it was called the "Serra Road")—the main houses of the town were arrayed: the carpenter's house, the Mestreprats', the barber's, the shoemaker's, the baker's, the ploughman's, the post office, the Bous' house, and then came the cinema. On the other side was just a row of bushy mulberries, and between each group of three, a bench.

Our meeting place was the bench in front of the town hall, an unlit whitish building, more imposing than modest, preceded by two rows of stone steps that first ascended in divergent directions, coming together at the top landing. When we played hide and seek, the easiest place to run was straight to the steps of the city hall to hide behind the undulating railings or between the plantings of the little garden at the large balcony to the side. Another possibility was to shoot for the *pujada de l'escola* and creep up the hillside to the school, where there was a little plaza with four olive trees and some swings. Finally, to the right of the city hall, past the Mestreprats' garage (where Quim Mestreprats's dad kept his tractor rather than the "Doscavalls" Citroën) there was the Casanoves' alleyway, a kind of narrow and resonant alleyway through which the bravest of us could dash into the darkness and appear, after a circuit of the town, via the school hill.

Little by little I moved away from the mulberry tree. In order for the game to have a point, I had to put myself at risk. Otherwise, it could go on forever and there was the danger that the other kids would give up from sheer boredom. When I was It, this was never a danger. Beyond the fact that I didn't mind being It, I was the fastest of our group and could run long distances. Now, so many years later, however, I'm struggling to understand our game. I don't understand, for example, what made us run so far if we only had to turn back. Wouldn't it have been better to hide ourselves at the start, behind some other mulberry tree, or beneath the baker's van or the Mestreprats's cars? Maybe I'm confusing this game with another that involved two teams which chased each other through town? But this can't be the case because on the night in question I was It all by myself. Maybe I pushed everyone so far for the pure excitement of escaping the watchfulness of the adults and exploring the back alleys of the town.

Whatever the case, that night, without a doubt, I was It by myself. Suddenly, between the plants of the little garden of city hall I saw some braids quaking.

"Mariona! I see you!" I said, sure that I wasn't wrong. Without turning, I backed up to the mulberry tree and said, knocking three times: "One, two, three, Mariona of the tailor's shop!"

"It's not fair!" exclaimed Mariona, pulling her head through the railing. "When you were counting, you were looking through your arm!"

I ignored her comment and waited for her to come down the city hall stairs. Then I asked her if there was anyone else with her.

"I don't think I'll tell you," she said in childish bad humor. But as soon as she sat on the bench, she spilled the beans: "There's Pere."

I thought that maybe she wasn't being entirely dishonest, the little snitch. Since several days before, Pere Estevet and Mariona had discovered that they liked each other and had been hiding together whenever they could. But if they liked each other, why would she rat him out? I crossed the street again. Between the plantings, something was moving, but I couldn't be sure that it was Pere. All at once I heard a noise behind me, a kind of muffled, light knock. I turned my head, and there, at the center of the road, beyond my mulberry, squatting like a toad, was Joan Forner.

He had just finished leaping from the only climbable mulberry tree—the only one *he* could climb (the rest of us couldn't climb at all)—and now he was considering running for it to save himself. Joan Forner was my best friend in town, though I'm not really sure why. He had a wild and indomitable character, and he almost never spoke. It's funny. This year he had begun helping his dad at the bakery. We looked at each other for an instant: both of us were about the same distance from the mulberry tree. We broke into a run at practically the same time. A moment before he could stretch out his hand and cry "safe!" I touched the tree and called his name.

"One, two, three, Joan Forner!"

Now I'd gotten two. I headed back to the garden.

"Pere, Mariona told me that you're back here! I know you're here, I see you." Someone was obviously moving behind the bushes, but I couldn't take the chance of saying the wrong name. I grabbed a handful of pebbles from the ground and flung them at random.

"Hey!" It was Pere's unmistakable voice. So I had a third.

I walked to the mulberry and rapped three times.

"One, two, three, Pere Estevet!"

I went on to call them all out: Quim Mestreprats (the Mestreprats' son), a boy who would die five years later, falling right off a cliff with his father's tractor; Amàlia Pastora; Roser from the Palets'; Vicent Pardall; I wasn't sure about Dolors Mussa and Eloi Pastor, two kids who lived on the other side of town and didn't play with us every night.

"Who's missing?" I asked as soon as I had them all together and seated on the bench.

"I'm missing," said Pere Estevet, raising his finger, repeating this joke as usual.

I didn't have to do a recount to realize that the only one missing was Clara Bou.

Clara was missing, and this was strange because for the past two summers she was the one who took the games least seriously. With hardly a glance I crossed the street, climbed up one set of the city hall stairs, and came down the other.

"Anybody seen her?"

"Keep looking, because I'm sure you know where to find her!" Mariona from the tailor's shop, still resentful, threw in my face. It so happened that everyone knew I was sweet on Clara Bou. Clara, however, was not sweet on me, nor any of the other boys in the gang. And even though this seemed a bit sad to me, in my heart I understood what my grandmother said about her: "Clara is becoming a woman"—a woman who doesn't hang out with little boys. I liked Clara a lot. I liked her eyes and her long arms. There was something in her gestures, in her way of talking, that intrigued me terribly. I couldn't take my eyes off her, was always spying on her. At times I was overcome and speechless around her. I grinned stupidly like a fool. Her wry face humiliated me and made me happy at the same time. At night, I hugged my pillow and imagined that Clara and I were telling each other our secrets. Yes, I was developing quite a crush on Clara Bou. Even so, in spite of the *platonic* cast of my feelings, during the town festival the summer before, I had worked up my courage to ask her for a dance. I went to a Catholic school and girls were scary. I suppose that in some way I felt that I had to live up to my duty as a romantic male. All of the boys took their girls dancing and I could do no less. The ball had begun. The tent was packed. Finally, I broke away from the boys and crossed the dance floor as cautiously as possible until I arrived at the girls' side of the floor and held out my hand:

"Do you want to dance with me?"

My boldness left her speechless. I remember her eyes widening in a light, mocking daze. Then she said to me, drily:

"No way."

And then came the laughter. Immediately, however, she stood, took me by the hand, and we began dancing a two-step that was playing just then. These were the four most painful minutes of my life. I was on tiptoes with my neck stretched so that she wouldn't look taller than me. But I couldn't keep the careless girl from steering me right into the middle of the dance floor, where the reputable married couples of the town wheeled in concentric circles, including my relatives and parents. "Look at the boy," I remember my mother saying into my father's ear. My dad turned his head and spread his moustache with a sort of smile that made me feel like killing him. I wanted to melt away. And then I imagined the entire tent, filled to capacity, with everyone laughing at the difference between the ever-so-womanly Clara and me, such a child. Fed up, I returned to my friends with my face red, and a sense of humiliation so vast that even today, when I think about it, the color rises in my cheeks. Despite what might be supposed, however, this predicament hadn't been enough to disenchant me with Clara Bou once and for all. On the contrary, after a few minutes I found the strength to look up, and I realized to my surprise that nobody was staring at me. I found Clara and kept looking at her until she noticed—and then she smiled at me. As always, she left me speechless, but this time as I tucked my head back down, I was even more hopelessly in love.

With the sense that the game had finished that night, I climbed up the school hill to see if I could find her up there, perhaps sitting on a swing and smoking a cigarette. Maybe I hoped she would invite me to sit with her and she would tell me some secret. But then I've already told you that Clara Bou was nowhere to be found that night.

"She's not anywhere," I said when I went back to the gang.

"She must have gone straight to her house," Joan Forner said coldly.

"What a spoilsport! What a jerk!" added Roser of the tailor's house.

"Come on! Leave her alone," said Amàlia Pastora protectively.

Besides being Clara's best friend, Amàlia Pastora was the bossy one of the group (but a kind and honest girl just the same) and she left us no choice but to do as she said. They made some room for me at the end of the bench, and we sat in silence for some moments, ruminating over what might have led Clara to go home. That night we played no more. With the bells ringing twelve times, we got up and said goodnight and went off to bed. It was an agreement we had with the adults: at midnight we'd be home. My house was the shoemakers' shop, and there, waiting for me, seated in a wooden chair outside, her hands folded on her lap, was my grandmother Lola, the nicest lady in the world. Grandpa Pau had died the winter before of a stroke and at my grandmother's side there was now only an empty chair. After helping her get up (not because she couldn't on her own, but because she had asked me), I brought in the two chairs, drank a glass of milk, and went upstairs. At the door to my room, my grandmother asked what I would like the next morning for breakfast.

"An ensaïmada bun with jam," I replied, "or a ham sandwich," because if I asked for something sweet one day, the next it would be salty.

"Okay then, goodnight child."

"Goodnight, Grandma."

I still hadn't fallen asleep when I heard the sound of voices coming from outside, and someone calling my name. I jumped out of bed and threw open the balcony doors. In the middle of the street, headed straight for me, were the sleepy faces of Joan from the bakery and Pere Estevet.

"It looks like Clara Bou didn't get home," they told me.

My room was the only one at the shoemaker's place that looked out over Serra Street. It took a moment for my grandmother to arrive.

"They say Clara Bou didn't go home," I told her.

We got dressed and went down to the street. At that point I had the sense that half the town was up looking for Clara. A nervous man said to me:

"Pau, they told me you were It during the game. Do you remember which direction Clara ran off in?"

I didn't have the least idea, but I wanted to help and told him:

"I think she went off to the Casanoves' alley."

"Well then, you have a look in the alley, and then check the soccer field."

With the anxiety of the good children we still were, we rocketed off for the alleyway and then shot up to the main highway. The soccer field was vast, but with one look we could see that Clara Bou wasn't there. We began searching through the neighboring meadows and stumpy abandoned vineyards, but soon we realized we were now looking for her as though we were looking for a corpse. All at once our eyes met. In the town above us, the air was full of voices. From time to time we heard someone cry Clara! and an echo replied, Clara! With a desperate determination, Pere Estevet took a deep breath and yelled, Clara! I imitated him: Clara! Joan looked at us and let out a laugh. Ignoring him, Pere Estevet again inhaled and yelled again. In the distance someone returned the same cry. We climbed back up to the highway and began a sweep through town. For a while we ran very fast. I'm not sure why we ran like that. Instead of looking for somebody, we were fleeing something. From time to time we stopped and made a search behind some bushes, at a roadside, inside an abandoned old manor. At times we crossed paths with the other people looking for Clara, and then made sure our most serious faces were on display.

Finally we returned to Serra Street. On the steps of city hall a group of people were talking. On the other side the girls of our gang were seated on the bench. From their faces I could tell that they hadn't found Clara. For some seconds we looked at each other. I remember that not everyone was worried—most of us were just sleepy. The one who was most worried was Mariona from the tailor's shop. She suddenly started bleating like an idiot. It made me so mad that I wanted to kill her.

"Why are you crying!" I wanted to yell at her. "Can't you see that Clara's just hiding?"

In fact, that was the conclusion that the mayor arrived at when he called for everyone from the steps of city hall a little while later. At the mayor's side, forming a wide half-circle, were the sheriff, Father Ramon, Mr. Ferrer, Ms. Marta, and Mr. Morral (the coach of the soccer team), the majority of my friends' mothers and fathers, some of the grandparents too, my grandmother Lola, Clara's father, her older sister and brother-in-law, and a bunch of other people I didn't know by name, though I remember they looked related. Much more than its streets, you couldn't escape the fact that those faces were the town. The mayor was a little man, but he had a reputation for intel-ligence. "The first thing we have to do is calm down," he said. "If we haven't found her it's obviously because Clara wants to stay hidden, and the best thing we can do is stop searching for her the way we've been searching for her." Some people agreed with him and others did not. To everyone's surprise, however, Clara's father was one of those in agreement. "It's true," he said laconically. Clara Bou's dad—everyone called him Bou—was a bit of a frightening man. He was a sullen farm worker with a bad reputation. For a long, long time we watched him to see if he would say anything else. "Yes, it's obvious that nothing's happened to my girl," he grumbled through his teeth, in a strangely humble tone, or maybe he was just uncomfortable, as if he didn't like the whole town hanging on his every word.

An intermediate solution was decided upon. While a small team would continue searching for her, the best thing the rest of us could do was go to sleep. As if I was four years younger than I was, my grandmother Lola took me by the hand and made me return home to the shoemaker's shop. It was the second time that we went to sleep that night. Before going to our rooms, she told me that I should say an Our Father and ask Our Lord God for my friend to be found safe and sound. That's what I did. Once again under the covers, I put my hands together and asked Our Lord (or the Baby Jesus—I don't remember who, assuming I even prayed to anyone specific in those days) for Clara to be found soon and for her to be safe and sound. Then I looked toward the balcony and listened for a few minutes to the voices coming from outside. Unlike Mariona from the tailor's shop, I didn't feel like crying. Rather, I felt fascinated, profoundly intrigued. "Where are you, Clara? Where are you hiding?" I began to ask under my breath, hugging my pillow. For a moment I imagined Clara coming out of my closet, with a naughty smile on her face, asking if I could make room for her. Half embracing, holding back our urge to laugh, we listened together to the barking of the dogs, perhaps a sign that she had been found. Little by little, however, the voices dropped off, or maybe I did. I suppose I ought to say that I couldn't sleep through the night, but I'm not so sure of that. I was a boy of twelve and sleep probably won me over. I got up late the next day, and after washing my face and combing my hair, I went downstairs. As I did, it seemed to me that today was no different from any other day. The harsh glare of July, the murmurs from the street, the scent of rope for espadrilles that permeated the house . . . My grandmother was in the shop helping a customer. I took a moment to say good morning and then went to the kitchen to eat up the ensaïmada bun with jam, or maybe it was the ham sandwich. Everything was so normal, even the words of my grandmother seemed unremarkable when she came back from the shop and told me:

"Child, they still haven't found your friend."

So it was. They didn't find Clara Bou. Even today, twenty-five years later, they haven't found her. Although I don't believe anyone is still looking.

TRANSLATED FROM CATALAN BY JAN REINHART

crisis

LEE ROURKE

Catastrophe

I'm sitting in my small room watching you all on my TV. I'm watching you committing the crime. I can see you all. I don't know why
this has become such a national event. Your crime is lousy. I certainly didn't plan it this way. But now you're all here, watching me, as
I watch you committing your crime. I'm sitting in my comfortable
chair in here. Just my chair. It's the only piece of furniture I have
now. I've thrown out everything else I own, except my TV. But you
know all that, you saw me flinging it all from my balcony, twelve
floors up, didn't you? You saw it all happen, one item after another,
falling . . . falling down to the tarmac below, where it smashed into
smithereens, smatterings of modern detritus still evident by your
booted feet, baptising the bitumen. You weren't aware that I'd barricaded myself in—even when you turned off the water and electricity
supply for the whole block, hoping to force me out like a rat. You
didn't realise that I'd already thought of that scenario, that I'd my
own generator and enough drinking water to last weeks upon weeks.
You didn't realise all that back then. You do now, though. I've heard
you all on the TV; I've seen the men and women in suits and hair-
dos talking about all this to the camera back in the studio. The whole
country knows about me now. They're watching with you, commit-

ting the same crime . . . waiting for the catastrophe. Well, I'm waiting for it with you. I'm waiting for it to happen, too. What have you
got down there? A swat team? Dynamite? What are you going to
throw at me? There's nothing you can do to stop me. I'll fall with this
building, your criminal act will not destroy me. I don't care. You don't
understand the lengths I will go to. I belong here. I will remain here
in this room until my last breath. I'll exist here in perpetual silence.
If that's what it takes. You'll see. You'll *all* see, down there, watching
me. You won't be able to stop me. I can see you all now, gathering,
enjoying the spectacle, the TV crews, the lights, the satellite dishes
beaming it all into the atmosphere.

**. . . . . HAS BARRICADED HIMSELF INSIDE THE TWELFTH-FLOOR
FLAT OF A BLOCK OF FLATS DUE FOR DEMOLITION THIS WEEK . . . . . .**

I can see you all down there. I'm watching you on my TV screen.
Committing your crime. You fit snugly within my 24" of plasma,
flat-screen technology. You're all in shot, in frame, enveloped in
some crude, everyday symmetry of waiting . . . of listening. And
what have you heard now? What? What? *I'm going to kill myself here!
I have a hostage here! I've killed someone here! I had difficulties in my
childhood! My mother didn't love me!* Is that what they're telling you?
Yes, they are. I can hear them on my TV telling you all about me, all
these things, all these retellings, these stories and clichés we've all
heard before. Repeated and repeated again. It's no wonder you all
crave this event, this moment . . . my downfall. It all makes sense
to me, if not to you. No, it can't make sense to you, your crime, if it
did you wouldn't be down there, you'd be up here with me, sitting
next to me, watching it all unfold with me. Waiting, anticipating the
final moments.

. . . . EAST LONDON AFTER A LONE MAN HAS BARRICADED HIMSELF INSIDE THE TWELFTH-FLOOR FLAT OF A BLOCK OF . . . .

You're all so bored, you're all somnambulists. You're living in a technological miasma of your own making and all you crave is the very same speed that, unknown to you, hurtles you towards the same beginning again and again anyway. One day it will forget you entirely, it will finally leave you behind, and then what will you do, without your entertainment? You'll kill yourselves, that's what you'll do. Stripped bare, that's all you'll have left to do.

. . . . BREAKING NEWS: POLICE HAVE BEEN CALLED TO A PROPERTY IN EAST LONDON AFTER A LONE MAN HAS . . . .

There you are again, in your studio, communicating your scripted thoughts, proselytising each hackneyed syllable to the nation. What are you going to say next? *That I'm mad? That I crave fame?* Is that what you've all been told to say? To think? I bet it is. Well, keep it. Your petty fictions. Keep all those thoughts, all those words, they're not enough for me anyway. It's all nothingness to me, but you won't understand that. *"Boredom," "humdrum," "apathy," "languor," "stolidity," "the blahs," "radium," "anguish," "ennui," "accidie"*—I've read these words, and others like them too many times. They've been used in essays, addresses, fiction and poems . . . they're not enough for me. So, use them for your own entertainment. Use them at will—you will never understand the weight that hangs above them, the weight that hangs above us all.

. . . . DUE FOR DEMOLITION THIS WEEK . . . BREAKING NEWS: POLICE HAVE BEEN CALLED TO A PROPERTY IN EAST . . . .

And all you policemen and policewomen down there, in your uniforms, some of you young enough to be my son or daughter. What is it you're all trying to guard? Why are you all just standing around? Surely you've got better things to do? Especially you there, coordinating it all, standing there, all proud like a peacock, with your plans, with your instructions and orders, your stupid walkie-talkie, transmitting more of your blather into the ether. What are you doing there? You look stupid. Your helmet is too big for your head. You'd rather be elsewhere. I can tell by the look on your face. You'd rather be at home, or in your local with your friends, talking about women and football. You'd rather be doing anything than be here, waiting for me, whilst committing your crime, down there, at the bottom of this tower block, waiting around for your orders to be followed. Well, your orders mean nothing. They're merely words. Sounds. Words force-fed into you by someone else who earns more money than you. Someone else who drives a bigger car, owns a larger house. This is all it is, this is the only thing that's happening here. The pursuit of money. Ha, what a farce. You underestimate the power of man's dwelling, the power of being somewhere in time: here, being here. You underestimate the sheer weight of it. And besides, deep down, you know this event cannot be narrated. You know this as much as I do.

. . . . LONDON AFTER A LONE MAN HAS BARRICADED HIMSELF INSIDE THE TWELFTH-FLOOR FLAT OF A BLOCK OF FLATS DUE . . . . . .

I'm made of thicker stuff than you. Look at you, pacing up and down, waiting for the event. Look at you rubbing your hands in gleeful expectation. Hoping whatever it is you've planned works and comes into fruition the moment you want it to. There you are gathering your fellow officers, manoeuvring them into position. Don't you see how obvious it is? Don't you see? If you were up here with me, looking down, you'd notice right away just how simple, fragmented and pointless it all looks. But you're not up here are you? You're down there, in the thick of it. Caught in the madness of it, seeing it all happen before your very eyes, in your so-called real life. You're caught. Caught.

. . . . **FOR DEMOLITION THIS WEEK . . . BREAKING NEWS: FINAL EVICTION PROCEDURES AND THE DEMOLITION OF** . . . .

But wait . . . what's that? Who's that you are talking to? And now, where've you gone? You've gone. Now we're back in that studio, with the suits and the hair-dos. What's that the presenter is saying? *Breaking news, breaking news.* What's all that about? What's that they're saying? I can't hear you properly. You're speaking too quickly. What's that? *Local council? Town planners?* I can't decipher what you're saying. *Reprieve?* Why a *reprieve?* Wait, wait, why have you cut back to the police down there? Why are people walking away? People are walking away. They're going away. Back home. Back to work. What's going on? Why's nothing happening? I don't understand, I thought something was meant to be happening? Today? The *event?* The *catastrophe?* The result of your crimes. Where is it? Where is the catastrophe? Why isn't the catastrophe happening? I want an answer. I want somebody to explain all this to me. I want somebody to explain to me why there is to be no event today. I want this to be explained clearly and slowly. Surely somebody knows?

. . . . **CONRAD COURT, IN HACKNEY, EAST LONDON HAS BEEN POSTPONED DUE TO "TECHNICAL DIFFICULTIES" AND A LAST-** . . . . . .

Can't you repeat to me what you just said? Can't you cut back to the studio so they can tell me one more time? Slowly? With meaning? So that I can understand why all this has suddenly stopped. So cruelly. And without any concern for me. Look, they're walking away. I don't understand why everyone is walking away down there. What shall I do now? How long do I have to wait now? Why can't they just get all of this over and done with? I cannot go through this again. Over and over again. *The catastrophe never happening again.* Their crimes repeating and repeating. Never reaching the point of no return—the point we are all waiting for. The moment we all secretly hope will come and envelop us all. Again.

. . . . **MINUTE REPRIEVE BROUGHT IN BY COUNCIL LEADERS AND CITY PLANNERS. IT IS UNKNOWN JUST WHEN EVICTION** . . . .

ANDREJ NIKOLAIDIS

The Coming

The smell of blood reached us even before we entered the house. There were no signs of a break-in at the front door. Clearly the murderer had rung the bell and a member of the household had opened up for him. I turned around to Janko: "Probably someone they knew." "Psssht!" he hissed—he must have been afraid the murderer was still in the house.

I looked back. Curious neighbors were already clustering around our patrol car behind the row of cypresses that skirted the Vukotićs' property. Some kids were tearing down the street in a souped-up yellow Fiat with music blaring and almost lost control at the bend. They spotted the crowd, slowed down, and drove back. "Turn that off," someone yelled at them, "there's been a murder here!"

I forced the door with my shoulder and took a step into the house. I gripped my pistol as tightly as I could, with both hands. It was cold, as if I'd just picked it up out of the snow. Janko came in behind. He lit the way for me with his flashlight. We heard a movement in the dark. Or at least we thought we did—who knows. We were on edge. Terrified, to tell the truth. It was my first murder, after all. Sure, I'd seen a lot of corpses before, but I don't think any sane person can get used to death.

When we heard the noise, or thought we did, Janko flashed his light into the kitchen. I stepped forward, ready to shoot. Then my legs caught on something and I fell. My cheek was warm and wet. "Fuck this," I called, "turn on the light."

I was lying in Senka Vukotić's blood. I found some paper towels in the kitchen to wipe my face and hands. Meanwhile, Janko photographed Senka. "I think I moved her," I told him.

There was a large wound on her head. It turned out that the murderer had dealt the first blow with an ax. Evidently that didn't kill her outright, so he knelt down and cut her throat. We didn't find the knife. The ax is at the lab in Podgorica for analysis.

The trail of blood led to the inside stairs. The lab later reported that the murderer had been wearing size eight rain boots with worn-out soles. As soon as he set foot on the stairs, Pavle fired at him. Two shots. We found the buckshot in the wall. It's incredible that he didn't hit him. We combed the house several times but couldn't find any trace of the murderer's blood. That's what fear does to you—Pavle was firing from above, from the top of the stairs, it can't be more than five yards. Before he could reload the shotgun the murderer was upon him. From what we've been able to reconstruct, it seems the first blow struck Pavle in the right shoulder. As the murderer swung the ax again to deal the mortal blow, Pavle dashed off into the bathroom and tried to hide.

Then something happened that makes us certain that the murderer knew the family and had been to the house before: instead of going after Pavle he went into the children's room. He knew they had children— that's the point—and he knew where to find them. He grabbed Sonja in the bed by the window. She was seven, Jesus Christ . . . One blow was enough for a small child like that.

Meanwhile, Pavle realized that he'd left the children at the tender mercies of the murderer. He ran into their room and found the intruder on the floor—the man had needed to set down the ax to grab Helena, who'd hidden under her bed. That was the second chance Pavle had that night.

He didn't get a third. Although he now had the ax, which put him at a clear advantage, the murderer overpowered him. And cut his throat, like he did with Senka down in the hall.

Helena tried to run away. She didn't get far. We found her body in the living room, on the couch in front of the television, which was on. Judging by the bloodstains, the murderer sat down next to her. Our psychologists are trying to unravel what that could possibly mean. One thing's for sure—he switched on Animal Planet.

Then he left. No one saw him, no one heard him, and he left no fingerprints or DNA. There won't be any more investigations because, as I'm sure you know, homeless people laid waste to the house and ultimately set it on fire.

"Quite a story, don't you think? I think you've got something for your two hundred euros!" Inspector Jovanović exclaimed.

"You can say that again!" I said, patting him on the shoulder. I ordered a beer for him, paid, and went outside. But I didn't manage to get away. Every day I go back to the pub, sit behind the same sticky bar, and listen to the same story like a bloody refrain I can't get out of my head.

I remember all of that this evening as I sit in a long line of cars and stare at the fire-blackened ruins of the library covered with snow like a white sheet spread over a dead body. It's meant to be hidden, but everyone knows there's a body underneath—everyone knows there's been a crime.

I'll need at least an hour to get out of this traffic jam, I thought. It's cold tonight, and the snow has turned to ice since there's no one to clear it off the roads. A driver probably failed to brake on time and crashed into the car in front. Even this evening they've managed to get into a fight about it. The police are coming now to restore order. I can see the blue rotating lights through the snow that's now falling ever more thickly. Luckily I filled up before the Ulcinj gas station closed and all the staff were sent home. When the gas station ran dry they rang the head office in Kotor to ask for another tankload.

They called all morning, and finally around noon they reached a guy. He told them everything was over—no one needed anything now, least of all gas. "I mean, what are people going to do with it? It's not like they can escape," the severely depressed man said. He complained that his wife had kicked him out of the house. She'd told him to get lost—she at least wanted to die without having him around. And with nowhere else to go, he went back to the office. He was alone, there wasn't another living soul at the Hellenic Petroleum depot. When the workers at the gas station finally realized that the end of the world also meant they'd lose their jobs, they divided up the money from the till. The gas cylinders that they'd sold to customers in happier times were now heaved into the trunks of their cars, and plastic bags full of candy, cigarettes, and bottles of whiskey were crammed into the back seats. They didn't bother to lock the door when they left. Now they're probably guzzling down Chivas Regal and their children are gorging themselves on candy till it makes them sick, so nothing will be left. Like they say: it's a shame to waste things.

The gas needle under the speedometer tells me I've got enough gas for all I need to do this evening. The motor rumbles reliably. I turn up the heating and put in a new CD. Odawas sings "Alleluia" while several men with long black beards march past in formation. They're rushing to the mosque—it's time for prayer. The lights on the minarets blink like a lighthouse. But it's too late now, I brood, we're still going to hit the rocks. You can crawl under the red altars, run into the minarets—slender rockets ready to take you away to a different world—but it will be as promised: tonight, no one will be able to hide.

Tonight would warrant an update of all our dictionaries, if only there were time, so as to add the definitive new meaning of *"dead-line"*: anything that anyone in the world still plans to do has to be done tonight. Working under pressure? I'm used to it, even though I initially imagined that being a private detective in a town as small and peaceful as Ulcinj would be *safe and easy*. Cheated husbands, suspicious wives—who could need my services apart from unhappy people in unhappy marriages? So I thought.

I rented an office in the center of town. I furnished it minimally but tastefully, I think you'll agree. Posters of good old movies went up on the walls: *The Maltese Falcon* with Humphrey Bogart, *Chinatown* with Jack Nicholson . . . The posters were to discreetly prompt clients to compare me with the best. A little pretentious, I admit, but it proved effective. A massive oaken desk dominated the room. Period furniture was to give clients the impression they were engaging a company with traditional standards—and people still believe in tradition, although tradition always betrays them if they don't betray it first. The desk sported a black Mercedes typewriter: a real antique—pure extravagance. I wanted everyone who came in to know that we didn't allow any newfangled gadgets like computers in the firm. I wanted clients to know that our methods were *time-tested*. A detective needs to seem timeless. I wanted people to think: wow, this a hard-boiled, old-school detective who can be a real tough guy where necessary—a Sam Spade type of character who's seen a lot and knows the mean streets but isn't afraid to jump back into the thick of things if circumstances require.

As soon as I opened my agency, though, it seems all of Ulcinj decided to start killing, robbing, abducting, and raping. And adultery—it must be a dozen marriages that I've torn apart. I'll always remember those jobs most fondly, given the rest of my blood-soaked career.

I'd follow the adulterers to their hotel, make myself comfortable in my car, and knock back a swig or two of whiskey—just enough to give them time to undress and get down to business. A few photographs as evidence, and the matter is settled. My own experience in such matters is rather scant, I should say, or at least not as extensive as I'd have liked it to be, but one thing's for certain—women cope with adultery much better. A woman sees her partner's adultery as a betrayal: she's angry and offended. But a man who's just found out his wife is cheating on him sees it as a humiliation—irrefutable proof that he's not man enough. When a woman finds out she's been cheated on, her femininity is abruptly heightened—it's as if she has a "femininity switch" that her husband inadvertently activates by having an affair. But a cheated man crumples like a used condom. Little in this world is as fragile as masculinity—I've learned that lesson well.

Another thing that quickly became clear to me: whether I'm solving *serious crimes* like murder or *crimes of the heart* (as one romantically inclined and, to my joy, promiscuous lady client once described adultery), the most important thing is to understand *what the client wants*. The ones who hire me to find out if their partner is cheating on them thirst for evidence that their suspicions are justified. If a wife is cheating on her husband, she's a sow; if she isn't cheating on him, he's a swine for suspecting her. Faced with this choice between a negative image of her and a negative image of himself, he always chooses the former. Each of us obviously has unlimited potential for swinishness—whether and in what form that potential comes out is just a minor technical detail. So I always make a point of presenting extensive evidence of adultery—a photomontage works wonders—irrespective of whether said adultery actually took place. If it didn't, it still could have, so in a way I'm communicating a *deeper truth*. And after all, the client comes first. If the client is satisfied, my own satisfaction is assured.

Things are more complicated with murder. To generalize a little, I'd say there are two kinds of murder-investigation clients: those who want to know *who* committed the murder, and those who want to know *why*. With the latter it's easy: you have a chat with them. When they drop in to inquire how the investigation's going, you invite them down to a local bar . . . People loosen up after a drink. Sooner or later they'll give you a hint as to their suspicions, and then the case is as good as cracked. From then on you just confirm the story they themselves have come up with. Tell them you're close to solving the case, but make them wait a little longer. For some reason people consider what they call *arriving at the truth* to be a thankless job. *The truth is a hard road*, several clients have said.

But those who want to know *who* the murderer was are hard to please. They usually want to take revenge, so you can't point a finger at the first passerby. I try to resolve the case but usually don't succeed. In the end I cancel the contract and just ask them to cover my expenses.

The way people think is to a detective's advantage. Tell them any old story and they'll exclaim: *I knew it!* Whatever tale you tell, even if it's got as many holes as Swiss cheese, people will say: *Yes, it's logical!* There's evidence for everything—all you need is a story to back it up. By way of illustration, let's take the World Cup football final. A penalty shoot-out will decide who gets to be world champion. The last shot is taken by the best player on the planet. Whether he scores or misses, people will say: I knew it! Because it's *logical* that the best player will score when it's hardest, just as it's *logical* that the best player will miss in a decisive moment because, as we know, fate is often unkind.

My point is that a detective's work isn't so much about finding out the truth as inventing a story that people will accept as the truth. It's not about discovering the truth but about discovering what truth is for those people. Truth always appears as a fiction and takes the form of a story. I am a storyteller.

Around that time, I recall, the first of the e-mails arrived that caused my *grand illusion* to collapse . . . At that time, too, I was caught in a long line of cars after leaving Inspector Jovanović with his beer and his inability to accept that the massacre he'd described to me did actually happen. An inability that fortunately didn't impinge on his ability to accept bribes. The massacre at the Vukotićs' will always be an "incident" for him—something that happened despite the fact that things like that don't happen. Or always happen to someone else. We're able to overlook the horror of our own lives, and we owe our strength to that blindness. It's only lies that liberate us: one drop of the truth would be enough to destroy what remains of our life.

It was every bit of 40 degrees centigrade, the wind had turned to a dry *jugo*.[1] The fishermen had hauled their boats up onto the sand the night before. They're people who sleep with radios to their ear. Ulcinj doesn't have a marina, so an accurate weather forecast and quick legs are all that saves their boats from the waves determined to smash them on the rocks. Radio Dubrovnik *got it right* again yesterday: the sea did rise after midnight.

It's as if someone's started a vacuum over the town. Everything under the sky is gasping for breath. I search for a whiff of fresh air in the park across from the pub. Then I go up to the bar. A whiskey with two ice cubes. All in vain: wherever I go I breathe in the heat. It's as if the world's turned into an oven that I'm leaning into, and it's open right in front of my face. But isn't it like that with every change: we decide on it not *because of* things, but *despite* them?

---

1 A term in Croatia and Montengro for the Sirocco wind from North Africa.

All the local schizophrenics are out on the streets—drinking Coca Cola, ranting, smoking as they walk, and often changing speed and direction as if they don't know where they're going. Indistinguishable from tourists. The town is full of people whose diagnosis is unknown but whose condition obviously requires immediate hospitalization.

A little later I'm driving through a horde of tourists. Like a herd of animals heading to a watering hole. That's how they go down the steep Ulcinj streets to the beach, knocking over and trampling everything in their path. They walk right down the middle of the road. It's wider than the sidewalk, so they can move faster, and speed is important because it allows them to occupy a spot on the beach closer to the water. They don't move to the side when a car comes—experience has taught them that the driver won't run them over. They don't react to the honk of horns and don't comprehend verbal abuse.

I saw on television that farmers in America have jeeps with rubber grill guards. The driver just drives straight ahead and anything in the way gets pushed aside. The vehicle doesn't injure the animals but directs the movement of the herd. Give a little gas, and then it's just straight ahead. *Go West*, eh? But America is far, far away. For someone who's decided to go to the pine forest today and get nicely drunk amid the pinecones and the scent of resin, the mistral and the shade, the problem is not just the pedestrians, not just the tourists—his *fellow citizens* are enough of a calamity. The ones with cars are the worst: they have driver's licenses, names, surnames, and even biographies. They have everything—except regard for other human beings.

People can rein in their desires. They really expect little of life. Simple things count—like getting in the car and driving to where there's lots of whiskey and ice. But however little we desire, we end up getting even less. I sit and wait in a line of cars hundreds of yards long. People are hot and edgy. They sound their horns, some curse and swear, others are calm because the priests have taught them to accept fate (another word for chaos). After one or two minutes that seem like one or two hours, the line gradually gets moving again like a giant snake. I know from experience that when there's a traffic jam in Ulcinj it's always because of some brain-dead neanderthal stopping and talking with another driver, or because he's parked in the middle of the road so he can go into a bookmaker's. We pass the culprit of today's stoppage: a square-headed young guy with a look of vacant stupidity who's stopped in front of the pita bakery and blocked the lane leading down to Mala Plaža. He ordered a pita from his car and waited for it to be made and brought to him. Then he didn't have the right change, so he waited—meaning *we* waited, for the *pita man* to go and fetch change for a twenty-euro bill. All this was done without any hurry, with the greatest philosophical composure, paying no heed to the other people and cars, to the heat and the horns blaring . . . Like a cow in serene Zen meditation—only cows on the road manifest quite the same indifference toward the surrounding world, a tranquility and resolve to do the first thing that comes into their heads: usually to dump a load of dung right where they're standing.

A person's degree of primitivism in an urban setting can be gauged by his indifference toward other people and their needs, by the firmness of his conviction that he's alone in the world and has a right to do whatever he wants here and now, regardless of the misfortune it may cause other people. His place is *nature.* There he learned that *to exist means to mistreat.* He's unburdened by the illusions of *Homo urbanus*—for him nature is not a delicate equilibrium, a sensitive and complex organism; nature has only mistreated him and his tribe through history, harassing them with droughts, storms, floods, and frosts; they've fled from nature and have brought nothing but nature with them—they *are* nature. A person's degree of primitivism in an urban setting can be gauged, I maintain, by the disturbance he represents for other people. A primitive person is unable to exist in quiet discretion: he always creates noise, unsightliness, and stench. He does everything he can to be noticed—he constantly *emits* his existence. His being is a blow to the senses and an insult to the intelligence. He mistreats us with his very existence. When he celebrates, a considerate, tasteful person unfortunate enough to live next door to him is bound to suffer. What a primitive person enjoys inflicts pain on the civilized.

I read in the paper about an Austrian in Vienna who shot his Bosnian neighbor. It turned out that the Bosnian had driven the Austrian out of his mind for years with the loud Balkan folk music that he listened to in his apartment every afternoon. The Austrian complained to the police several times, and they intervened in accordance with the law, but that didn't prevent the Bosnian from continuing to mistreat the Austrian. When he realized that all legal possibilities of protecting his calm and privacy had been exhausted, the Austrian shot the Bosnian in the head and calmly turned himself in to the police.

This story has stuck in my mind because it tells us that the law can't protect us from the primitive, who's nothing but a walking disaster. However brutal the law is, it cannot compare with the brutality of nature. When law is about revenge, as in the case of capital punishment, it's closest to nature—and thus farthest from the law.

That's why it's so unbearable here: primitivism is not some random excess but the very *essence* of local culture, which therefore isn't a culture. If you're not primitive here you're a foreign body and you'll be made to feel it every day. With a lot of effort, luck, and money you can construct a fortress and preserve your own order of things inside it—for a while. You can erect high walls, dig moats, and build drawbridges to shut off your world *for a while*. But they'll find a way in: like in Poe's "Masque of the Red Death," their *nature* will get through and wipe your little world off the face of the earth.

Here people dump trash by the roadside and turn the landscape into a landfill. Their sheep and goats, which they need in order to survive in their suburbs, wander the asphalt and graze the parks, or what's left of them. Their children imitate the cherubs in fancy fountains and pee in flowerbeds in front of the passersby. They shit on the beaches and in neglected recreation centers. Music is the form of art they like most because it doesn't demand interpretation or reflection. Like the salt strewn on a vanquished ancient city they sow the world with noise—their repulsive music lasting late into the night, which they need in order to enjoy themselves. Walls and billboards are plastered with pictures of their big-titted women with frightening faces and grimaces that we can only assume are meant to suggest lust but which actually attest to nothing but stupidity and vacuousness. The males of the species thrust their ever-erect organs into that void, and from that nothingness *their* children are born to ensure the continuation of *their* world, nation, family, and culture—of *their* kind.

There are times like that day, stuck amid all those people, every one of them a nerve-grating nuisance, when anger grips me so tightly that no insult I could ever think of and no salvo of sarcasm I could fire at their civilians—their *women and children*—could bring relief. Those are the times when anger grips me so tightly that I can't move, as if the black monolith from *2001* was weighing down on my chest, times when anger is all that exists—when I'm anger itself. Then I think: death. What comes next has to be death. If there's anything after and beyond anger, it can only be that. Those were my thoughts that day as I nestled into my car seat, gripped the steering wheel—and waited.

It's fascinating that something as dependable as death becomes so utterly unreliable if we dare to count on it for release—as a rule it arrives too late. A mitigating circumstance is that, because it takes its time in coming, we're never truly disappointed. They say that *Homo sapiens* is an animal endowed with reason. I'd say that, despite his reason, he's an animal punished with optimism. Because as soon as they remove the pistol from his forehead, lift their boot from his neck, and pull the blade from his belly he thinks: things will get better. But before he can even cross himself and pronounce *faith, hope, and love* a few times, he'll be cast face-down in the mud again, and then death won't seem so terrible and unfair.

Nope, not this time either—everything's as it was before, I said to myself, and noticed that the people around me were starting to get out of their cars. They raised their eyes to the sky, called out to one another, seized their heads in their hands, and spread out their arms in wonder. Then the first flake fell on the windscreen. I opened the window and peered out: as serene and dignified as a Hollywood White Christmas—snow fell on Ulcinj that June day.

TRANSLATED FROM MONTENEGRIN BY WILL FIRTH

MICHAEL STAUFFER

The Woman with the Stocks

I

The woman with the stocks had a mother.

This mother had thought she could make the woman with the stocks, who was still a little girl at the time, happy by buying her the stocks.

The stocks were meant for later in the woman's life. The investment consultant had assured the mother that the stocks would appreciate a great deal in value over the years without the mother having to concern herself too much with them.

The mother of the woman with the stocks and the woman with the stocks had always trusted the investment consultant and had never had any doubts about the growth of the stocks.

The woman with the stocks left the stocks sitting in the bank for twenty years.

The woman with the stocks had managed for years not to think about these stocks.

Then one night the woman with the stocks had a dream:

Sitting with her mother in a fast-food restaurant, she won €500,000 with the purchase of a pizza. At least that's what it said on the bottom of the pizza box. Instead of being happy, the woman with the stocks looked again and again at the bottom of the pizza box, checking to see if the proof she had won was still there.

Instead of thinking about how much of her winnings she could give away and to which of her friends, and how she might best celebrate her win, the woman with the stocks disbelievingly ran her hand again and again over the writing that guaranteed she had won and hoped this writing would never fade.

When the woman with the stocks awoke from this dream, she was seized by the desire to interpret it.

In connection with the interpretation of this dream, the woman with the stocks thought about checking on the progress of her stocks, which were still sitting in the bank.

Thus began the woman with the stocks's personal crisis.

II

The woman with the stocks's investment consultant advised her to wait. She just had to wait! And she shouldn't blame herself because everything was going badly now!

The investment consultant told the woman with the stocks a terrible story about a young woman who had been really depressed because she couldn't have children. And that this woman had then taken poison, and as she was dying had said that she had a perfect right to die.

The investment consultant said that the woman with the stocks shouldn't act as rashly as that young woman had.

The European stock markets had once again closed weak. The US stock market was spreading its losses out, dragging down the European markets with it.

Shortly after she had checked on the progress of her stocks again for the first time in twenty years, the woman with the stocks received, as if by coincidence, a letter from the cemetery superintendence asking if she wanted to turn over her mother's grave for someone else's use, as is customary in much of Europe.

After twenty years, as stipulated in the cemetery regulations, the deceased's survivors had to decide what should be done with the grave because at that time the official period of rest for graves expired. Turning over the grave at this pre-appointed time would cost nothing.

The gravestone would be held for pickup for one year, after which time it would be destroyed. Otherwise a yearly payment of 500 CHF was required for grave maintenance.

The woman with the stocks attempted to discuss the matter with her brother. But he didn't care either way.

The woman with the stocks ultimately signed the letter, confirming turnover of the grave, because she was afraid she would no longer be able to make the yearly payment.

The woman with the stocks felt like a terrible daughter for agreeing to the turnover of her mother's grave for financial reasons.

The mother had been fully aware back then that she would die soon. While on a walk, she had seen the perfect gravestone and had shown it to her daughter.

It was a serpentine stone block, smoothed by water over a long period of time.

The mother of the woman with the stocks wanted a stone that would last for a long time.

The woman remembered that it had been very difficult to transport the stone.

From the streambed to the stonecutter to the cemetery. In silence, all her mother's brothers had helped.

III

A magpie regularly flew by the woman with the stocks's window. When the woman with the stocks stood near enough to the window, the magpie would land on the windowsill, as if to look at the woman with the stocks.

The woman with the stocks wanted to give the magpie a name and so called it Pia.

The woman had rarely before racked her brain over whether she had enough money or not.

Now she would think for hours about nothing but money. She followed the development of her stocks' market value, which had not interested her for twenty years, and it was as if the woman with the stocks's life now only developed in step with this value.

The woman with the stocks read the numbers and didn't know where the missing money had gone, but she could not help thinking that it had to be somewhere.

The woman with the stocks felt personally responsible for the decline in her stocks' value, even though she knew that she had had nothing to do with it. Her fear that she had no future grew.

The woman with the stocks dreamed of her mother more and more.

She sat with her again in a restaurant. She heard a lonely violin playing a funeral dirge somewhere in the restaurant.

Suddenly there were a lot of popping sounds, and shortly thereafter a person in a suit lay stretched out on the floor. On a screen hanging above the counter a video was playing in which a grasshopper was sucking the innards out of another insect.

The woman with the stocks continued eating and watched what was happening on the screen, spellbound.

The mother of the woman with the stocks likewise continued eating but only looked at her plate and admonished the woman with the stocks to pay attention to her food, saying she shouldn't always shovel everything into her mouth so greedily.

American currency and fiscal policy led to a continuously plummeting dollar, which put even more pressure on European exporters.

IV

The woman with the stocks's mother had always said that the stocks were meant for emergencies.

Those were the mother's words: If the woman with the stocks or her brother ever had an emergency, then they could sell the stocks and would be taken care of.

The brother, back when the stocks were still up, had bought a large condo for himself with his share.

It had not really been an emergency. Now he had an apartment and a girlfriend, whom he had met through the Internet.

The woman with the stocks's brother sat with his girlfriend from morning until night on a pull-out couch. The woman with the stocks often thought how she had done everything wrong, compared to her brother.

The woman with the stocks thought for hours about what her mother had wanted to say with these stocks. Did the stocks stand for the maternal hearth and the feeling of security it brought? Or were the stocks a promise of warmth?

The woman with the stocks visited the investment consultant again, who attempted to calm her down. The depreciation of the stocks' value did not mean that the woman with the stocks had nothing in the bank.

It just wouldn't be advisable to sell the stocks because then she would realize her losses.

She should just have a little patience, and everything would get better soon.

The woman with the stocks told the investment consultant that she couldn't calm down, that she needed consolation for her losses, that he should console her, that he should give her a hug, and that in the future she expected him to hug her regularly and warm and console her.

The banks in the Euro Zone had to enter losses of more than 283 billion euros in their books.

It became clear that European banks in Asia and Eastern Europe were more heavily involved than had previously been supposed.

V

The woman with the stocks went to the main entrance of the exchange. People were streaming out of the doors. On the steps a few schoolchildren were sitting and eating. The woman climbed up the stairs. She passed through the doors and stopped under the display board. She was looking for stocks followed by a red arrow pointing down.

The woman wanted to hear the sounds of the falling values. She wanted to hear the sound of the financial system crashing.

As she left the exchange, she patted the outside of the building and wished it good luck.

At home the woman with the stocks watched the magpie intently as it took a little walk along the windowsill, strutting around as if on an exclusive boardwalk among big shots.

Then all of a sudden the magpie said, "Hello there!"

The woman with the stocks didn't know where the magpie had learned to make this noise.

All she knew was that it had said, "Hello there." The woman with the stocks looked at the magpie for a long time and then asked in return: "Where are you building your nest? And would you happen to have some room there for when I have to leave my apartment because I can't afford it anymore?"

"I'll show you how to build a nest, so you can build one for yourself if you need to," the magpie answered.

Then it told the woman that bulky, black limousines had often been driving by the central bank of late, and that men wearing black would get out, go into the bank, and come out with big, heavy briefcases.

The traffic of big, heavy limousines had been picking up, the magpie said. And she speculated that the men were carrying material out of the central bank to build nests for themselves elsewhere.

VI

The woman with the stocks ate warm oatmeal every morning.

The magpie now came regularly for dessert. The woman with the stocks and the magpie would then sit in bed, stretch their legs out, and eye their potbellies.

The magpie said that its birthday was coming up. The woman promised to decorate the windowsill with freshly cut banana slices and paper strips for the occasion. And she promised to write the magpie a poem.

The woman no longer believed in a stock market recovery at all. She had come to realize that her investment consultant was a completely average person who wanted nothing more for himself than for the stock values to recover by New Year's or the beginning of spring.

It had become clear to her that, for this reason, the investment consultant would do anything to make it look as if the stocks had really improved.

VII

The woman with the stocks dreamed about her childhood home, about her mother and her father.

The woman with the stocks had furtively taken a drag on a joint in the dream.

When her father popped up, he only said, "I won't have you smoking that stuff under my roof!"

That was all. The woman with the stocks had been terribly ashamed when her father caught her smoking pot and woke up.

The woman with the stocks finally saw that, if you didn't take any risks, soon you didn't have any to avoid, because you were no longer alive.

The woman with the stocks wanted to live and forget about her worries over nothing. She wanted to give a witty reply to the whole system and ask: If money was everything, then what was nothing?

The investment consultant began giving the woman presents every time she visited his office. Hungarian salami, for example, and ring-shaped apple chips too. The woman understood he had a guilty conscience. After all, he had her whole fortune on his conscience, so why not let him worry himself a little on her behalf?

The investment consultant repeated that the prognosis for the coming year was exceedingly positive. Everything would be on the rise, and soon enough the woman with the stocks would be able to buy a nice condo like her brother.

The woman laughed aloud: "'A nice condo,' 'a nice condo.' With what my stocks are still worth, best case scenario I could buy a hole in the ground. A hole in Afghanistan, got it?"

Snow lay on the street. Many banks had fences staked off in front of them, and there were many police officers standing between the fences and the banks.

The woman with the stocks saw cameras and reporters. On a banner she read: A TURKEY'S LIFE IS PRETTY NICE, AT LEAST UP UNTIL THE END.

On a corner a demonstrator was demonstrating ways to set expensive cars on fire.

Other demonstrators had brought their own gallows and were attempting to hang a banker in effigy.

The rope they had tied around the effigy's neck passed through a ring on one end of the gallows, ran under the crossbeam through a second ring, and then down to the foot of the gallows where a barrel could be hung as a counterweight.

The activists were throwing coins and worthless stock certificates into the barrel.

This devalued junk pulled the effigy up high into the air. Various bank logos had been pasted on the side of the barrel.

VIII

The woman with the stocks wanted to take the blame for everything. She wanted the money to have disappeared because she had acted like an idiot.

The woman with the stocks wished the losses she had suffered could be traced back to something she understood.

If she had laid all the money on a table in front of an open window and then been surprised when a strong gust of wind swept everything away, the woman with the stocks would have understood that.

The magpie told the woman with the stocks that the men dressed in black didn't appear at the central bank anymore, and the big, heavy limousines had likewise disappeared without a trace. Now there was a giant peacock standing in front of the main entrance, with a bald head and deep, dark bags under its eyes.

The magpie also said she thought the bank had been cleaned out and the men with the suitcases didn't come anymore because they had gathered enough material for their nests.

The woman told the magpie that she'd found a flier in the park: *We're looking for our dog, Pavel. Our child's lost his favorite pet.*

Next to the text were photos of Pavel in various poses. Sleeping in the car, lying on the kid's bed, a close-up, lying on the living room floor. It was pretty bad if even dogs were being stolen nowadays.

The woman with the stocks often wanted to gorge herself, and always gave in to this desire. With devastating speed she devoured everything in her path.

The emptier her stomach was, the worse her mood. The woman with the stocks was depressed.

She wanted to scream out loud. Instead she stuffed herself with vegetables and mustard. Everything caused the woman with the stocks pain. She felt ugly and poor and grubby.

The woman with the stocks could no longer find her equilibrium. She often went to the refrigerator and took a strawberry from its container. There was nothing nicer than strawberries, ripe and freed from the earth.

The woman with the stocks crammed a whole container of strawberries in her mouth one by one. The woman with the stocks hated herself for it. The woman with the stocks cried a lot and spent a lot of time lying in bed, and as if that weren't enough, none of her pants fit her anymore.

Politicians forced the central bank to make way too much money available to speculators and borrowers. It should have been the central bank's job to close these help-yourself money stores, instead of continuing to support such madness.

The central bank poured even more rum in the punch and turned the music up even louder, instead of recommending a little thought and reflection.

The central bank sang the loudest:

Pedal to the metal, pedal to the metal, pedal to the metal!

IX

The woman with the stocks sat at the kitchen table and attempted to concentrate on the improvement of her stocks. The name of the game: wait and see gains again.

There was no alternative. She tried to focus on this vision and used clear tape to stick account statements to one another. She taped a lot of account statements to one another until a sort of rug formed. The woman with the stocks took this rug and attempted to lay it on the ground and walk over it.

She sat at the table and painted the account statements.

She painted all positive trends red. On the trend lines she painted sitting figures.

These figures all looked like they were made of heavy potato sacks.

She painted smiles on their faces.

The figures only ever sat on the upward-pointing segments.

On the downward-pointing segments the woman with the stocks painted tufts of grass.

She wanted to take one of these drawings to the investment consultant and tell him he was a small-time crook and had been on antidepressants too long and that really he hadn't been able to do his job for a long time.

She wanted to ask him if he'd had to pull the noose from around his first client's neck? Had one of his clients already thrown herself in front of a train?

X

The magpie had chicks.

The woman with the stocks had already visited the magpie's nest a few times and had even watched the magpie's chicks for her a few times.

The woman with the stocks wanted to move. She wanted to invite all her friends to dinner one last time and tell them she'd begun building her nest.

The woman with the stocks sat in the local train and thought about how someone should shake all the passengers and tell them they ought to wake up and take to the streets.

This crisis isn't going to pass, the woman with the stocks wanted to scream to the train.

The woman didn't say anything, however. Instead, she simply pulled on the emergency brake. The train stopped abruptly. People fell on top of each other. The woman with the stocks got out!

TRANSLATED FROM GERMAN BY DUSTIN LOVETT

work

SANTIAGO PAJARES

Today

There's something strange about today. I can feel it in my toes as
I shuffle my feet across the carpet. I can feel it in the alarm clock,
which I let beep for more than half a minute before turning it off, believing that it'll somehow turn itself off. I look around at my house,
empty as always, and I tell myself that I've got to, just got to set
aside some time to vacuum and dust. Dirt is collecting in the gaps
between the tiles of the bathroom floor and the lettuce in the fridge
has more brown leaves than green ones. I know that it's all a disaster,
if a minor one, but I think—as I did with the alarm clock—that if I
just leave it alone, it'll get resolved without my help somehow. I don't
know why I think that, but that's what I think. There's something
strange about today.

I have a tough time tying the knot on my tie and I have to do it over
and over and over. My name is Jack, and I have six ties. I have six ties,
three suits, and five hundred books. I don't know what else you could
want to know about me.

Today it's exactly one and a half years since Claudia left me. We
talk every once in a while, and she's already dropped the news, as
if it were nothing, that she's with someone else now. I've told her
that I'm happy that she's putting her life back together, even though

that's not true. She's also asked me—as if it were nothing—if I was with someone, and I told her I was, but that we hadn't been together long. Lies, lies, lies, but I know that hearing it makes her feel better, and that now she'll stop thinking that she abandoned me, which she did. But I don't blame her. Not today.

I think I've been brushing my teeth for a few minutes, focusing my thoughts on Claudia and the carpet in the bedroom. The bristles of the toothbrush feel like strands of straw in my mouth, but I keep brushing. I keep going because that's what I have to do. I keep going because that's what I've always done. I've been alone for a year and a half.

It's not that I haven't gotten laid in a year and a half, of course that's not it. I've had sex with three women. I met all three in a bar—not in the same bar—and I asked all three if they wanted to get breakfast the next morning, but they all declined. They had to get to work. All three of them worked on Sunday.

So, every day I walk to the bus stop and see the same people, and never say anything to them, even though we see each other five days a week. I get on the bus and then, before I sit down, look around for elderly or pregnant women. I like giving them my seat. It gives me a good feeling in the pit of my stomach, which usually lasts me until I arrive at the office and see one of my colleagues. I say hello to them, and they say hello to me as well, and I like it, but not as much as I like offering someone my seat on the bus.

Sometimes there's a woman on the bus who glances over at me. She raises her eyes slightly—hidden behind small, thick-rimmed glasses—over the top of her book. She has brown, vivacious eyes. I know this because I've stared at her eyes as they swiftly scan the lines on a page. I've also glanced back at her a few times, while she was looking at me, but neither of us has ever done anything about it. We never do anything.

Since before Claudia left me, well before, I've been taking paroxetine and halazepam, as advised by my doctor. Maybe since I was twenty-five, if I'm remembering right. Ten years on antidepressants is a great burden for someone like me, as I imagine it would be for anyone. I don't believe in antidepressants anymore. I think the doctor prescribed them for me because he didn't know what was wrong with me, because he didn't know who I was. I can't blame him. Ten years later I'm still in the process of figuring it out myself. Maybe on the day I figure it out, I'll go crazy. Maybe I won't do anything at all. At any rate, I never do anything.

I work for a technology company, a midsize company that's been acquired by a large corporation, so that even though I still work in the same office, and the majority of my colleagues are still around, our logo is different now. They gave me a transparent plastic jewel case containing some small business cards with my name embossed on them and the logo of the new company to the side. I looked at them for a few minutes and asked myself if those cards were me, if that was the answer to my question. I had to run to the bathroom and sit on the toilet and put my head between my legs and try to control my breathing until the cold sweats stopped. When I returned to my office I put the business cards in a drawer and I haven't looked at them since. It's not a big deal, of course; after all, I'm never going to go anywhere. Though that's not quite right, now that I think about it. Before I put them in the drawer, I slipped one in an envelope and sent it to Claudia. I never received an answer, but that's what usually happens to me when I don't ask any questions.

For eight hours a day, nine if I count the hour we have for lunch, I work side by side with my colleagues in the department. We talk about the problems we have to solve in order to finish a project, and the obstacles we face, imposed by the company or by our own bosses. Sometimes we get it done, sometimes we don't, but we always try. I like to eat something light at lunch, while my colleagues, the closest thing I have to friends, chew their enormous fillets and baked potatoes. I stuff pieces of lettuce and tomato in my mouth while I pretend to listen to them and hum Brahms symphonies under my breath. So far, nobody has noticed. Sometimes they give me a friendly punch in the shoulder and tell me that I don't talk much, but I just smile and that seems to be enough for them.

Some days, whenever we don't get out of work too late, or sometimes precisely because we get out late, we go to a nearby bar and play darts. I like darts. I like how they sound when they hit the board and the applause that follows. I've got good aim, the best out of all my colleagues. Everyone wants to be on my team. There's always someone who brings me a beer and then knocks the neck of their bottle against mine whenever I make a good throw. It's not that I'm a beer-lover, but it feels odd to drink a soda when everyone else is drinking alcohol. I don't always drink, though; sometimes I just let my beer get lukewarm on the tabletop, next to the small army of empties. Nobody notices. If they did, they would certainly drink it. And I wouldn't tell them it was my beer. I never say anything in those types of situations. They usually resolve themselves. It's a pity that the same isn't true for my bathroom, which needs a good cleaning.

We see a lot of women on these occasions when we all go out. Just like us, they go out to have a few beers after they're done with their day's work. My colleagues pounce on some of them, the most attractive or the drunkest, and try to strike up a conversation. At first they're usually laughing and the women aren't, but after a few drinks the situation typically balances out. There have been a few times when I've found myself doomed to talk to one of the women after being pressured by my colleagues. In the beginning they'd go over first and pave the way for me, but now I've learned to do it myself. It's not terribly hard, I just have to start talking and ask them a question, and then they get carried away talking and a few minutes later they tell me that I have really kind eyes and ask me why I don't talk very much. I respond that I prefer to listen and this spurs them on to talk even more. What normally happens is that after a half an hour they tell me that they have to go, or I tell them I have to go. Then I go back to my group and tell them: She was married, can you believe it? And they all applaud as if I'd just made a nice throw at the dartboard. They all seem happy. Everyone but me.

When I get back home I usually listen to some music and read a book. I like The Clash and The Who, but I like other bands too. I read one of the books that I take from the bookshelf at random, where they pile them up without rhyme or reason. It doesn't matter if it's a book I've already read. For me, it's like talking to someone I've talked to before. It gives me a very pleasant feeling of familiarity. Whenever I don't like a book, I usually leave it on one of the benches I pass on the way to the bus stop. When I come back in the evening it's already gone. Sometimes I tell myself that if I were a better person, I'd leave the ones I like. I also sometimes watch movie trailers on the Internet. It's not that I don't have time to watch the whole movie, just that I prefer the trailers. A trailer is like a first date with someone. It's an attempt to condense all the good experiences of one life down to a few minutes. If you don't like it, you don't have to see the rest. One time, out of curiosity, I saw one of the movies, but experience has taught me to opt for the shorter version. I feel the same way about people. Except for Claudia.

Before I go to bed I usually think about things like the marooned ocean liners in Mauritania. I try to bring to mind their rough, rusty metal surfaces. Or I think of Kolmanskop, the city that was overtaken by sand in the Namib Desert. I know it's odd to think of these things before going to sleep, and I know this because I've asked other people what they think about. For that reason I've never mentioned this to anyone. Well, that's a lie. I mentioned it to Claudia, but she didn't think it was weird. Maybe that's the type of thing that made us a good couple, in my opinion. In her opinion we weren't a good couple, but I can't blame her. After all, she never thought about things like that before she went to bed.

But today is different. I can feel it in my toes as I shuffle my feet across the carpet. I can feel it in the alarm clock, which I let beep for more than half a minute before turning it off, believing that it will somehow turn itself off. I look around at my house, empty as always, and I tell myself that I've got to, just got to set aside some time to vacuum and dust. But I know I won't do it today. Because today marks eight months since I last took a halazepam or a paroxetine. Because today, for the first time in a long while, I'm not afraid to get out of bed, and I don't feel a knot in my stomach while I'm tying one of my six ties. Maybe that's why I find it so hard to tie. I savor the buttered toast and run my tongue over the surface of it, a mixture of crunchy and creamy textures. I drink the coffee from my coffee maker, the first of the three cups that I'll drink during the day, and I don't feel it gurgling in the pit of my stomach. Even better, it's almost tasty.

It's a cloudy day today, but it doesn't matter to me. Today it's exactly one and a half years since Claudia abandoned me. I see that she left me a message on my answering machine while I was at work, but I don't listen to it. It will be just like all the others, to assure me that I'm doing all right. I'm not, but now I know it. Now I know it.

I take a few of my favorite books down off the shelves and put them in one of the plastic shopping bags that accumulate in my kitchen, which I never know where to put, one of those non-biodegradable plastic bags that take four hundred years to break down in the environment. I put Dumas, Hobbes, Palahniuk, and Tolstoy in there. I head out the door, and it doesn't bother me that it's started raining; I leave one book on each bench and watch the raindrops land on their leather or plastic covers. When I get to the bus stop I'm drenched, and there's rainwater dripping from my bangs and forehead. The people there look at me out of the corners of their eyes, and I look straight at them until they look away. It's a new feeling, like seeing specks of dust floating in the air for the first time. It seems like magic, but it's not; it never has been.

I take my cell phone out of my jacket pocket and text Claudia, telling her that I'm not seeing anybody, that everything I'd told her was a lie. I don't tell her that I'm sorry, because that's not true. After I send it, I turn off my phone, open the bus window, and throw it out into the street. A woman looks at me curiously, and I respond by shrugging my shoulders and smiling, as if there was nothing else I could have done. She smiles back and then returns to her book.

I spend my day in the office handing out my business cards. I go down the aisles, shake the hands of everyone I come across, tell them my name, and put one of my cards in their jacket pocket. Sometimes they laugh, other times they give me strange looks, but the fact is that after a couple of hours I've given away all of my lives. I throw the plastic jewel case into the garbage and never think about it again. They send me a report to revise, but instead of doing that I stick it to the wall with a thumbtack, pull out the box with my three darts in it, and toss them at the report from across the room, landing one right next to the other. A bunch of my colleagues applaud and pat me on the back between peals of laughter. It's just like we were in a bar, except I don't feel out of place. At lunch I eat a T-bone steak and French fries, and I get so full that I have to loosen my belt. In the afternoon my drowsiness gets the best of me, and I fall asleep during a strategic planning meeting with one of my bosses. I don't know if it bothers him, but it doesn't bother me, of course. At the end of the day, I think they're going to fire me, but I'm not sure. No matter what happens, I don't know if I'll come back to the office tomorrow. I don't gather up anything before leaving. There's nothing I want to keep.

After I leave I stop by a bar, alone, and ask for a shot of tequila. I drink it down in one gulp, and when I go to pay the bartender, he tells me it's on the house.

I stop by the supermarket before heading home and buy food that I've never bought before. I put hot chilies, barbecue sauce, and basmati rice into my basket. A bottle of triple-distilled vodka as well. When I get to the cash register, I walk right past the metal arch of the anti-theft device without stopping and it doesn't beep. Nobody stops me.

I get on the bus and see the woman with the brown eyes and thick-rimmed glasses near the back. She isn't reading her book like she usually does in the morning. She looks tired. I sit down beside her, despite there being many other open seats. She glances over at me out of the corner of her eye, but she doesn't dare say anything. So I tap her on the shoulder.

"What do you think about before you go to sleep?" I ask. She stares at me in silence, surprised. I smile at her. "Seriously."

"Hmm, I don't know."

"Make something up, the first thing that comes to mind."

"Boats," she responds, right away.

"Boats that are marooned in the sand?"

"No, boats out in the water."

"Oh," I reply. "Does it seem odd to you that I think about boats marooned in the sand?"

"No more than anything else would," she says.

"My name's Jack." I reach to give her a business card, but I don't have any more.

"I'm out of cards," I tell her.

"No problem."

"What's your name?"

"Maria."

"Do you like The Clash?"

"No."

"What about The Who?"

"Don't like them either."

"Well, maybe now I don't like them either."

I invite her to my place. She accepts, but she warns me that nothing is going to happen.

"Nothing ever happens," I reply.

"Your place is really dirty," she tells me.

I glance around, looking at the house as if it were a hotel room.

"I thought the same thing this morning."

TRANSLATED FROM CASTILIAN BY RHETT MCNEIL

SERHIY ZHADAN

The Owners

. . . This story was told to me by one of the original owners of the
club. I'd heard about these clubs quite a bit, but never actually visited
any, which, after all, is not that surprising, considering the specific
nature of these institutions. But rumors about the first official gay
nightclub, accompanied by a variety of names and addresses, had
been circulating for a few years now, and since no one knew exactly
where it was located, every joint fell under suspicion. They talked the
most about the club at the Dynamo sports stadium; the right-wing
youth of the city who came to watch the games positively condemned
all such institutions, and kept threatening to set fire to the nightclub
together with all the gay people gathered there for their so-called
parties. Once during the soccer season of 2003–2004, they even set
fire to Pinocchio, a coffee shop near the stadium, though the police,
of course, didn't think to connect this incident with the activities of
the rumored gay club, because, think about it, what kind of gay club
would meet at Pinocchio, which was such a homophobic name?

On the other hand, the media often mentioned the nightclub in
its various cultural bulletins or features about the rough-and-tumble
club scene in the city. As a rule, these bulletins from the city's club
scene were reminiscent of letters from a war—first toasts, then ma-

chine-gun fire rang in the video reports on the subject, and sometimes, when the cameraman didn't neglect his, ahem, professional duties, getting shit-faced on cognac on his expense account, he'd actually catch the machine-gun fire before the wedding speeches and violent profanities had finished, and show the tracer bullets perforating the warm Kharkiv sky like a salute to loyalty, love, and other things that nobody cares about on television. In this context, reports about the gay club intrigued the audience because there was never any mention of standoffs between the "criminals" and the authorities; the reports said: there was a party at the gay club, everything was civil and calm, there were no casualties. There had been interest for a time, but then the club's reputation began to wane, which wasn't too surprising; there's only so long a lack of excitement can seem novel to the general public, especially when our city has far more exciting establishments, like our tractor assembly factory. Anyway, the problems of a sexual minority in a country with such serious financial problems could hardly hold anyone's interest long. And when word got out that the nightclub was under the governor's official protection, the general response was muted—who expects the government to behave? Just mind your own business— the most important things are a clear conscience and getting your taxes done on time.

I met San Sanych during the elections. He looked to be forty, though he was actually thirty-two. Biography is simply stronger than biology, and Sanych was a clear case in point. He wore a crisp, black leather coat and carried a handgun—a typical run-of-the-mill gangster, you know what I mean. Though a little too melancholic for a gangster; he almost never used his cell, except to call his mother every so often, and as far as I can remember, nobody ever called him. He introduced himself as San Sanych and gave me a fancy business card that read, in gold lettering, "San Sanych, Civil Rights Advocate." Underneath, there were several phone numbers with a London dialing code. Sanych said they were office numbers; I asked whose, but he didn't answer. We hit it off right away. After the introductions, Sanych pulled a gun out of his pocket, said that he was all for honest elections and informed me that he could get as many of these guns as necessary. He had his own idea of honest elections, and why not? The thing was, he knew someone who worked at the Dynamo stadium and could get starter pistols there and make regular guns out of them at home. Look, he said, if you saw off this crud—he indicated the place where, apparently, the crud that had been sawn off used to be—it can be loaded with regular bullets; but the coolest thing is that it's only a starter pistol: the cops have no complaints when you buy them. If you want, I can hustle up a batch, forty bucks a piece, plus ten on top for sawing off the crud. If you want—to make it totally legit—I can even hustle up a Dynamo sports club ID for you. Sanych loved guns, and even more than guns he loved talking about guns. After a while, I became his best friend.

One time, the gay club came up. He just let it slip, at one point. Before becoming a civil rights advocate and defending honest elections, he had been in the nightclub racket and, it turned out, was directly involved with the first official gay club, the same phantom institution that our ever-so-progressive city youth had been trying to burn down for so long, and so ineffectually. So I asked him to tell more and he agreed, said no problem, okay, it's all water under the bridge, sure, why not.

This was the story he told me.

Turns out he used to be a member of the Boxers for Justice and Social Adaptability Association. He told me a little bit about the group.

They'd started at the Dynamo sports club as a civic union of former professional sportsmen. It's unclear what the Boxers for Justice actually did, but they certainly had a high mortality rate; once a month one of them was inevitably gunned down and then opulent wakes with delegations from the police and regional government were held. From time to time, about once every few months, the Boxers for Justice had unofficial "matches" with an equivalent Polish organization. Anyway, that's what they called them. Several buses would come to the Boxers' office, the boxers along with great numbers of domestic appliances piled into them, and then the caravan would set off for Poland. Regional heads and coaches went separately. Upon arriving in Warsaw, the boxers went to the local stadium, which doubled as a market, and sold their merchandise in bulk, after which they celebrated another wonderful victory for their team. The catch was that Sanych had never been a boxer. Sanych was a wrestler. His grandfather, who had been a serious professional wrestler after the war, and even participated in a USSR Peoples' Spartakiad, during which his arm was broken, and of which he was particularly proud—not the broken arm, participating in the Spartakiad—got Sanych started in freestyle wrestling. Eventually, his grandfather brought him to Dynamo. Sanych started making progress, participated in city competitions, had great promise, but in a few years his arm got broken too. By that time he'd already finished college and was trying to start his own business, though unsuccessfully, especially after the broken arm. That's when he found the Boxers for Justice. The Boxers looked at his arm, asked him whether he was in favor of justice and social adaptability and, upon his confirmation thereof, received him in their ranks. Right away, Sanych got into a brigade that controlled the markets in the tractor-assembly-factory district. It turned out that it wasn't too difficult to make one's career in this business—as soon as your immediate supervisor was killed, you took his spot.

In a year, Sanych commanded a small subdivision, and had great promise again, but, in the end, he just didn't care for the business: much as he excelled at it, Sanych had a college degree and didn't much like the idea of meeting his end before he turned thirty at the hands of some disgruntled black-market mule carrying a secondhand grenade. The work seemed especially unattractive since his business affairs took up all his time and he simply didn't have any private life anymore—notwithstanding the prostitutes that he picked up at the market on occasion. But Sanych didn't think they counted, and I think they probably didn't consider it much of a family life either—a temporary cohabitation on economic grounds, perhaps. And so Sanych began seriously reconsidering his future. The bulletproof vest incident made up his mind. At one point, in the depths of a prolonged alcoholic stupor (apparently it was some kind of a holiday, Christmas most likely) Sanych's employees decided to present their young boss with a bulletproof vest. They had acquired it by trading a new Xerox machine—the very latest model!—with some Kiev state security force officers. Sanych and his men drank yet another toast to this gift and then decided to try the thing out. Sanych pulled on the vest, his men pulled out a Kalashnikov. And you know what, the vest turned out to be legit—Sanych survived the party with only three moderate bullet wounds. But that was the end of it: he decided to stop right there. His career as a freestyle wrestler had been a failure, and now his career as a fighter for justice and social adaptability didn't come out right either. He had to do something about it . . .

■ ■ ■

So that's how Sanych found himself back on the streets without either a business or a family, albeit with fighting experience and a college degree, though the latter was of no interest to anyone. And during this critical period he met Goga, aka Georgy Crowbar. He and Goga went to the same school when they were kids, after which

Sanych went to wrestle and Goga went to med school. They hadn't seen each other much, recently—Sanych, as indicated above, being actively involved in the social adaptability of boxers, and Goga being a young professional out in the Caucasus participating in the Russian-Chechen war. Indeed, it was hard to know which side Goga thought he was on, while he was out there, as he had been buying medicine from the Russian Ministry of Health and selling it to the Georgian children's clinic. Goga got busted when he ordered a recklessly large shipment of anesthetics, which gave the Ministry of Health all the reason it needed to open the books and start asking the obvious question: why would a regional children's clinic in whose name all the receipts had been made, need such a huge amount of narcotics? Which is why Goga had to come home, trading shots with his irate Caucasian buyers all the way. Immediately upon his return, he acquired a few lots of drywall. It wasn't a bad business, but Goga had already gotten a new idea, and it began to crowd out his other fantasies and projects: he decided to go into nightclubs. And it was at this critical moment that our heroes encountered each other again.

"Listen," said Goga to his childhood friend, "I'm new in this business, I need your help. I want to open a club." "Well, you know," said his buddy, "I don't know much about it, but if you want, I can ask around." "You don't understand," Goga said, "I'm not interested in asking around, I know what I need to know myself—what I need's a partner, get it? I want you to come in on this with me—I'd like that. See, I've known you since my childhood, I know your parents, and I know where to look for you, just in case you decide to stiff me. And the main thing is, you've already worked with everyone here. You'd be a real partner." "And you really think you can make money on it?" asked Sanych. "Sure, I can make money on anything," said Goga. "But look, you think I'm doing it just for the dough? I have five boxcars of drywall at Balashov Station—I could sell them in an instant and go off to Cyprus if I wanted. But—see my dilemma?—I just don't care for Cyprus. Do you know why I don't want to go to Cyprus? I'm almost thirty, after all, just like you, right? I've had businesses in four countries; I'm wanted by the public prosecutors of more than a few autonomous republics and was probably supposed to die somewhere in the tundra from scurvy a long time ago; three times I was caught in the crossfire; Chechnya's general himself bought my syringes; the Krasnoyarsk special police squad nearly executed me; once lightning hit my car while I was driving it (I had to get a new battery). I pay alimony to a widow I know in Northern Ingushetia, though the others don't get anything; half of my teeth are implants, and once I almost agreed to sell my kidney for the money to buy up a batch of machine tools. But look, I came home, I'm in a great mood, I sleep well; half of my friends have already been wiped out, but half are still alive; you, for example, are still alive, though what are the odds of that? See, somehow we've survived, and since I'm still alive, I thought, okay Goga, okay, now everything's on the right track, now everything will be fine. If the Krasnoyarsk special police squad didn't manage to execute you, and the lightning didn't kill you either, why bother with Cyprus? And suddenly I realized what I'd really wanted all my life. Can you guess?" "What?" San Sanych asked. "All my life I've just wanted to own my own club, see, my own club, where I can sit every evening and where no one will kick me out even if I start puking onto the table. And so what did I do? Guess what I did!" Goga started laughing. "I went ahead and bought this fuckin' club, how d'you like that?" "When did you buy it?" Sanych asked. "A week ago." "What kind of club?" "Well, it's not a club yet, it's just a sandwich shop for now . . ." "What?" Sanych asked. "Well, do you know that café, the one that's just called 'Sandwiches'? There's a hell of a lot of work that still needs doing, but the location's nice, it's in the Ivanov neighborhood. So I'll sell off the drywall, do a renovation, and leave all my troubles behind. But I need a partner, you understand? So, do you like the idea?" he asked. "I like the name," Sanych said. "What name?" "The name of the place. 'Sandwiches.'"

So they agreed to meet at the soon-to-be club next morning. Goga promised to introduce his new partner to his prospective art director. San Sanych came on time, but his partner was already there waiting at the doors of Sandwiches. The exterior of Sandwiches left much to be desired: the last renovation seemed to be done about thirty years ago, and since the entire building couldn't have been more than thirty years old, it was probably safe to assume that the last renovation had been never. Goga opened the padlock and let San Sanych go in first. San Sanych stepped into a half-lit space crammed full with tables and plastic chairs: Here we go, he thought sadly, should have stayed with the Boxers for Justice . . . But it was too late to retreat—Goga followed him in and closed the door behind them. "Our art director should be here any minute now," he said and sat on one of the tables, "Let's wait."

The art director's name was Slavik. Slavik turned out to be an old junkie; he looked around forty too, but maybe that was just the drugs. He was half an hour late, complained about traffic, then said he'd taken the subway—in a word, he was making excuses. He wore an old jean jacket and huge, idiotic-looking sunglasses, which he refused to take off even in the dark basement, on principle. "Where did you find him?" Sanych whispered while Slavik was walking around and examining the space. "Mother's recommendation," answered Goga as quietly. "He used to be art manager at the Pioneer Club; they kicked him out, I think, for corruption." "Well, it wouldn't have been on account of his religion . . ." said Sanych. "All right, just trust me," answered Goga. "So how's it going?" he yelled to Slavik. "Do you like it?" "Overall, I do," said Slavik. Preoccupied by something, he came back over and sat on a plastic stool. I'll give you a quick lesson in aesthetics if you don't, thought Sanych and even turned off his phone, so that no one would interrupt (though nobody ever called anyway). "Well," said Goga, obviously enjoying himself, "what do you say, any ideas?" "All right then," Slavik exhaled heavily and pulled out a suspicious-looking cigarette. "All right then." He didn't say anything else for a moment. "Georgy Davydovich," he addressed Goga formally, "I'll be frank with you." Oh Christ, Sanych thought. Goga went on squinting happily in the twilight of his sandwich shop. "I'll be frank," Slavik repeated. "I've been in show business for twenty years, I worked during the Ukrconcert epoch, I'm well known among the musicians, I've babysat the great Grebenshchikov, I've even coordinated a U2 concert in Kharkiv." "There was a U2 concert in Kharkiv?" San Sanych interrupted.

"No, they cancelled," answered Slavik, before going back to ignoring San Sanych, "and this is what I've got to say, this is my opinion, Georgy Davydovich—it was a *cool* idea to buy this club." "You think?" Goga asked, as though doubtful. "Yes, really a *cool* idea. I'm telling you this in all sincerity, there's nothing I don't know about show business, I even organized the first jam session in this city." Here he apparently remembered something, lost his train of thought, and was quiet for a time. "So . . ." Goga prompted, unable to stand it any longer. "Yes," Slavik nodded, "yes." Shit, he's wasted, Sanych thought, increasingly annoyed. "Yes what?" Goga asked. "*Si*," Slavik started nodding his head again, "yes . . ." San Sanych reluctantly reached for his phone. In principle, on his previous job, he'd simply killed this kind of a freak, but here the situation was different, it was a different business, they'd have to figure it out without him. Slavik suddenly started talking: "I'll tell you what, Georgy Davydovich . . ." unexpectedly coming out with the following whopper:

"The nightclub business," he said, working up a head of steam, "is pretty hairy . . . first of all because the market is already established, you know what I mean?" Everybody pretended they did. "Small businesses are to blame. You know, those motherfuckers spring up all over the place . . . they get in ahead of you! So, then, what, you buy your own place . . ." he seemed to be addressing Goga, "you want to open a nice, regular club, fill it with nice, regular customers, with nice, regular cultural programming—well, fuck, why bother?" "Slavik, get on with it," Goga cut him short. "All right," Slavik went on, "So how do you do it? How do you bring people in when they've already got all they want? What's the *hook*? What's the hook in any part of show business?" Goga gradually stopped smiling: "The hook is the format!" he offered. "Sure, sure," Slavik nodded happily and even gave Goga a short round of applause: "*Si*, that's it . . ." he trailed off. "So . . . what about it? What about the format?" asked Goga after a long pause. "Oh, the format's totally fucked," Slavik said. "Like I said, in this business, everything's been taken by now, every goddamn angle," he laughed. "The market is saturated, get it? It's like, you want to sell fast food? Great, go ahead, but the city already has a hundred fast-food joints; you want to open a bar, hell, let's open a bar, I can come up with all the cultural programming you want, no problem; or, why not, you want a dance club, let's do a dance club; an old-timey pub, we'll do a pub. Only, you won't make a fucking cent on the thing, Georgy Davydovich, excuse me for being so frank, not a fucking cent." "And why is that?" Goga asked, obviously hurt. "I told you, because the market is saturated, you'll just get squashed. You have no one watching your back, right? You'll go up in smoke, right along with your club." "So what are you suggesting?" Goga asked, nervous, "do you have any ideas?" "*Si*," said Slavik apparently pleased with himself, "*si*, there's one *cool* idea, a really *cool* idea." "And what is it?" asked Goga, smelling trouble. "We should take the last unoccupied niche, if you follow me. And in this business there's only one niche left—we will have to open a gay club." "A *what* club?" said Goga. "Gay," Slavik answered, "a club for gays, that is. We don't have a single one. It's a niche that's just got to be filled." "Have your brains finally leaked out once and for all?" asked Goga after another pause. "Are you for real?" "And why not?" asked Slavik cautiously. "I just don't get it," Goga grew more and more agitated. "You really want me, Georgy Crowbar, to turn my dream place into a gay club? You'll get us all killed! That's it, you're fired," he said and jumped off the table. "Wait, wait, Georgy Davydovich!" Now it was Slavik's turn to be nervous. "Nobody's asking you to put *Club for Fags* in big letters over the front door, okay?" "Oh yeah? And what would you call the place instead?" asked Goga, putting his coat on. "We'll call it an 'Exotic Recreation Club,' for example," Slavik shouted. "And we'll give it a flashy name, that'll appeal to our target demographic. You know, like 'Peacock'!" "*Staphylocock,*" Goga sneered. "So who's going to come to your 'Peacock'?" "I'm telling you. People will. The niche is empty, see? There's not a single gay club in a city of two million! It's a gold mine. We don't even have to find our audience, they'll come on their own, all we have to do is open the doors!" Goga cringed in disgust, but sat back at the table (though he left his coat on). Slavik took this as a good sign, pulled out another cigarette, and continued, "I was just as shocked as you, when the idea came to me. It's a fortune, just lying in the street—anyone could come over and take it. I'm still amazed it hasn't occurred to anyone else—and I promise you, if we wait, a month or two, somebody will steal the idea, I bet you anything they'll steal it!" Slavik was only getting more and more worked up; apparently he was sincerely worried that someone would steal it. "But right now, we're ahead of the competition!" Then he finally noticed Sanych: "Say something!" he pleaded, seeking his support. "Okay," said Goga at last. "In principle, it's not a bad idea." "Wait a minute," said Sanych, "are you serious?" "Well, why not?" "Obviously, why not!" Slavik yelled in excitement. "Slow down," Sanych interrupted again. "Listen," he told Goga, "you and I are friends and all that, but I'm against this. I've been working for the Boxers for Justice almost two years—they'd put a curse on me if they heard about this, are you kidding? We agreed to start a normal business, not open some *peacock*." "No one's talking about peacocks," said Goga, "nobody is really planning to call it Peacock. We'll come up with a regular name. Or we'll keep the old one." "Which?" asked Sanych. "Sandwiches! Why not?" Goga smirked again. "Doesn't that sound good? *Exotic Recreation Club Sandwiches?* Eh, sweetheart?" Slavik the Sweetheart nodded, then nodded again. What else could he do? "Don't sweat it," Goga turned to his partner, "he'll take care of the customers," he pointed at Slavik, "you and I just have to worry about finishing the renovation before summer, then we'll see. After all," he added, speculating aloud, "why *not* a gay club? At least there'll be no whores around."

So everyone rolled up their sleeves. Goga sold his drywall off, Sanych introduced him to the right people, and they started the renovation. Slavik, in his turn, volunteered to register the gay club as a "youth initiatives club," so as not to pay all the usual fees for opening a commercial venture. It turned out that Slavik was indeed well known—and since everyone knew him, they did their best to avoid dealing with him. Early in the morning, Slavik would go to the local government headquarters, stop by the cafeteria, have his tea there, and shoot the breeze with the checkout girls; thereafter he'd go to the cultural administration office. They wouldn't let him in, Slavik would act offended, run back to Sandwiches, get into a fight with the construction workers, scream that he'd been in show business for twenty years, and then threaten to invite the great Grebenshchikov to opening night just to show them. As for opening night, by the way: spring came and went, and finally the renovation was finished; they could open the club. Goga called a meeting, this time in his newly remodeled office. "Well," he asked, "any ideas about opening night?" "Georgy Davydovich, I do have a few ideas," Slavik began, all businesslike. "First of all, fireworks . . ." "Next," Goga cut him off. "All right," Slavik was calm enough, "I suggest Japanese food." "Where will you get it?" asked Sanych. "I have acquaintances," Slavik answered with dignity. "Japanese acquaintances?" "No, Vietnamese, but they'll look plenty Japanese for our purposes. You know, they bring in shipping containers at the Southern Station: every time, there's one for making fur coats and one for food." "Keep talking," Goga interrupted again. "Vaudeville striptease," Slavik blurted out victoriously. "What kind of striptease?" "Vaudeville," Slavik repeated. "I have my eye on four chicks in bikinis, they do a show every third week, can't do it more often, they also work at the Pioneer Club on the side." "Look," Goga broke in, "that's out. I've told you—no whores in the club. As though our audience would be interested anyway!"

"So are you done?" he added a moment later. Slavik pulled out one of his cigarettes, lit it, let the smoke out, sighed heavily, and started again: "Very well," he said, and then paused for effect, "very well, Georgy Davydovich, I understand where you are going, okay, well, I'll talk to Grebenshchikov if you insist, only, I think, even for me, he wouldn't do it for free . . ." "Fine, fine," Goga waved him away, "Sanych, do it for me, get me some musicians, okay? And you," he said to Slavik, "figure out who we'll be inviting." "What do you mean, who?" Slavik asked, brightening: "Firefighters by all means, tax administrators, and somebody from the culture administration. We'll feel them out, in a word." "All right," Goga agreed, "but in addition to all those fags, do try to get us a couple of decent gay guys, okay?"

The opening was held in early June. San Sanych hired a group that usually played in a hotel restaurant: they had a well rehearsed set, were reasonably priced, and didn't drink at work. Slavik put together a guest list, only about a hundred people. Goga studied the proposed list for a while, then narrowed it down a little more, crossing out the cafeteria girls from the local government headquarters and the four striptease artistes from the Pioneer Club. Slavik attempted to keep the cafeteria girls at least, but yielded after a long argument. Goga invited his old business partners, from whom he had bought his drywall wholesale, as well as his childhood friends and the Leekhooy brothers. San Sanych invited his mama, and wanted to invite an old friend, a former prostitute, but then thought about his mama and dropped the idea.

The opening came off beautifully. Slavik got wasted in half an hour; San Sanych asked the guards to watch him; Goga ordered everyone to relax—was it a party or what? San Sanych's mama said that the music was too loud and soon left. Sanych called a cab for her and came back to celebrate. The wholesale guys took off their ties and were drinking to the owners' health; Slavik sang loudly and kissed the representatives from the tax administration—indeed, all in all, he was acting gayer than anyone else in the crowd—gay, in any case, as he understood it; he was definitely doing it on purpose, to get the crowd going. And it sort of worked: the Leehooy brothers started a fight with the wholesale guys in the men's room, just your usual kind of brawl, what else had they paid for? Grisha Leehooy's offended screams—"Now who's a fag!"—came from the bathroom, and everyone knew that his brother was backing him up. The fight was quickly contained, Sanych pulled everyone apart and drunken wholesale guys went to finish the party at a striptease club, since Sandwiches didn't have any girls on stage. The tax administration people also went to a striptease joint, and they didn't take Slavik along so as not to ruin their reputations. Almost everyone left, and after a while there was only some girl at the bar and a couple of middle-aged men whispering to each other in the corner. They looked exactly like the tax administration representatives, though maybe that was only because it seemed so difficult to say anything definitive about their appearance.

"Who're those guys?" Sanych asked Slavik, who'd started sobering up and was now remembering who he'd been kissing. "Ah, them," he said, squinting. "I don't want to offend anyone present but . . . I think that's them. I mean, the gay guys." "Do you know them?" Sanych asked, just in case. "Sure," Slavik nodded. "It's Doctor and Boosya." "What kind of doctor?" Sanych asked. "Just a regular doctor," Slavik answered. "Come on, I'll introduce you. Hi, Boosya!" he addressed the guy who looked younger and more taxman-like; "And howdy to you, Doctor." He shook hands with the somewhat more respectable looking of the two—that is, the one who looked less like he worked in the tax administration. "Meet Sanyok here." "San Sanych," San Sanych corrected him sheepishly. "Our manager," Slavik insisted. "Nice to meet you," said Doctor and Boosya both, and invited them to their table. Sanych and Slavik sat. A silence fell. Sanych was getting nervous, while Slavik reached for his cigarettes. "So, Slavik, you're here now?" Doctor started in, hoping to ease the tension. "Yes," said Slavik, lighting his cigarette and then smothering the match in their plate. "My friends asked me to pitch in, and I thought, why not, I have a free slot in my calendar just now. Clearly they could use a little guidance," he went on, taking the doctor's fork and spearing some salad. "Take tonight, for example . . . you could really do it right, with some sort of cultural program . . . I even had Grebenshchikov set up . . . But it's not a big deal, it turned out fine," he put his hand on Sanych's shoulder, "just fine. I give them some advice here and there, you know, and I think things will work out fine, yes . . ." Sanych carefully removed Slavik's hand, got up, nodded to Doctor and Boosya, wished them a pleasant evening, said he was sure they'd talk again soon, and moved to the bar. "Who are you?" he asked the girl who had just ordered another vodka. Her lip was pierced, and whenever she took a drink, the metal balls clinked against her glass. "I'm Vika. You?" "San Sanych," said San Sanych. "Gay?" asked Vika matter-of-factly. "Owner," said Sanych defensively. "I see," said Vika, "can you take me home? I'm totally wasted." Sanych called a taxi and, after saying good-bye to Goga, took the girl outside. The taxi driver turned out to be some hunchback. Sanych had seen him around. The guy seemed overjoyed to see them, and asked, "So, are you from the fag club?" "Yeah, yeah," San Sanych answered uneasily. "Where to?" he asked Vika. As they drove, Vika got queasy. "What," the hunchback asked, "planning to puke?" "Everything's fine," Sanych said, "no puking here." "Whatever you say," said the hunchback, seeming somewhat disappointed. "So where are we going?" Sanych grabbed Vika by the shoulder, turned her to face him, checked the inner pocket of her leather jacket, and pulled out her passport. "Try this," he said to the hunchback, giving him her registered address, and off they went—right back to Sandwiches. Vika lived next door. It would have been easier to carry her home, but who'd known? Sanych pulled her out of the car, asked the hunchback to wait, and carried her into the house. At the apartment door he stood her on her feet. "Are you all right?" he asked. "All right," said Vika, "all right, give me my passport back." Sanych took it out and looked at her photo. "You look better without the piercing," he said. "If you want, you know," said Sanych, "I'll stay with you." "Mister," said Vika smirking, "don't you get it? I'm a lesbian. And you aren't even gay. You're just the owner. You know what I mean?"

She kissed him and vanished behind the door. Sanych felt the cold taste of her piercing on his lips. Like a silver spoon . . .

TRANSLATED FROM UKRAINIAN BY ANASTASIA LAKHTIKOVA

evil

CLEMENS MEYER

The Case of M.

So you talk to the girl. No problem, you know her don't you, you did
an internship at her school, at the after-school club. Did you plan it
all back then? I mean, not at the after-school club, I mean at that moment when you decided to lure her to your—well it's not really your
apartment to be precise, but anyway, where you live. Or did you want
to wait and see how things turned out? You used to jerk off when you
thought about it, and you always had to take a break in the middle
and listen in case your mother was creeping around outside your
bedroom door. You used to see her walking home alone. "I've got
something for your mom," you say. "Your mom said you're supposed
to come and pick it up from my place." And she goes with you; you
reach for her hand but then let go again, feeling how warm it is.
You're nervous, not much farther now, just around the corner; no
one takes any notice of the two of you, you keep your head down and
hope you don't meet anyone you know. And you don't meet anyone,
not even when you're both standing outside the house where you live
with your mother. Did you know my mother used to live across the
road, right there by the last bus stop? I grew up there, did you know,
I lived there with my mother too; well, my sister was there too, and
let me tell you, living under one roof with two women could be hell

at times, and I got caught masturbating more than once; nearly ten years I lived there, I didn't move out until I was nearly twenty-one— oh, you see, you're twenty-one now too; no wait, you're only nineteen, and now it's too late to move away, or let's say move out; you're away from your mother now, in August 2009, but almost exactly a year ago you knew very well she wasn't at home. "Hello Mum, can I introduce you to my new girlfriend?" No, that's no good; you weren't really one for the girls, were you? I wasn't either at your age, by the way. When I was a kid I told my mother I wanted to live in a house in the forest when I grew up, with my friend J. H., who was my best friend back then but he's dead now, sadly. Yes, she said, that's perfectly normal; some men love each other too. Did my mother think I was going to be gay? But by the time I reached my big porn-mag phase between thirteen and eighteen she must have thought differently; it's not all that easy to hide porn mags in an apartment full of women. Did you have porn mags too? Or at least the soft stuff: *Praline, Neue Revue*, and that kind of thing? Or did you—you must have sensed at some point that you have . . . let's just say: a slightly different focus—did you buy those nudist magazines? Because, don't get me wrong, there are a whole load of naked little girls in them. No, no, it's fine, I bought one of those mags myself once, although I'm not even sure they still exist. But there's still *Landser* and *Junge Freiheit* for the Nazis among us, so you must be able to get the other stuff too; mind you, we're living on the Internet now, there are different ways to get hold of jerk-off material nowadays. And it was really expensive, that nudist magazine; I took it to the forest to have a wank and it was so embarrassing in the paper shop; who buys those things anyway, potential kiddy-fiddlers or uptight pedophiles? It was at a chess championship in the Black Forest, there was always so much going on at the youth hostel that I never got a chance to jerk off. I was fourteen back then, I think. Did you have Internet access at your mum's place? Wait, let me have a look . . . well there you are at the computer, but as soon as I get closer you go all tense; oh shit, now I see, you're playing *Monkey Island* because none of the new games will work on your ancient computer. No, sorry, I don't want to be cruel, I'm just interested . . . I'm a voyeur of the first degree, you see, I'm really fascinated by things like that, especially things that get out of hand, so I'm pretty interested in the . . . let's say the human soul. So I just want to take a careful look inside of you . . . by the way, of course I'm interested in the carnal side of things, if you get what I mean, I even had a bit of a sick obsession for a while; mind you, *sick* is taking it a bit far. But I want to put myself in your shoes so to speak, and I can, there's no need to be scared, you just go ahead and trust me . . . IF HE'S SICK HE SHOULDN'T BE ALLOWED OUT (*Leipziger Volkszeitung*, 18 August 2009), MY CLIENT WAS AL-WAYS AN OUTSIDER; I used to stand on the windowsill, it must be nearly ten years ago now so I was about twenty-two, with the blinds down, and believe it or not with my pants down too; mind you, I can't say *that* for sure after all these years . . . anyway I always had my binoculars at hand; they were good binoculars, I still take them to the races nowadays, not always though because they make you look like some dumb tourist or retiree; wedged a match between two slats of the blind and had the best view of the school sports grounds across the way. Well you know the school don't you, that's where she came from on 18 August 2008, she came from day camp. I didn't even know there was such a thing anymore, I thought day camp was one of those old East German things; when I was her age, so nine, she was nine, right? Or have I dropped a year, more or less? When I was her age we used to go to the vacation day camp, me and my sister, we had one of those—what did they call it again?—a vacation pass; we made radios that only picked up one station, watched movies, painted pictures, once we went to the German Library for some special screen-printing thing, and we did all sorts of arts and crafts, and then there was some talk in the old town hall about myths and legends, and I remember now, some loser from a children's home; sorry, that's nothing to do with you, believe me; some kid put his hand up and said something about werewolves in helmets, yeah helmets, what a load of shit. We were very close back then, me and my sister, I mean; later we backed off a little. Can you imagine I dreamed a couple of times, it's a while ago now though, I dreamed I fucked my sister? I don't like talking about it—see how much I trust you?—but you can't help what you dream about, can you? And I always think we've backed off a little now, but in a good way, I'd say; it's because of the divorce as well, because we lived with my mother under one roof right then, at that critical age I mean when your hormones run riot and everything; Jesus, that was an absolute nightmare, the women were constantly on the rag, you know, and me constantly jerking off; it was never going to work out. And I was a bit out of kilter back then anyway, used to steal and started drinking too young, problems at school all the time; it was always like that, even back in the East, but then they wanted to kick me out of school twice, at grammar school, and back in the East my mother had to take me to a shrink a couple of times: "Now draw your parents as animals and yourself as well," IF HE'S SICK HE SHOULDN'T BE ALLOWED OUT, Jesus, can't you all just shut up! Hey wait, stay, I haven't fin-ished yet, where was I? Right: on the windowsill and the sports grounds across the way. I went to that school too, you know. And you weren't just an intern there (you wanted to be a Social Assistant, re-mind me to ask you what that is exactly), you were there yourself right from when you were an A-B-C-darian, what a stupid name, do you remember? First day of school and all that, I remember it any-way, and you stayed there until the end. I don't think you'll know the teachers I had there, they're all somewhere else now or dead. Mind you, I'm only thirteen years older than you; some of them might still be there. And you must know the school caretaker, Shimmy we used to call him; no idea what his real name was. He used to say the same two things all the time, practically crazy he was, he used to shout them more like: "Your ass is gonna get busted!" when he was angry; old Shimmy was always pissed off about something; and "Heeme!" We spent ages puzzling over what that *heeme* meant. All it means is "at home" in Saxon dialect, and he said it in almost every sentence. "Your ass is gonna get busted, heeme!" And at some point us kids figured out what he meant by his *heeme*. He used to live there, at the school, I mean, with his family. And when he was out and about there, on his home ground so to speak, taking care of everything, doing all sorts of technical stuff, repairs and organization and who knows what else for us children and teachers (and back then for the Pioneer leaders and all the party bigwigs, but that won't mean much to you)—and the guy was popular with us, believe you me—he just felt so goddamn at home: *heeme*. He was a funny guy, that Shimmy.

And not long ago, in July 2009, to be precise, just so we don't get confused—we're actually still outside your building—there was a fire on the school grounds, right where the garage is with Shimmy's car in it. I didn't notice, even though it's only five hundred yards away from my apartment, and the firemen must have been working on it all night while I was asleep. The fire was between the front building for the primary kids (boys and girls) and the gym. The flames must have been good and tall, and Shimmy's car burned of course; no one knows how the fire broke out, some kind of spontaneous combustion, they say. I can still see the soot-stained façade with the black windowsills when I walk past the school complex. AN INEX-PLICABLE CRIME. In the old days you couldn't have seen the building from my side of the road, there were tower blocks in between but they've been knocked down now. PUPILS VERY UPSET. Anyway, where was I? There was a link a minute ago, I'd found something in the word-flow to take me back to where I wanted to go in the first place, or where I'd already been . . . Yeah right, windowsills, the soot-stained windowsills! And there's me on my windowsill again, standing there with my binoculars and watching the little girls playing sports . . . but they were fifteen or sixteen, toward the end of high school, I mean I'm not a goddamn pedophile; sorry, nothing against you, you seem to be a special case, my young friend, we'll get to that soon enough; but I do like a nice pair of breasts and the girls I used to watch had them under their tight sports tops, and big ones too, sometimes; maybe there were a couple of fourteen-year-olds once in a while, how should I know; it's not like they have their age printed on their shirts, and some of them you'd swear were over eighteen. It was different in my day but they're real sex bombs at fifteen and sixteen now, and so there's me on my windowsill; sometimes I stand there all through gym class and sway my binoculars to and fro, left to right, and they're doing long jumps down there now, what a gorgeous bounce you get from that, and my biggest fear is getting caught. What about you? Weren't you scared someone would knock or ring while the two of you were in there? And first of all you have to get into the room with her; you're still going up the stairs now. In my building there's—wait, let me think—there's me all on my own down on the ground floor, but I don't count; to meet myself I'd have to get caught in a time loop like the space traveler Ijon Tichy, so let's start again: upstairs the couple, then the Arab, one guy's in jail right now, should be out again soon though so we'll list him as present and accounted for; so four people, and that's it—the apartment above me is empty, there's only one apartment on the ground floor and the first floor, it's a very narrow building. So that's four people, and very, very often—I have to say so because it surprises me how often it is—very often I meet one of them when I come home. What would you have done if the woman next door had suddenly been standing on the staircase, or the man from upstairs on his way out to go shopping? "Good afternoon," or "Hello," or maybe "How's things?"—people liked you, at least that's what I read, even though you used to get bullied of course, what with your disability. I mean it's all right to say that, isn't it; it's not a real disability though, you went to a proper school, just slight problems with your motor skills and your speech a bit slow sometimes because of some genetic thing, trisomy 8, and you must be a mild case I suppose because you're not such a Jerky Joey as other people who have it, *extended thorax, peculiarities in the number and width of ribs, extraneous nipples, high, narrow palate, cleft palate, broad nose, frequently upward-pointing nostrils, sagging of one or both eyelids, short fingers, narrow wing of ilium, liquid accumulation in the neck area* . . . holy ghost and Jesus H! You'd be a right Franken-stein, but you look more like a cuddly teddy; I saw you in the court-room; no, I was right at the back, and yes, really, you look like a nice kid: a bit awkward, a bit chubby, but pretty much the boy-next-door type; my mother told me she saw you at the Schlecker drugstore a couple of times, she thinks so anyway, she just doesn't know if it was *before* or *after*; you were down there every now and then chatting with the girls at the register: how awful it is what happened to that poor girl and how you can't imagine anyone . . . I've lost the thread again: "Good afternoon"—no, because nobody came by, and you and she walked past the little closet in the corridor that used to be the outside lavatory, where you propped her up later on, I think, for several days even, at least two days or so; I don't want to check my material again right now, it's not nice digging and delving in all that, take my word for it; and then your keys jangle; can't someone stick their head out and see what those voices are in the corridor? Voices, voices, in your head, there has to be . . . I'm not quite sure . . . absolute calm? Or chaos? Jesus, you know, when I had my first girl; I mean that was nothing like you of course, she was my age, my young friend, the way things should be; I nearly mixed her up with my second girl: she was older than me, it was in a brothel, some old decrepit apartment building and inside it a woman in every apartment; it was at Christmas, some time in the '90s, with my friend M., he's dead too now; but I was nervous both times, couldn't think straight, trembling all over; Jesus, you've been imagining it all those times and then all of a sudden . . . SHOCKING PHOTOS OF THE VICTIM—CORONER APPALLS COURT WITH AUTOPSY FINDINGS.

So I can stand right next to you, I know exactly what's coming; you don't like that, do you, someone else being in the apartment? Don't worry, I won't do anything. What interests me is, where did you get the funnel from? I mean, who has a funnel in the house nowadays? I haven't got one. And when I went around to dinner at my mother's place the other day I asked her if she happened to have a funnel, a—is that what you call it?—a *kitchen funnel*. I remember us having a funnel, but we used to live somewhere else back then. I used to play with that funnel, it was blue, I think, and there's plenty of things you can do with a funnel: I put it on my dolls' heads like a hat; the tin man in *Alice in Wonderland*, no, *The Wizard of Emerald City* (that's the Russian version of *The Wizard of Oz*) had one of the things on his head too, but that wasn't a kitchen funnel, it was a metal one for oil and petrol and all that; if I put the funnel on the floor between my Indians and knights it was the roof of a mystical temple where an evil spirit lived, who could rise up and down through the pipe, depending on what mood he was in, and if he had to kill knights and Indians dead outside he'd go in, out, in, out; and the best thing was to hold that multi-purpose funnel in front of your mouth or up to your ear, and everything sounded strangely clear but with an underlying sound of static, and with the funnel up to your mouth you could shout and yell like hell! "Ladies and gentlemen, here come the champions BSG Chemie Leipzig, a big round of applause for Captain Manfred Walter as he holds the cup up in the air with the trainer Alfred Kunze! And the 30,000 people in the audience are singing, their voices rising in a joyful chorus . . ."

CAUSE OF DEATH: SUFFOCATION. You'd got the packing tape ready beforehand, I know that: brown adhesive tape, maybe you even bought it at the stationer's by St. Martin's Bridge, or at Schlecker, they have that kind of thing there too, I think. Or maybe your mother had it at home anyway, it always comes in handy: Christmas packages, cleaning and mending; she had a funnel too, didn't she, it was a well-run household, you can't say a word against her on that front. HE PLANNED TO SEAL HER MOUTH WITH TAPE TO SMOTHER HER CRIES FOR HELP. And this is where you start losing me, no matter how hard I try to understand you. Because there are a hell of a lot of dead ends in your planning. You got so greedy for her body, I'd say, that you could only keep your eye on a certain area, you could only concentrate so far. I mean who hasn't been through it, not that I mean to compare the two: you meet a woman at a club or wherever, and even though you're in a relationship, happily married if you like, you end up at her place or your place, and all you think about is all the exciting stuff coming up and what it'll feel like, not all the dominoes that go *clack, clack, clack*, tipping over one after another and making a mess of everything. Not meaning to compare the two though. *Clack, clack, clack.* You had enough time, mind you, you spent days watching her, imagining over and over what it must be like, how it must feel, but when you've done what you're planning with her, what then? And where do you put her? You didn't think of convincing her to keep quiet, like some pedophiles do, did you? No, you came straight out with the tape when she'd only been sitting on the sofa for two minutes. But I've said already that you're a special case, not a real pedophile I assume in the scientific, medical, and whatever else sense; I suppose we'd have to dissect your mind and poke a long thin needle in there to really get a look at your thought-streams . . . and look, I've got something, an image, or more like a sound, "Granny and Mommy, Granny and Mommy, Granny and Mommy, Granny and Mommy!" Jesus H. Christ, does it never stop, let's pull that needle out quick, sever the contact; and look, just because you grow up with your granny and mommy, have a slight genetic problem, are sexually frustrated and don't know about the birds and the bees . . . no, let's stick to the facts. Facts. Facts, facts, facts. ISOLATED EVEN IN JAIL.

You wouldn't last a minute; the murderers, thugs, and thieves would beat the shit out of you, and maybe even worse than that. A friend of mine told me how they showed a rapist what's what in Torgau, I mean in the prison there, Fort Zinna it's called; a rapist who raped women like normal, the ones who rape children CHILDREN ARE DEFENSELESS INFO@LEIPZIG-CHILD-PROTECTION.DE get sent somewhere else to be on the safe side, like you now. You'll be out in ten years if you're lucky, you can get tried as a minor up to the age of twenty-one if need be and you're only nineteen, but you're retarded enough—sorry, I didn't mean it like that, I wanted to stick to the facts, I really am interested in how everything works inside of you, looking over your shoulder a little, having a little chat . . . Weren't you scared, by the way, when they set up that kind of vigilante group in our neighborhood, just after they found her body out by the pond; *death penalty for child molesters* it said on the T-shirts, in old German typeface; someone offered me one but I said no. One evening they marched through the neighborhood with flaming torches, there were candles as well and a couple of normal enraged and grieving citizens, *death penalty for child molesters*. The stupid thing was that her uncle, on her father's side I think, is a well-known neo-Nazi around here. And then the NPD was on the case pretty quick, drinking beer on the torch-lit march through the neighborhood, starting at the school and then out to the pond you chose. Did you know I used to play there a lot as a kid? It's in a little wooded area, isn't it, that pond, it's called Stötteritz Copse; we didn't like walking through it once it got dark. And believe it or not, right by the lake was a wooden playground, it's not there anymore and it was pretty rundown already back then, the drunks used to hang around there; believe it or not a man showed me his dick there once, I must have been eight or nine, maybe ten. He was standing by a bush to have a piss, and I came past with my friend J. H., who I wanted to live with in a house in the forest back then (but not in this wood, we were thinking more of Mecklenburg in the countryside), remember? We had a cart with us and we wanted to go up the hill, you must know it, and race down it in the cart. We used to do that a lot, I was usually the pilot and he just pushed us off, and I used to have awful accidents with that cart, it's a wonder I never broke any bones. And this dirty bastard comes along and blocks the way, standing right on the path, his tool hanging out—it didn't look healthy, I remember that—dangling out of his trousers. Grinning at us, and us standing there with our cart and not knowing what to do. It's a narrow path, so the two of us back up and run away from him quick. It was an autumn afternoon, dark. You must have passed by the spot, that night when you took her to the pond.

So all sorts of paths crossed there, between the years: yours, mine, the torch-lit march, the police bringing up the rear. No, I don't want to insult the grief of ordinary people, that's not my style. You know what I said to them when they wanted to push one of their *death penalty for child molesters* T-shirts on me? I said I think it's better if they lock people like that away—I wasn't thinking of you in particular—because that's when an animal suffers most, isn't it? But don't worry, I only said that so I didn't look like a wuss—take my word for it, most people around here want to see you dead, now more than ever, and they didn't even know you back then, didn't know about the funnel. DEGRADATION OF THE VICTIM.

And you know what, they've got a point, it's hard for me to deal with too, no matter how much sympathy I can find for you. I DIDN'T SEE ANY SIGN OF REGRET. The teddy bear, the teddy bear, he's on the brink of deep despair . . . I'm scared if I turn around there'll be two little girls standing hand in hand in the middle of my *study*, staring at me wide-eyed. Like in that film, you won't know it: *The Shining*. Do you know what it is, the "shining" in the film? It's not unlike what I did before with the long thin needle . . . images and sounds, telepathy, you get it? But the two of us don't have that gift, I hope. And me in the apartment, and you in the apartment, and her in the apartment. Why *two* little girls, you'll ask me, when you only had room in your heart for that one girl and got so attached that everything else . . . I can't tell you why exactly. There's this little bar inside the station, Leipzig Central Station, where the dead sit; I saw her there once and there was another little girl with her . . . but no, you must know her too, her creator was inside with you; I mean, creator just means it was his *fault* she was in the bar. Back to the beginning. And you met him in jail; well, *met* might not be the right word, but the guy was the only person they dared to put you together with. Because they have to stop you from getting lonely and going stir crazy—there's a medical term for when people go mad in solitary confinement and deteriorate mentally but I can't think what it is right now. So they let you have a little chat with him now and then, eat your meals together and that kind of thing, because he's just as much at risk as you, when it comes to loneliness and getting beaten to death, or let's say getting assaulted at least. The two of you weren't all that different after all, even though the guy was in his late thirties; I mean, you were probably as different as night and day but there's that one thing that changed everything, everything there is . . . Especially for the girls of course, the ones I saw in the bar where you see things you're not supposed to see; but that's not why I'm here today, is it? THE CHRONOLOGY OF THE DRAMA.

I have to admit it: I'm a gambler. A betting man. I like putting a little on the horses. I like to try and back a winner, and the second and third place too. It's all a matter of probabilities, you see. Calculations, that's what we tell ourselves: calculations, statistics, and probabilities. But in reality it's also a matter of something as profane as Lady Luck and coincidence. I was at a race not long ago, the horse bolted and threw the jockey just before the start, and this trusty steed galloped and galloped because it couldn't do anything else and it didn't know anything else . . . but I meant to tell you about the race where my favorite horse—mind you, that's going too far, I've got a couple of favorite horses, Mharadonno, Overdose (the wonder horse from Hungary), Secret Affair, Dream Star, Deep Sleep, Westphalian Storm . . . NOW SHE'S A STAR IN THE SKY. Children like horses.

But the one I'm talking about is my favorite horse, Califax. I really like him because he once won a race called the "Clemens Meyer Cup." I'd backed the old boy on the nose a few weeks before, two hundred euros; oh yeah, that's a lot of cash, isn't it? And then he only came in second. He didn't quite make it that time around. And then there's this other race I want to tell you about, he was in with good odds on that one. Looking at the probability, he might have—it was pretty likely actually because he knew the track in the city of L. and he liked it—he might have been first past the post. And then: WHAM, the horses come out of the starting boxes, and my boy falls back instantly. Something's not right, I think. And that's exactly it, he gets stopped, something wrong with his bones and his tendons, the race goes on without him; those are just the Ifs, the Ifs, the Ifs. What's that got to do with you, you ask? With *her* and with you? I don't know what made me think of it either, it's just that those are the things that go right through and through you, and you have to, you just have to react to them, I mean talk about it. Because here's me standing behind you, well not right behind you, you're still in the other room and I'm quite a way back in the hall of this place where you live with your mother, who's not here now. No, you can't see me; the spool runs and runs, the projector clatters, flashes of light on the edge of your vision, and I'm the man who makes the odds, who weighs up the probabilities, and hopes for Lady Luck.

And she's out of the room while you're still fumbling with the tape. And for someone whose motor skills are . . . let's say "limited," you're up out of your seat pretty damn fast. Starting box: WHAM. Throw the good expensive tape away. (Don't forget to tidy up before Mother comes home!) Maybe she didn't run all that determinedly (wasn't sure if she had to run or just say "I want to go home"). And even if you can't hear it, I'm screaming back in the hall: "Go, go, go!" and "Just the last few yards!" and she really is almost out of the front door by the time you come toddling up. Now I have to turn around, my face to the wall; I don't know if she had her hand on the door handle. Probably did, I think; when a teddy like you turns into a grizzly all you want to do is reach out for the door handle, and she must have noticed, now at the very latest, that the teddy who was always so nice at school . . . but I can't watch anymore; I'm turning away at the back of the hall, my face to the wall, even though I promised you before I'd look over your shoulder, but my favorite horse, Califax—he was dead too soon after. You start to stutter, "I-I-I-I . . . i-i-i-it j-just ha-ha-happened, I didn't me-me-mean . . ." ("Granny and Mommy! Granny and Mommy! Granny and Mommy! Granny and Mommy!") If only she'd gotten out into the corridor somehow, luck and probability, and you're not the fastest mover, are you? But then I hear the sounds, pretty muffled and dull, and no screaming, just a gurgling, something crunching and breaking, and I don't dare to turn around in my study, and her face in the photo next to me, a grin I have to hide between my books. And when I do turn around everything's empty, and I hear you fumbling around in the kitchen. They're sounds that go through time and space. Something crunching and breaking. Was that in the hall just now or not until the kitchen? There's a clanking and a jingling; you're going through the kitchen cupboards. The funnel. TEETH BROKEN, LOWER JAW DISLOCATED.

What on earth where you thinking? I don't mean *in general*, just in that situation. I'm asking you very carefully, putting two fingertips on your shoulder just as carefully. You twitch because you don't want to think about it. You know, there was alcohol involved with my first girls, but not that way, you know, not that way at all . . .

Left, right, left, I have to get my strength together and march around the hall, back and forth, back and forth, boots slamming against the ground, *death penalty for child molesters*, while you, while you . . . Jesus, I need a drink, and I'd like to ask politely, and I do ask you politely, but the wine bottle's empty now, half empty at least; and I don't want to drink from it anymore, even though your mouth wasn't even on it. All right, I say, all right, if that's the way it is I'll go then. But there's no way out, no way out . . . and you don't see me, and you don't hear me, and because I'm there where I am I have to see everything, and I do see it, even if I turn away, my face to the wall: *The Shining.* 0.083 PERCENT BAC.

There's not much left for us to tell, is there? You couldn't even get it up, just used your fingers once she was already dying, after the funnel and the wine and the beating and the strangling. It's not that easy, is it? When sex was always so far away, in the mind and in the flesh. And then everything was spick-and-span again by the time your mother came home; how quickly a person can be propped up in the closet down half a flight of stairs. And a quick kick of the fallen tooth under the fridge. Did you ejaculate? They didn't say anything about that anywhere, you see, not even in court . . . but I was only there the one day, and I was a little distracted at times, I have to admit. By you, some of the time, I mean, the way you squatted there, the two cops behind you, arms folded, not that you could have held them any other way, what with the cuffs around your wrists—

In August 2009 the trial began of the defendant Daniel V., who pleaded guilty to murdering eight-year-old Michelle in Leipzig a year previously.

TRANSLATED FROM GERMAN BY KATY DERBYSHIRE

BERNARD QUIRINY

Rara Avis

The painted eggs of Jacques Armand have made him famous the world over. After starting out his career on flat surfaces, he decided at the age of thirty to practice his art only on eggs. "The egg," he said, "is the purest, most perfect, and most beautiful of nature's creations. It surpasses by far the pyramid, the cube, and the sphere." His first works soon met with success; in a few years, he became one of the best-known artists of his time, and "the eggs of Jacques Armand" were spoken of in the same tones as "Buren's stripes," "blues by Klein," or "the compressions of César."

All his works were cataloged in the same way: title first, then type of paint, the species of egg, and lastly its dimensions (in millimeters) and its weight (in grams) before being hollowed out. The most famous were as follows: "*Zambezi Landscape*, oil on ostrich egg, 193 x 143 mm, 1650 g"; "*Sad Woman Bathing*, egg tempera on chicken egg, 53 x 43 mm, 60 g"; "*Small Swarm of Black Flies*, charcoal on lark's egg, 25 x 17 mm, 4 g"; and "*Homage to M. C. Escher*, soft pencil on swan's egg, 115 x 76 mm, 350 g." Their prices reached astronomical heights and collectors spent millions at a fell swoop in their struggle to own the most expensive pieces.

I met Jacques Armand when the National Museum of Modern Art devoted a retrospective to him in 1987. He was eighty years old and would die soon after; and yet my memory remains one of a jaunty, mischievous man, as smooth a talker as he was a great painter. At the time, I was working for an art magazine. The editor-in-chief had decided to devote two pages to Jacques Armand. The artist was willing to meet me, but rather than having me over, suggested we take a walk through his show one evening after the museum had closed. It seemed a good idea to me, and I went to our rendezvous accompanied by the magazine's photographer.

The retrospective was spread out over eight rooms and gathered three hundred and fifty works. It included the first egg Jacques Armand had ever painted, his most celebrated series, and a dozen or so exceptional achievements lovingly displayed, like ten sunfish eggs painted with a needle under a microscope, no more than a millimeter and a half in diameter, viewable through magnifying-glass globes. One learned from the catalog that eighty species of birds and ten species of fish were represented, and that Jacques Armand had used more than thirty-five different techniques, some of his own invention.

The photographer did his job, then left; Jacques Armand and I stayed, alone in the museum—or almost, for an overweight night watchman was shuffling from room to room. Stuffed into a woolen cardigan, his lips hidden by a white beard and mustache that made him look like a druid, Jacques Armand walked from one egg to the next, keeping up such a steady stream of chatter that I hardly ever had to ask him any of the questions I'd prepared—he guessed them all and sometimes asked them himself, as though struck by some doubt about his own work. Then he would seek my opinion with a worried air, and silently mull over my reply while staring at the ceiling.

He told me of expeditions he'd made to Pacific islands in search of rare eggs, bizarre specimens sent to him from the four corners of the earth, the extravagance of certain collectors who wanted portraits on hummingbird eggs ("I wore out my eyes") or biblical frescoes on ostrich eggs; he also treated me to several philosophical orations in which the meaning of life always came down to a matter of eggs, as though eggs contained the solution to all humanity's problems since Parmenides. "God," he declared solemnly, raising his index finger, "is a cloud of luminous goodness in the shape of an egg. He contains the universe."

He also recounted several legends. People in the villages of Siberia believed that wizards were special beings who emerged from giant iron eggs that mythical birds had brooded. In France, it was said that an egg laid on Good Friday and eaten on an empty stomach Easter Sunday protected you against all disease for the rest of your life. Finally, he treated me to a long lecture on Fabergé's eggs, whose splendor he admired, he explained, but which hadn't much to do with his own work. Try as he might to seem indifferent to the Russian goldsmith, the other man's fame clearly rankled.

We were still walking among the artworks when Armand paused at the sight of a large egg adorned with a blue arabesque; he seemed troubled, as though he'd just glimpsed the ghost of a long-lost friend. Then he coughed and asked me what we'd been talking about.

"That egg—" I murmured, without following.

I approached the work: what had seemed an arabesque was in fact an ideogram. The egg was about twenty centimeters tall. I read the placard: "*The Monster*, oil on egg, 198 x 151 mm."

"Strange," I remarked. "Neither the type of egg nor its weight are specified."

"That's because I never knew," replied Jacques Armand, walking back toward me.

I had the feeling he didn't want to say any more about it, but that at the same time, was begging me to question him, as though he wished to confide his secret in me. I insisted.

"It's a long story," he said. "I don't think it will interest your readers."

"I'd like to know."

"As you wish. But . . ."

He looked around then, as though afraid we were being watched. I pictured the overweight watchman hiding behind a blackbird's egg and couldn't keep a smile from my face.

"I'd like you to refrain from including it in your article," said Jacques Armand. "For this story to stay between us, and for you not to tell anyone else. Promise."

I promised, intrigued.

■ ■ ■

Twenty years ago, a woman named Doris brought me the egg. She knocked on the door to my studio in Montmartre, and held out a hatbox. Inside, nestled in Styrofoam peanuts, I found the egg you see before you. When I removed it from the box, I found it weighed almost nothing. It had already been hollowed out. I was irritated, since I like performing this act myself: hollowing the egg out is the first step of an artistic process, much like readying a canvas for paint. Most of the time, when other people do it, they damage the shell. The hole at the top is usually fairly neat, but the bottom one three times bigger than necessary. But that wasn't the case with this egg, which had been hollowed out with great delicacy.

"What species is it?" I asked Doris. "A species that lays no eggs," she replied. I stared at her, uncomprehending; there was something like fear in her eyes, as though the pale shell I held between my fingers terrified her. "Tell me what you mean," I said, offering her a chair.

■ ■ ■

"This was in December, 1950," she began. "I was twenty-three, and worked in a girls' boarding school not far from Nevers. There were two housemistresses per floor, in charge of watching over ten rooms of four boarders apiece. My colleague was a lady of forty named Suzanne, ugly but quite kind.

"One morning, Suzanne came looking for me in my quarters. 'Michelle is sick,' she announced. 'She's complaining of stomach pains and doesn't look like she's in any state to go to class.' The infirmary was closed that day and the snow made getting around impossible. Michelle was thus confined to bed; we stopped in to see her every hour.

"Michelle remained in bed all day. At lunchtime, I brought her some soup; she refused to eat a thing and, that evening, only managed to swallow the dried end of a loaf of bread and a quarter of an apple. The next day, she complained again and refused to get up. We wanted to call for the doctor, but she protested; I put my hand on her forehead and, noticing that she had no fever, began to think she was pretending. I ordered her out of bed, but she began to cry; to put an end to it, I threatened to call the headmistress, Mrs. Charming (whose name alone usually set the students trembling), and warned her that she had better be washed and dressed by the time I came back, at ten o'clock recess. Of course she was still in bed when I came back. Furious, I raised my voice. 'You asked for it,' I said. 'I'm going to call Mrs. Charming.'

"Mrs. Charming's arrival failed to frighten Michelle. The headmistress lost her temper right away: she pulled the sheets back violently and seized Michelle by the arm. Michelle struggled a bit, screaming, and received a resounding slap. At that moment, Suzanne burst into the room. Together, we immobilized the young girl, tore her from her bed, and threw her to the floor. What we saw then astounded us: the white sheets were horribly soiled, as was the girl's nightgown; there was blood everywhere. In the middle of the filthy bed, we found an egg, *that* egg, striped with long brownish stains. Kneeling on the floor, Michelle was weeping and staring at the ovoid monster she'd no doubt wished to brood. 'Give me my baby,' she murmured between sobs.

"Mrs. Charming was the first to react: she calmly said that we should send Michelle home, destroy 'that thing,' and make sure word of this got out to no one. She ordered us to take care of it immediately and then, with an uncertain step, left the room and returned to her office.

"Suzanne and I gathered the revolting sheets and stuffed them in a bag, which we threw in the trash. Then we took Michelle for a shower and called her parents to come get her. We answered their questions simply by saying she had the flu. When order had been restored, the headmistress summoned Michelle's roommates to her office. Had she left the school, gone into the surrounding woods, or said anything at all that might have seemed strange to them? Each of the three girls interrogated gave a different answer. The first, Marie, insisted that Michelle had not left the school all week and that her pains had begun the night before. The second, Renee, maintained that Michelle had gone out two days earlier, after the end of class and before dinner; she'd come back holding her coat rolled up in a ball against her stomach, as though hiding something. The third, Clotilde, declared that she'd quarreled with Michelle the week before and had been deliberately ignoring her since.

"Baffled, Mrs. Charming dismissed them. The egg intrigued her, but more than anything else, she feared scandal: this affair must not be allowed to harm the school's reputation. She asked us what we'd done with 'the thing,' as though she still couldn't bring herself to call it by its proper name. I explained that Suzanne and I had hidden it in the closet by my quarters. She requested we get rid of it as soon as possible, however we chose, and then never to speak of it again."

■ ■ ■

I interrupted Doris's story. "You violated her orders, since the egg is intact, and you're telling me everything now."

"My story is not yet finished," she replied.

■ ■ ■

"Suzanne wanted to destroy the egg as soon as possible: for her, it amounted to an abomination, and should not be seen by anyone. However, neither she nor I managed to take action; I don't know why, but we hadn't the courage to get rid of it. After a few days, the subject became kind of taboo: something we had to do, but refused to discuss. Suzanne was clearly as frightened as I was. I considered acting alone, but couldn't.

"I regret that today, for the memory of what happened next still torments me. One night, a month after we'd found the egg, I was woken by noises nearby. At first I thought mice had gotten into the attic, but I soon realized it was coming from the closet where we'd hidden the egg. Uneasy, I put on my slippers, grabbed a flashlight from the nightstand, and headed out; the door of the closet was open. I aimed the beam inside: Suzanne was standing there, naked, the bottom of the egg pressed to her lips; she'd put two holes in the shell and was sucking out its contents, a trickle of translucent, sickening liquid running down her chin.

"Surprised in mid-desecration, she glared at me with contempt. As I remained silent, she finished off her vile feast unhurriedly, depleting the inside of the egg with sucking noises. When she was done, she put the hollow shell back where we'd hidden it, left the closet, and went back to her room without paying me the slightest heed, even burping when she shut her door. Dazed, I stood there, flashlight in hand. Unable to decide what to do, I went back to bed. I fell asleep almost immediately. The next day, I confirmed that it hadn't been a dream: there was the egg, in the closet, clean and light as a ping-pong ball.

"There it stayed till the end of the year. When the school closed its doors for summer, I hid it in my suitcase, wrapping it in clothes, and brought it back to my house. I found another job, and never returned to the school. I never saw Suzanne again."

■ ■ ■

Jacques Armand fell silent. Pensively, we considered Michelle's egg before being torn from our contemplation by the watchman, who passed nearby, whistling. I felt like I'd just seen a very disturbing movie, unable to think of anything else. I tried to imagine how the egg had looked when Doris found it in Michelle's soiled bed, and wondered if her story could be believed.

"Do you think it's true?" I asked.

"I have no doubt about it," replied Jacques Armand. "I'm sure Doris never made up a thing. The only thing I don't know is if Michelle really laid the egg. Doris was convinced of it, but she had no proof. It's unbelievable that a young girl could have found it in the woods: no bird is capable of laying an egg that size. But in the end . . . I'm not certain of anything. Did she meet a monster in the woods? Perhaps she was the monster."

"Is she still alive?"

"Michelle? No idea. I suppose she went mad. You'd have to go through the records of all the asylums in the area; maybe you'd pick up her trail. Unless she grew feathers from her arms, her feet turned into talons, and she flew off from the balcony of her room. After all, an adolescent who lays an egg could very well turn into a bird."

This joke left me ill at ease.

"Did you know right away what you'd paint on the shell?" I asked Armand.

"No. In fact, for a long time I had artist's block because I didn't know what had been inside—white and yolk, as in a chicken egg, or a fetus, as in a woman's belly, or even some combination of the two. The uncertainty paralyzed me; I found it indecent to seek beauty in material that might once have housed a human life."

He paused, then corrected himself.

"No, to be precise, what stopped me wasn't strictly speaking the uncertainty, but the possibility of *knowing*. The fear that if I painted it, Suzanne would walk into my studio and announce she'd been digesting the contents of the egg for twenty years and now wanted to regurgitate it back into the shell. Absurd, yes, but I felt like the egg belonged to her, and I couldn't appropriate it by making it an Egg by Jacques Armand. In a nutshell—and forgive me if I'm unclear—I would have been terribly disappointed if I'd learned the egg wasn't human, and completely terrifed if I'd been certain it was. In either case, I couldn't paint it."

"What happened?"

"Two years later, I received a letter from Doris in which she told me of Suzanne's death. She'd run into her again, a few months earlier: the poor old woman was retired now and living alone in Paris. They had tea, and chatted the hours away. Finally, Doris could not resist her desire to bring up the egg. Suzanne laughed mysteriously and barked something like, 'Of course, the egg. What a story, right?'"

"How disappointing."

"Indeed. Yet on the other hand, it was a relief. As I just mentioned, Doris told me in her letter that Suzanne had died shortly thereafter. 'Had the egg been laid by a woman or a bird? Now no one would ever know.' She was right and, strangely, this freed me. I'd been unable to paint the egg for fear of finding out it was well and truly human; now I would be able to because I was convinced it was, though I'd never have the proof. Strange, isn't it? In the end, I finished the work very quickly, in three nights. I made it very simple, so that it wouldn't attract attention, or be noticed except by informed connoisseurs. I want it to preserve its secret. It is perhaps the least known of all my pieces, but when I look at it, I find it one of the most beautiful."

"Does what's painted on the shell mean anything?"

"Yes. It's a Chinese word referring to a mythical bird that, so it's said, kidnaps babies from the cradle to devour them."

I admired the egg, which now seemed to give off a more intense glow.

"Perhaps one day I'll set this story down on paper. Until then, promise me you'll never say anything about this to anyone."

I promised, and the visit drew to a close. I took my leave of Jacques Armand, wondering if he hadn't played a trick on me. Six months later, he died. I think of him whenever I pass a pregnant woman in the street and muse on whether her belly perhaps houses an egg. If it has a painted shell, then Jacques Armand is in heaven, and he has breathed into the Creator's ear an idea for a new monster born of woman, fashioned by the hand of God, but adorned by his brush alone.

TRANSLATED FROM FRENCH BY EDWARD GAUVIN

Index by Author

Index by Country

Author Biographies

For additional information on the authors and countries included in
Best European Fiction 2012, *visit www.dalkeyarchive.com.*

ZSÓFIA BÁN was born in 1957 in Rio de Janeiro, Brazil, and grew up in Brazil and Hungary. A writer, literary historian, and critic, she made her fiction debut in 2007 with her much acclaimed book *Night School: A Reader for Adults* (forthcoming in German). Her stories have been widely anthologized, and she is working on a new volume of short stories and a novel. She lives and works in Budapest, where she teaches American literature and visual studies at Eötvös Loránd University. She has received several national prizes for her essay and fiction writing, and she was one of the writers representing Hungary at the 2009 PEN World Voices Festival.

MUHAREM BAZDULJ was born in 1977 in Travnik, Bosnia and Herzegovina. He received a degree in English and American studies from the University of Sarajevo. He has published several award-winning short-story collections, including *Druga knjiga* (2000; *The Second Book*, 2005), and *Čarolija* (*Magic*, 2008), from which the two stories in this anthology were selected. Bazdulj's texts have been featured in a number of prestigious international anthologies such as *The Wall in My Head*, published on the occasion of the twentieth anniversary of the fall of the Berlin Wall. His short stories and essays appear in *World Literature Today*, *Creative Nonfiction*, *Habitus*, *Absinthe*, and other literary reviews.

PATRICK BOLTSHAUSER was born in 1971 in St. Gallen, Switzerland, and grew up in Schaan, Liechtenstein. After high school he went to the University of Bern to study biology. During this time he began to work for several theater groups as actor, dramatic adviser, director, and playwright. In 1996 he completed his diploma in behavioral ecology. Since 1996 several of his plays have been performed in Austria, Germany, and Switzerland. After spending several years in Berlin, he lives in Zurich, writing his second novel with the working title *Meander*.

BJARTE BREITEIG was born in 1974 in Kristiansand, Norway. Bjarte Breiteig's three short-story collections combine simplicity and density, often dealing with the experience of loss and longing. His first book, *Fantomsmerter* (*Phantom Pains*), was published in 1998 to glowing reviews. "Down Here They Don't Mourn" was taken from his second collection, *Surrogater* (*Surrogates*, 2000). In 2003 Bjarte Breiteig was one of five authors included in the European literary project Scritture Giovani's *Borders* anthology. His third collection, *Folk har begynt å banke på* (*Someone's Knocking at the Door*, 2006), introduced a more epic dimension in his writing, probing deep into his characters while making incisive insights into differences of social class and social realities. Breiteig has won numerous literary awards in his homeland.

DUNCAN BUSH was born in 1946 in Cardiff, Wales. He was educated at Warwick University, Duke University, and Wadham College, Oxford. He has won numerous awards for his poetry collections *Aquarium, Salt, Masks,* and *Midway;* his most recent collection is *The Flying Trapeze.* He has published three novels, including *The Genre of Silence,* set in the USSR during the Civil War; *Glass Shot,* a psychological thriller in South Wales during the 1984/85 Miners' Strike; and *Now All The Rage,* which unfolds in an obsessive imaginative borderland between fame and obscurity. He teaches and currently divides his time between Luxembourg, France, and Britain.

ARNO CAMENISCH was born in 1978 in Graubünden, Switzerland. He writes in both Rhaeto-Romanic (Sursilvan) and German. He debuted in 2005 with *Ernesto ed autres Manzegnas,* but is best known for his award-winning novels, *Sez Ner* (2009) and *Hinter dem Bahnhof* (*Behind the Station,* 2010)—the first two parts of a widely acclaimed trilogy. A brilliant performer of his own work, with links to the Spoken Word scene in Switzerland, he has recently been publishing poetry in literary magazines and anthologies. In 2010, he was awarded both the ZKB Schillerpreis and the Berner Literaturpreis for *Sez Ner.* He maintains a website at arnocamenisch.ch.

MARIE DARRIEUSSECQ was born in 1969 in Bayonne in the French Basque Country. After graduating from the École Normale Supérieure with a doctorate in French literature, she became a writer and a psychoanalyst. Since her 1996 best-selling debut, *Truismes* (*Pig Tales,* 1997), she has published ten novels, several short stories, and a play; she has also contributed frequently to art magazines in Paris and London. She lives primarily in Paris and is a mother of three children.

DANILA DAVYDOV was born in 1977 in Moscow, Russia. He is best known for his poetry and also writes short stories, essays, critical articles and reviews, and philological studies. A graduate of the Literary Institute in Moscow, he completed a PhD on "Russian Naïve and Primitivist Poetry: Genesis, Evolution, Poetics" in 2003. He is currently writing a doctoral thesis on "Russian Poetry of the 1930s–'60s as a Sociolinguistic and Sociocultural Phenomenon." Davydov is widely published in Russia and abroad in such periodicals as *Strelets, Chernovik* (New Jersey), *Vavilon, Vozdukh, Oktyabr, Arion, Novy Mir, NLO, Reflection* (Chicago), and many others. He is a coeditor of several magazines and often compiles collections of contemporary poetry.

AGUSTÍN FERNÁNDEZ PAZ was born in 1947 in Vilalba, Spain. Having graduated in educational science, he became a primary school teacher and later taught Galician language and literature in a Vigo secondary school; he retired to devote himself exclusively to writing. During his writing career, he has published over forty books in Galician, including the best sellers *Cartas de inverno (Winter Letters*, 1995) and *O único que queda é o amor (Nothing Really Matters in Life More than Love*, 2007). This latter collection, from which the story "This Strange Lucidity" is taken, won him Spain's National Prize for Literature in 2008.

DAVID-DEPHY GOGIBEDASHVILI was born in 1968 in Tbilisi, Georgia and is a poet, novelist, performer, and multimedia artist. He graduated from Tbilisi Academy of Fine Arts (Faculty of Architecture). During the Rose Revolution he was one of the leaders of the disobedience movement, and during the Russian invasion in 2008, he joined a volunteer army to set up the headquarters for civil solidarity. He is the creator and copyright owner of the famous slogan

"STOP RUSSIA." His writing has been praised by Georgian critics as being full of innovative ideas and new sounds; his novels and poetry have become a cult event for the new Georgian generation.

RÓBERT GÁL was born in 1968 in Bratislava, Slovakia. Having resided in various cities as a student (Brno, New York, Jerusalem, Berlin), Róbert now lives in Prague, Czech Republic. He is the author of several books of philosophical aphorisms and two novels, *Krídlovanie* (*On Wing*, 2006) and *Agnomia* (2008), both of which are forthcoming in English translation.

BRANKO GRADIŠNIK was born in 1951 in Ljubljana, Slovenia (formerly Yugoslavia). He received his MA in creative writing at Lancaster University, England. Once the originator of Slovenian metafiction with acclaimed collections of short stories *Zemlja zemlja zemlja* (*Earth Earth Earth*, 1982) and *Mistifikcije* (*Mystifictions*, 1986), he started—in novels like *Leta* (*Lethe*, 1985) and *Nekdo drug* (*The Other One*, 1991)—to lean toward suspension of disbelief; his lifelong endeavors to breach the divide of faction and fiction have reached their acme in the diaristic *Roka voda kamen* (*Hand Water Stone*, 2007), an extraordinary bildungsroman exploring the interplay of nature, society, history, the Self, and the Other.

SANNEKE VAN HASSEL was born in 1971 in Rotterdam, the Netherlands, where she lives and writes short stories. She studied history of civilization and theater studies and was a member of the theater collective 't Barre Land. She made her literary debut in 2005 with the short-story collection *Ice Rain*, followed two years later by the collection *White Feather*. For both collections she received the BNG New Literature Award. She wrote *Pieces of Sarajevo* (2006) and the novel *Nest* (2010), about a teenager with an unwanted pregnancy.

She has organized and curated an international short-story festival in Amsterdam, Hotel van Hassel. She maintains a website at www. sannekevanhassel.nl.

DESMOND HOGAN was born in 1950 in Ballinasloe, Ireland. He has published five novels: *The Ikon Maker* (1976), *The Leaves on Grey* (1980), *A Curious Street* (1984), *A New Shirt* (1986), and *A Farewell to Prague* (1995), as well as several books of stories: *A Link with the River*, introduced by Louise Erdrich (1989), *Larks' Eggs* (2007), and *Old Swords and Other Stories* (2009). *The Edge of the City*, selected travel and review pieces, appeared in 1993. In 1971 he won the Hennessy Award, and in 1977 the Rooney Prize for Literature. He won the John Llewellyn Rhys Memorial Prize in 1980 and was awarded a DAAD Fellowship in Berlin in 1991.

MAJA HRGOVIĆ was born in 1980 in Split, Croatia. She studied theater and women's studies. Since 2003 she has worked as a journalist in the culture section of the *Novi List Daily*, and has been a member of the editorial board at *Zarez—a Journal of Cultural and Social Affairs*, where she publishes literary reviews. In 2009 she was awarded first prize for journalistic excellence organized by the Balkan Investigative Reporting Network (BIRN). Her work has also been published in magazines and news portals such as *Nulačetvorka, Cunterview, Kulturpunkt, Op.a, Grazia,* and *Libela.* She regularly writes for the portal *ZaMirZINE*, concentrating on women's rights and their treatment in the media. Her first collection of short stories, *Pobjeđuje onaj kojem je manje stalo* (*He Wins Who Cares Less*), was published in 2010.

MARIJA KNEŽEVIĆ was born in 1963 in Belgrade, Serbia (formerly Yugoslavia). She earned her MA in comparative literature from Michigan State University. She has published thirteen books ranging from poetry and essays to stories and novels. Her novel, *Ekaterini* (2005), was also published in Austria and Poland. Her poetry has been included in *New European Poets*. The story presented in this selection belongs to her as-yet-unpublished story collection, *Fabula rasa*.

ARMIN KÕOMÄGI was born in 1969 in Moldova. He received his BA in economics from the Technical University of Tallinn. Since 1992 he has been an active entrepreneur mainly in the fields of trade and logistics. In 2003 his first short stories were published in several literary magazines; the short story included in this anthology, "Anonüümsed Logistikud" ("Logisticians Anonymous"), received the Tuglas Award in 2006. His first novel, *Pagejad (The Runaways)*, was selected as one of the best novels in 2009 by Cultural Foundation of Estonia. Kõomägi has also supported and sponsored several Estonian art and film projects.

JIŘÍ KRATOCHVIL was born in 1940 in Brno, Czech Republic. He is a distinguished Czech novelist, short-story writer, essayist, dramatist, and publicist who has won the Tom Stoppard Prize (1991), the Czech Booksellers' Prize (1993), the Prize of the *Literární Noviny Weekly* (1993), the Egon Hostovský Prize (1996), the Karel Čapek Prize (1998), and the Jaroslav Seifert Prize (1999). His works have appeared in eleven languages. His recent novel *Slib. Requiem na padesátá léta (The Promise: Requiem to the Fifties*, 2009) has been enthusiastically received in its German translation, *Das Versprechen des Architekten*. He lives in Moravský Krumlov as a freelance writer.

GERÐUR KRISTNÝ was born in 1970 in Reykjavík, Iceland. She graduated in French and comparative literature from the University of Iceland in 1992. After a course in media studies at the University of Iceland from 1992 to 1993 she trained at Danish Radio TV. She was editor of the magazine *Mannlíf* from 1998 to 2004, but is now a full-time writer. Gerður Kristný has published poetry books, short stories, novels, and a book for children, and has received the Halldór Laxness Literary Award and the Iceland Literature Prize. She lives in Reykjavík with her husband and two sons.

MARITTA LINTUNEN was born in 1961 in Savonlinna, Finland. She holds a Master of Arts in music. Lintunen has been nominated for several Finnish literature awards since 1999 and she was awarded the WSOY Literature Foundation Prize for her literary achievements in 2010. She describes herself as writing in three languages: those of poetry, short story, and novel. Her experience as a musician comes through in the skillful and controlled rhythm of her writing. As a result, her language doesn't give in to unnecessary vanities, and the characters in her short stories struggle, try to be brave, and continue to strive.

PATRICIA DE MARTELAERE was born in 1957 in Zottegem, Belgium, studied philosophy at the K.U.Leuven, and worked as a writer and professor of philosophy. Between 1988 and 1992 she published four novels: *Nachtboek van een slapeloze* (*Night Book of an Insomniac*, 1988), *De schilder en zijn model* (*The Painter and His Model*, 1989), *Littekens* (*Scars*, 1990), and *De staart* (*The Tail*, 1992). She received the J. Greshoff Award and the Belgian State Prize for Essay and Criticism for her essays. In 2004, she published another novel, *Het onverwachte antwoord* (*The Unexpected Answer*), to wide critical acclaim; the first section is included in this anthology. De Martelaere died in 2009 from complications of a brain tumor.

DONAL McLAUGHLIN was born in 1961 in Derry, Northern Ireland, and has resided in Scotland since 1970. His short-story collection, *an allergic reaction to national anthems & other stories* (2009), was longlisted for the Frank O'Connor Short Story Award and nominated for the EIBF Readers' Best First Book Award. He is a recipient of the Robert Louis Stevenson Memorial Award, was Scottish PEN's first *écrivain sans frontières*, and is a former Hawthornden Fellow. His translations include a stage version of *The Reader* (with Chris Dolan), the poetry of Stella Rotenberg, and over one hundred writers, to date, for the *New Swiss Writing* anthologies. He is currently translating three books by Urs Widmer. Donal has also edited anthologies of Slovene writing (with Janice Galloway), Latvian writing, and contemporary Scottish writing. He maintains a website at donalmclaughlin.wordpress.com.

CLEMENS MEYER was born in 1977 in Halle/Saale, East Germany, and now lives in Leipzig. He studied at the German Literature Institute, Leipzig, and he has worked as a security guard, forklift driver, and construction worker. Seen by many as a star among young German writers, he won a number of prizes for his first novel, *Als wir träumten* (*As We Were Dreaming*, 2006), in which a group of friends grow up and go off the rails in East Germany after the fall of the Berlin Wall. He has also published the Leipzig Book Fair Prize-winning *Die Nacht, die Lichter* (*All the Lights*, 2008) and *Gewalten* (*Forces*, 2010), a diary of 2009 in eleven stories.

ANDREJ NIKOLAIDIS was born in 1974 in Sarajevo, Bosnia and Herzegovina. In 1992, he came to Ulcinj, Montenegro, as a Bosnian refugee, and currently lives there. He has written for *Monitor*, *Vijesti*, and the Bosnian magazine *Free Bosnia*, and is a columnist for zurnal.info and e-novine.com presently. He wrote a scenario for the motion picture "If There Are Dead" (in production), and he has translated works by Noam Chomsky and Slavoj Žižek from English to Montenegrin. His works include *Mimesis* (2003), *Sin* (*The Son*, 2006), and *Dolazak* (*The Coming*, 2009).

SANTIAGO PAJARES was born in 1979 in Madrid, Spain. At the age of twenty-three, he wrote his first novel, *El paso de la hélice* (*The Path of the Helix*), which was published in 2004. The book was discovered, translated, and brought to publication in Japan by Borges's Japanese translator. Pajares wrote his second novel, *La mitad de uno* (*The Other Half*), the next year, and his third, *El Lienzo* (*The Canvas*), two years later. Santiago Pajares also writes and shoots short films, and has received nearly twenty awards in Spain for his cinematic work.

PEP PUIG was born in 1969 in Terrassa, Spain. An heir to Mediterranean tradition—writing with the perpetual backdrop of a mythical summer and from a state of permanent adolescence—his work moves ambiguously between sentiment and irony. After his first novel, *L'home que torna* (*The Man Who Returns*, 2005), he published *Les llàgrimes de la senyoreta Marta* (*Miss Marta's Tears*, 2007) which received a great critical reception, *La Vanguardia* praising it as "the best novel written in Catalan in many years."

BERNARD QUIRINY was born in 1978 in Bastogne, Belgium and lives in Burgundy, where he is an academic, specialist in public law, and author of a thesis on the political thought of Cornelius Castoriadis. He has contributed to several publications, including *Le Magazine littéraire* and *Chronic'art*. In 2005 he published his first collection of stories, *L'angoisse de la première phrase* (*Fear of the First Line*), followed by a second in 2008, *Contes carnivores* (*Flesh-Eating Fictions*), with a preface by Enrique Vila-Matas; this collection garnered numerous prizes. His first novel, *Les assoiffées* (*The Thirsty Ones*, 2010), is a satire about a group of French intellectuals on an official expedition to a Belgium that fell in the 1970s under a feminist dictatorship.

NOËLLE REVAZ was born in 1968 in the canton of Valais, Switzerland. She is the author of numerous short stories and two novels, *Efina* (2009) and *Rapport aux bêtes* (*With the Animals*, 2002), which is forthcoming in English. This novel, which has been adapted for the stage and the screen, is the story of a frustrated peasant in an invented spoken language. She has also written radio plays, including a monologue, *Quand Mamie* (2007). Besides her work as a writer, she teaches creative writing at the Swiss Literature Institute at Biel/Bienne, where she lives.

GABRIEL ROSENSTOCK was born in 1949 in Kilfinane, Ireland, and is the author/translator of over 150 books, including 13 volumes of poetry and a volume of haiku, mostly in Irish (Gaelic). A member of Aosdána, he has given readings in Europe, North, South, and Central America, India, Australia, and Japan. He has also taught haiku at the Schule für Dichtung in Vienna. He has brought out Irish-language versions and translations of poems of Francisco X. Alarcón, Seamus Heaney, Rabindranath Tagore, Günter Grass, Zhāng Ye, Michele Ranchetti, Michael Augustin, Peter Huchel, Georg Trakl, Georg Heym, and numerous others. *Uttering Her Name* (2009) is his debut volume in English.

LEE ROURKE was born in 1972 in Manchester, England. He is the author of the critically acclaimed debut novel *The Canal* (winner of the *Guardian*'s "Not The Booker Prize" 2010), the short-story collection *Everyday*, and a work of nonfiction, *A Brief History of Fables:*

From Aesop to Flash Fiction. His literary criticism regularly appears in the *Guardian,* the *Independent, TLS, New Statesman, RSB,* and *3:AM Magazine.* His second novel, *Amber,* is forthcoming. He lives in London.

JANUSZ RUDNICKI was born in 1956 in Kędzierzyn-Koźle, Poland. In 1983 he moved to Germany for political reasons, studying Slavic and German literature in Hamburg. He currently divides his time between Hamburg and Prague. He is a frequent contributor to *Twórczość* and *Machina.* His novels include *One Can Live* (1992), winner of the St. Piętak award for a debut; *My Wehrmacht* (2004); *Come On Everyone, Let's Go* (2007), which was nominated for the NIKE Award and the European Literary Prize; and *The Death of a Czech Dog* (2009), which was a finalist for the NIKE and nominated for three other prizes. Collections of his stories have been published in Germany and the Czech Republic.

MICHAEL STAUFFER was born in 1972 in Winterthur, Switzerland, and has won numerous international awards for his varied work. He has published four novels, over twenty radio plays, and six plays. He writes fiction and drama, does performances, recites poetry, and improvises. He teaches literature at the Swiss Literature Institute at Bern, and he lives and works in Switzerland and Europe. His most recent titles include: *Ich begrüsse mich ganz herzlich* (*I Welcome You Heartily,* 2011), *Kleine Menschen* (*Little Men,* 2010), and *Hinduhans* (*John the Hindu,* 2010), which was nominated for the "Best Fiction" category of the German Audio Book Prize.

SERHIY ZHADAN was born in 1974 in the Luhansk Region of eastern Ukraine. He currently lives in Kharkiv and writes poetry, prose, and essays. He is the author of the poetry collections *the very, very* *best poems, psychedelic stories of fighting, and other bullshit* (selected poems, 1992–2000), *History of Culture at the Turn of This Century* (2002), *UkSSR* (2004), and *Lili Marlen* (2009), as well as the story collections *Big Mac* (2003), *Anarchy in the UKR* (2005), *Hymn of the Democratic Youth* (2007), and the novels *Depeche Mode* (2004) and *Voroshilovgrad* (2010). His work has been translated into twelve languages as well as being featured on Poetry International's website.

RUI ZINK was born in 1961 in Lisbon, Portugal. He received a PhD at the New University of Lisbon, where he currently teaches postgraduate courses in text publishing. Over the last decades he's been dealing with the several possibilities of the fictional word and the novel format. He is well known as an *agent provocateur* in Lisbon's cultural scene, and is the author of more than twenty books, including *A arte suprema* (*The Supreme Art*, 1997), the first Portuguese graphic novel, and *Dádiva divina* (2005), which was awarded Portugal's prestigious PEN Club Award. In 2009 he was Endowed Chair and writer in residence at the University of Massachusetts at Dartmouth.

Translator Biographies

ARTTU AHAVA, unusually for a native speaker of Finnish, translates from Finnish into English, rather than the other way around. Arttu has a degree in English from Helsinki University, and has done postgraduate studies at Oxford University. He is currently working in Helsinki as an English-language journalist and translator.

CHRISTOPHER BURAWA is a poet and translator. His awards include the 2010 Joy Harjo Poetry Award, a 2007 NEA Literature Fellowship for Translation, and a 2008 American-Scandinavian Foundation Creative Writing Fellowship. He is the Director of the Center of Excellence for the Creative Arts at Austin Peay State University in Clarksville, Tennessee.

GERALD CHAPPLE has a PhD from Harvard University and taught German at McMaster University in Hamilton, Ontario. His translations of Günter Kunert, Barbara Frischmuth, David Wagner, Anita Albus, and others have appeared in *Fiction, Agni, Grand Street, Osiris,* and *Antioch Review.* He won an Austrian government Translation Award in 1996.

MARGARET JULL COSTA has been a literary translator for over twenty years, translating, among others, Javier Marías, Eça de Queiroz, and José Saramago. Her work has brought her various prizes, the most recent of which was the 2010 Premio Valle-Inclán for Javier Marías's *Your Face Tomorrow III: Poison, Shadow, and Farewell.*

JOHN K. COX is professor and department head in history at North Dakota State University in Fargo. He earned his doctorate at Indiana University. *The History of Serbia* (2002), *Slovenia: Evolving Loyalties* (2005), and translations of novels by Danilo Kiš and Ivan Cankar are among his chief publications. He is currently writing a study of the fiction of Ismail Kadare.

JENNIFER CROFT is a PhD candidate in comparative literary studies at Northwestern University, where she is writing her dissertation on duels in twentieth-century Western literature. Her translations have appeared in *Words Without Borders, Wag's Revue, Two Lines, Washington Square,* and elsewhere. She lives in Buenos Aires.

KATY DERBYSHIRE comes from London and lives in Berlin. She has translated various contemporary German writers including Clemens Meyer's short-story collection *All the Lights* (2011), Helene Hegemann, Dorothee Elmiger, and Inka Parei. Katy runs a blog on German writing by the name of *Love German Books.*

BRIAN DOYLE teaches Hebrew at the K.U.Leuven in Belgium, and has translated a variety of academic and literary works from Dutch/ Flemish into English. His recent literary translations include Christiaan Weijts's *The Window Dresser* (2010) and Tessa de Loo's *The Book of Doubt* (2011). He also translates poetry and literary nonfiction.

JONATHAN DUNNE translates from Bulgarian, Catalan, Galician, and Spanish. His translations include work by Tsvetanka Elenkova, Manuel Rivas, and Enrique Vila-Matas, and have been nominated for major literary prizes, including the International IMPAC Award and the Warwick Prize for Writing. Most recently his translation of the *Collected Poems* of Lois Pereiro was published by Small Stations Press. He is currently working on a bilingual *Anthology of Galician Literature, 1981–2011*.

WILL FIRTH was born in 1965 in Newcastle, Australia. He studied German and Slavic languages in Canberra, Zagreb, and Moscow. Since 1991 he has been living in Berlin, Germany, where he works as a freelance translator of literature and the humanities. He translates from Russian, Macedonian, and all variants of Serbo-Croatian.

MICHAELA FREEMAN was born in 1975 in Prague, the Czech Republic. She is a freelance translator, writer, web designer, digital artist, and creativity coach. She focuses on specialty and creative translations from Czech to English. For this, she teams up with her husband, Jim Freeman, a writer, proofreader, and editor. She maintains a website at michaela-freeman.com.

TSISANA GABUNIA graduated from the Tbilisi State University of Foreign Languages in 1962. She teaches English at TSUFL (now Ilya University), and has taught at Georgetown University and Boston University. Her translation work includes radio plays for the Radio of Georgia, a film script, a libretto of a children's opera, novels by David Dephy and Eva Babel, and articles for the magazine *Modi to Georgia*.

EDWARD GAUVIN has received fellowships and residencies from the NEA, the Fulbright Foundation, the Centre National du Livre, Ledig House, the Banff Centre, and ALTA. His work includes *A Life on Paper* by Georges-Olivier Châteaureynaud and publications in *Joyland, Conjunctions, Subtropics, World Literature Today, Epiphany, Tin House, The Southern Review,* and the *Harvard Review.* The winner of the John Dryden Translation prize, he is the contributing editor for Francophone comics at *Words Without Borders.* He maintains a website at edwardgauvin.com/blog.

SEÁN KINSELLA is from Ireland. He holds an MPhil in literary translation from Trinity College, Dublin, and he has previously translated work by Frode Grytten and Stig Sæterbakken into English. He currently lives in Norway with his wife and two small daughters.

TOMISLAV KUZMANOVIĆ earned his MFA in literary translation from the University of Iowa, and has translated Zoran Ferić's *The Death of the Little Match Girl,* and Igor Štiks's *A Castle in Romagna,* co-translated with Russell Valentino. His translations from Croatian have appeared in *Granta, The Iowa Review,* and *New European Poets.* He currently teaches literary translation at the University of Zadar.

ANASTASIA LAKHTIKOVA is a native of Ukraine. She is a Lecturer in the School of Literatures, Cultures, and Linguistics at the University of Illinois, Urbana-Champaign, where she teaches courses in literary translation.

DUSTIN LOVETT, a Fulbright recipient, graduated from the University of Illinois with a degree in comparative literature and German as well as a Certificate of Translation Studies. His translations have appeared in previous editions of *Best European Fiction* and on the *Guardian*'s website. He currently resides in Vienna, Austria.

DONAL McLAUGHLIN *see under* Author Biographies.

RHETT McNEIL has published numerous translations from Portuguese and Spanish, including short fiction by Machado de Assis and Enrique Vila-Matas, and novels by Gonçalo M. Tavares, A. G. Porta, and António Lobo Antunes. Currently, he is translating novels by Juan Filloy and Luis Chitarroni, and completing a PhD in comparative literature at Penn State University, where he teaches courses in language, literature, and film.

CHRISTOPHER MOSELEY teaches at the School of Slavonic and East European Studies at University College, London and translates from Estonian, Latvian, Finnish, and Swedish. He is the author of *Colloquial Estonian* and coauthor of *Colloquial Latvian* for Routledge. He has coedited the Routledge *Atlas of the World's Languages*, edited their *Encyclopedia of the World's Endangered Languages*, and completed the third edition of an atlas of endangered languages for UNESCO.

ANDREW OAKLAND is a translator from Czech and German who lives in Brno, Czech Republic. His recent translations include Radka Denemarková's *Money from Hitler* (2009) and Michal Ajvaz's *The Golden Age* (2010). He has just finished translating a novel by Martin Reiner.

PAUL OLCHVÁRY has translated twelve books from Hungarian, including Vilmos Kondor's *Budapest Noir*, György Dragomán's *The*

White King, and Ferenc Barnás's *The Ninth*. His translations have appeared in the *Paris Review* and the *Kenyon Review*. A recipient of grants from the National Endowment for the Arts and PEN American Center, he lives in North Adams, Massachusetts.

JAN REINHART specializes in the translation of Catalan, Spanish, and Portuguese literature into English. He has degrees in Spanish, Portuguese, and journalism, and is finishing his masters in translation. Currently he manages the film and music libraries of Rutgers University. Previously he was a newspaper reporter and cultural journalist.

URSULA MEANY SCOTT is a literary translator based in Dublin and working from French and Spanish. Her translation of Claude Ollier's novel *Wert and the Life Without End* was published in 2011. She holds an MPhil in literary translation with distinction from Trinity College, Dublin and was awarded a literary translation fellowship by Dalkey Archive Press in 2009.

ARCH TAIT studied Russian at Cambridge and Moscow Universities and since 1986 has translated eighteen books and many stories and articles by today's leading Russian writers. His most recent translations are Anna Politkovskaya's *Nothing But the Truth* and Ludmila Ulitskaya's *Daniel Stein, Interpreter*.

LIZ WATERS translates literary fiction and quality nonfiction from Dutch into English. Her most recent translations include *The Crisis Caravan* by Linda Polman, *The Burgher and the Whore* by Lotte van de Pol, and *Immigrant Nations* by Paul Scheffer. She lives in Amsterdam.

JEFFREY ZUCKERMAN works in book publishing. He holds a degree in English with honors from Yale University, where he studied English literature, creative writing, and translation. He has translated several Francophone authors, from Jean-Philippe Toussaint and Pauline Klein to Édouard Levé and Frédéric Beigbeder.

Liberté • Égalité • Fraternité
RÉPUBLIQUE FRANÇAISE
AMBASSADE DE FRANCE
AUX ETATS-UNIS

Service culturel

 CYNGOR LLYFRAU CYMRU
WELSH BOOKS COUNCIL

 Estonian
Literature
Centre

 N O R L A

HUNGARIAN BOOK
FOUNDATION

POLISH
CULTURAL
INSTITUTE
www.PolishCulture.org.uk

MINISTRY OF CULTURE
AND MONUMENT PROTECTION
OF GEORGIA

GOETHE-INSTITUT
NEW YORK

 Bókmenntasjóður
The Icelandic Literature Fund

swiss arts council
 pr◌helvetia

 SPAIN
FOREIGN
CULTURAL
COOPERATION

PRINCIPALITY OF LIECHTENSTEIN

FILI
FINNISH LITERATURE EXCHANGE

J A K | JAVNA AGENCIJA ZA KNJIGO REPUBLIKE SLOVENIJE
SLOVENIAN BOOK AGENCY

Acknowledgments

Publication of *Best European Fiction 2012* was made possible by generous support from the following cultural agencies and embassies:

The Arts Council (Ireland)

Communauté française de Belgique—Promotion des lettres

Cultural Services of the French Embassy

Cyngor Llyfrau Cymru—Welsh Books Council

Embassy of the Principality of Liechtenstein to the United States of America

Embassy of Spain, Washington, D.C.

Estonian Literature Centre

Finnish Literature Exchange (FILI)

The Goethe-Institut New York

Hungarian Book Foundation

Icelandic Literature Fund

The Ministry of Culture and Monument Protection of Georgia: Program in Support of Georgian Books and Literature

NORLA: Norwegian Literature Abroad, Fiction & Nonfiction

The Polish Cultural Institute of London

Pro Helvetia, Swiss Arts Council

The Slovenian Book Agency (JAK)

Rights and Permissions

Zsófia Bán: "When There Were Only Animals" © 2011 by Zsófia Bán. Translation © 2011 by Paul Olchváry.

Muharem Bazdulj: "Magic" and "Sarajevo" © 2008 by Muharem Bazdulj. Translation © 2011 by John K. Cox.

Patrick Boltshauser: "Tomorrow It's Deggendorf" © 2011 by Patrick Boltshauser. Translation © 2011 by Gerald Chapple.

Bjarte Breiteig: "Down There They Don't Mourn" © 2000 by Bjarte Breiteig. Translation © 2011 by Seán Kinsella.

Duncan Bush: "Bigamy" © 2011 by Duncan Bush.

Arno Camenisch: excerpt from *Sez Ner* © 2009 by Arno Camenisch. Translation © 2011 by Donal McLaughlin.

Marie Darrieussecq: "Juergen the Perfect Son-in-Law" © 2006 by P.O.L éditeur. Translation © 2011 by Jeffrey Zuckerman.

Danila Davydov: "The Telescope" © 2011 by Danila Davydov. Translation © 2011 by Arch Tait.

David Dephy: "Before the End" © 2011 by David-Dephy Gogibedashvili. Translation © 2011 by Tsisana Gabunia.

Agustín Fernández Paz: "This Strange Lucidity" © 2007 by Agustín Fernández Paz. Translation © 2011 by Jonathan Dunne.

Róbert Gál: excerpt from *Agnomia* © 2008 by Róbert Gál. Translation © 2011 by Michaela Freeman.

⊡ SELECTED DALKEY ARCHIVE PAPERBACKS

PETROS ABATZOGLOU *What Does Mrs. Freeman Want?*

MICHAL AJVAZ *The Golden Age* ▪ *The Other City*

PIERRE ALBERT-BIROT *Grabinoulor*

YUZ ALESHKOVSKY *Kangaroo*

FELIPE ALFAU *Chromos* ▪ *Locos*

JOÃO ALMINO *The Book of Emotions*

IVAN ÂNGELO *The Celebration* ▪ *The Tower of Glass*

DAVID ANTIN *Talking*

ANTÓNIO LOBO ANTUNES *Knowledge of Hell* ▪ *The Splendor of Portugal*

ALAIN ARIAS-MISSON *Theatre of Incest*

IFTIKHAR ARIF AND WAQAS KHWAJA, EDS. *Modern Poetry of Pakistan*

JOHN ASHBERY AND JAMES SCHUYLER *A Nest of Ninnies*

ROBERT ASHLEY *Perfect Lives*

GABRIELA AVIGUR-ROTEM *Heatwave and Crazy Birds*

HEIMRAD BÄCKER *transcript*

DJUNA BARNES *Ladies Almanack* ▪ *Ryder*

JOHN BARTH *LETTERS* ▪ *Sabbatical*

DONALD BARTHELME *The King* ▪ *Paradise*

SVETISLAV BASARA *Chinese Letter*

RENÉ BELLETTO *Dying*

MARK BINELLI *Sacco and Vanzetti Must Die!*

ANDREI BITOV *Pushkin House*

ANDREJ BLATNIK *You Do Understand*

LOUIS PAUL BOON *Chapel Road* ▪ *My Little War* ▪ *Summer in Termuren*

ROGER BOYLAN *Killoyle*

IGNÁCIO DE LOYOLA BRANDÃO *Anonymous Celebrity* ▪ *The Good-Bye Angel* ▪ *Teeth under the Sun* ▪ *Zero*

BONNIE BREMSER *Troia: Mexican Memoirs*

CHRISTINE BROOKE-ROSE *Amalgamemnon*

BRIGID BROPHY *In Transit*

MEREDITH BROSNAN *Mr. Dynamite*

GERALD L. BRUNS *Modern Poetry and the Idea of Language*

EVGENY BUNIMOVICH AND J. KATES, EDS. *Contemporary Russian Poetry: An Anthology*

GABRIELLE BURTON *Heartbreak Hotel*

MICHEL BUTOR *Degrees* ▪ *Mobile* ▪ *Portrait of the Artist as a Young Ape*

G. CABRERA INFANTE *Infante's Inferno* ▪ *Three Trapped Tigers*

JULIETA CAMPOS *The Fear of Losing Eurydice*

ANNE CARSON *Eros the Bittersweet*

ORLY CASTEL-BLOOM *Dolly City*

CAMILO JOSÉ CELA *Christ versus Arizona* ▪ *The Family of Pascual Duarte* ▪ *The Hive*

LOUIS-FERDINAND CÉLINE *Castle to Castle* ▪ *Conversations with Professor Y* ▪ *London Bridge* ▪ *Normance* ▪ *North* ▪ *Rigadoon*

HUGO CHARTERIS *The Tide Is Right*

JEROME CHARYN *The Tar Baby*

ERIC CHEVILLARD *Demolishing Nisard*

MARC CHOLODENKO *Mordechai Schamz*

JOSHUA COHEN *Witz*

EMILY HOLMES COLEMAN *The Shutter of Snow*

ROBERT COOVER *A Night at the Movies*

STANLEY CRAWFORD *Log of the S.S. The Mrs Unguentine* ▪ *Some Instructions to My Wife*

ROBERT CREELEY *Collected Prose*

RENÉ CREVEL *Putting My Foot in It*

RALPH CUSACK *Cadenza*

SUSAN DAITCH *L.C.* ▪ *Storytown*

NICHOLAS DELBANCO *The Count of Concord* ▪ *Sherbrookes*

NIGEL DENNIS *Cards of Identity*

PETER DIMOCK *A Short Rhetoric for Leaving the Family*

ARIEL DORFMAN *Konfidenz*

COLEMAN DOWELL *The Houses of Children* ▪ *Island People* ▪ *Too Much Flesh and Jabez*

ARKADII DRAGOMOSHCHENKO *Dust*

RIKKI DUCORNET *The Complete Butcher's Tales* ▪ *The Fountains of Neptune* ▪

For a full list of publications, visit: www.dalkeyarchive.com

SELECTED DALKEY ARCHIVE PAPERBACKS ⑤

For a full list of publications, visit: www.dalkeyarchive.com

☐ SELECTED DALKEY ARCHIVE PAPERBACKS

DANILO KIŠ *Garden, Ashes* ▪ *A Tomb for Boris Davidovich*
ANITA KONKKA *A Fool's Paradise*
GEORGE KONRÁD *The City Builder*
TADEUSZ KONWICKI *A Minor Apocalypse* ▪ *The Polish Complex*
MENIS KOUMANDAREAS *Koula*
ELAINE KRAF *The Princess of 72nd Street*
JIM KRUSOE *Iceland*
EWA KURYLUK *Century 21*
EMILIO LASCANO TEGUI *On Elegance While Sleeping*
ERIC LAURRENT *Do Not Touch*
HERVÉ LE TELLIER *The Sextine Chapel* ▪ *A Thousand Pearls (for a Thousand Pennies)*
VIOLETTE LEDUC *La Bâtarde*
EDOUARD LEVÉ *Autoportrait* ▪ *Suicide*
SUZANNE JILL LEVINE *The Subversive Scribe: Translating Latin American Fiction*
DEBORAH LEVY *Billy and Girl* ▪ *Pillow Talk in Europe and Other Places*
JOSE LEZAMA LIMA *Paradiso*
ROSA LIKSOM *Dark Paradise*
OSMAN LINS *Avalovara* ▪ *The Queen of the Prisons of Greece*
ALF MAC LOCHLAINN *The Corpus in the Library* ▪ *Out of Focus*
RON LOEWINSOHN *Magnetic Field(s)*
MINA LOY *Stories and Essays of Mina Loy*
BRIAN LYNCH *The Winner of Sorrow*
D. KEITH MANO *Take Five*
MICHELINE AHARONIAN MARCOM *The Mirror in the Well*
BEN MARCUS *The Age of Wire and String*
WALLACE MARKFIELD *Teitlebaum's Window* ▪ *To an Early Grave*
DAVID MARKSON *Reader's Block* ▪ *Springer's Progress* ▪ *Wittgenstein's Mistress*
CAROLE MASO *AVA*
LADISLAV MATEJKA AND KRYSTYNA POMORSKA, EDS. *Readings in Russian Poetics: Formalist and Structuralist Views*
HARRY MATHEWS *The Case of the Persevering Maltese:* *Collected Essays* ▪ *Cigarettes* ▪ *The Conversions* ▪ *The Human Country: New and Collected Stories* ▪ *The Journalist* ▪ *My Life in CIA* ▪ *Singular Pleasures* ▪ *The Sinking of the Odradek Stadium* ▪ *Tlooth* ▪ *20 Lines a Day*
JOSEPH MCELROY *Night Soul and Other Stories*
THOMAS MCGONIGLE *Going to Patchogue*
ROBERT L. MCLAUGHLIN, ED. *Innovations: An Anthology of Modern & Contemporary Fiction*
ABDELWAHAB MEDDEB *Talismano*
GERHARD MEIER *Isle of the Dead*
HERMAN MELVILLE *The Confidence-Man*
AMANDA MICHALOPOULOU *I'd Like*
STEVEN MILLHAUSER *The Barnum Museum* ▪ *In the Penny Arcade*
RALPH J. MILLS, JR. *Essays on Poetry*
MOMUS *The Book of Jokes*
CHRISTINE MONTALBETTI *Western*
OLIVE MOORE *Spleen*
NICHOLAS MOSLEY *Accident* ▪ *Assassins* ▪ *Catastrophe Practice* ▪ *Children of Darkness and Light* ▪ *Experience and Religion* ▪ *God's Hazard* ▪ *The Hesperides Tree* ▪ *Hopeful Monsters* ▪ *Imago Bird* ▪ *Impossible Object* ▪ *Inventing God* ▪ *Judith* ▪ *Look at the Dark* ▪ *Natalie Natalia* ▪ *Paradoxes of Peace* ▪ *Serpent* ▪ *Time at War* ▪ *The Uses of Slime Mould: Essays of Four Decades*
WARREN MOTTE *Fables of the Novel: French Fiction since 1990* ▪ *Fiction Now: The French Novel in the 21st Century* ▪ *Oulipo: A Primer of Potential Literature*
GERALD MURNANE *Barley Patch*
YVES NAVARRE *Our Share of Time* ▪ *Sweet Tooth*
DOROTHY NELSON *In Night's City* ▪ *Tar and Feathers*
ESHKOL NEVO *Homesick*
WILFRIDO D. NOLLEDO *But for the Lovers*
FLANN O'BRIEN *At Swim-Two-Birds*

For a full list of publications, visit: www.dalkeyarchive.com

SELECTED DALKEY ARCHIVE PAPERBACKS ⬜

For a full list of publications, visit: www.dalkeyarchive.com

⬛ SELECTED DALKEY ARCHIVE PAPERBACKS

For a full list of publications, visit: www.dalkeyarchive.com